"UNC
COME AND ST

He didn't hesitate. He did not even appear to be surprised by my command. I built the pentacle of protection around us, completing it just as the attack swept into the room.

The ice wind crackled against my pentacle's walls, and whirlwinds danced in the depths of the mirrors. With a snap, the long dining table split in half and crashed against the stone floor. Porcelain dishes and crystal goblets shattered. The mirrors began to bleed from every crack. Frost splattered the glass, then melted in red runnels that soaked the ancient rugs.

An arrow of ice raced toward me from distant amber clouds within a broken mirror. The barbed white tip pounded through my barricade, scattering blue and silver dust into the hurricane of frost. The wind numbed my fingers. I fumbled with my philter purse, but I could not gather the powder that I needed. I could not speak even a simple spell to slow the freezing of my skin. . . .

SABLE, SHADOW, AND ICE

Cheryl J. Franklin

DAW BOOKS, INC.
DONALD A. WOLLHEIM, FOUNDER
375 Hudson Street, New York, NY 10014

**ELIZABETH R. WOLLHEIM
SHEILA E. GILBERT
PUBLISHERS**

First Printing, June 1994
1   2   3   4   5   6   7   8   9

For the people of DAW Books,
especially Sheila, who takes good care of me

*Forty-five cards guide the
Mages of Avalon.*

---

*There are five suits:
Blood, Brass, Ice, Sable,
and Shadow.*

---

*There are nine faces:
Prince, Mage, Dom, Cat,
Everyman, Hound,
Ghost,
Mixie, and Dreamer.*

---

*With these cards, a Mage
may see visions of truth.*

Prologue
Aroha/Ch'ango

Summer's oppression ends at last, mused Aroha, as a gust of cold wind wrapped his silk Mage robe against his legs. A cloud-spattered afternoon sky, cleaner and drier than the usual late-Tiunu weather, streaked the hectic streets of Tathagata with alternating bands of brilliance and darkness. Between shadow and light, Aroha's robe shifted from deep indigo to violet, the color that proclaimed him as a duly elected Mastermage. A flash of sunlight made the silver marks of Aroha's advanced Mystic status glitter across his muscular forearms.

Mages of the Avalon School would call this a Shadow day, observed Aroha with a thin smile of satisfaction, *a changeable day, an auspicious day for a Tangaroa Mage, whose symbol is Shadow.*

A thin crown of Tangaroa aquamarines bound Aroha's thick black hair. He fingered the aqua roll of Mage tools chained to his waist. He had studied the methods of all five major Mystic Schools, but he did not advertise his mastery of the other Schools by displaying their colors. Most Affirmists, including influential members of the House of Doms, distrusted Mages who flaunted their Mystic power beyond accepted bounds. Aroha had amassed enough enemies without provoking needless quarrels of protocol.

He strode briskly among the true shadows cast by the multistoried shops and office buildings. Strong planes composed his bronze face; keen eyes of sea-mist green returned the appreciative gazes of passersby with a practiced air of amused self-confidence. Many of his fellow pedestrians watched him with a furtive pretense of disinterest. Outside of Tathagata's aloof government district, violet was rarely seen, though a strong color attracted less wonder in Tathagata than in any lesser city. In Tathagata, clothing of Affirmist browns and the rainbow hues of Mystic affiliations nearly outnumbered the neutral shades of cream and white, since Tathagatans generally interpreted the Mystic/Affirmist social contract to satisfy themselves. Tathagatans could afford to flout the customs that governed the rest of the world, because Tathagata housed the World Parliament, which issued the laws and controlled their enforcement.

"Good journey, Mastermage Aroha," greeted a passing Mage of the Inianga school, pausing in an eager attempt to initiate a conversation. Astute information brokers paid well to track the activities of notorious Mastermages like Aroha. The tacit protection of the government district did not extend to the rest of Tathagata.

"Grow in wisdom," replied Aroha with firm courtesy that extended no invitation. The orange-garbed Inianga Mage, knowing himself dismissed by a superior, continued on his way in disappointment, his greedy curiosity unassuaged.

Aroha derived minimal pleasure from the authority that his status granted him over the older, less-marked Mage, though such small examples of his influence had once satisfied him. Three years in Tathagata had jaded him to such trivial forms of power. Pursuit of more sophisticated ambitions had brought him to the ignoble shopping district near Xilonen Plaza, because Mastermage Ch'ango had advised him to spend his afternoon in this unlikely location.

She had refused to give him a reason, but a woman of Ch'ango's extensive influence seldom explained herself. Aroha had complied readily because Ch'ango had taught him much of the ways of power, and he hoped to gain much more from her. He had not expected to find himself listening to the nearly illegal rantings of a street preacher, a spindly boy who could not be more than sixteen.

"The Intercessor offers you wisdom and joy!" proclaimed the towheaded youth, flinging his arms wide with enthusiasm. He had climbed onto a curved plastone bench to address those who passed him on the busy Tathagatan street. He wore a simple gray robe, such as Tathagata's Mystic monastery issued to its less fortunate supplicants. The boy's features were arranged pleasantly enough to have intrigued a few speculative admirers, but most of those admirers shifted their attention when Aroha arrived. Aroha possessed a much more compelling style of attraction, augmented by the implicit status of Mastermage violet and the impressive arrays of bright silver Mage marks.

Aroha seated himself cross-legged on the narrow strip of patchy lawn that bordered the street. He held his back stiffly erect in the manner of a long practitioner of meditative Mystic arts, though the well-toned muscles beneath his silken robe showed the effects of unusual physical development for a professional Mage. His expression became warily attentive as he watched the street preacher.

The boy did know how to use his voice effectively. Aroha granted him that slight tribute. However, Aroha regularly heard better speakers in the World Parliament. Ch'ango surely had some other reason for recommending that her protégé devote an afternoon to listening to this young radical.

The reason for Ch'ango's recommendation could be as simple as suspicion of the truth: Aroha *had* intended to spend this day with another of his mistresses. The familiar concern over discovery taunted Aroha, and he tightened his jaw imperceptibly. He argued inwardly against his own worry: No, Ch'ango was not that tolerant, and Aroha guarded his secrets much too carefully from Mage spells, as well as from conventional betrayal. Aroha never left his house without barricading himself against spell seekings, and his house was a veritable spell fortress. Aroha never juggled the favors of more than two influential women at one time, and there were no more than three people in Tathagata who even knew about Tua'ana, the whore who was Aroha's only self-indulgence apart from his relentless ambitions. No, if Ch'ango ever suspected the breadth of Aroha's interests, nothing short of his lifeblood would satisfy her desire for vengeance. Ch'ango had sent him here to learn, and a wise man never rejected an opportunity to improve his lot.

Aroha forced himself to truly listen, though the sun-warmed ground encouraged laziness, and the boy's stern style bore an irritating resemblance to the lectures of Aroha's father. "What do you achieve by all your worldly struggles?" demanded the boy. "Do you think your wealth makes you better than the people you claim to rule?"

"Do you think your Mystic schemes will make you better than the rest of your kin?" demanded a memory of Aroha's father, his strong face stubborn with anger. *"Do you think a Mage is better than a fixer?"*

"Yes," muttered Aroha beneath his breath, though his father had not lived to see Aroha become Mastermage of

Purotu at a precocious twenty-three years of age. A deadly
fall from a scaffolding cheated both father and son of any
chance for reconciliation. His father's death did not free
Aroha of the compulsion to succeed beyond the inglorious
family trade and his father's scornful expectations.

The lanky young preacher seemed to hear Aroha's ironic
whisper, though the streets were noisy with chattering pedestrians and rumbling autobuses. The boy turned his thin,
pale face toward Aroha and aborted his sermon. He jumped
down from the bench and crossed the paved walkway with
a gangly lope. Uninvited, he joined Aroha on the sparse,
sickly lawn. Few members of the boy's abandoned audience
dispersed. Most chose instead to observe with heightened interest and to whisper speculatively as the preacher approached the Mastermage.

The boy pointed awkwardly at the elaborate Mystic
embroideries of Aroha's robe, the golden lizards, fish, and
birds that filled Tangaroa legends and inspired the shape of
many Tangaroa spells. "I rarely have a Mastermage in my
audience."

"Since you denounce the entire Mystic pantheon," remarked Aroha austerely, "I could arrest you for unlawful intolerance of accepted creeds." The boy, all pale and earnest,
looked even younger from close vantage. The abundance of
rapt witnesses demanded a stern demeanor from the Mastermage, but Aroha's honest reaction was amusement that the
boy approached a Mastermage with such confidence.

The boy nodded without evident dismay. "The Intercessor's words have lain too long unheard." He extended his
open hand, a gesture halfway between a Mage truce and an
Affirmist greeting. "My name is Benedict."

Since the boy's wrists wore no silver Mage marks, Aroha
met the boy's hand in the Affirmist style. "Aroha,
Mastermage of Purotu." With the brief touch, Aroha probed
the boy and found no obvious threat, no practiced Mage
skills, no antipathy—nothing noteworthy at all, except a
sense of undeveloped Mystic potential strong enough to impart an unpleasant chill to Aroha's lotus marks.

"Why do you listen to me, Mastermage Aroha," asked
Benedict, "if you are already so certain that you disbelieve
me?"

"If I never listened, I would never learn," answered
Aroha, maintaining a careful Mystic guard against the atten-

tive ears of any potential enemies. Incautious conversation with a radical could result in political embarrassment or worse, depending on an enemy's ingenuity and dedication to mischief.

"Is knowledge what you value?"

"I value what knowledge can give me."

"Wealth and power?" asked Benedict with a faint smile. "Is that what you want?"

"For a start," replied Aroha equably.

Benedict bowed his head, as if the Mage's brief answer required deep consideration. Benedict's golden strands of straight, short hair created a haloing effect that Aroha observed detachedly, until the tingling of Mage senses altered the view into spontaneous Mystic vision. The pale hair curled in the light, and it framed a feminine counterpart to Benedict's face—a little softer, a little finer. The vision passed as quickly as it came, and Aroha disciplined himself to conceal its occurrence.

Aroha kept his arms relaxed by force of concentration, though his Mage marks stretched his skin taut. His Mage senses burned with the certainty that Benedict and the unknown girl would hold prominent places in his own life. It was a strength of connection—neither good nor bad, but potent—akin to that which his first meeting with Mastermage Ch'ango had stirred in him.

"And will all that wealth and power give you control over your own existence?" demanded Benedict. "Will you be able to summon an autoboat any faster? Will you be able to feed yourself without a supply cube's aid? Will all your wealth and power mean anything to the thousands of ordinary people who live without hope of anything beyond their next E-unit fantasy?"

"I shall have far more control than a poor man," answered Aroha dryly, "and the world is filled with people who envy me already." Because Mage vision had transformed the boy from stranger to inevitable acquaintance, Aroha took the trouble to elaborate, "If wealth and power were not desirable, you would see no public Mages, shopkeepers, lawyers, cargo movers, caretakers, servants, scroungers—or privateers, prostitutes, and fixers. If wealth and power were not desirable, we would all be E-unit addicts, migrating from town to desolate town, until we exhausted all the resources that the late Empires left us."

"The world is not far from that sorry state of existence."

"If wealth and power were not desirable," continued Aroha, undeterred by Benedict's interruption, "you would not preach antiquated religion on a Tathagatan street corner. Like Empire science, the exclusionist religions were outlawed because they carried too much destructive potential. Mages are limited by their Mystic skill and tools, and Doms can rule only to the extent that their inherited wealth allows, but a lone messenger of 'divine' inspiration could usurp unlimited personal power, if he succeeded."

"Is that why you think I preach? To acquire personal power?"

Aroha replied with sardonic equanimity, "Why else?"

"To share the gift of joy that comes with understanding." The boy met Aroha's cynical disdain with a level gaze. "Ten months ago, I experienced a dreadful prophecy, portending a cruel injustice by and against people who are dear to me."

Aroha raised his dark brows in eloquent skepticism. "You are not a Mage."

"No," agreed the boy, "I am not a Mage. Hence, no one would advise me regarding my prophecy. I became discouraged and desperately lonely—nearly to the point of ending my own life. My sister, Marita, the one person who had always been my support and companion, was unavailable to hear me." Benedict shrugged. "She has taken residence with a jealous Mage, and his endless demands preoccupy her. I came to Tathagata to seek counsel from my parents, and they only reiterated the hollow legal tenets of Affirmism. 'Tend yourself, as pleases you best, and condemn no one for doing likewise,' they told me, instead of listening to me. They dismissed my prophecy as a bad dream."

"You might have consulted a public Mage for confirmation or contradiction of that possibility." Personal confidences generally made Aroha uncomfortable, because he preferred to bury his own feelings deeply, but Benedict's outpouring served to enhance the indefinite Mage sense about the boy's significance. During the instant of its speaking, the name *Marita* caused Aroha's Mage marks to burn with elusive portent.

"My Affirmist family trained me to distrust the services of public Mages. My sister's disavowal of our Affirmist training was the one point of my story that *did* interest my parents. The news of her intention to convert to Mysticism upset them deeply, but they refused to dissuade her, because they feared that someone might accuse them of intolerance. Verbally, my parents affirmed all that I told them, but they understood nothing."

"Where families are concerned, emotion tends to preclude rational discussion," muttered Aroha, bitterly recalling his own experiences with family conflict.

"My family values the sort of wealth and power that *you* esteem so highly, and those things mean nothing to me. When I discovered the Intercessor's words, they gave me a reason to live, a reason that will *never* fail me. The Intercessor gave me hope when the world gave me none."

The boy's idealism inspired only scorn in Aroha. However, because Aroha sympathized with the hurt of a parental rift, he curbed his acerbity. "Does anyone share your peculiar understanding of this 'Intercessor'?"

"The Intercessor will enlighten others—in time." Displaying an astonishing disregard for social custom and ordinary caution, Benedict touched the twin silver scarabs atop Aroha's wrists. "Perhaps *you* will receive the blessing of the Intercessor's wisdom."

Danger! shrieked Aroha's Mystic senses, and he snatched his arms away from the boy's gentle invasion. With cold fury, he scolded the boy, "Never touch a Mage's silver without permission. Do you know nothing of Mystic customs?"

"Very little," admitted Benedict. "I apologize for hurting you."

"Your insulting familiarity did not *hurt* me," retorted Aroha, but he did not complete his answer. Mage barriers, lowered by the unexpected Mystic impact of the boy's touch, gave access to more deliberate Mage forces. Ch'ango's sending flared in Aroha's mind, blinding him to the world around him. He saw Ch'ango, robed in clinging violet and clenching a bright, curved sacred blade. She raised her wiry arm high and drove it downward into the flesh of the squirming sacrifice, a pathetic creature already mutilated beyond recognition as cat or hound or rodent. The blood spurted high, a crimson fountain that beaded her austerely elegant face. "The boy cannot claim you, Aroha, because you are mine," she gloated, "and you will never leave me."

Aroha felt the tug of her power tearing at his soul. He muttered a counterspell and a curse, but blood magic was potent, and Ch'ango was strong. He unleashed his ever-present store of anger into his own magic, and he cast it against her in retaliation. Abruptly, she released her stranglehold, and he gasped at the sudden freedom. Ch'ango's laughter teased him, denying the cruelty of her double-edged jest.

Aroha's Mage vision blackened, brightened, and returned to its unobtrusive form of pseudo-reality. His anger lingered. He detested Ch'ango's Mage games, though he gained strength from them. He particularly loathed her liberal use of blood magic, especially when she bestowed its power on *his* behalf. She had mocked him the first time she offered a sacrifice in his presence, because he had disgraced himself with his squeamishness. Even for the sake of his ambitions, he could not overcome his inherent revulsion for blood magic. Ch'ango worked to cure him of his aversion.

Aroha blinked to clear the blur of her Mystic sending from his physical sight, and the fine bones of the pink-cheeked young radical confronted him anew. The boy's eyes, a rare blue-gray, observed Aroha critically. "You have need of wisdom," declared Benedict with the earnest conviction of opinionated youth.

The boy arose clumsily and returned to the curved bench. He glanced once more at Aroha, before clambering back atop the bench to resume his interrupted preaching. *He sensed Ch'ango,* concluded Aroha in ill humor, *though he lacks the Mage marks that would enable him to appreciate her grisly expression of endearment.*

Having lost his taste for any further lessons of the day, Aroha grimaced, but he did not leave. He did not enjoy Ch'ango's concept of affection, but he refused to let her think him weak and unworthy. The powerful, manipulative woman who was Mastermage of Rit had advised him to listen to a street preacher, who had more untapped Mystic potential than most Mastermages. Suppressing his irritation, Aroha listened.

"Truth has slept too long!" proclaimed Benedict. "We have forgotten too much of what once was known across the world."

And how have you remembered, young idealist? wondered Aroha, all of his cynicism revived by Ch'ango's sending and Benedict's inadvertent offense. As the son of "fixers," those socially despised individuals who repaired Empire devices to the minor extent that the law allowed, Aroha could not recall ever having sufficient leisure time to cultivate any ideals. His parents had set him to work as soon as he could hold a tool. Aroha had labored continuously as a fixer from age five to age twelve, when the Mage Center accepted him on probation. Purotu Mages had continued to exploit his fixer skills until his sixteenth birthday gave him the right to affiliate himself as a legal Mystic.

"The Empires protected themselves by denying the value of any truths but their own," continued Benedict. "They persecuted the Intercessor's faithful and tried to destroy His holy words by flame and flood, but worldly forces cannot conquer the Intercessor. The holy words may be charred and stained, but they survive! Hear them, and rejoice!"

Aroha's interest intensified enough to overcome damaged pride. *Words, charred and stained? Was the boy a Scribe? Was that why none of the Mystic Schools had managed to convert him?*

Aroha craved Scribe skills as fanatically as he did potent Mage spells, though Mystic teaching labeled the two brands of power incompatible. Aroha, like any sane Mage of consequence, dreaded the possibility of weakening his Mystic power, but knowledge exerted a siren's force over him. If Benedict could provide access to Scribe lore, the boy's significance to Aroha could exceed anything that a momentary Mystic vision might predict.

Aroha had once succeeded in seducing a Scribe, but she had refused to compromise her Guild vows, and even his Mage spells had failed to persuade her. Aroha regretted the resultant inconvenience of Scribe Talitha's enmity, since the Scribes were clannish and formidable. However, he would willingly have tried the same approach on every woman and man in the Guild if he had thought another Scribe would be less stubborn than Talitha. Aroha would have risked life itself to acquire the Scribes' Guild's secrets.

"Heed the Intercessor's words!" cried the boy. "Turn away from anger and envy. Affirm *love*, not the convenient insincerity of telling people what they want to hear. Submit your Mystic spells to the Intercessor's wisdom, and know the joy and strength of doing what is right in *His* sight."

The boy is a fanatic, thought Aroha disparagingly, but he acknowledged his own compulsion as an equivalent madness. Scribe skills could cripple him; even Ch'ango feared to study the true Scribe symbols. Though she paid scroungers generously for any ancient text with a Mystic icon on the spine, Ch'ango hoarded such volumes primarily to protect their secrets from potential rivals. Aroha's father would have equated such fear with superstition, but Aroha's father had derided all Mage lore as quackery.

Having earned twelve lotus marks, ten shells, and the scarabs that signified the most powerful Mage specialty, Aroha had long ago vanquished his own doubts regarding Mystic potential. Only incompetent Mages—a plentiful class, in Aroha's critical view—resorted to trickery in their professional dealings. Mages like Aroha and Ch'ango did not need to exploit illusion and deceit, except to augment their political standing with Doms and other Affirmists, who could not appreciate true Mystic skill.

For a second time, the boy interrupted his preaching abruptly. Aroha glanced behind him to see what had distracted Benedict, but the pedestrians were too plentiful to be individually informative. A cluster of brown-coated Affirmists debarked from an autobus, but Aroha recognized none of them; he had little social contact with Affirmists. When he saw Benedict trot down the street, away from the Affirmist shoppers, Aroha sighed at opportunity's postponement.

Ch'ango's Tathagata home was large, drafty, and dim, festooned with snarling gargoyles and cold with the onyx chips that tiled floors, ceilings, and walls. The heady smoke of sandalwood incense spiraled through the pillared halls and lofts. Curtains of silver chimes, tiny round bells chained into bondage, shivered at the arched windows, singing an erratic melody. Mage glow softened the harsher Empire light bowls to hazy yellow. Furnishings of rare ebony and ivory, concise of line and intricately assembled, adorned select walls and corners in understated magnificence. The Lung-Wang Mage honored her early training with a nacreous shrine dedicated to the Dragon Kings. If anyone observed the unlawful porcelain figures of Hangseng Emperors among the lawful Mystic displays of Lung-Wang affiliation, no one dared to make mention of that fact to Ch'ango.

As a young woman, Ch'ango had made the choice to display her Hangseng Empire heritage proudly, and she had never retreated from that bold stance. She guarded the creamy pallor of her skin. She coiled her black hair tightly, freeing the soft oval of her face from any distraction. When she could find no standard garments that suited her, she had fitted and stitched her own silk sheaths to display her compact body to best effect.

She had cultivated her dark regality rather than imitate the conventional beauty of neutrality. Her style had matured well, though after a quarter century as Mastermage of Rit, she adorned herself too heavily with arrogance. Her eyes, black and deep and elongated by thick lines of kohl, disdained nearly everyone. She even treated Aroha coldly, though she valued him above all others. She cultivated many handsome young men, but none of them matched Aroha either in Mage skills or intelligence. As far as she was capable, she felt affection for him.

She regarded Aroha now across the black marble table where they had shared a cold supper. Her patronage was the only major compliment she ever bestowed on him, but privately she admired him with a ferocious passion. "What did you think of the boy?" asked Ch'ango with cool amusement. Her dexterous fingers stroked the bright-winged dragons of Lung-Wang citron that garnished her violet robes, and she imagined Aroha's strong hands upon her.

"Educated," replied Aroha crisply. He did not elaborate, because he did not wish to display his ignorance before Ch'ango. He had accrued his own reasons for interest in young Benedict, but Aroha still did not know why Ch'ango had sent him to hear the boy's preaching. He gave much attention to the shadow-gray cat that purred contentedly in his lap.

Ch'ango would not tolerate Aroha's reticence; she recognized its cause as pride. "And?"

Reluctantly, Aroha conceded the impression that continued to chill his silver Mage marks, "Dangerous."

Watching Aroha maneuver under pressure energized and enthralled Ch'ango, because the exercise asserted her own formidable Mystic power. Even by the standards of Tathagata, where most of the world's powerful gathered, Aroha had demonstrated a rare aptitude for subtle intimidation. His invincible attitude had first drawn him to Ch'ango's attention.

She delighted in puncturing Aroha's conceit, for she had learned its fragility. A trivial investigation of his origins had revealed his fixer past. From that knowledge, she had fashioned the spell that laid bare his severe, utterly unexpected insecurities. Despite his achievements as a Mage, he regarded himself as a fixer's son, eternal slave of the defunct Empires. He zealously avoided any mention of his family.

Ch'ango, in her own conceit, believed that she alone had sufficient Mystic insight to understand a man as determinedly reserved as Aroha. She dismissed Affirmist perceptions altogether. Believing that she understood Aroha, she gained a Mystic advantage over him, which let her feel safe in cultivating him instead of undermining him as a potential rival. "Why is the boy dangerous?" insisted Ch'ango.

She forced him to concoct a quick rationale. "The old religions were inherently divisive," he answered with the excessive, calculating rapidity that masked some of his most uncertain moments. "Since the boy is educated, he knows that any revival of such extreme beliefs would threaten the Mystic/Affirmist social contract. Since he preaches in Tathagata, he intends to make his presence felt in powerful quarters. Since he has not been arrested, he has more personal power than is evident."

Ch'ango curled her lips in her rare smile of approbation. "You perceive well, Aroha-purotu." She appended his home city to his name only when she felt particularly generous. She knew that he disliked the usage, which he regarded as condescending—for "purotu" meant "pretty" in the dialect of Tangaroa spells—but he was quite willing to accept that annoyance in trade for the practical benefits of Ch'ango's patronage. His tolerance of her whims also pleased Ch'ango, because he tolerated little from other Tathagatans. "The boy belongs to the Family of Doms," she informed him. "He is the only son of my Affirmist counterpart, Dom Hollis of Rit, who intends to keep the seat of Rit in the immediate family."

"Heir of Rit," murmured Aroha pensively. Ch'ango savored the sense of his disciplined mind and Mage spell, as he reconstructed the afternoon's conversation in light of her revelation. "Young Benedict takes an unconventional path for one to whom power is assured by birth."

"The greatest gains require the greatest risks. Rit has traditionally attracted the most cunning members of the Family, most of whom have contributed to Benedict's lineage. No one has managed to break the direct succession for several generations."

"Benedict intends to be more than the Dom," murmured

Aroha, sincere interest vanquishing his usual reluctance to speculate aloud. "He intends to become the prophet of a new religion."

"Not new," retorted Ch'ango, slightly piqued that Aroha had matched her startling insight so easily. "Very old. Very influential, until the Empires disbanded its organizations and discredited its leaders. Both Empires worked tirelessly to eradicate its traces, even in its indirect forms. The postwar riots dismantled the rest."

Absently, Aroha amended her claim, "The traditions of the Avalon Mages still include some obscure references, particularly among the grail myths."

Ch'ango concealed her amazement behind a complacent smile. She never accustomed herself to Aroha's breadth of knowledge, for he was so young, and his origins were so humble. She replied as if she knew the Avalon mythologies as well as he, and she resolved to coax more information from him later, "Though minor today, Avalon was once a formidable Mystic School. The Empires devoted much effort to diminish its prestige, largely because of the former dominance of its traditions and adherents. Avalon survived by excising any religious references that the Empires consid ered significant." Ch'ango folded her spidery hands. "The boy *is* dangerous. He must not become a Dom. Hollis must designate another heir."

"Affirmists have their own political priorities, as we have ours. Elections are arranged accordingly."

"Elections can be rearranged."

"With a Mastermage of your caliber to defend him from other Affirmists, Dom Hollis would seem to be invincible."

"I *influenced* Hollis' father successfully, and I shall influence Hollis by whatever means are necessary."

"Using Mage arts against your Affirmist counterpart violates the social contract and could antagonize even your Mystic constituents."

"Be not naive, Aroha," snapped Ch'ango, relieved to resume her position as superior. "One who seeks true power cannot afford to be intimidated by archaic customs. Do you believe that the zealous Benedict, if he became Dom, would honor the Mystic/Affirmist contract on *my* behalf?"

Because Aroha of Purotu was in no sense naive, he did not take offense at Ch'ango's sharpness. The full, false arrogance of insecurity burdened Aroha, but he had intelligence enough to know when to listen. "Do you intend to discredit the boy, the father, or both?"

"I shall reason with Dom Hollis," replied Ch'ango, and her black eyes glittered with secret discomfiture at Aroha's quickness. "Hollis will cooperate or suffer my displeasure. The boy is barely sixteen. I have time enough to prepare an alternative for *him*." Her fingers rippled with a flicker of violet Mage light, contemptuously discarding the difficulties and illegalities of manipulating Affirmists. She would not share the rest of her plans with Aroha, since he insisted on anticipating her instead of applauding her cunning. She had better ways of taking pleasure from him. Her Mage light caressed Aroha's face, trickling seductively down his body.

Though he hungered only for information, Aroha did not risk antagonizing Ch'ango by pressing her when her interests had moved elsewhere. Of all the influential Tathagatan women he cultivated for his personal gain, Ch'ango was his most prized acquisition. She would kill him in a moment if she ever recognized how callously he used her, but Aroha took great care to keep Ch'ango satisfied—and ignorant of his other mistresses.

Aroha smiled, plying the charm that empowered him as effectively as his considerable Mage skills. Inwardly, he steeled himself against revulsion for the grasping fingers and parchment skin of Mastermage Ch'ango. Physically, she disgusted him. Ch'ango was a cold, aging woman with an excessive fondness for blood magic. As the most dreaded Mastermage of the World Parliament, she offered inestimable value to Aroha and his ambitions. Political worth did not always arrive in pleasant packages.

Sometimes, political worth arrived in the guise of a disheveled youth preaching history on a Tathagatan street corner. Aroha appreciated Ch'ango's concern over Benedict's dangerous prattle, but Aroha dismissed that issue from his personal agenda. Ch'ango would ensure that Benedict never entered the World Parliament. The certainty that elated Aroha owned an entirely different nature, and it sang through every Mage-trained nerve: *The only son of the Dom of Rit shares the knowledge of the Scribes.*

17 Years Later

Marita

Twenty-seven hours remain until the execution. I have not slept at all this past night, and the sheets have twisted around my feet. My eyes feel like sand.

A man will die tomorrow. The people of my blighted home, the island city of Rit, have laid him on the altar of their fear. I would like to blame Uncle Toby, Lar, or Talitha; I would like to accuse my influential family or our distant, ruling Parliament with its equally corrupt Houses of Doms and Mastermages; but we have all condemned Benedict equally. I thought I knew the reasons. I do know the laws. I, too, am Benedict's executioner.

It is not Benedict we fear. It is the past, the future, and the merest suspicion that Benedict is wiser than our comfortable laws can tolerate. If Benedict is even a little wise, then the rest of us are worse than fools.

The death will be humane. Talitha would tolerate none of the protracted methods of blood magic that Lar might prefer. A little powder will dissolve in a golden wine, staining the liquid pink. A clear, undecorated glass will be handed to Benedict, and the wine will be poured for him. His deathbed will be ready: a soft mattress clothed in the white sheet that will become his shroud. I have seen the room. It is paneled in plastiwood of an oaken hue. The room is plain but comfortable.

Each spring, we Mages prepare an offering of resins, herbs, and philters, and we burn it on an altar made of gold. We dance the ancient stories, beat drums, and raise our voices in an eerie chant derived from the cultural myths of the five dominant Mage Schools. The ceremony of offering casts an emotional spell of empowerment upon participants and observers alike.

The offering recruits new Mystics without condemning alternative beliefs and offending the Law of Affirmation. It also serves to remind us cynical, established Mages that Mysticism has a true beauty that persists despite all the unscrupulous members of our profession. If the offering ever had a deeper purpose, we have buried it beneath the unified Mysticism that has equalized all our world's mythologies into an uneasy whole.

Benedict once asked me: "To whom is the offering made?" I had no answer for him. He has his faith, as I have mine, and the philosophy of reason is inadequate to explain such fundamental, personal judgments. I wish I were as confident as Benedict. I sway too easily with the hearts and minds of those who surround me.

Benedict, my brother, will die tomorrow. He did not protest the verdict. He seems content to accept his punishment. He has admitted guilt of every charge against him—from defying the Law of Affirmation to abetting a smuggler. I do not understand my brother's serenity, except as proof of his zealotry. He does not expect any unforeseen benefactor to save him from this most final act of justice. He has exhausted his value to those who have used him, and he acknowledges that he is alone but for his Divine Intercessor, relic of a single-minded type of religion that only Benedict remembers.

Benedict's faith comforts him, but its impracticality has condemned him. My frail, remaining hope takes the more prosaic form of a man. I expect to be as disappointed as my brother.

My hope is the enemy, Andrew, though I would not want to know how, if he chose, Andrew might save my brother. Elusive, enigmatic Andrew has stirred the past that all of us dread. My brother will pay for those crimes, still protecting Andrew as a friend.

Andrew does not earn—or need—loyalty. He possesses that ill-defined quality of dominance that outweighs common sense among susceptible persons like my brother. Andrew needs nothing from anyone, except restraint, but Andrew is too clever for the traps set against him. Even if Benedict had agreed to aid in the capture effort, as Uncle Toby once hoped, Andrew would discover the means to survive.

My brother will die in the place of this man, this criminal against humanity, who defies the entire Mystic/Affirmist social contract. Lar, as Mastermage of Rit, cites many Mystical traditions that make the death of a servant an effective form of attack against the master. As a Mystic, I cannot argue with Lar. I have witnessed the power of blood magic too often, little as I like its use. Talitha and Uncle Toby make an equally convincing case against Benedict from the Affirmist perspective: My brother is an accessory to treason against society, and he must be punished accordingly.

By giving my brother the fatal cup, Lar will enact a powerful spell against Andrew, and the Affirmists will eliminate a lawbreaker with their characteristic pragmatism. Benedict does not object to death, for he considers it only an interlude in a journey to meet his Intercessor. The execution of my brother is such a satisfactory solution from everyone's viewpoint, except mine. I am outnumbered; therefore, I must be the fool.

Not even I can truly wish to see Andrew assume my brother's role in that plain, quiet room, awaiting execution. I, too, am susceptible to Andrew's brand of influence.

Feti'a will welcome the day soon, and I should not miss the ritual. If I believed in my professed creed, Benedict would tell me, I would now rise eagerly from my bed to join my fellows at the pentacle, where I would find solace from my Mystic faith.

The morning is too cold and damp. I shall lie here beneath the soft, silk-and-down quilt that rewards me for betraying my brother. I shall not open my eyes. My mind will replay those same five days, three months ago, that have assaulted me throughout the night, and I shall wish that I could sleep.

I.

MAGE CARDS:

Blood Mage

Sable Prince

Brass Dom

Ice Dreamer

Shadow Cat

Marita

Uncle Toby extends invitations as commands. He does not request confirmation; he assumes it. He has been Dom of Rit since my father's death, and the rank of Dom carries authority over Mystics as well as Affirmists. I have met worse Doms, but Uncle Toby does savor his superior status.

My relationship with Toby is complex with respect to both lineage and personal interactions. By birth, he is my second cousin, and I adored him for the first ten years of my life. He was an appealing adolescent, who often tended my brother and me. He devastated my childishly romantic ideas when he married my mother's older sister, Nan, instead of waiting for me to mature.

When Uncle Toby invited me to lunch at the Stone Palace, which our family has owned for several generations, I expected an unpleasant afternoon. After his marriage, Uncle Toby never had much use for me, even when the rest of the family still considered me their own. In fairness to him, he treats me as well as he treats anyone, but Uncle Toby does not remain Dom of Rit by squandering kindliness.

I approached the Stone Palace on foot, since Rit's intra city trams and buses have not functioned in years. The lack does not greatly trouble us. Nothing worth visiting is far apart in Rit. The Stone Palace is only a quarter hour's walk from my office, which is a similar distance from the Mage Center, where I live.

I took the straight inland streets, an ugly route. The most scenic road, which overlooks the ocean, is broken and cluttered with the rubble of centuries. The neighborhood of the Stone Palace, like most of Rit's central district, consists chiefly of abandoned, high-density apartment complexes that date from the era of population excess. Just prior to the great Hangseng-Nikkei War, construction of the Stone Palace represented the intended first step in a full district renovation.

The rest of the renovation never occurred. Empty row houses, boxy things of plastiwood and yellowed stucco, still crowd the grounds beyond the Stone Palace's high, outer wall.

Toby, despite his populist politics, relishes the aristocratic sound of the "Stone Palace," although the building served originally as a hotel for affluent travelers. Its name may be affectation, but the foundation of its impressive facade consists of true, quarried granite instead of molded plastone.

The Stone Palace upholds its name better now than in its original design, judging by the old pictures. Once, graceful trees and flowers broke the hard lines of a stronghold built in the tense, dismal days before the war. Since the contamination from the war destroyed most exterior plants of sophisticated growth habits, the planter boxes are empty except for dark patches of string-moss. Flood lines, dating from the first years after the war, stain the gray stone of the walls and wide walkways, and the inner courtyard is etched to chalky white from the fouled seawater that once scoured Rit Island. Though the gardens now thrive only in Aunt Nan's sequestered greenhouse, the Stone Palace has endured atop its lonely hill. It is only a two-level structure behind its shallow facade, but the Stone Palace maintains a forbidding presence.

The gatekeeper, a man of inoffensive, medium size and coloring, squinted at me from his lofty chair in the wall turret. He made a great show of tugging on heavy chains to part the blue-green copper-clad gates for me, as if they constituted an actual barricade. In fact, the gates have enough deeply hammered ridges to allow easy climbing, and the weedy ground beyond the wall provides a resilient—albeit scratchy—landing.

The gatekeeper allowed me to enter without challenge, though tradition makes it rare for a Mage to enter an important Affirmist's dwelling without escort. The staff of the Stone Palace seems to change each time I visit, but all of them recognize me without introduction. It is, I suppose, Toby's way of reminding me that I remain a member of a significant family.

Does he imagine that I could forget? My family controls most of the world's supply factories, as well as most seats in the House of Doms. If I had remained an Affirmist, I could have pursued a candidacy for personal power, if I had cherished such goals. I would surely have been a coveted prize for political alliance, since the era of creating new parliamentary seats for every outstandingly ambitious Affirmist ended with my grandfather's generation. Even members of my family—the Family of Doms, as it is often called by envious outsiders—must now contend for official parliamentary positions.

As a Mystic, I have removed myself from the direct struggles, but I am not immune from their influence. I have few friends, since few people can accept me apart from my birthright. I cannot enjoy any man's attentions without questioning his motives. I cannot pursue my own relatively simple life without awareness that the Family still observes me, judges me, and pursues serious debates regarding the nature of my personal aspirations.

Because my father, grandfather, and great-grandfather were Doms of Rit, I must exert more care to be socially correct than less visible citizens. I rebelled against my family's political affiliations and aims, but I remain exceedingly careful not to offend. I understand the fundamental Law of Affirmation, and I obey it, for I value my survival. I acknowledge openly and often that my Mystic beliefs represent a strictly personal choice, and I do not try to spread my creed beyond accepted bounds. I am not entirely impractical, and I am well aware of the reasons for the Affirmist laws of our world. The Empires' catastrophic demise taught us that lesson, at least: We must tolerate each other if we hope to survive as a species.

I understand the Affirmist perspective of my upbringing, but I also share the Mystic awareness of subtly pro-Empire traces that would horrify staunch Affirmists. Post-war riots eradicated most overt Empire images, but every Mage knows the prevalence of Nikkei symbols in a city like Rit, where the princes of the Nikkei Empire ruled for so along. As Dom, Uncle Toby governs against any resurgence of anti-Affirmation Empire ideas, but his home is rife with Empire legacies.

From the untended grounds that surround the Stone Palace, a broad passage, guarded by a dilapidated, wrought iron gate, leads to the inner courtyard. Wind hisses through the passage like the whispers of the dead, and the wind carries an odor of perpetual mustiness. Marble statues line that long walkway, their hollow eyes fixed upon gardens that no longer exist. First rioters and then vandals beat all clear features from the white, weathered figures of men and women from our disparaged past. The statues' vacuous faces now seem sad and innocuous. Their nameplates have all vanished. Only one pedestal is empty.

Affirmists seldom understand the significance of that missing figure, because Affirmists do not cultivate the senses that read the anger of the past. As I pass that pedestal, I feel the biting frustration of the rioters who toppled its tenant centuries ago, condemning an impotent statue for the cataclysmic war that eradicated most of our planet's life. Aunt Nan taught me the peculiar nature of the charge against that statue: The empty pedestal supported the forbidden image of the Nikkei prince who engineered the Stone Palace's utility and convenience systems. I cannot walk through that passageway without grieving: for the rioters, for their frustration, and even for the Nikkei prince.

This day, since I walked alone, I avoided the statues and the distress they always caused me. I tramped through loose dirt and gravel, scuffing my sandals, and circled the palace to reach a less disturbing route. Behind a sticky curtain of string-moss, I found the copper doors that I'd discovered years earlier during childhood explorations. The doors were as solid as those in the outer wall, but this bolt had broken long ago, and no supply factory produces a replacement bolt to fit the broad, opulent scale of the Stone Palace. There is little enough reason to regret the loss of the fastener. The rooms on this side of the Stone Palace are dark, their utilities inoperative, and the windows so deeply scratched that they are as opaque as the flexsteel draperies behind them.

Out of courtesy to my Affirmist host, I did not use a Mage light. I could feel my way easily enough to the nearest of the Stone Palace's many atriums, a shuttered room that once held a water garden. Thin light spilled through the atrium's broken, overhead lattice. Little clouds of mica dust glittered, swirling at my feet. I crossed the arched plastiwood bridge over a dry streambed and opened the banded iron gate.

Uncle Toby awaited me in the main courtyard, the focal point of most of the Stone Palace's habitable rooms. Along each of three sides, a dozen distinct balconies open from the individual guest rooms of the old hotel. A single, continuous balcony with a private stairway crosses the fourth side. That is Aunt Nan's private territory.

I crossed the etched cobbles to meet my uncle, and we sat on the cold edge of the central fountain. Stone dolphins leaped endlessly from the half-empty pool, the dizzy mechanism of their dance surviving long after their originals have vanished from war-tainted oceans. "Thank you for coming, Marita," gushed Toby with his warm smile. "It is good to see you so well. You are prospering."

Uncle Toby has the looks of a simple man. He has a forthright face, mischievous hazel eyes, a ready smile, and a comfortable manner. During his years as Dom, he has become plump enough to seem nonthreatening, yet he has not gained enough weight to appear decadent. He is as uniformly brown in skin, eyes, and hair color as any Affirmist could desire. He seldom wears anything more formal than an oversized, sleeveless robe over bulky shirt and trousers. He conveys honesty. Perhaps he has convinced himself that he believes in what he does.

I tried to match his geniality, replying, "There is always a market for love philters, and mine are more successful than most." I touched my philter purse, a roll of canvas and emerald silk that holds many vials, but I did not unbind it from the silver cords at my waist. A Mage cannot be too careful in the presence of any Affirmist, especially a Dom like Toby. Legal claims against the unsolicited application of magic often succeed on the weight of popular appeal, since practicing Mages are envied by the bitter jurists in a decaying city like Rit. Most Affirmists imagine that all Mages are wealthy, because Affirmists do not realize how much our Mastermages charge us for our spells and supplies.

I had purposely worn a simple, short-sleeved sheath that offered no concealment for wands or other threatening apparatus. My arms wore no jewelry that might hide my Mage marks: above each wrist, a crescent, and on each forearm, an incomplete triangle of ten silver lotus blossoms with the three-lotus base positioned near the inside of the elbow. I never keep my hair long enough for the secretive coils that many Mages favor, because my hair is too distinctively blonde for the tastes of my Affirmist family. I had likewise chosen neutral, inoffensive colors—the traditional cream and white—except for the philter purse that I dared not leave unattended. Uncle Toby wore a robe of rich Affirmist brown, but he is Dom and can afford small gestures of incorrectness.

"You succeed well in persuading your clients to trust you," murmured Toby, skillfully expressing his disbelief in Mysticism while affirming my personal choice. "You inherited the full portion of your father's charisma, to your brother's misfortune."

"You flatter me unduly," I replied, "and do Benedict a disservice. He was always Father's favorite, as you may recall."

"I recall that I preferred my niece even then, and time has proven my judgment sound." I did not believe my uncle—save to the extent that gender had made me Toby's potential ally and Benedict only a rival. In those days, Benedict was everyone's favorite, because he was delightfully considerate even in rebellion, and I was a stubborn child. "How long has it been since you've seen your brother?" asked Toby, studiously casual.

"Two or three years," I answered, restraining a sigh. If Toby insisted on speaking as my uncle instead of as my Dom, the law said he deserved the same openness from me. Toby's familial claim only curtailed my customary rights of privacy. I did not like to discuss my few personal relationships with anyone, and Uncle Toby's affections were at best sporadic and opportunistic.

"Your brother had some difficulties in Malawi."

"Did he?" I tried to sound disinterested, but Toby's plump cheeks furrowed in warning. I continued reluctantly, "I'm sorry, but I'm not surprised. Benedict abandoned all diplomacy years ago, when he discovered his 'Divine Intercessor.' He has become chronically rude and difficult."

"He has returned to Rit."

"Has he?" I whispered, too shocked to immediately believe that Benedict had come home, and I had not known. Our contact had waned with distance, since Benedict could not (or would not) afford to hire a member of the powerful Scribes' Guild as courier. However, I had not thought he would return without telling me.

"I am surprised that you had not heard. He has been speaking in the forum. There have been complaints." A glimmer of Toby's old, cunning charm brightened his eyes as he acknowledged, "Perhaps I succeeded too well at keeping Benedict's name from circulating. I did not intend to hide the news from *you*."

"I hear little news, aside from my clients' private concerns. I have little contact with any events outside the Mage Center, where no one discusses 'the Family' in my presence." I expected my rival Mages to keep secrets from me—and most Mages are rivals in some respect—but Benedict could have sent me some token of greeting. A twinge of hurt made me sound cold. "If Benedict is abusing his right to express opinions, issue an injunction against him."

"I would rather avoid legal action, if possible."

"You're due for reelection soon?" It was an honest, if cynical, question. I deliberately avoided issues of politics, especially regarding such blatantly corrupt examples as the Doms' elections. I knew how thoroughly my family choreographed the distribution of Affirmist power. I also knew that Lar, as Mastermage, defended Toby from the schemes of Affirmist rivals and received a similar political service in return. Everyone expects the parties of Mystics and Affirmists to be internally corrupt but immune to each other's influence because Mystics and Affirmists revere different types of wealth. The balance of mutual advantage and independence has sustained the parties' uneasy alliance since the Great War.

"Next year," replied Toby, unembarrassed by the contrivances of government. "If you could talk to Benedict, I would be appreciative. I have invited him here several times, but he consistently declines."

Toby's appreciation held limited value for a registered Mystic, but his enmity could destroy a Mage's career. "I'd be happy to help you," I answered with a strained smile, "but I doubt that Benedict will cooperate with me. He may not even agree to see me."

"I respect your right to practice your creed."

I nodded in reluctant understanding. Uncle Toby had granted me permission to use Mage's arts in dealing with my brother. It was not quite a formal commission, but it comprised a significant concession from a Dom. As a Mystic, I was pleased by the implicit tribute to my beliefs. As an individual, I felt angry at being trapped so neatly between Uncle Toby and my obligations as a Mage. "I shall do what I can within legal limits."

"I have confidence in you, Marita. You always had more influence with Benedict than anyone else in the family did."

"That was years go." I bit my lip. I had received an informal commission from the Dom. I could not let self-pity entrap me. "Can you tell me anything about his recent history?"

"Your parents taught you your letters, didn't they?"

I nodded again although I disliked the question nearly as much as the commission against my brother. If I had been less sure that Toby already knew the answer, I would have lied and sealed the lie with a spell. Outside of the tightly controlled Scribes' Guild, literacy is illegal, since it can lead to just such radical ideas as seduced Benedict.

The Scribes' Guild tolerates few exceptions to their exclusive rights, but wealth and rank in Parliament carry many privileges. Several branches of our prominent Affirmist family still educate their children in the old ways. Doms and their kin—and we are an incestuous lot—claim to have need and wisdom enough to handle the responsibility of reading the few documents that survived the war. In truth, the Chief Scribes are rewarded well for tacitly including selected Doms as members of the Guild. In return, literate Doms guard their secret knowledge as jealously as the official Scribes.

The existence of a literate, practicing Mage would appall the Scribes if they thought any other Mages knew about me. Since the earliest use of Mage marks, Mystic lore has remained unwritten except in the most obscure of private symbolisms, and literacy is commonly supposed to cripple the natural gifts of Mysticism. Perhaps my diversity of training did stultify my Mage skills, but I am reasonably successful in my profession. My example could inspire a few reckless Mages to try to impinge on the Scribes' domain, and that occurrence would please neither Scribes nor Doms.

My family never registered me—or my brother—with the Scribes' Guild. Our parents left the task to Aunt Nan, who taught us our letters, and Nan chose to forget, year after year. The omission seemed fortuitous when I discovered my Mystic affinity. I have wondered if Nan predicted that Affirmism would not satisfy me forever.

I made a solemn, binding vow to my parents that I would not disclose my reading ability outside my family, neither to teach others nor to enable others to benefit from what I knew. Uncle Toby's question was a warning of how easily he could injure me by reminding significant Doms or Scribes of the danger I could present to our society. It was a secret of which even Scribe Talitha, who was Uncle Toby's assistant and a formidable political power in her own right, remained ignorant.

Having made his quiet threat, Uncle Toby smiled benignly. "Your skill will be convenient in this instance," he remarked. "I shall show you Benedict's file." Uncle Toby stood and stretched, suggesting confidence in our family bond by his relaxed attitude. The pose did not convince me, because I knew Toby too well, but I matched it by swinging my legs over the fountain's edge and dipping my bare feet into the cool, shallow water. One of Nan's birds cried "keerau" and fell silent.

Talitha

Scribe Gavilan, Tathagata:

Our informants were correct: Aroha is here in Rit. Having some experience at recognizing his handiwork, I expect to find him soon. We shall not lose him again, as we did in Malawi, by relying on our control of the ports and the local authorities. We shall lure him carefully and defeat him with the last of the true Empire weapons, which the Family has guarded all these years in case of such an emergency. The Protectorate's decision to use the weapons sickens me, but the only alternative may be the blood magic that Ch'ango recommends.

If Toby fails, we may yet be forced to resort to Mage methods. Lar is convinced that Toby will fail and is making his own preparations accordingly. Lar has ordered several senior Mages to deploy destructive philters along the likely privateers' routes. He has concocted a variety of creative lies—from delicately placed rumors regarding stolen spells to crude exploitation of anti-Affirmist sentiments among lesser Mages—to ensure that his Mystics alert him to any vulnerabilities in Aroha's organization.

I cannot fault Lar for excessive measures. Even bereft of his Mage skills, Aroha has already caused too much damage by his cunning and treachery. As Ch'ango has often said, Aroha's ruthlessness demands harsh measures in return.

How I hate the depths to which Aroha and his accursed "Empire Prince" force us! If I did not fear that they might actually succeed in restoring their tyrannical Empire, I would despise what we are doing to combat them. We must defeat Aroha. I dare not imagine the alternative.

Grow in wisdom,
Scribe Talitha, Rit

Marita

White sky bleached the forum's sandy colors. The benches, warmly toned on brighter days, encircled the speaker's platform like the scrapings of ashes around a doused pyre. The outer wreath of fallen monoliths, the forum's original proud framework, seemed to breed unnatural shadows, strewn by past angers instead of by the weak sunlight. Scavenging dogs, bone and brindle mongrels, sniffed and scratched among the weeds.

The man who stood on the speaker's lonely, cracked stone dais had the same pallor as the sky. He was a gaunt man with overly defined bones that might have made him beautiful, if they had been allowed to develop undamaged. Skewed by old breaks, the bones gave him an insubstantial, unfinished appearance. The dampness of the evening's early fog had darkened his yellow hair and flattened it against his skull. He wore a long, gray robe, a fine woolen garment edged and cinched with crimson rope, tightly gathered around his narrow waist. His eyes reflected the indefinite hue of his surroundings.

"Hear me," cried this gaunt man, who was my brother. "There is no darkness, no despair that the Intercessor cannot lift from you. A greater life is yours forever, if you will take it. This joy is the Intercessor's gift to us all!"

A few more members of the audience drifted away from the forum, wandering back into the city's dark alleyways. Of the audience that remained, two had stretched out on empty benches to sleep, four played a game with colored stones, and the others talked among themselves. They had identified this speaker as a radical. They did not want to appear to listen.

"Affirmists!" persisted Benedict. "You know your unhappiness. Your creed dictates a belief in everything, but this means you believe in nothing. You who are Mystics, by considering yourselves capable of godhood, become either dishonest or disillusioned."

"They only become disillusioned if they're too honest to become rich!" taunted a young man with the unadorned wrists of one who is ignorant of the Mage's arts. A childish compulsion to speak his mind made him reckless, or he would not have spoken publicly to a radical. "The rich don't stay in Rit, and we poor have no reason to be happy."

Benedict's attention latched eagerly onto the young man. "All your worldly needs are met," argued my fervent brother. "You are only poor in spirit." Benedict spread his arms to encompass his scattered audience. "Why is joy so difficult to accept? You build walls against it, stacking high your bricks of disbelief, mortared by anger and insecurity. You see the world's history of injustice and choose to look no further. You doubt each other and yourselves. You refuse to know that you are wealthier than any city's Dom or Mastermage, if you will only accept the love that the Intercessor freely gives to each of us. That acceptance is the only law that any of us needs."

"I'd rather accept a Mastermage's gold," mocked the young man, and his companion, a girl of similar age, laughed with him. They both wore the bone-colored tunics and trousers that were the uniform of the inoffensive, but they had not yet learned to clothe their thoughts with equal care. I was once that young.

Years ago, I had heard my brother speak of his odd creed, but I had never imagined that he would carry his convictions from adolescence to adulthood—especially in a public forum, where our grandfather had once issued proclamations as Dom. Benedict had frozen in time, unchanging except for physical wear that was all too evident. I could see my own rash youth in him, but it was a remote perspective, distorted by my brother's unnatural ideals. Knowing our family's fondness for polemics, I had half expected to find a man who used unconventional tactics solely to gain attention. Benedict still sounded sincere.

Perhaps Uncle Toby's concerns were justified. Benedict had a hungry look, and he had acquired some unsettling mannerisms, shaking his hands toward his audience and raising his steel-blue eyes repeatedly to the sky. His bones had never been brittle; those mishealed breaks could not all have occurred by accident. In childhood, Benedict and I had often been mistaken for identical twins, because our family had properly declined to distinguish between our genders, and Benedict was only older by a year. Though the basic similarities of thin, sharp bones and pale coloring remained, I doubted that anyone would even recognize us as full siblings now, so faded and skeletal had Benedict become.

At the least, I could understand why Uncle Toby found Benedict an embarrassment, best confined within the family. A prominent Affirmist like Uncle Toby could forgive nearly anything but incorrect sincerity. I wondered how many Affirmist relatives Uncle Toby had sent to Benedict before recruiting me, the family's lone Mage, as reluctant accomplice. Uncle Toby had surely exhausted all other options short of official injunction. He certainly knew that Benedict and I had ceased to be close.

Cautiously, I delved into my philter purse. Mysticism is a respectable creed, but public displays are discouraged in Affirmist cities like Rit. I wear my Mage marks openly, which assures me the right to practice the spells of my rank under proper authority, but I do not flaunt my magic even for the sake of the Dom. Though the forum has received little use since the argument between my grandfather and Mastermage Ch'ango, it is still an official site for political expositions. It is also tainted by the memories—visible in every scorched, tumbled stone—of the Mystic impact of that same, infamous argument.

I mixed three of the jewel-toned powders in the palm of my hand, and I whispered the words of binding. When the blend satisfied me, I blew the fine dust in the direction of my brother. The motes sparkled briefly above his head, but neither he nor his inattentive audience seemed to observe the haloing effect or its source.

Benedict passed a hand across his eyes, and he stepped down from the speaker's platform. My spell would not last long, but Benedict would cease his proselytism for the day. He stumbled on the hem of his robe.

Gold blazed startlingly across the gray-on-gray scene, reaching swiftly to steady my brother. Emerging from behind one of the few standing stones, the gold accompanied a man of such remarkable appearance that he might have materialized from some extravagant Mystic legend. The stranger had the evenly bronzed skin and heavy black hair of most of the world's population, but his resemblance to the

ordinary ended there. This was no E-unit addict, drifting
from dreams into daylight only long enough to let his entertainment god perform self-maintenance. Neither did the
man's heroic proportions conform to the carefully neutral
mold of social servants such as myself. He had the strong,
impressive musculature suggestive of a manual laborer, a
rare being in this pampered age. Rarer still was the ostentatious panoply of gold bracelets that decorated his arms.

Fixers are strongly built, but the law forbids them to own
so much as a golden bead. Transient ship workers, employ-
ees of my influential family, occasionally visit Rit to carry
special goods for the Dom or Mastermage. Such workers,
hand-selected by the Family, are allowed to prosper in exchange for loyal silence. I assumed that the man belonged to
that rare class, though he did not display the usual token of
affiliatory brown. The cream shades of his vest and trousers
were politically neutral.

If I had not been on my uncle's errand, I might have offered the man a commission to stand for an hour in front of
my office building. He could have inspired a drove of new
business in love philters. He could have inspired interest
from an E-unit addict.

He nearly stunned me into immobility when I realized that
he was more than a helpful stranger to my brother. He exchanged quick words with Benedict, then determinedly ushered my brother from the forum. I left my position in the
shadow of a fallen stone and followed them hurriedly.

Befuddled by my spell, my brother could not move speed-
ily, but his companion compensated with strong, steady support. I was just able to observe the pair of mismatched men
turning toward the wharfs. The stench of the polluted sea became thick and noxious, but I did not take the time to
cleanse the air around me with a philter powder. I nearly lost
sight of my quarry in the shadowy alleyways between the
brick row houses, most of which were as empty as the majority of Rit. If the curling white fog had descended any
lower, I would have needed a spell to track my brother's
course. The Mages' Luck stayed with me, and the journey
proved short.

The two men entered an unprepossessing waterfront
house, a narrow building the color of the wet sand beyond
the plastone tide-wall. To the height of four levels, the house
was indistinguishable from its neighbors. A single, warped

plastiwood door adorned the ground level, and a single square window and unguarded ledge indicated each upper-level apartment, three per floor.

At the fifth level, this house—unlike its neighbors—had a plastone extension, which reached to within a finger's breadth of the adjacent buildings. The fifth level's windows were large, irregularly spaced, and darkened by plastiwood shutters. The top-heavy structure looked too unbalanced to stand alone. Indeed, it seemed to lean slightly toward the east, an ominous direction from my perspective, as a ten-lotus Mage of the Avalon School.

The front door opened to me without resistance. A glint of my sapphire philter powder mingled with the sand on the steep stairway. I climbed to the fourth level, where the traces stopped at a charcoal door adorned with coarse white characters that spelled Linden. It was an old name in our family, nearly as old as the alphabet that my brother had used in claiming his place in Rit.

I could pretend that Benedict had hired a Scribe to write the name legally, though I was sure he had done nothing so sensible. The naming did not even represent a practical use of his secret knowledge, since any of the standard pictorials would have served better as identification. Trust Benedict to revive a dangerous, abandoned relic from the past without thought of the consequences. He had always loved our games of delving into the cobwebbed city storerooms and trying to identify the former purpose of what we found, despite repeated warnings from our parents.

My brother opened his door to me before I knocked. Benedict and I had once shared a twinlike awareness of each other's essence, but I had hardly expected him to retain any of that old perception. I had been trained in such arts, but I could no longer distinguish my brother from other men except by the ordinary senses of sight and sound.

Benedict grabbed me and hugged me, though he had usually been undemonstrative when we were close in feeling. After our last bitter meeting, when our opposing philosophies had erupted into cruel recriminations, I had feared that he might refuse to speak with me at all. My inner cynic's voice told me that he still sought only to win a convert to his Intercessor, but I nearly cried with gladness that my brother did not shun me. I had always felt lonely without him.

"Marita, I am so delighted to see you," blurted my

brother, as excitedly as a child. "You look wonderful! You
have not changed a bit, except your hair is curlier."

"Thanks to the liberal use of a philter I developed last
year," I replied wryly. "The philter has not sold as well as
I hoped, so I apply it to myself."

Reminded of my Mystic status, Benedict released me
from the hug, but he clung to my hands. "Please, come inside. I can offer you real chocolate. I remember how you enjoy it."

Without attempting to reply, I allowed Benedict to usher
me into a room that was as unexpected as his enthusiastic
welcome. The usual appliances were missing. He had no
E-unit, no supply cubes, no environmental regulator. I had
visited (and occupied) many apartments where the appliances no longer functioned, but I had never seen a living
space where the entire central console had been removed,
leaving only tarry scars that peered from beneath a woven
chestnut rug. A plastiwood table with three matching chairs,
a tall, black enamel cupboard, and a low cot, covered by an
old-fashioned, white thermal blanket, served as the only furniture. The window's opalescent shade was raised, and the
clear panes were folded outward onto the narrow ledge. The
salt scent of the ocean seemed stronger here than below,
where the oily refuse at the water's edge predominated.

"Please, sit," offered Benedict eagerly. "All three chairs
are stable. My friend found them for me. The apartment was
empty when I moved into it."

Apparently recovered from my spell, Benedict glided to
the tall cupboard and removed a small parcel from a well-
stocked shelf. I watched him curiously. He might look worn
and battered—as was understandable for an outspoken
radical—but his step was eager and his energetic movements
belied the remnants of my philter. Reverentially, he removed
the clear wrapper from a solid block of dark chocolate,
which he laid in front of me with quiet pride.

"I haven't seen chocolate in a decade," I murmured. The
offering impressed me, though I was too innately suspicious
not to question its presence in Benedict's home. Chocolate
had been unavailable from supply cubes in this part of the
world since Factory One failed. The single factory failure
did not justify a relocation effort, since Tathagata's process-
ing centers still produced and distributed the majority of our

basic foods and other goods, but the loss of local resources had limited Rit's selections.

I had lived close enough to Doms and Mastermages to know that the laws restricting supply distribution applied only when convenient for the wealthy and influential. My own special privileges had ended when I chose to become a Mage, breaking my ties with Affirmist Doms like Uncle Toby. I had not risen high enough among the Mages to regain what I had lost. However, I had fared much better than Benedict overall. I asked him, "Where did you obtain chocolate?" and I tried not to place too much insulting emphasis on the pronoun.

"My friend Andrew gives it to me," replied Benedict without a pause. His smile held only innocent pleasure, and his voice rippled with boyish delight. "Andrew lives upstairs. He is the friend who found this furniture for me."

Dryly, I observed, "Andrew sounds like a very useful friend." I revised my assessment of Benedict's gilded companion at the forum: more than a prosperous ship worker for the Family; more likely a privateer—a raider of supply factories or a trader in the pilfered stock. Perhaps his presence in Rit would not be so good for my business, after all, since my timid and conservative customers tend to hibernate at the mention of criminals. "I am glad to find you living so comfortably, Ben. I heard reports that indicated otherwise. I was concerned." I *had* felt concern, although I would not have acted upon it without Uncle Toby's inarguable urging. My status was not so secure that I could lightly risk association with a known radical.

If Benedict had contacted me, of course, I would have accepted the risk of meeting him without hesitation. He had extended no such courtesy. That sign of my brother's indifference had inflicted a wound which his present warmth did not heal.

Benedict's smile drooped a little sadly. "You heard that I was imprisoned for a time." He studied the distended knuckles of his left hand, and I felt the remembered pain of their breaking.

Beset by his pain, I could not maintain any resentment against him. I yearned to share my brother's hurts and make him whole again. "I'm sorry, Ben." My Mage crescents, shiny silver against my sun-browned arms, burned with sorrow for him. "Would you let me try to help you?"

"There is no need, Marita." All pain vanished, swept away by a bittersweet joy that excluded me and forced me to realize how deep the rift between us had grown. My brother's smile blossomed anew. "Andrew paid for my release."

Kind of him, I thought sardonically, too aware of my upsurge in loneliness to feel charitable. Andrew evidently had no fear of facing the law that he flouted, which only indicated that he knew how to place an effective bribe. What could a prosperous privateer hope to gain from Benedict? A real ability to embarrass Uncle Toby, I supposed. Many ambitious Affirmists in the family, as well as some Mystic rivals, would pay well to discomfit Dom Toby of Rit. No one was likely to displace a seated Dom, but someone was always willing to nudge the foundations of power in small ways. "You still live dangerously, Ben. You give speeches that could offend most of the world's populace."

"Have you heard me?" He seemed pleased by the idea. He scraped his chair a little closer to the table.

"I heard you today."

"Ah." Benedict rested his lean jaw in his battered hand. "Andrew said that a Mage had caused my faintness. I appreciate your concern for me, Marita, but it is neither necessary nor wise."

"You know that you'd be arrested again if you were not the Dom's nephew."

"I have been blessed with an ability to speak the truth more freely than my fellow believers. I must not waste the gift." His thumb scraped his chin's pale stubble. "Rit is a difficult audience for me. It is hard to preach in one's own home."

The grief of watching Benedict, knowing he hurtled toward self-destruction, made my throat feel tight. "You take advantage of Uncle Toby. He cannot continue to be so generous to you, if you insist on flouting all the accepted standards of conduct. You have no right to claim a unique understanding of truth. Tolerance is the foundation of our society." It was our old argument. I was surprised at how deeply I still felt the injury of Benedict's narrow vision. "You have *no right* to claim to be better than anyone else."

"I have never claimed to be better than anyone else," answered Benedict gently.

"You claim that your creed is the only acceptable set of

beliefs. What worse statement of your intolerance and bigotry can be made?"

"I do not love you less, sister, for my recognition of the hollowness of your Mystic philosophies. I try to teach you, because I love you. I try to teach others, because I love them."

"Your idea of love brings only hurt."

"Love is not always gentle."

I shook my head and whispered bitterly, "I do not want to argue with you, Ben. I love you better than *that*, even when you behave outrageously."

Surprising me, Benedict relented, "Tell me of your own life, Marita. I see that you have earned your tenth lotus pair. I knew that you would succeed in whatever you chose to try. I am glad for you."

I turned my forearms, embedded with the silver lotus emblems of my rank. "I have crescents as well," I said, displaying the metallic symbols affixed permanently to my skin and nervous system. "Crescents are not the most prestigious specialty, but Mage Feti'a told me that I lack the natural skills to earn scarab marks. I hope to achieve another lotus of power eventually, and perhaps some agility shells."

Benedict stared at me unblinkingly, as if to pierce my soul with his clear gaze. "Do not covet what you lack. The scarab skills are dangerous and much too tempting. They are a force for corruption."

"You almost sound like you believe in Mysticism, brother." I should not have taunted him. I had come here to reason with Benedict, and I could do nothing but argue with him.

"I recognize the existence of the Mystics' powers. I disagree with the usage and the philosophy that elevates such powers to the central focus of life."

"You prefer that we ignore our potential."

"Self-development serves no purpose, until it reaches beyond the self."

I broke a tiny corner from the chocolate and tasted it slowly, savoring the bittersweet richness and trying to quiet my resentment. According to Uncle Toby's file, Benedict had been officially declared irrational at the time of his imprisonment in Malawi. I could not expect Benedict to understand the impropriety of criticizing my lawful beliefs. He deserved my pity, not my anger. If he were not my brother, once the dearest friend of my life, I would not have felt such frustration. I made an effort to detach myself and view him as a stranger or a particularly difficult client.

With a sigh, Benedict crossed his arms and leaned away from the table. "Did Uncle Toby send you here?"

I answered in my coolest, most professional voice. "Uncle Toby hoped that I could persuade you to keep your beliefs within the bounds of correctness. He shares my concern for you."

"I may believe what I like, as long as I make no claim that my beliefs are true?" The zealot's fervor returned, and the gray-robed man in front of me again became the preacher from the forum. "I cannot live that way, Marita. I do not dispute anyone's right to disagree with me, but I shall not pretend to esteem all philosophies equally. That stance negates the value of every creed. As a practicing Mystic, you must surely concur with me in this point, at least. We both rejected the all-accepting, all-demeaning tenets of our Affirmist upbringing."

"Uncle Toby is a Dom. If he advises you to be silent, you should heed him. How often do you expect your friend Andrew to pay for your crimes?" I could have stated my assessment of Andrew's opportunistic motives, but I knew that Benedict would not believe me.

"Andrew makes his own choices, as I make mine." Benedict's smile returned for an elusive instant. "Would you like to meet him?"

Without hesitation, I answered, "Yes." Perhaps I could reduce Friend Andrew's eagerness to abet my uncle's enemies. Perhaps I could even influence Andrew to help control my brother's injudicious ways.

Benedict walked lightly to the window and tapped on one of the open panes. The sound was small. Almost before it faded, Benedict returned to the chair beside me.

From the ensuing pounding, an entire parade might have been descending the stairs. Benedict's door flew open, striking the wall and jarring the room. Instead of the man I had expected to see, a boy stood beneath the lintel.

Children are rare enough in fading cities like Rit. This boy was a mixie, one of that unfortunate breed that sometimes results when a food factory first begins to go bad. The boy had the classic rough orange skin, shriveled features, and dark, dilated eyes. He looked to be on the verge of adolescence, which would indicate that he was near the end of his brief mixie life.

Around the boy danced a long-haired white puppy, a waist-high brindle hound, and a smoke-colored cat that any Mage would have coveted immediately. I had never seen another cat outside of the Mastermage's chambers, where cats are kept for spells and ceremonial purposes only. Cats, even more affected by the war's contaminants than humans, are rarely fertile now. Few mammals, except the mutated hounds and rodents, still maintain any stability of population.

Neither the boy nor his animals crossed the threshold into my brother's room. "Andrew's gone fishing," said the boy, eyeing me suspiciously from beneath his shaggy russet hair.

No edible fish have occupied the oceans near Rit in the two hundred years since the war, but my brother nodded. "Cris, this is my sister, Marita."

"The Mage," answered the boy, and he gathered the cat into his arms. The animal curled contentedly against him, but a glint of green eyes shone at me from amid the satiny fur. "Andrew doesn't trust Mages. He says most of them are cheats and liars."

I ignored the boy's rudeness, though it verged on a criminal breach of Affirmation. "I'm pleased to meet you, Cris. May I know the names of your friends?"

"Milk, Sand, and Iron," he responded brusquely, leaving to me the sorting out of the respective labels. "Those aren't their secret names. Andrew told me never to tell secret names, especially to a Mage."

"I do not practice blood magic, Cris, but I understand your caution." The sacrificial arts had always troubled me, although many respected Mystics considered blood magic a basic requirement for advancement. My rigid attitude was undoubtedly a remnant of my Affirmist upbringing.

"Will you join us for some chocolate, Cris?" asked my brother with exactly the same warmth of hospitality he had shown me.

"Nah. We're seeing Lillie, and we promised Andrew we'd return before the tide covers the sandbar." The boy settled his chin against the cat. "Will you need us, Ben?" I had a strong suspicion that the boy was offering to help remove me from the premises. The great she-hound, whom I assumed was Sand, had paid little attention to me, but she looked like a formidable opponent.

"No, Cris. Thank you."

At my brother's words, the boy allowed the cat to leap from his arms. The improbable family of boy, dogs, and cat bounded noisily down the stairway. I could hear one of the dogs bark gleefully as they reached the lower level and raced outside.

"I should leave also," I informed my brother. The boy had made me feel uncomfortable, and my stilted mood lingered. "Uncle Toby has invited us both to dinner tomorrow evening."

"The invitation is intended as a command, I suppose," replied Benedict with a faint, sad smile.

"He is the Dom. You have already tried his patience dangerously." I paused, hoping that my warning would take hold. "Thank you for the chocolate, Ben. I shall see you tomorrow."

"He won't change me, Marita."

I was tempted to scatter a powder of protection around my foolish brother, but I decided not to waste further valuable resources on a futile cause. I had done all that Uncle Toby had asked of me. Perhaps Uncle Toby could convince Benedict of the seriousness of the situation.

Perhaps I would go home and let my tears flow freely. Honest tears have power for those with the gifts of the Mage crescents. Little remained of what Benedict and I had shared as children, but I could still cry for him.

Hiroshi

20 Tenuare, 510

My friend, Andrew,

The shipment is smaller this month, but we have improved our products. We have redesigned our basic power supply and consolidated the packaging of the control modules for several of the toys. I think you will share my satisfaction with the results. With the next shipment, we should be able to compensate for this month's shortage. I hope the delay does not inconvenience you. I rely on your unfailing ingenuity and charm to appease our customers.

We have translated most of the Malawi text that you sent us. It contains several significant Hangseng medical formulas. Ellen is enthused about the possibilities for improving the health of the mixies.

Other news is less sanguine. I have received disquieting reports about the activities of the Protectorate, confirming the worst of your predictions. A friend of our cause informs us that several of the most troublesome Protectors are headed for Rit. I cannot view the timing of such a visit as coincidental.

We have always assumed that our enemies would eventually set aside their differences for the purpose of fighting us, but I dread the prospect of such a war. I reiterate the advice that I gave you when you decided to follow Benedict to his birthplace: Do not force the prophecy. Do not let the Protectors press us into conflict. Above all, be alert for Ch'ango's deceptions. I would beseech you to fulfill our contracts quickly and return to us.

I know that you will do as you deem best for our cause. Anavai sends her love.

Hiroshi

Marita

"From Rit will rise destruction!" I could see my brother's haggard face so clearly, hear his impassioned voice so distinctly. He wore his drab gray robe. Yet he spoke as a Mage, gifted with vision, before a sea of Inianga orange and Kinebahan crimson.

In the seething shadows above his head, a jar of glazed sable clay took shape. Crimson eagles, bears, antelopes, and other spirit symbols of Kinebahan mythic history patterned the jar's curved walls. The animal symbols leaped and lived.

"The condemned will gain release by righteousness, and those who obey the law of sin will be enslaved," declared my brother with the dire certainty of true, grim vision. Violet smoke engulfed the spirit jar, and the smoke became a leather-winged serpent of muddied ocher hue with fangs and talons of polished brass. The dragon breathed its fire upon the jar and fractured the ancient pottery.

The spirit jar tilted, and the crimson symbols bled from its sides and flowed thickly from its maw. Where the dark tide splattered, the robes of the listening Mages turned ashen gray to match my brother's ragged garment. Some of the Mages, Iniangas as well as Kinebahans, shriveled out of human form and became the animals that had adorned the spirit jar. All were gray and wounded.

"Power is real," my brother assured his damaged audience. His fervor had not dimmed. *"The evil ones understand this too well. Those who should be champions of the good have forgotten, because they accept the lies of the evil ones, and they use power wrongly. With deceit, the evil ones have defeated many of us, but we who remain will not fail. The evil ones rely on deceit, because they know the truth. The strength is ours."* He spread his arms and banished Mystic illusions. The Mages before him resumed their original colors and shapes. Each face resembled the Avalon card that

symbolized respectively the Kinebahan or the Inianga school: Mage of Sable or Mage of Blood. Dragon, smoke, and spirit jar were gone, and the sky became quiet and blue.

With the sense of my brother's presence so strong, waking alone in my own cot to a silent, sultry morning was a shock. The coarse fibers of my bed's linens bore little resemblance to the silken smoothness of my childhood, but I still reached blindly for long-gone companions, a bear of brown boiled wool and a patchwork strip of fur that I had named Snake. When my fingers found only the hard, slick wallboard, I forced open my eyes and groaned.

My cell provided a harsh greeting on the best of mornings. It was a box, just large enough to contain my bed and cupboard. The narrow strip of plastiwood floor barely sufficed for me to stand and dress. Even the colors had become unpleasant with age. The white walls had turned to murky yellow, and the blue trim had faded to pinkish gray. The cell was miserable, but the automatic cleaning and temperature controls still functioned fairly well, which made the cell more desirable than larger quarters that had failed after years of heavy usage. Such were the privileges that ten lotus marks and Avalon seniority had earned for me. On such mornings, I sometimes regretted abandoning my family's material advantages.

On this morning, I could barely reconcile myself to the lapse of time and my altered circumstances. Not since childhood had a dream ever seemed at once so real and so ordinary to me. My brother had spoken, strewing more of his wild ideas before an unlikely audience. The Mage illusions were disturbingly complex but not beyond displays that I had seen Lar perform.

Dream interpretation is a prerequisite of the fourth Mage's lotus, but such lesser Mage methods of interpretation are usually based on deep symbolisms and spells of insight. A powerful Mage might have interpreted such a strong dream as Mystic vision, but I was a lesser Mage who had never attempted to master the advanced Mystic arts. From interpretative methods, I could find nothing significant in my dream, but its clarity of expression disturbed me. The testiness of my resultant mood was itself an omen of misfortune.

The final words were unquestionably Benedict's, for who else did I know who would speak of good and evil, as if the world could be divided into clean halves? The final speech was probably one that I heard from Benedict years ago, though my conscious mind had forgotten it. In the chaotic manner of dreams, Benedict's speech had mingled with a skewed version of a prophecy that Mage Shamba had issued last year—a hard to translate prophecy that had inspired the abrupt departure of the Inianga and Kinebahan Mage Schools from Rit.

Benedict loomed understandably large in my present awareness, but the inclusion of Mage Shamba's prophecy made no sense to my waking mind. That prophecy had not affected my life, except as it diminished the Mystic presence in Rit. Seething resentments over Lar's contrived election, rather than any profound Mystic truth, had presumably inspired the drastic step of Mage withdrawal. The Kinebahans formally challenged Ch'ango's unilateral designation of Lar as her successor, and she sealed their enmity by confiscating their spirit jar—amplifying her own spells with the unique power of stolen magic. The Inianga and Kinebahan schools have traditionally supported each other against Lung-Wang or Tangaroa encroachment.

I had few facts to support my cynical beliefs—and I had a real desire *not* to know too much about the cause of the schism. My dream of the prophecy bewildered me.

The second call of the Pan flutes pushed aside stale concerns. I had overslept, which was unlike me. I dressed hurriedly in the sleeveless, V-necked emerald robe of an Avalon Mage, not even trying to arrange the braided silver belt and philter purse to hide the frayed pleats. I left my sleeping cubicle and joined the throng of Mages crowding toward the courtyard pentacle, where the Mastermage would personally initiate the day. Most of the robes around me were aqua for the School of Tangaroa, or citron for the Lung-Wang School. The dawn sounds consisted chiefly of rustling robes and the thud of bare feet against the pavings, since no Mage is supposed to speak before day's greeting.

The Mage Center, where most local Mages choose to reside, has not dwindled as badly as Rit proper. The Mage Center at Rit was never large, but its founders prospered at the time of its development. The builders used land extravagantly in the Center's design. The entire complex sprawls all on a single level, each room opening onto the courtyard or the street that surrounds the Center. Most of the building and its pavings are constructed simply from mottled gray plastone, but the steep roof is tiled in an Empire blue ceramic that makes the entire edifice distinctive. The courtyard pentacle is tiled in the same deep sapphire, polished even brighter by the bare feet of countless Mages.

I took my place among the Avalon Mages. We stood according to our ranking at one point of the pentacle, all of us attired in the sleeveless, belted emerald robes that were our uniforms during the warm seasons. I had become senior of the Avalon School in Rit, now that Dory, our matriarch of the last fifty years, was gone. We numbered only five: myself with ten lotus marks; flame-haired Janine, one of Rit's most successful populist Mages, with eight; Kurt and Rodolfo, bickering rivals and occasional lovers, with four and six, respectively; and sweet, mousy Lilith with three. All of us claimed some measure of European ancestry, which had led us to our particular school of study. Each of us had blue eyes, an aberration in this era, and Kurt, our darkest member, was fair enough to acquire freckles after just a hour spent in sunlight. The Avalon mythos is no longer popular, except among a few of us who are visibly of that ethnicity. Though Dory never expressed regret over having accepted me, I knew that the presence of a member of the Family had accelerated Avalon's deterioration in Rit.

Tangaroa is nearly as pure as our School, but Tangaroa takes pride in its zealous adherence to its Oceanic origins. Where Avalon has dwindled into the least of the Mage Schools, Tangaroa has become the greatest, since the cataclysmic Hangseng-Nikkei War and the angry aftermath spared most of Polynesia and little else. Few inhabitants of the world's major continents, especially in the northern hemisphere of the planet, survived those dreadful times. For that reason, the Dragon Kings of Lung-Wang, formerly the most restrictive of Mystic organizations, now include every brand and blend of racial types. The African Inianga and Amerind Kinebahan make some claims of purity, but their standards for qualifying ancestry have become notably lenient.

Spicy yellow smoke rose in slender spirals from the five points of the pentacle, although only three of the five great schools were represented at the gathering. Following the prophecy that my dream had recalled, most of the Inianga and Kinebahan Mages withdrew from Rit, dispersing to other Mage Centers around the world. Those few who re-

mained have overcome traditional rivalries and given their
allegiance to Lung-Wang or Tangaroa.

Though a diligent Mage never ignores a potent dream, I
regretted my slumbering revival of a prophecy that I had
only heard reported in rumors. I wanted to forget my dream
altogether, as I had dismissed the original prophecy's verac-
ity. However, recollections rumbled annoyingly through my
mind with every Mage who arrived at the pentacle. Amid the
citron and aqua, I visualized the darkly dignified Mage
Shamba leading his fiery Inianga, and I imagined the crimson robes of Kinebahans taking their places behind their
massive patriarch, Mage Pachacamac. Mage Shamba would
have become Mastermage instead of Lar, if Mage Pachacamac had succeeded in his challenge against Ch'ango.

If he had predicted the target of her retaliation, I doubted
that Mage Pachacamac would have jeopardized Kinebahan
spirits by issuing the triad of mildly threatening gestures that
constituted a formal, irrefutable Mage challenge. Ch'ango
neither apologized nor explained her unconventional tactic
of stealing Kinebahan magic instead of meeting Pachacamac's challenge in direct contest. Ch'ango was never noted
for explaining herself. She retired to Tathagata after months
of angry confrontations with infuriated Mystics, including
some of her own Tangaroa allies, and left Rit with Lar as
Mastermage—as she had undoubtedly intended from the
start.

After contending with Ch'ango in her final term, Lar's
original opponents saw his weaknesses as a blessing. Having
initiated the conflict, Lar had managed to transform himself
into the restorer of peace. Lar has always been adept at seiz-
ing opportunity, as I have good cause to know and to regret.

Personally, I had trouble caring greatly who served as my
Mastermage, since the Mastermage of Rit tends to live almost exclusively in Tathagata. I know—better than most—
how little our popular elections mean. Past hurts sullied my
feelings toward Lar, but my very limited contacts with the
arrogant Ch'ango had not endeared *her* to me either. Dory
had never expressed a strong opinion on the subject, which
suggested only that Dory valued Avalon neutrality too much
to take an official stance.

As if summoned by my bitter memories, Lar, robed in the
violet of his rank, appeared abruptly at the center of the pentacle amid a shower of golden fireworks. It was a simple ef-

fect that would not have impressed any of the Mages who watched it if Lar's own magnetism had not made the gaudy display seem so appropriate to him. Lar is a striking man: tall and well-built, his black hair touched by silver, his jaw strong and stubborn, his deep eyes a clear, caramel brown. His lotus marks may have been earned less by Mage's knowledge than by political acumen, but no one disputes Lar's legislative influence within the World Parliament, both in the House of Mastermages and the House of Doms. Rit may be small and meager, but Rit's leaders remain a formidable force in world government.

"We welcome the spirit of the morning," announced Lar in his ringing voice, and he raised high his staff of burnished rosewood entwined by a silver serpent. "As morning follows night, let us walk forward and never look back." The early light sparkled from the amethysts that formed the serpent's eyes. The serpent's scales had darkened with age, for the staff was old, worn so smooth that the metal serpent and the wood blended together as if of one substance. The Rit staff was one of the few personal artifacts of natural wood that I had ever seen in daily use. Nearly all of the old trees died after the war, and those that have sprouted since are spindly, twisted things, too soft and splintery for fine carving.

"Grow in wisdom," finished Lar, as he touched the tip of the staff to the ground in each of the five directions of the pentacle. Each School's members bowed as the staff pointed toward them and they acknowledged Lar's greeting.

We of Avalon bowed in turn and replied appropriately, "Good journey." The sweet smoke of incense swirled about us, reinforcing the delicate scent that never leaves a practicing Mage of Rit.

On normal mornings, when Feti'a welcomes the day on Lar's behalf, the ceremony ends informally. The orderly rows of Mages dissolve into milling, gossiping groups that wander toward the commons for breakfast, where most of the Center's few dozen children are already collected. Feti'a, an imposing woman whose Polynesian ancestors must surely have mingled with an Amazon, laughs raucously, lightening the mood of all around her.

Feti'a did not laugh in Lar's presence. Our rows did not dwindle and merge. We turned from the pentacle nearly in unison and walked to the commons with a silent, measured pace. Lar did not join us, but his presence was felt. We

Mages are more conscious of our power and importance on the rare occasions when Lar occupies his rooms at the Center. We are prouder but more solemn.

Awareness of my status did not improve my spirits, as I crossed the tile expanse to the commons. My visit with Benedict still disturbed me, as witnessed by my dream. My forthcoming report to Uncle Toby weighed on my mind. And I could not believe that coincidence brought Lar and Uncle Toby simultaneously to their sad little domain of Rit.

Uncle Toby might have come home to secure his reelection as Dom, but the outcome was assured, though the process might run a rough course over Benedict's pitiful carcass. Lar lacked even that feeble excuse. His position as Mastermage could not be challenged for at least three years, even if another ambitious twelve-lotus Mage established residence in Rit today. I hated the political maneuvering on which my family thrived. Thoughts of my family's generations of scheming did little to inspire in me any appetite for breakfast.

The Mages' commons resembles most public eating places, although it functions a little more reliably than most of Rit. Pale banks of food units, constructed like narrow lockers with shelves for each meal of the day, occupy one end of the commons. Mages scramble through the aisles, trying to reach their designated units and escape to their assigned tables with their meals intact. The children are sequestered at one end of the commons, but their noise pervades the entire room. Eating is not the most dignified part of Center life, which is why outsiders are never allowed to dine among us.

I accepted bread and sweet-tea from the food unit allotted to me. Beside me, Kurt stared glumly at the lump of unbaked dough that his unit had produced. Kurt has an expressive face and a dramatist's flair for conveying emotion with his lanky body. His current pose would have broken the heart of an unsuspecting stranger. "Haven't you reported these failures yet?" I asked him.

"All the working units seem to be set for poi, mush, or grits," sighed Kurt. "I might as well eat raw bread dough."

I took pity on him and offered him one of my crusty rolls. Kurt beamed immediately, but Rodolfo thrust his arm forcibly between us and shook his head at me sternly. Short and slight, Rodolfo looks soft, but his dainty features are deceptive. He defends his opinions with aggressive determination. "Marita, you should know better than to waste your sympathy on this greedy infant," scolded Rodolfo. "Kurt is too lazy to prepare the new philter that Feti'a asked in payment for a new unit. He deserves what he gets."

Kurt grinned sheepishly, and I snatched my roll back from his tray. I seated myself beside Janine at the long plastiwood table reserved for the Avalon School. The five of us made a lonely group at the end of a table designed to seat fifty.

Janine admired herself in a pocket mirror, carefully verifying that the lines of kohl adorned her wide eyes perfectly. Lilith, whose childlike face and muted taupe coloring could never support Janine's bold style, watched the operation with envy.

"Stop preening, Janine," complained Rodolfo. "Vanity before breakfast is unbearable." With his cascading golden hair and graceful lines, Rodolfo is prettier than any of the Avalon women, and he knows it.

Kurt rolled his eyes. "You should try to be more tolerant of yourself, Rodolfo," he said.

"I lack your experience in enduring personal flaws," retorted Rodolfo.

Janine laid aside her mirror and reached across the table to slap the hands of both men. She turned to me. "Did you see your brother, the lunatic?" she asked. Lilith, whose ideas of proper decorum would put most Affirmists to shame, looked pained by the careless words, but she would never speak against Janine. To the best of my knowledge, Lilith has never argued with anyone. She would be an ideal Affirmist, if an abusive parent had not prejudiced her against the entire Affirmist party.

"Don't worry, Lilith," I said, before delving into Janine's troubling question. "My brother *is* irrational. Legal truth does not offend." At times, Lilith's weakness of spirit annoys me, but I feel a nagging obligation to reassure her. She *has* suffered; she *did* struggle to become a Mage; she *does* work exhaustively to maintain a clientele. Few Mages share Lilith's patient sympathy for life's perpetual victims, whose helplessness often extends to an inability to pay their bills. "Yes, I saw Benedict."

"What will you do next?" asked Kurt, attacking his unbaked dough with a tentative prod of his thumb.

"I shall report to Uncle Toby and receive my reward of a

fine dinner and general approbation," I answered. "I have discharged my duty."

"But you're unhappy," said Lilith, distorting her undistinguished face with a woeful frown. "Is your brother very miserable?"

"Not at all." I struggled to contain my temper, though Lilith's probing of sensitive emotional territory did irritate me. I needed to divert the conversation before I snapped at Lilith and made *her* miserable. "He seems quite contented with his ravings. He has friends, as well, who apparently take very good care of him." I tore an edge from my roll and thought of Benedict's chocolate. "Have any of you heard of a waterfront privateer named Andrew?"

"The waterfront is a society unto itself," replied Rodolfo with visible distaste. "We city Mages don't have much contact with them." Lilith murmured in agreement, as if she actually related to Rodolfo and his sophisticated customers. Kurt, who cultivates Rodolfo's clients whenever possible, grinned at Lilith's posturing, but he did not unmask it. Hinting broadly, Kurt propped his chin on his hand and leaned toward Janine.

Janine shoved Kurt's elbow to upset his precarious balance, but she answered equably, "I don't know any names, but I've seen signs of increased smuggling recently. A few of my customers have been paying me with wood and chocolate. A lawyer even offered me a bicycle in exchange for a favorable trial reading."

"Did you accept?" asked Rodolfo.

"No. The man wanted me to pay for the tires. When I refused, he threatened to sue me. Dissuading him cost me two grams of my best philter blend and an all-night spell chant." All of us shook our heads in commiseration. "Is your brother associating with smugglers?" asked Janine.

"Possibly."

"Then he can't be entirely crazy. Smugglers are particular."

I nodded slightly. That contradiction had troubled me, too. Illegal trade moves more merchandise worldwide than official supply lines, but the insiders select their compatriots— and their targets—cautiously.

A young Polynesian girl, a one-lotus Mystic enrolled in the Tangaroa school, approached us. She wore the violet armband that signified her present status as an attendant to the Mastermage. She extended her empty hands to me, and I stood to meet her formal greeting in kind. "The Mastermage wishes to see you, Mage Marita," she informed me.

On Uncle Toby's behalf? I wondered, but a thrill of nervousness gripped me. Not even the senior member of a Mage School receives spontaneous invitations from her Mystic leader, and Lar does not flout custom lightly. The fact that I knew Lar rather well in his humbler days did not help at all. As Mastermage, he had far more legal authority over me than Uncle Toby. Kurt and Rodolfo smiled at me supportively, while Lilith looked frightened, and Janine flirted with an inquisitive Lung-Wang Mage at the next table. I gave my uneaten roll back to Kurt, and I left the commons.

We crossed the yard, silent now in the absence of any other Mages. The sunlight glared blindingly off the polished pentacle. My young escort did not speak to me. I tried to remember her name, but my nerves made my mind foggy. She left me at the medieval doors that guard Lar's quarters.

The Mastermage's chambers are lined with polished wood of varied colors and grains, engraved with runes and mystical symbols from floor to ceiling on every wall. The teak floor is likewise decorated, although a glossy varnish protects it and its carvings. The furnishings consist of rare figurines of ancient mystical beings, magicians' cabinets with their diverse illusions, and tall glass-front cases filled with talismans, crystals, and wands from every country and every age of Mysticism.

The huge black cat known as Spider occupied a violet plush lounge. She watched me from yellow eyes that were half-blind, for Spider had come to these chambers during Ch'ango's reign. I thought of the gray cat held protectively in the arms of the mixie boy, Cris, and I suddenly felt sorry for old Spider. I doubted that anyone had ever touched her with affection. She was valued and pampered, but most of her kittens had been offered as blood sacrifices—for deeply serious causes of the Mastermage, of course—and she was likely to end her own days as a blood offering. I approached her with an outstretched hand, but she hissed at me, and I did not insist.

"Spider is very conscious of her superior status," murmured Lar. "She has even torn my flesh on occasion."

I turned reluctantly, feeling the rush of heat that his nearness had always stirred in me. I still found him unbearably handsome, though I had reason to know that his passions were only constant toward his ambition. "You asked to see me, Mastermage."

His full lips twisted. "Please, Marita, don't be so formal with me. We know each other too well for that sort of role-playing." He shrugged, and the violet silk of his formal robe rippled with Mage glow. I knew which philter blend caused that subtle glow, just as I could identify the herbal incense that wreathed him, but his powerful presence still affected me. He touched my frayed belt with a slight, amused shake of his head.

The reminder of former intimacy, so long abandoned, doubled my uneasiness. What did Lar want so badly of me at this diminished stage of my life? I might have risked a spell against him once, though he was senior to me in every Mage ranking, but he *was* my Mastermage—and he wore scarab marks. I doubted that he deserved the scarabs any more than he did his twelve lotus pairs, but I preferred not to learn by direct example. I witnessed a full scarab spell only once, as a young child, when Mastermage Ch'ango toppled the great monoliths of the Rit forum in her anger over a speech of the Dom, my grandfather. My grandfather was not a man to be intimidated easily, but he relinquished his position as Dom to my father as a result of Ch'ango's unsparing, unlawful threats.

"It has been a long time since you remembered me, Lar."

His voice trembled with emotion—or contrivance. "I have never forgotten what you meant to me, 'Rita. I have wondered if you thought of me fondly or bitterly."

I stared past him to the serpent staff that he had left upon a broad, black marble altar. "I am grateful to you. Because of you, I became a Mage."

He took hold of my chin and forced me to look at him. "Would I be impertinent to kiss you as a friend who has missed you?"

I summoned all my resolve and retreated from his cool hand. "You would be very impertinent. We were lovers, Lar, but never friends."

His clear caramel eyes smiled at me like every phantom lover I had ever summoned. He could have won me with a single word of apology, but he did not pursue the past. Having stabbed a painful rent in my emotional defenses, Lar left my side to hang his serpent staff on massive silver wall hooks. "How is your brother, Marita? Does he still preach nonsense?"

I answered cautiously, "Yes, but he is well enough otherwise."

"I would enjoy seeing him again. He always amused me. Invite him to the next public ceremony."

Lar knew that my brother would refuse to participate in any Mystic rite. "I shall convey your invitation, if I have an opportunity before you leave us again."

"I expect to remain in Rit for a few months. I have stayed away too long. The World Parliament is harder to escape than a clinging lover." He smiled wonderfully, presumably to suggest approbation. I had often stormed, but I had never clung. "I need some time to renew my bonds with the people I represent. I hope to spend some of that time with you. Will you dine with me tonight?"

How could I believe wistfulness from Lar? He had barely spoken to me since leaving my bed fifteen years ago for a tryst with someone else. Lar must have thought that I was still as gullible as that romantic adolescent he'd betrayed, although he should have learned something from the fact that I did not wait meekly for him to return that night. "Sorry. I can't. I'm having dinner with Uncle Toby."

"Ah."

I waited for Lar to suggest another occasion, while I tried to decide if I dared to refuse him outright, but no further invitation came. Nor did Lar remark on Toby's presence in Rit, the next elections, or any of the subjects that I might have expected to cause his abrupt remembrance of me. Benedict interested Uncle Toby: Was that sufficient justification for Lar's summons? I certainly did not believe that Lar was motivated by nostalgia, despite the longings of my ego.

"Perhaps another time," he said.

"Perhaps."

He laid his hands on a golden statue of Kuan-Yin, goddess of fecundity, and he stroked her gilded face. He nodded, dismissing me with a coldness that made me feel very small and lonely. He watched me leave, as superior and aloof as Spider.

Andrew

2 Fepuara, 510

Most Excellent Hiroshi,

As always, my friend, your talents produce astonishing fruits. How could I complain of a temporary shortage, when you give me so much with which to satisfy our customers? I am only sorry to waste your marvels on the ignorant wretches who trade with me. They understand nothing but the profit they can gain by selling forbidden oddities. They lack even the imagination to question my sources.

I should not complain. It is you who are the creator, denied the honor due you. If I achieve nothing else of value with my sinful life, I shall make these self-styled Protectors respect what they have rejected. If Ch'ango objects to the competition, so much the better. The witch needs to realize that her brand of power is subservient to yours.

Regarding Dom Toby: He has indeed arrived in Rit, along with the faithful Scribe Talitha and Lar, that sham of a Mastermage whom Ch'ango vengefully foisted upon the World Parliament. I feel positively flattered by such abundant attention. Our esteemed members of Parliament seem finally to have reached a unified decision in our regard. Such a miracle of cooperation could almost inspire me to believe in Benedict's Intercessor. (Ask Anavai to forgive my profane reference to her creed. I remain a corrupt and heretical pirate, despite all of Benedict's efforts to reform me.) The presence of so many old friends should enliven my visit, which has been relatively uneventful up to now.

I shall force nothing. However, the war does exist, and it will continue as long as Ch'ango controls the Protectorate from the safety of her false "retirement." Battles are inevitable. Do not worry unduly about me because of a prophecy neither of us understands. Toby, Talitha, and Lar have all tried unsuccessfully to destroy me in the past. I think their alliance will make them even less effective, because their methods are too dissimilar. They will trip over each other in trying to entrap me, and they will damage only their own assets.

Regarding a more immediate bit of awkwardness: The Family is displeased with Benedict (and they do not even know enough to blame him and his prophecy for *my* presence in Rit). They have recruited Ben's sister, the Avalon Mage, to express the Family's concern. Ben trusts her. I question her neutrality—for obvious reasons. She was an early attachment of Lar the Lesser, which is not a tribute to her judgment. However, she has not conformed to the Family's self-serving conventions. She has a reputation for conscientious Mage work of a humble sort. For Ben's sake —and ours—I shall evaluate her.

A.

Marita

I arrived at my office just minutes before my first appointment of the morning. My office occupies a professional suite in the Sumi Tower, a plastiglass structure that once housed the Nikkei Empire's local overseers. The offices are large, airy, and well equipped, although they tend to contain an excess of unusable devices, the gadgetry of the past. Window offices like mine are also expensive, but I have a large number of prosperous clients, who would never consult me in any less impressive setting. Dark, draped corners of musty, half-ruined buildings may profit the populist Mages, but I have never felt comfortable portraying myself with such mystery.

I use the emerald color of my school freely in my office, for the signs of affiliation are appropriate to a place of work. Since all of the intrinsic furnishings and accoutrements are white and unobtrusive, the green silk of chairs, tablecloth, and draperies need not compete with any extraneous symbols. A plastiglass cabinet displays the overt instruments of my trade: wands, candles, oils, herbs, crystals, and cards. Cascades of tiny silver bells and green silk ribbons hang from the slanted ceiling. I cause the bells to chime or the ribbons to whisper, according to the needs and sensibilities of my clients.

My first appointment was a simple request for renewal of a luck philter prescription. I listened dutifully to the old woman's plaints and praises, modified the blend slightly to meet her changing tastes, and sent her away with a promise to consider accepting her neighbor as a new client. I told her to have her neighbor set an appointment for appraisal with Llewella, the matronly Scribe who is the domineering receptionist for all the Mages on the seventh floor.

I was distracted all day, pondering the puzzle of Lar, Uncle Toby, and Benedict. Snippets of an inferior form of

Mage vision, fashioned from the past, accosted me repeatedly. After a difficult bespelling of a client recovering from his lover's death, I slipped into the past so thoroughly that I kept my next client waiting for half an hour.

I was a girl again, seated on my lace-covered bed in the house that my parents maintained just outside of Rit proper. A spindly tree, which my father had purchased at great cost, scraped against the window driven by storm winds, and the ocean thundered. I was crying, because Toby was to marry Nan.

"She is too old for him," I complained.

"He loves her, 'Rita," replied my golden-haired mother staunchly, and she held me to give me comfort. We both recognized her lie. Even at the age of eleven I understood that Toby had married solely to advance his claim to a seat in the World Parliament. I also realized why Toby had previously taken such trouble to endear himself to me, the daughter of a Dom, and I felt a personal hurt. The House of Doms is more dynastic than democratic, but our influential family competes fiercely for choice positions. Rit, though small, carries special parliamentary privileges dating from Empire traditions.

"I could have given him the seat of Rit," I argued, airing my injured pride, "since Benedict doesn't want it."

"Your brother will change his mind," my mother answered, but I felt her tremble. "Benedict will be the next Dom of Rit."

I could not understand my mother's fear, for she was not a timid woman. "Does Aunt Nan love Toby?" I asked wistfully.

"I don't know, 'Rita. My sister does not share her feelings easily. Nan has always had odd ideas." My mother bestowed on me one of the wide, lovely smiles that had earned her many admirers. "You are much like her in character."

"Am I?" The idea soothed my damaged ego slightly, because I respected Nan. My mother nodded, still holding me.

My crying altered to deeper grief, as my memories shifted forward to my parents' memorial service, held in the outer yard of the Stone Palace. From time's detached perspective, I saw myself at sixteen, thin and gangly and as pale as my white funeral shift, my bare arms banded with the brown velvet circlets of Affirmist mourning. My eyes were swollen and red, for I had not stopped crying since learning of my parents' deaths. I had not seen them for over a year, and I had looked forward so feverishly to their return. I had wanted so much to explain myself to them, to hear them affirm the decisions that had so upset Benedict, to exchange with them something more personal than that last cold, secretive, written vow to conceal my literacy from any Mystic. Not even their bodies had returned to give me solace, because the autoboat had failed en route from Tathagata, and their bodies were not recovered.

Cousins, many of them Doms, shuffled past me without a word. I had recently declared myself a Mystic, and they disapproved. They would never voice such an incorrect attitude of intolerance, but they announced it clearly by their indifference to me. They acknowledged even my brother more freely, and he had developed a strange religious fanaticism that frightened *me*. Lar, my Mystic lover, had declined to attend the Affirmist service, and I felt terribly alone. Only Nan had chosen to stand beside me, though Toby had glared his disapproval. Nan had said nothing, but I felt her share my pain, and I loved her for it.

When she taught me the lessons of my childhood, Nan had seemed as bright and vivid as her beloved flowers. Since her marriage to Toby, she had faded gradually, but I had not noticed the depth of change until we stood together in common sorrow. Newly introduced to the elements of the Avalon Mage school, I realized that Nan's significator card was the Shadow Ghost. My grief, already too great for my mind to comprehend, expanded to encompass her.

With the sad, pallid image of the Shadow Ghost before me, my self-inflicted memory spell faded, but it lingered disturbingly in my consciousness. For several years, I had convinced myself that I had successfully separated myself from my family's manipulative lifestyle. Janine, who is ambitious, thinks me spoiled and foolish to discard my connections to so much wealth and power. She has often remarked on how far she would have advanced if she had been given my opportunities. She cannot understand, and I am not allowed to teach her.

When Benedict and I were children, Aunt Nan educated us carefully to understand the importance of our family's position. We did learn to expect a standard of living that far exceeds the world's norm, but wealth alone does not make a Dom. Those like Janine, raised to bitter parents in ordinary circumstances, seem to imagine that the Doms train their children to become oppressors, but the truth is not that simple. Most of us are taught to become responsible protectors, which is why we learn the history that created us. We are not trained to be corrupt. We are simply as vulnerable as anyone else to selfishness and greed, and we are in a much better position to profit from those traits.

Janine and others grumble, but they do not act. Their dissatisfaction is largely recreational. They elect their familiar Doms and Mastermages consistently, for they have little incentive to change. Most of them live the bulk of their lives in the false reality of their E-units.

No one truly suffers from the avarice of Doms and Mastermages, since our world has an abundance of housing and supply units to accommodate its diminished population. No one is hungry, homeless, or deprived of entertainment. Those who crave nonstandard luxuries provide services to each other or to the Mastermages, who rule the Mystic powers, and the Doms, who control the automated factories and devices that still survive from the Hangseng and Nikkei Empires. Factory failures have increased in the last fifty years, but the total production of goods still exceeds the world consumption, even excluding the remote factories that only supply adventurous privateers. The Empire Princes built well, and they built for a much more populous world.

Have I ever regretted my choices? Of course—for minutes at a time. I have told myself that I could govern as well as any man of my family (and most of the Family's parliamentarians are male, despite Affirmist denials of such incorrect bias). I have imagined claiming a Seat for myself and making Lar regret his abandonment of me. Then I remember how deeply he hurt me, and I resolve again to have no more regrets.

Like Benedict, I have unconventional ideas. One of our cousins calls us throwbacks, maintaining that my brother and I represent a dangerous abnormality, made evident by Benedict's madness and my personal rebellion. That cousin is a self-serving opportunist whom I particularly dislike, but he is reasonably observant. Benedict and I *are* rarities. Even among the actively dynastic, dominant families, few couples manage to produce more than a single child. My profligate grandfather sired half a dozen children, but no woman ever managed to bear more than once for him. Benedict and I are full brother and sister.

Even now, I love my brother beyond reason, but he is strange by any ordinary definition. While I do not like to put myself in the same category, I realize that Janine is not alone in considering me a fool. Somehow, the teachings that were intended to create responsible behavior in the heirs of a Dom went astray in us. Maybe it was the abnormal closeness that Benedict and I shared as children; maybe it was Aunt Nan's odd, independent perspective that infiltrated our education. Benedict became a philosophical idealist. I became a romantic idealist. Lar taught me disillusionment, but he cost me my faith in my own family as well as in the influential Mages. No one had ever performed a similar service for Benedict.

As I arranged the Avalon seer's cards, I personalized the reading, even as I tailored it orally for my client. I explained to the man that recent breaks in his comfortable routine would discipline his pride, while I pondered the possible meanings of the card of the Ice Hound in my own life. What was the crucible in which I might earn the sorrowful wisdom of the Sable Mixie? Shared memories rested in the Blood Ghost: Benedict, presumably. The Shadow Everyman spoke of magic hidden in a mundane guise; it could refer to most Mystics and many Affirmists. I know that the Brass Dreamer appears most often in a symbolic sense, as the sacrifice of willful, misguided ideas rather than the physical trauma suggested by the card's fiery image, and I so informed my client. I did not tell him that the card of the Brass Dreamer felt hot to me.

As the hazy sky turned scarlet with the approach of night, I changed from my emerald robe to the neutral tunic and trousers that were more acceptable for a dinner with Affirmists. I closed the silken draperies and seated myself at my desk. I had finished all of my appointments for the day. Uncle Toby did not expect me for another two hours. I removed my personal deck of Mage cards from my desk and unfolded the fragile, raw silk wrappings that guarded the cards from the influence of other Mages.

The edges of the cards were ragged from frequent handling. The cards had been one of my first Mystic tools. I had consulted them often through the first few years of my Mage training, rigorously obeying Dory's advice. I had gradually lapsed from all the early disciplines, as cynicism eroded my initial faith. Of all the Avalon Mages in Rit, I suspected that only Lilith was still young enough as a Mage to read the cards regularly. For me, the cards had become merely another tool of my profession.

Holding them now, shuffling them and retuning them to myself, I regretted my lack of recent practice. Client readings never demanded as much as a reading with a personal involvement. Though I positioned the Ice Mage, my significator, carefully on the unfolded silk, all my continued shuffling of the cards failed to stir any of the sense of *rightness* that should precede the layout. Accurate use of the Mage cards to clarify and resolve my own problems required a concentration that I seemed unable to conjure at the moment. Frustrated, I laid aside my too-long neglected deck. I would achieve nothing without a preliminary cleansing of my Mystic senses.

I lit a white candle for myself. I stared at the flame, trying to shut out all distractions. I opened myself to receive whatever impressions might come.

For an instant, I thought that I had forgotten to cover the windows, because the scarlet sky seemed to surround me. I yielded to the flood of color, letting it carry me to its focus. Lines of darkness began to flicker across my vision. The contrast throbbed through me, touching anger that I did not choose to face. I maintained a calm focus with difficulty.

The chords of anger discouraged me from my first path, and I shifted my attention to explore a quieter direction. I reached for the healing color of my school, but no sooner had I relaxed into a new receptivity than the scarlet surged around me again. The flashes of darkness were quicker, sharper, and more painful. The anger became mine, and I cried against Lar's betrayal, against my parents' deaths, against a sense of friendlessness that named my brother as its instigator. I hated all of them, who took from me and hurt me and gave me nothing.

I had lost control of the seeking completely, which is an error that no Mage of more than eight lotus marks should ever make. I had heard of Mages who entered seekings so irrevocably that radical personality changes, severe physical afflictions, or even death resulted. I had never had difficulty with control even in my earliest lessons, which had made me reckless. Entering a seeking spell without an initial focal point is considered dangerous, because the lowering of general barriers can allow a cunning enemy to penetrate a seeker's mind.

I had never worried about enemies. As far as I knew, I had none. With the thread of self-awareness still within me, I realized that I was now under an attack as vicious as any I had ever heard recounted.

Red is the color of the Kinebahan School, but the Amerinds employ elemental magic, according to personal totems. Theirs is the power of nature, fierce and hard but not warped by human cruelty. No lawful Kinebahan Mage would vandalize a victim.

I was in no condition to try to identify the intruder, who was filling me with bitterness, anger, and hatred. Lies, built on distorted truths, crippled me. I knew that I was defeated.

"The evil ones rely on deceit," said a voice that sounded like my brother's, "because they know the truth. The strength is ours."

I yelped with pain and snatched my hand away from the flame of the guttering candle. A volcano of wax erupted around the wick and extinguished the fire. I sat in the darkness, nursing my wounded confidence.

I had narrowly escaped something that meant me no kindness by the intervention of an equally unknown savior. I found poor consolation in identifying the reason that my early morning dream had troubled me: It was not a dream but a vision, a thing rarely experienced by a lesser Mage—or it was a sending from someone or something with far more than a ten-lotus Mage's skills. But why would either a Mystic vision or a sending use my brother's voice?

My office door opened, admitting the shadow figure of a man against a stream of white fluorescent light. I could see Llewella's bronze-colored desk in the reception room. My failed seeking must have lasted over an hour, for the desk was fastidiously cleared and Llewella had gone. The office doors of my Lung-Wang neighbors were closed, and the sense of emptiness that accompanies after-hours workplaces was strong.

My visitor touched the switch that illuminated my office for mood readings. The rosy haze of light sufficed to let me recognize my brother's impressive rescuer from the forum. "Promptness does not seem to be one of your many virtues, Mage Marita," observed the man whom I had privately identified as Andrew. "Your uncle may wonder if you delivered his invitation, and it is seldom wise to insult a Dom." His voice was wry, but it suggested detached humor rather than displeasure. "I have been waiting for you downstairs. I had begun to think you were avoiding me, which would make a most unpromising beginning for our relationship."

Andrew still wore a preponderance of gold, although he was otherwise attired conservatively in cream-colored trousers and open vest. The bright metal nearly covered his arms, the engraved bands of assorted widths extending from wrist to elbow and from elbow to shoulder. From a wide gold sash at his waist hung many strands of gilt-tipped black shells, a variation on a design favored by several Tangaroa Mages of my acquaintance. A crown headband, woven of metallic threads, constrained the black hair that hung to his shoulders. He had the basic coloring and structure of a Polynesian, but his skin was unusually golden, his strong cheekbones would have suited an Amerind, and the light gray-green of his eyes suggested at least a touch of European. Such assorted ancestry had combined to form an attractive package, but it did little to help me evaluate his cultural background. His colors were all properly neutral.

"Did my brother send you here?" I asked. Had my brother sensed that I would need rescue? No, that was absurd. Benedict was not a Mage, and I could hardly expect prescience from him.

"Benedict felt unable to attend the dinner tonight," replied Andrew with an enchanting smile. "I am his delegate." The smile conveyed the unspoken message: *You and I know the truth. Benedict has refused Dom Toby's invitation.* The implication was clear. Andrew and I, barely acquainted, had already become conspirators on my brother's behalf.

I forced myself to recall my original reasons for consulting my Mystic senses: Benedict, Uncle Toby, Lar. The arrival of Andrew as substitute might not please Uncle Toby, but the custom was socially correct and could not be protested graciously. Whether the inspiration was Benedict's or Andrew's, it did offer a solution to a difficult situation. At best, it might convince Uncle Toby that Benedict's wits could still function at rational levels. At worst, it proved that Benedict had one capable supporter.

Guiltily, I folded the silk across my cards, mentally scolding myself for having left them so vulnerable. I did not

know if Andrew had enough Mystic presence to affect
them—and I was too shaken to assess him at the moment—
but the scarlet enemy could have corrupted them irredeem-
ably. I would be unable to trust them again without a
protracted cleansing spell and the liberal use of several expensive philter blends.

"I hope you find me acceptable as your escort," continued
Andrew with a half-bow that made his gold flash dazzlingly.

He did not seem to require my approval, so I offered no
reply. My silence appeared to trigger a change in his approach. He left his position in the doorway and crossed to
my display cabinets. He studied the contents for a few moments, but he did not follow his inspection with the normal
handscan of a Mystic. He seated himself in the cream satin
chair that my primary clients used.

He informed me crisply, "Your brother said that you expressed an interest in meeting me. Benedict is not the type
to encourage my overly developed ego with a lie." His eyes
watched me intently, either in appreciation or in challenge. If
my wits had been functioning normally, I might have known
which conclusion to make. "For my part, I feel quite honored to meet Rit's most successful purveyor of passion's
secrets. You fulfill the image of your art, Mage Marita."

The flattery did not impress me, since I doubted its sincerity. I returned my stock professional reply, "Image is essen-
tial for a Mage to succeed in an Affirmist community. I
specialize in love philters because that is what is expected of
me." My response held almost as little truth as the hollow
compliments of a privateer. I had my share of admirers, but
I had no illusions of being a great beauty. My bones are
good, but I have always been too thin and too colorless. The
fact that my father was a Dom tends to glamorize me in the
eyes of many clients, and my philters give better results than
those of most public Mages.

"Your business skill evidently supports the image."

"Are you interested in making a purchase?" I asked. My
muscles tingled as I rose to my feet, but I walked smoothly
to the variegated display of my Mage's wares. I opened the
glass case and touched several samples, stirring the musk-
scented glitter dust that impressed my customers. I pocketed
an amulet of protection, though I had fashioned it of simple
herbs that would not thwart the powerful Mage who had at-

tacked with scarlet anger. Nonetheless, the emerald velvet packet comforted me.

"I have a terribly outmoded attitude about personal relationships," drawled Andrew. "I like to believe that high romance is achievable without resorting to powder and smoke."

Such sarcasm might have seemed insulting from another man, but Andrew managed to make it a tantalizing promise. "High romance is the essence of my form of magic."

"I do not doubt that a sense of romance inspires many of your customers," answered Andrew, "but that form of inspiration is not a function of Mystic arts." His smile, brilliantly white against his dark skin, had a captivating effect that masked his implicit criticism.

"You are not a believer in Mysticism?"

He gave me gallantry instead of an answer. "You might educate me about your viewpoint during a private consultation."

I did not need the training of a Mage to understand him. After the near-disaster of my candle seeking, a flirtation with my brother's benefactor was sufficiently ridiculous to make me wonder if my mind were still intact. Yet Andrew's mock courtship seemed to flow naturally, diverting the remnants of my emotional upheaval into a less threatening channel.

I am usually more suspicious of strangers. I am almost always more suspicious of men who display immediate interest in me. Seeing Lar again may have made my emotions more vulnerable than usual, but Andrew would be difficult to ignore under any circumstances. It was a further measure of Andrew's overpowering brand of charm that I did not question his motives—or the timeliness of his arrival—until considerably later.

Confronted by his smile, his charm, and his overt sensuality, I was sorely tempted to indulge myself with this enigmatic seductor. My professional expertise does not imply a particular adeptness with my personal liaisons, as Lar proved. I certainly did not need to attach myself, however briefly and impulsively, to a probable privateer who happened to know my brother. I answered briskly, "Make an appointment with my receptionist."

Andrew continued to smile despite my brusqueness. He

extended his open hand to me in a gesture of truce. "We must not keep the Dom waiting any longer."

I accepted his hand, Affirmist-style, with misgivings. He had a strong grip that did not reassure me. The man who had cultivated my brother so effectively seemed to be making an uncompromising foray to conquer me, and he was visibly equipped to succeed. Perhaps he had a prediliction for my family—it was not an unprecedented affinity—and expected the same immediacy of attachment in return.

He deserved to be confident. If the occasion had been unencumbered by family obligations and dire Mystic attacks, I could have welcomed a dinner engagement with him. Under the present circumstances, I could only gird myself for an unsettling evening.

Benedict

2 Fepuara, 510

Dear Hiroshi,

Please use your influence with Andrew to persuade him to exercise more personal caution. He is overly protective of me at his own expense. I assure him that the Intercessor will guard me, but Andrew has not learned to share my faith. Andrew tries to handle every problem alone.

Andrew has insisted on taking my place at a dinner with Uncle Toby tonight, and I fear the consequences. Yes, I realize that Andrew is well able to take care of himself, but Ch'ango is cunning, and she knows Andrew's weaknesses as well as his strengths. I trust my sister, but I fear that others may use Marita to tempt Andrew back into his old ways. We both know how catastrophic the results of such a lapse could be.

He listens to no one but you. Please, urge him to be cautious. He could so easily become the prophesied force of destruction, and that would serve only Ch'ango's evil goals.

May the Intercessor guide you,
Benedict

Marita

As we walked to the Stone Palace, the damp air curled around us, and Rit's tired workers scurried past us to their homes. We did not suffer the usual awkwardness of strangers, although Andrew's company was not what I could call comfortable. Andrew talked of the dingy buildings that we passed, dissecting their tired architecture and mundane composition as if they were wondrous monuments; he discussed plants and animals, extant and extinct, of Rit and elsewhere; he spoke of music, history, and art, but he never lingered on any subject long enough for me to reply intelligently—or even to absorb the full sense of what he was saying. His speech was rapid; the pace at which he shifted topics was bewildering. I had never considered myself slow-witted, but Andrew's mind seemed to function on an entirely different scale.

"Kano designed those plastone ledge boxes," he said at one point, waving a gold-encased arm toward a shabby hostel, "to provide a sustained source of water for the flowering plants that were popular during the early Empire era. Kano altered the usual plastone formula to increase porosity for the inner shell. Kano's clients included some of the Empire's greatest architects, though his designs never became popular in the northern states. He offended a significant overlord in his misspent youth and became a target of a form of *tabuu*. The Empire overlords adhered strictly to their Empire rules, but they had considerable flexibility in the execution of the laws. Some of the methods were benign. Others were ruthless. A famous example of the latter school was Shomadai, who shunned his own daughter because she failed to meet his expectations. She was a musical prodigy, widely respected as a performer, but the experts denigrated her compositions as trite. Too sensitive to endure harsh criticism, she abandoned her art altogether, and her family abandoned her.

Criticism, like praise, must be used judiciously. Don't you agree?

"Mm," I answered unintelligibly, comprehending his question long after he had transitioned to another subject. I nearly suspected that he concocted his "facts" spontaneously from his own imaginings. I had never heard—nor even read in secret family archives—any histories of such comprehensive scope.

As we neared the Stone Palace, I finally began to catch pace with his conversation, either from practice or increased familiarity with the topics. "When all the power and recycling elements functioned," he explained, "the Stone Palace produced enough resources to sustain the entire present population of Rit. Fruit grew prolifically in the orchards surrounding the main buildings. Ocean water was channeled into fish hatcheries and sea-vegetable beds, filtered and desalinized for human consumption, and reprocessed for irrigation. Nothing was wasted in those days."

"As opposed to the present?"

"How many people live in the Stone Palace today? One dozen? Two dozen? The Palace is your uncle's home, but he spends nearly all of his time in Tathagata."

"A Dom's duty is to represent his people in the World Parliament."

"Of course. But as a result, Rit's most luxurious private residence remains largely unused."

In my triumph at having matched Andrew's rapid rhythm, I forgot my usual reluctance to discuss my family. "My Aunt Nan lives in the Stone Palace. My mother was raised there. My brother and I both spent a large portion of our childhood there. I'd hardly say that the Stone Palace is wasted. How many dwellings in Rit can boast continuous usage?"

"Almost none," grinned Andrew. "Benedict has told me that the Stone Palace was a marvelous playground for a child."

"It seemed less grim in those days. Seeing it now, I would select Rit's most squalid domicile over the Stone Palace. The Stone Palace is too well suited to the Shadow Ghost." Meanly, I hoped that my Avalon imagery gave Andrew as much bewilderment as his conversation caused me. "I do not share my Aunt Nan's wish to retire from life."

He neither questioned nor acknowledged my Mystic refer-

ence. "Your parents must have been less partial to Tathagata
than Dom Toby."

"My mother preferred to live near Rit, and my father often joined her. When they did go together to Tathagata, Benedict and I generally resided with Aunt Nan. She was our
teacher."

I continued to talk, because Andrew listened with as much
energy as he spoke. Except for Kurt, who is probably my
closest friend, I trust few people enough to confide my
thoughts to them. By the time I remembered ordinary caution, I had told Andrew much more about myself than he deserved to learn. From that moment, I tried to give no more
information than I received, but I had an uneasy feeling that
Andrew already knew a great deal more about me than I
knew about him.

I learned nothing more about Andrew himself than I had
already discovered from my brother's comments and my
own superficial observations, except that Andrew had a fac-
ile tongue and an encyclopedic breadth of knowledge. On a
personal level, Andrew proved to be as glibly uninformative
as the most successful politicians of my acquaintance, either
Mystic or Affirmist, and better informed than any Scribe.
Andrew's ability to overwhelm my own vocal inhibitions
was unnerving.

As we approached the Stone Palace, the narrow streets became ours alone, and I felt my earlier uneasiness revive in
full. My fingers played with the amulet in my pocket and the
philter purse at my waist, though I did not know what tool
I should prepare to use. I distrusted Andrew, but I did not
fear him; my Mage crescents did not shiver with warning in
his presence. My Mage marks did not lead me to fear thieves
either, though Andrew's panoply of gold might easily have
attracted violence. The streetlights brightened to greet us and
faded behind us, detecting no other motion near us on that
still night.

We arrived without trouble, no later than was fashionably
correct. The official escorts, who were simply well-dressed
guards, had not yet acquired the glazed look of lengthy waiting. I did not try to explain Andrew to the gatekeeper—
another stranger to me—but we were admitted without
delay. I had already decided to let Andrew handle any explanations to my uncle.

As we entered the hallway of statues, Andrew became silent. I glanced at him, wondering if he shared any haunting Mystic sense of the past, but his strong face remained impassive. The age-dimmed lamps flooded our path with more shadows than light, and the ghostly dance made Andrew appear as remote and romanticized as the statues. I felt reluctant to try a Mage technique to evaluate him. The scarlet onslaught in my office had shaken my Mage confidence badly.

When we reached the courtyard, the cleaner lights of moon and stars relieved my uneasiness briefly, until the balcony lamps intruded with yellow brightness. Talitha, a statuesque and uniformly impressive woman of African ancestry, came forward to meet me with open arms. She is Scribe and chief aide to my uncle, as she was briefly to my father, and I doubt that there is anyone in either governing House of Parliament who knows more about the methods of power. Since the Family values her, she could easily be a Dom herself, if she chose to trouble herself with the annoyances of popular election. She usually treats me with a maternal protectiveness, though she is not much older than Toby. I would not like to cross her.

"Marita, you are too thin," she chided, hugging me warmly. "You have not been taking care of yourself. I warned you about the habits of those Avalon Mystics." Away from sensitive political circles, Talitha does not worry about offending with her views. She is an Affirmist by name and influence, but among her intimates she is as independent in her own way as my brother. Not for her the bland colors of neutrality: She wore a flowing, beaded robe striped equally with shades of Affirmist brown and Inianga orange. In the cold courtyard of the Stone Palace, she looked like a singular blaze of life.

"I have been deprived of your good influence for too long," I answered.

Talitha flashed her bright smile, but the expression froze when her black eyes moved toward Andrew. Talitha can glance once at a man and describe him in detail a year later. When she measures a man for more than a few seconds, she is weighing him either as a potential lover or as an enemy. She watched Andrew for a full minute, a duration that left me squirming, though Andrew seemed unperturbed. He matched her challenging stare with a mild, slightly impudent grin and the unmistakable, unconscious arrogance of a pow-. erful man.

I hesitated to interrupt their intense, mute exchange with an introduction, realizing only at that moment that Andrew had never actually named himself to me. We had walked and conversed together under the apparent assumption that I knew his identity. Observing Talitha's predatory reaction to him, I first weighed the disquieting ramifications of his arrival at the moment of my seeking's ending, but concern barely touched me at that point. Andrew presented a striking enough figure to elicit attention from any woman. I attributed Andrew's mysteriousness to a privateer's professional caution.

"You came as Benedict's delegate?" asked Talitha at last. Her voice sounded oddly stiff.

"Benedict felt unwell," replied Andrew. His even gaze did not leave Talitha, but he twisted one of the gold bands around his muscular arm with a purposeful care. The wire-mesh bracelet resembled an Inianga design. "He suffered a fainting spell yesterday."

Talitha glanced at me, but I admitted nothing. I could not bring myself to protest that Andrew used half-truths on my brother's behalf. I did wonder if Benedict would approve of his friend's casual guile.

"By what name should we call you?" asked Talitha bluntly. The reflection of her Inianga-colored robe kindled her dark eyes into ferocity.

"Andrew." He clipped each syllable with care. "Of Purotu."

Talitha smirked, as if Andrew amused her in a cold fashion. "You have strayed far from your beginnings," she said with the composure that I had often admired. Talitha's lean, straight height and dignity always gave her a regal air. With her hair coiled into a crown of braids, she stood almost as tall as Andrew, and their pride seemed equally well matched.

Andrew rolled one strong shoulder in a desultory shrug. "Fast ships still cross the oceans."

"You have not selected a popular destination."

"Rit has attractions."

"What attracts you, *Andrew* of Purotu?"

Andrew's smile acquired a rakish slant. "Family affiliations," he answered crisply.

"Yours?"

"Every family has its points of interest." Reverting suddenly to a bewilderingly rapid, staccato style of speech, he again wrapped his attention around me. "My heritage, for example, consists of a Pacific island assortment with several doses of Amerind—and traces of every other ethnicity you might care to name. My antecedents were never too concerned about cultural purity. There is even a guilty rumor in the family that a Nikkei prince once made himself at home among us, while hiding from the Protectors of civilization after the Great War."

Andrew's response renewed my earlier impression that his mind functioned in mysteriously oblique ways, but Talitha did not pursue the subject of his purpose in Rit. She said only, "You do not wear the colors of a Mystic."

"Not lately."

"You claim to be an Affirmist?"

"Not particularly."

Talitha emitted an abrupt and humorless laugh. "You will understand if I insist that you remain under official escort this evening."

"Of course."

Despite Andrew's circumspect replies, Talitha had elicited more information from him with her few terse queries than I had even thought to ask. The three of us, followed by two discreetly distant escorts, crossed the courtyard. The moonlight treated the weathered building with kindness, but the fountain looked more empty than usual, for the shadows hid the water. Andrew paused to watch the turn of the dolphins.

"The fountain leaks," I explained, although I did not know why I should defend the sorry state of the Stone Palace's courtyard. Andrew's earlier accusation of wastefulness had not consciously affected me. "It drains to that level within a few minutes of being filled."

"And there is no functioning automaton to repair the cracks," observed Andrew. "How sad for the Dom." His tone was not quite sarcastic, but it came near enough to qualify as incorrectness.

"Who can reassemble stone?" asked Talitha, curiously tolerant of the insult.

"Who indeed?" Andrew slid his arm caressingly around my shoulders, making Talitha purse her lips with thoughtful care. I experienced the pleasing sort of shiver that brings many clients to seek my love philters. Having observed the results of my clients' intemperate passions, I know that such tempting sensations are best ignored. I tried to discipline my reaction accordingly.

The chill of my crescents also made me suspect that Andrew's gesture represented more a statement of defiance than dalliance, and I tried to evaluate it from that impersonal perspective. I wondered again if my brother had sent Andrew as my rescuer—from Uncle Toby's expected irritation at Benedict's uncooperative attitude? I reached no conclusion. I had trouble enough following Andrew's thoughts when he voiced them.

We entered the wide room that had once been a lobby. The Stone Palace had originally faced the ocean, until floods blocked the main entry with the deposited sweepings of the lower city. The lobby retains a fine atmosphere, gracious in a style that has become rare. The green marble floors and columns have endured, even if the mirrors are cloudy and the peach brocade furnishings are musty. The colors, even in their current faded state, would be too controversial for use in a gathering room today, but age has made them respectable.

Uncle Toby did not wear his displeasure openly, except by the faintest tightening of his jaw. Although he declined to rise from his armchair, he smiled thinly at Talitha, and he nodded to me. He turned his attention to Andrew with an expression that suggested wary suspicion rather than anger.

I slipped away from Andrew in order to offer a formal family greeting to my uncle. "Don't be cross, Uncle Toby," I whispered, as I bent to kiss his cheek. "We both knew that Benedict might not come. We should respect his courtesy in sending a delegate. It's a promising concession to social graces."

"By what right does this man present himself here?" demanded Toby tensely. From the fixed way he stared at Andrew's arms, Toby seemed far more interested in the gold than in the wearer. Toby tugged at his own rings, an expensive Affirmist assortment of colorless jewels and brown metals that seemed tawdry beside Andrew's blatant wealth. If an assayer had been handy, I think Toby would have assigned him to perform a full analysis.

"This is Andrew," I answered, breaking my intention to distance myself.

"Benedict's friend," added Talitha dryly.

By a glance, Toby and Talitha exchanged a silent message that I could not decipher. Toby leaned back in his chair, not quite relaxed. "Benedict disappoints me," said Toby without emotion. "I had hoped to see him again. It has been so long."

"I'm sure he is equally grieved," replied Andrew. He tapped the crystal prisms of a wall sconce and scattered a rainbow across the mirrored room. Toby squinted as the light danced across him. Andrew smiled easily, either oblivious or indifferent to the prospect of Dom Toby's displeasure.

Talitha, the diplomat, declared firmly, "You must not make your guests feel unwelcome, Dom Toby. It has been long since you have had an opportunity to talk at length to your niece." She turned to Andrew. "May I provide you with a tour of the Stone Palace? It is an edifice of considerable history."

"I would be delighted to see it," responded Andrew with a courtly bow that seemed to tease at an aura long missing from the elegant room. Smoothly confident, he joined Talitha, the two of them shadowed by the dutiful young man who had been assigned as Andrew's "escort." I would have followed them, but my uncle stopped me with a sharp utterance of my name.

"What do you know about this 'friend' of your brother's?" growled Toby, his voice barely above a whisper, though there was no one present to hear us but his own hired guardsman, a stoic, unprepossessing figure who probably wished he could spend the evening with his family.

"Almost nothing," I answered truthfully, "except that Benedict could speak of little else but his friend, Andrew."

Toby lowered his head and seemed to gnaw at my words, as if they had a sour taste. "The man is a privateer."

"You recognize him?"

"He has a reputation in Tathagata, as well as in other sites of his prior exploits. That ostentatious display of gold is a trademark. A show of riches impresses the criminal element."

Andrew's notoriety did not surprise me. I only wondered why Janine had not heard of him, since she is usually better informed about Rit's "criminal element" than Toby. "He does flaunt his success unabashedly," I agreed. "Any Mage who displayed that much wealth would be accused of theft, fraud, and destructive magic."

Toby grimaced, probably the most sincere expression I had seen on him of late. Toby's subsequent sigh was far less revealing. "As far as we can tell, Andrew arrived in Rit about the time your brother returned. None of our local informants admits much knowledge about him, except that he *is* a successful privateer." My uncle arranged a comfortable smile as carefully as he might set the part of his cropped brown hair. "I will be appreciative if you keep me informed of anything he tells you."

The casual request jarred at my battered Mage senses. "Did you expect Andrew to come tonight in Benedict's place?" I asked. As moments of silence passed, I felt increasingly misused and resentful.

"It was a possibility," acknowledged Toby at last, losing his smile. "The man has a long history of making insolent gestures, and Benedict seldom complies with family requests."

"I am a Mage, Uncle Toby, not an investigator of trade infractions." Since my singular defection from the ranks of Affirmists, I have rarely defied a prominent member of my family with such directness. Toby's intended use of me, however, exceeded all bounds of legal correctness. "If you want information about local privateering, assign one of your staff members to the task. I have no intention of maintaining regular contact with either my brother or his disreputable friends."

Toby hissed through his teeth and pried himself out of his chair. With a curt gesture, he dismissed the lurking guardsman. "Join me in my office for a moment, Marita," the Dom commanded, and I followed, my curiosity overcoming my irritation.

Toby's office is surprisingly simple for a man who chooses a palace as his home. The overhead lighting is excellent, and the room is comfortably equipped with padded brown fibron chairs and a plastiwood desk, but the Stone Palace has a variety of offices that meet similar criteria with more visible luxury. Toby's choice of office reflects some trait in him that I have never quite managed to identify.

The utilitarian design did not originate with him, of course, having belonged to some long forgotten hotel official. Toby does not even know the purpose of most of the devices embedded in the satiny beige walls. I doubt that he uses any of the wall units except the safe, an undisguised square of plasteel with a nearly invisible locking mechanism.

He approached the wall safe now. He unlocked it with a card key and removed a white enamel box of the padded type often used for fragile gifts. The box formed a cube, less than two decimeters in each dimension. Toby laid the box carefully on the glazed surface of the desk. "Open it," he told me.

Wishing that I felt less like Pandora, I released the side latches. The top panel of the box slid back automatically. Coarse foam bulged from the interior of the box, which cradled a toy truck.

I glanced uncertainly at Uncle Toby. He nodded, and I removed the truck from its clinging nest. The cold metal had endured the centuries remarkably well. The truck's red body shone, and the silver details remained untouched by tarnish. I had no idea why an antique toy held special interest for Toby. He was not a man to indulge in simple pleasures.

"It functions," he informed me. "It is an Empire toy that, according to all our records, has not been manufactured in the past three hundred years, and it functions."

Not yet impressed, I asked, "What sort of function does it perform?"

"Set it on the floor," said Toby, "and push the rear lever once."

I complied dubiously. The tiny lever had been designed to fit a child's hands and required some delicate maneuvering on my part. Trying to envision Toby's broad fingers managing the toy's control, I smothered a grin. I had barely removed my hand from the lever, when the truck raced across the floor, stopped, and spun in a circle. I jumped back from it in surprise.

Side compartments of the truck, which had appeared seamless, opened, and the truck began to unfold itself into a propeller-capped vehicle such as I had seen once in a very old history book. The toy, no longer a truck, spun again and raced back to where I had set it, but it did not stop. Lifted by twirling silver blades, it rose nearly to the ceiling and flew three circles around the office, veering away from the walls as if it sensed them. I could not suppress a laugh of delight. Kurt would have adored Toby's little treasure.

With a whir and a rattle, the flying machine returned to where it had begun. The propeller blades folded inward, and the toy again became a truck. I touched its polished sides with new respect.

Uncle Toby remarked quietly, "The last documented flying vehicle of any sort failed a hundred and fifty years ago."

"This was obviously overlooked," I said, blinking at the solemnity of his reminder. I gathered the toy into my hands with care, trying to detect any visible sign of its dual nature. "It is astonishing, Uncle Toby."

"It is appalling," he replied. He struck a proud pose, as if making a formal address to his fellow members of Parliament. "Between them, the Hangseng and Nikkei Empires maintained direct control of all technology. Manufacturers of supply units, factory robotics, and even sophisticated toys were located only in the areas that the war converted into the Deadlands. Such areas were critical targets of attack for both sides. *Nothing* survived."

"The Mystics of that era warned against such a cataclysm," I interjected, perhaps injudiciously. "The pressures of uncontrolled population growth could not be contained indefinitely by Empire edicts."

"We all agree that the Empires were flawed, Marita." Toby wrapped his large hands around mine, protective of the treasure that I held. I relinquished the toy with regret. I would have enjoyed a lengthier opportunity to examine it. With the toy back in his possession, Toby resumed his pontificating, "We who survive are fortunate that our subject countries were equipped with sufficient supply units and factories to meet our world's continuing needs for food, shelter, clothing, medicine, entertainment—everything our race now requires and desires. In the centuries of the two Empires, the war and the riots that ensued nearly destroyed our species, but the Empires' costly mistakes left us with a more perfect world."

"I recall my history lessons, Uncle Toby."

"Then I do not need to explain to you how dangerous the technology of the Empires proved to be. Such sciences were forbidden in the subject countries long before the war, and our survival clearly justifies the present laws against any efforts to revive those black times."

"We couldn't re-create Empire technology if we tried. Are you afraid that some angry Mage will use this toy to deliver a cloud of poison philter powder to a distant enemy? I assure you, Uncle, advanced Mages already have more effective ways of killing from afar, but an Affirmist with a sharp knife could do more extensive damage in a few minutes than most Mages could produce in a month. Such powerful spells and philters require lengthy preparation and considerable resources."

"I am not afraid of the Mystics, Marita. Our philosophies differ, but we understand each other. We understand the balance of the society we created together from the rubble of the Great War." Uncle Toby paced toward the toy. His shadow loomed over it. "I am concerned about the persons who control the unit that produced this toy, because this toy is not an antique. It is only one of several such toys that we have confiscated in the last few years, and the toys are surfacing more frequently all the time."

"Privateers have recruited fixers in the past, despite the severe penalties for tampering with factory devices."

"*Repairing* a factory is a serious crime. *Rebuilding* a factory requires more than fixer skills," grunted Toby. "It requires Empire knowledge. The World Parliament convened an emergency session last spring to assess the problem and determine its source. As a result of that session, Mastermage Lar and I have returned to Rit. We believe that the source is located near here, but our agents have been unable to uncover any specifics."

"You think Andrew is connected to these people?" I asked slowly.

"He is a privateer. He knows local distributors. I imagine that he is also aware of local competitors." Uncle Toby wrung his hands, a nervous gesture that I had never seen him use. "These rascals protect each other, but eventually one of them will tell us what we need to know. I am only asking you to help in that effort for the defense of all of us. If one undocumented factory unit exists, there may be others that can produce devices of greater danger than a toy truck that flies. Even this toy has the potential to produce a plague of incorrect thinking. It inspires curiosity and wonderment, which are extremely dangerous attitudes."

"Why didn't you tell me any of this yesterday?" I was not sure I wanted to hear Toby's speculations now, but I had indeed opened Pandora's box.

Uncle Toby shrugged, but he failed to look nonchalant. "I had hoped to recruit your brother, for he is already familiar with this *Andrew.* However, Benedict is evidently not a viable ally."

"I am a Mage," I reminded him again.

My protest seemed to revitalize Toby. "If you are concerned about aiding an Affirmist cause, please be reassured: Mastermage Lar will confirm what I have told you. Indeed, he and I consulted extensively on this possibility before I asked you to seek your brother. We were obviously uncertain about Benedict's rationality, and our fears have proven true. I, rather than Lar, have approached you, because we decided that a request from family would be more courteous and less likely to alarm you. We agreed, however, that you should be informed fully if Benedict failed us. We trust you, Marita, and we believe that you can help us."

"I am not a spy."

"You are a talented Mage with valuable expertise. You can surely gain Andrew's confidence. Your personal charms seem to have made an impression already, but you may choose to concoct one of your Mage philters. I would not presume to dictate your methods."

"Is this a legal commission?" I asked, although no legal blessing would make me like it.

Toby pursed his lips in displeasure, but he grunted, "If you wish."

"I do." I was sure that I could not decline my uncle's request without severe penalties, but I could at least try to protect myself against his future forgetfulness. The legal dangers of meddling with privateers outweighed Toby's silent threats. I preferred a more tangible defense than verbal promises from a man who had lost my trust long ago.

"I shall have the contractual seals readied for exchange by morning." Toby returned the innocuous toy truck to its box and resecured it in the safe. He rubbed his hands together, a little too obviously self-satisfied for my taste. "Shall we join the others for dinner?"

"Would you mind if I sat here alone for a few minutes? I need some time to assimilate all that you have told me."

Toby frowned slightly, but he nodded. "Don't be too long," he warned and left me.

As soon as he was gone, I darkened the room and sat cross-legged on the floor. By feel, I selected three philter powders from my purse and blended them in the palm of my hand. I preferred to mix my philters by careful measurements in my own office, but I carried mostly love philters, luck philters, and common oils and powders to impress my customers. If Uncle Toby intended to continue these outrageous commissions, I would need to revise my assortment of prepared philter blends.

The powders grew warm, and they glowed, softly at first, but brightening quickly to create a sphere of phosphorescent light around me. I moistened one finger with my tongue and dipped the finger in the powder. Gently, I touched the floor at five points. When I raised my hand from the fifth touch, I whispered the spell, and lines of light arched from point to point to form a pentacle around me.

I breathed more easily once I had established my protection. I should have used such caution before my candle-seeking earlier, but at least I would not repeat my carelessness. Now I knew that the menace existed.

I focused on my own construct of light before reaching for the awareness of other essences. I moved cautiously, leery of detection, though few members of my uncle's household were capable of recognizing my efforts. I did not know how sensitive my brother's rascally benefactor might be to the Mystic arts. I did know that Talitha had a minor gift of perception. If she observed me, she would not let my probe remain secret. She does not tolerate anyone's unauthorized use of magic in my uncle's vicinity.

Talitha's roseate aura glowed with pale luster, the only brightness I detected. The mundane world bound my uncle's essence too tightly to create much impact on the Mystics' plane, and he had presumably chosen his staff to resemble him in attitude. Aunt Nan had dimmed with each year of her retreat from life, though she had once held the potential of a lesser Mage. Of Andrew, I sensed an unusual *nothingness,* a cleanly marked void observable only because I searched specifically for him. Andrew was either more worldbound than Toby and the household staff members, or a costly, extraordinarily potent spell protected him.

I envied the skill that might produce such a spell. Despite my efforts at self-protection, I became increasingly conscious of my own vulnerability. Training exercises in Mystic defense had never prepared me for the obstacles that fear created. Each time my concentration wavered, the lines of my pentacle rippled and thinned. I awaited attack from the scarlet menace, and I doubted my ability to withstand it. Doubt weakened me.

I hurried my assessment, sacrificing thoroughness to complete my search without interference. I raised my arms, and my pentacle faded. I scattered a golden powder of sealing to eliminate the traces, both mystical and worldly. I had not learned as much as I had hoped, but that is generally the way with magic. It is difficult, unreliable, and dangerous. It seldom justifies the effort put into it, but a Mage always hopes for the rare, spectacular success. Only those Mages who wear legitimate scarab marks expect consistency from the esoteric forms of their craft.

In darkness, I sat and stilled the throbbing of my nerves. a misguided insect strayed across my ankle, and I had bludgeoned the tiny beast before I recognized its harmlessness. Humbled by my overreaction, I called myself several unflattering names.

In an unpleasant mood, I left my uncle's office to be rejoined almost immediately by my silent, unobtrusive escort. I nodded at the dour, mocha-colored man, but he gave me no acknowledgment in return. When I inquired about my uncle's whereabouts, my escort led me through the musty hallway without a word of reply.

My uncle awaited me in the dining salon, a long, mirrored room lined with too many silver-gilt chairs and the inadequate light of a half-functioning crystal chandelier. Several of the mirrored panels wore cracks of varying lengths. Talitha and Andrew had not yet returned. Black porcelain settings for six dressed the table. "Are you expecting other visitors?" I asked.

"I thought it would be equitable to let the escorts dine with us," replied Uncle Toby with a magnanimous smile that I did not trust for a moment. Escorts/guards at dinner suggested prisoners rather than guests. Did my uncle really think that the mysterious Andrew posed such a threat?

I assumed the seat on my uncle's right. We waited. I felt uncomfortable talking in the presence of my guard, despite the man's apparent disinterest. Uncle Toby did not seem to feel conversationally inclined either. He polished his nails with a square of buffing cloth, either demonstrating rudeness or familial ease, depending on the perspective. I chose not to take offense.

A young, wiry-haired servant wearing a white uniform

tightly stretched over her ample figure cracked open the kitchen door to inquire about dinner. Uncle Toby waved the woman away. We continued to wait.

The impatient servant returned. Uncle Toby allowed her to pour wine for the two of us. With a condescending nod, Uncle Toby permitted the guard to sit at the table with us, but the hired man received only water to drink. I wondered if the man shared my unfavorable opinion of Uncle Toby's autocratic manners.

"Talitha is providing a very thorough tour," I remarked, as I drained the last of my wine half an hour later.

Uncle Toby scowled, jumped to his feet and strode to the door. "Talitha!" he shouted into the echoes of the stone courtyard. His only answer came from Nan's raucous birds. Toby gestured curtly toward my escort. "Find them." The guardsman uncoiled like an overly taut spring and departed in haste.

Uncle Toby wagged his bland, brown head at me, as if settling a long argued point. I tried to look wise, as befitted a Mage, but I had no idea what point Toby expected to convey. Personally, I had begun to suspect that Andrew had used his charm to better effect on Talitha than on me. I might envy Talitha the experience, but carnal indulgence was hardly sinister. I did not want to admit that a more general uneasiness nagged at me more with each passing moment.

I had never claimed to be a prophet. As a Mage, I considered myself a competent alchemist, but my psi skills had never received a particularly strong rating from Feti'a. Perhaps I was simply nervous from my earlier fright. Perhaps the Mages' Luck walked with me in full. Without preamble or conscious thought, I arose and stepped away from the table. I shook two philter powders—silver and blue—into my hand. "Uncle Toby, come and stand beside me," I ordered, "quickly."

Toby did not hesitate. He was a staunch Affirmist and a Dom, but he was practical, and he evidently trusted me where family safety was concerned. He did not even appear to be surprised by my peremptory command. I built the pentacle of protection around us, completing it just as the attack swept into the room.

The ice wind crackled against my pentacle's walls, and whirlwinds danced in the depths of the mirrors. With a snap, the long dining table split in half and crashed against the stone floor. Porcelain dishes and crystal goblets shattered. The mirrors began to bleed from every crack. Frost splattered the glass, then melted in red runnels that soaked the ancient rugs.

An arrow of ice raced at me from distant amber clouds within a broken mirror. The barbed white tip pounded through my barricade, scattering blue and silver dust into the hurricane of frost. The wind numbed my fingers. I fumbled with my philter purse, but I could not gather the powder that I needed. I could not speak even a simple spell to slow the freezing of my skin.

A vision of my brother's gaunt face gathered in the tumultuous air at the door of the room. Benedict sighed, and the gentle sound carried like a song, even above the raging of the Mage wind. He extended his left hand toward us. It bled, where the tip of the smallest finger had been severed, a common practice in sacrificial blood magic.

Drops of his blood beaded every spiral of the hurricane. My ears rang with a voiceless whisper, a few notes of an old folk song that my brother used to sing, and a rumble like a distant Mage gong. My arms ached from the burning of my Mage marks, tight against my skin.

The wind passed into the mirrors, carrying with it the ice, the blood, and my pentacle's powder all in a swirling cloud. The vision retreated into the mirror's dark depths. I muttered a spell of clear-sightedness, until I could see only the reflection of the room, the table, the chairs, my uncle, and myself.

The table was not broken. My brother was not with us. I did not know how much of what I had seen consisted of Mage's vision, how much was reality. *Something* had occurred to make Toby grow pale. "Uncle Toby," I began.

He glared at me, even as he downed the rest of his wine with trembling hands. I did not know how to question him. He was a strict Affirmist. He might accept a Mage's protection, but he would not admit to a Mystic seeing. "We must find Talitha," he said.

And Andrew, I thought, but I only nodded. I crossed the room behind him. We entered the courtyard to see Talitha approaching us, her tall, proud body erect and angry. She walked alone.

"Where is he?" she snapped at me.

"Andrew?" I asked inanely.

"Did you bring another?"

"I did not *bring* anyone. Andrew came."

"And left. Having opened every basement vault."

"You let *him* outwit you?" demanded Toby with an anger that I had never seen him show to Talitha.

She did not take Toby's criticism kindly. Her glare would have felled any lesser man. "You hired the guards, Dom Toby, and you extended the invitation that let this man come. You approved our safety procedures, which clearly did not suffice against *him*. Despite our precautions, he managed to administer some Mage's foul brew to drug me and Guardsman Lee." She transferred her glare to me, and I flinched. "I have not yet taken inventory to tally the missing items, but this Andrew, who 'came,' is a thief."

As far as I knew, the Stone Palace's basement vaults had seldom been opened since the day Benedict, as a child, was caught delving into them. Our mother had chastised him for unseemly curiosity, and the vaults had henceforth remained securely locked. From what Benedict had told me, the vaults had contained nothing but the discards of the Palace's varied owners. It seemed unlikely that even Talitha would be able to determine what might have been taken.

Except as an insult, I could only believe that such losses were insignificant to my uncle, but he roared as if his life had been threatened by the theft, instead of by a Mystic's attack. "Find *Andrew* and bring him to me—in chains, if you must. Question Benedict."

I did not know who was meant to receive the orders. My erstwhile guard lurked visibly near the room from which Talitha had emerged, but he seemed too distant to be Toby's point of focus. A shadow at a window of the upper level might have been Nan, but she was certainly not a part of my uncle's plans.

Talitha answered my question. She crossed her arms sternly. "You brought the thief, Marita. You are responsible for reparations. That is the law."

That *was* the law, though it was seldom enforced. If Talitha wanted an indentured Mage, however, she could not have arranged a better form of entrapment. The prospect stunned me.

From a cynical perspective, it provided a credible motive for the theft of worthless relics. Recognizing a well-known privateer, Talitha could easily have arranged a "tour" to persuade Andrew to cooperate in a small charade. She was cunning and very protective of Uncle Toby, even at the expense of his family. If Toby was under attack by the Mage that I had now encountered twice, I could not blame Talitha for taking extreme measures to recruit Mystic help, but I could condemn her approach. I expected better of Talitha.

I had admittedly jumped to a dubious conclusion. I did not, however, feel like being just to Talitha, when she was so busy blaming me for the actions of a man I had barely met. Talitha had often treated me like a child, and I had been more amused than annoyed, but she had never before trespassed on my legal rights—or my professional pride.

I wondered if the unknown Mage of the ice wind knew—or cared—about Andrew, the flying toy, and Uncle Toby's speculations. Both Talitha and my uncle could undoubtedly have clarified a great deal for me, if they had been willing. There was no use in trying to talk reasonably to Affirmists about matters of magic. Amid the present atmosphere of anger and fear, there seemed little hope of talking reasonably to either Toby or Talitha on any subject.

I wanted to escape them both before I let my temper compound my troubles with them. I also burned with eagerness to return to the relative safety of the Mage Center. Even Janine's caustic tongue would comfort me at this point.

I did not have my fine dinner with my uncle, the Dom. I ate a cold piece of meatcake from a public supply unit. By the time I reached the Mage Center, I was sniffling from the chill that had settled in my bones. I set a protective pentacle around my bed before I dared to sleep.

Talitha

Scribe Gavilan, Tathagata:

Aroha's insolence never ceases to amaze me! He came to us openly tonight, daring us to move against him. I tried to oblige him, but he escaped, despite the weapons that Dom Sevrin procured for us. Now, we have nothing to use against Aroha except those stunners that were with the shore patrol—which was scouring the coast in search of *him* while he strolled so freely in and out of our midst. (The patrol continues to deny finding any unauthorized smugglers, probably because Aroha's conspirators have bribed key officers. Our proven allies cannot cover the entire coast without local aid, so our efforts are crippled. A man of Aroha's resources and experience inevitably exploits such weaknesses as avarice.)

Worse by far, Aroha stole as many of our weapons as he could carry, and he destroyed the rest that we had hidden. You know how I argued against accepting the weapons from dread of such a catastrophe. Who can stand against Aroha in a direct confrontation? We cannot defeat him by employing his own evil tools, because he is too much their master. Aroha breached even the Empire-crafted locks of the Stone Palace's main storage chamber. He forced me to watch his work, as he exercised his devilish skills for sabotage. His free usage of forbidden Empire methods sickens me. He is utterly unrepentant and indifferent to the damage that his schemes will bring to the world. Ambition blinds him.

To our misfortune, Aroha has not lost his ability to blind others with his glib speeches and obsessively cultivated charisma. Dom Toby insists that a Mage assault occurred while Aroha ransacked the Palace. I have seen no evidence to confirm the attack, and Marita said nothing about it—though my sharp tongue may have alarmed her into reticence. I did not handle her well; she is usually quite compliant. I would not like to think that Aroha could have corrupted her already, but lonely women like Marita do have a particular susceptibility to his brand of influence. I hope that we have not erred by choosing to involve her.

I can*not* believe that Aroha could have initiated the Mage attack against Toby. Even if he were not preoccupied at the time, flaunting his Empire skills in front of me, all of our reports concur that he sacrificed his own Mystic abilities in his greed to absorb the fiendish teachings of Prince Hiroshi. Perhaps Aroha has acquired another Mage as ally, though most powerful Mystics resist the lure of Empire science for fear of losing their Mage skills. I could better accept the hypothesis of alliance, if I were less troubled by the certainty that Aroha would scorn to recruit help to attack Toby—or me. The alternative suggests that the attack was not truly Mage-generated, which would indicate that Prince Hiroshi has concocted yet another of his abominable creations. Neither prospect is palatable.

I suppose that I should relent and accept more direct contributions of aid from Mastermage Lar. Ch'ango has consistently vouched for his abilities, and she is as dangerously clever as Aroha in her own way. Even Toby disagrees with my determination to thwart Aroha without active Mage help. My father's dislike of Lar and the resultant rift with Ch'ango has undoubtedly prejudiced me. How I miss my father's counsel!

My reservations about Lar might diminish if I knew what Ch'ango told him after the Protectorate's meeting last Novema. His attitude toward me changed abruptly from patronizing condescension to eager accommodation. I would like to trust him; I would like to think that there is at least one Mage who can exert some restraint on Ch'ango. Please, try to discover diplomatically what the other Protectors have heard.

I do feel uneasy about Ch'ango's intentions, since she is fanatical where Aroha is concerned. Yes, I share her fanaticism—and many of its reasons—but I do not share her partiality to blood magic. This purported Mage assault against Toby, coinciding with Aroha's visit and our recruitment of Marita, has rekindled my worries about Ch'ango and her protégé, Lar. If Toby's "Mage attack" did occur, it may have been aimed against *Marita*. From her position both as Benedict's sister and as a Mage in contact with Aroha, a sacrifice of Marita's blood could enhance many of the spells that Ch'ango favors. If Lar initiated such an assault in order to improve my chances against Aroha, I am ungrateful—and nearly glad that the effort failed.

I do not know what to do about Marita, short of leashing her for the duration of our stay in Rit. In the past, I have always managed to manipulate her without much difficulty, but I wish that Toby had not decided to involve her. She bends easily, but she has a proven threshold of rebellion—sudden and complete—that Toby overlooks. Toby also overestimates her ability to influence Benedict. Toby has, however, taken my advice regarding Aroha: We have told Marita nothing about that devil or his history. Lar did aid me in this instance, insisting that Marita is too idealistic to be entrusted with the truth. Aroha, of course, will deceive her, because that is his way. Benedict continues to represent the unpredictable element. He serves Aroha, but he does love his sister. If forced to choose, which of them would Benedict sacrifice?

I trust your good judgment, Gavilan, in determining how much of this letter to share with Ch'ango. She is a crucial asset to the Protectorate, but she takes little account of individuals and much care of herself. If I thought we could eliminate the danger of Aroha and his prince without her, I would petition the other Protectors to remove her from our core council. She has a strong streak of viciousness in her.

It has been a frustrating evening, Gavilan.

Scribe Talitha, Rit

Marita

Mystic law required me to report the attacks to the senior Mage in Rit before discussing them with any other Mages. Normally, that would have been Feti'a, as local delegate of the Mastermage. Since Lar himself was present in Rit, legal obligation compelled me to give my report directly to him. Though Feti'a and I are not friends, I would have greatly preferred to discuss my troubles with her.

However, the use of illegal magic was the business of the Mastermage, and the decision of how to react was his to make. I requested an appointment as soon as the day had been greeted. Since I did not relish the prospect of another private meeting with Lar, I did not describe the matter as urgent. Shortly after breakfast, which I ate alone in my room, Lar's Scribe notified me that Lar had granted me an appointment that evening. I faced the prospect of another full day without the guidance of a Mastermage, and I felt only relief.

My own schedule for the day was light, and none of my customers had critical, immediate needs. I sent a courier to Llewella, asking her to reschedule my morning clients, though I dreaded facing Llewella's disapproval when next I saw her. Jun, one of the Lung-Wangs who shares Llewella's services, has good reason to call her Mage's Bane: Llewella is a natural tyrant. Grimacing at the thought of Llewella's inevitable lecture to me, I wrapped a neutral cloak over my Avalon green, and I headed for my brother's flat.

Two shaggy russet hounds slunk from my path as I approached the main wharf, but I saw no other travelers. The hour was early, but I had expected to see more activity near the docks. The yellow foam of polluted water drifted sluggishly, undisturbed by any trading vessel. Rit had a dozen ports, most of which had lain idle throughout my life, but this wharf had formerly served as a major supply point for the town. I had not stopped before to consider how much a single factory failure might diminish the port traffic. The loss saddened me.

I love Rit, although I hardly know why. It is a dismal community. Few of its inhabitants relish their assignment to it. Those who can afford to choose their homes seldom stay without ulterior motives, such as the politics that inspire Toby and Lar. Rit is noisome, dilapidated, and generally ugly. It is my home. Every lessening of Rit hurts me. I entered the waterfront building where my brother lived, and I imagined how fine it must have looked when it was new, clean, and proud.

I pounded loudly on my brother's door, hoping to rouse his neighbors—if they existed—in order to meet them. Neither they nor my brother appeared. I rattled the lock of my brother's door. Every apartment I had ever occupied could be opened more easily by judicious meddling than by key. Benedict's rooms were no better secured.

The apartment was very neat and very empty. I wished that Benedict had been so orderly as a child. In our younger days, Benedict had intruded frequently on my territory.

I searched the ebon cupboard first, mentally cataloging the chocolate, fresh fruit, and other smugglers' delights. I found nothing resembling Toby's flying truck. Nonetheless, if I used my discoveries to calibrate Andrew's influence on my brother's life, the scope of material evidence was disquieting. I had tallied an impressive inventory when I felt a soft pressure near my ankles. I looked before jumping. The gray cat rubbed against me.

I bent slowly, extending my hand for inspection without reaching too suddenly. Evidently, I did not appear threatening. The cat—Iron?—accepted my touch, guided my fingers to the soft fur behind her ears, and began to purr loudly. Entranced, I sat on the rug, as the cat circled me, butting her head against my hand to demand my continued attention. She balked when I tried to gather her into my lap, but she resumed purring as soon as she had made her point. Eyes slitted with pleasure, she regarded me with serene approval.

"You are a confident one," I whispered, so as not to offend her sharp ears. "Are you another smuggled prize from Andrew?"

Iron circled me lazily, directing my hand to her ear or chin or back. The luxury of her company made me covetous, until I recalled the mixie boy. A mixie inspires pity or discomfort but never envy.

A door slammed somewhere in the building, shattering the cat's contentment. Her hind claws raked my hand as she jumped away from me. Using the table as a convenient ladder, Iron leaped daintily to the top of the cupboard. She disappeared into the wall.

My hand stung, where a line of blood welled, but I did not begrudge the cat her instincts. Disappointed at her departure, I took comfort from the informative method of it. "You are a Mage's friend, Iron," I murmured, craning my neck in an effort to see her hidden exit.

I tested the stability of the plastiwood chair before trusting it as a footstool. The chair wobbled only slightly, and the legs seemed solidly attached. I reached above the cupboard and probed the wall. The slight stickiness of old grease brought a mutter of revulsion to my lips. I felt the opening, though it was narrow, accessible only because the cupboard tilted forward at the top. Even Iron, more fur than solid substance, must have squeezed to pass through the hole.

I leaned my full weight against the cupboard, and it did not budge. Determinedly, I began to empty the bulky piece of furniture, removing contents, drawers and shelves. Even as a hollow shell, the cupboard was heavy for me, but I managed to shove it a small distance away from the wall. Exhaling, I wedged myself into the space that I had made.

Iron's escape hole may not have represented any part of the original architecture, but the room's design did include a neatly fitted door and transom window. Someone had carefully removed one pane of the transom, perhaps on Iron's behalf. The door sported a flat, hinged plasteel handle instead of a protruding knob. The door was locked.

I tried my skill at lock-jiggling, but this smoothly set mechanism presented a more resistant obstacle than the front door's common fastener. I resorted to my philter purse, mixing a paste of powders and elixirs that I seldom used. I squeezed a few drops of an inflammatory oil into the keyhole beneath the hinged handle, inserted a string as wick, and sealed the opening with my paste. I lit the wick with a Mage flash spell. The method was not subtle, but it worked quickly and well. With a pop and a gust of pale, sour smoke, the lock mechanism broke in half. I pulled open the door.

The dim closet that I entered first held a bare, spring-based cot and nothing else, but the door beyond the closet opened onto a sizable room, well lit and stacked with gray plastic crates. Thick layers of epoxy sealed the crates and prevented casual inspection. I tried to lift one crate but abandoned the effort rather than strain a muscle. Unmarked by any identifying emblems, the heavy crates did not resemble legitimate cargo. I assumed they held smugglers' wares, as harmless as the contents of Benedict's cupboard or as insidious as Uncle Toby's winged toy. I could have opened the crates by use of Mage tools, as I had breached the door's lock, but I chose to inspect the remainder of the suite first.

A spiral, plasteel stair led me up one flight to the fifth floor of the apartment building and the wide, windowed room that I had noticed from the street. The windows wore tight shutters, but rosy ceiling panels brightened automatically. Shocked, I completed my ascent slowly.

A filigree screen that looked like real gold, patterned with twisted wire leaves and the shining, hammered wings of mythical birds, enveloped the top of the staircase. Through the gleaming lace, Iron gazed at me from atop a voluptuously stuffed cushion of sapphire stain. She sniffed the air delicately. Having identified me, she returned to the careful grooming of her facial fur.

I pushed aside the filigree screen. The room could have competed well against the most exotic salons of Rit's populist Mages. It could have held its own in comparison with Lar's elaborate suite at the Mage Center.

A rainbow of tall glass cases, shimmering with oils, powders, and living, flowering herbs, each lit by its own invisibly suspended fragment of sunshine, lined three walls. Blue satin cushions, like Iron's chosen perch, were scattered strategically. Waist-high ebony cabinets, inlaid with pearl dragons, surrounded a black marble table littered with vials, crystals, and candles. Iridescent, multihued feathers filled five tall, gold vases, arranged on the floor at the points of an onyx pentacle. Incense, heated in a gold censer on the table, spiced the air with a richly masculine fragrance. I had seen many Mages' offices, but none more boldly proclaimed their owner's prosperity and pride.

I drooped onto a stack of the satin cushions and sank into feathery softness. *Does Benedict know that his neighbor is a Mage?* I wondered first, then followed that question with a more sobering suspicion about the identity of the Mage. The smuggler's crates downstairs belonged to this suite.

"You need not have broken my lock," announced Andrew from behind me. His voice had the clipped sound of annoyance, and I could hardly blame him. "I would have admitted you by the front door, if you had bothered to ask."

I turned to see him climb the last turn of the circular stair as lightly as the cat before him. He still wore the gold bracelets, but his gray denim trousers were designed for hard work, his black hair was braided tightly, and he carried a torn canvas shirt. Patches of salt and sand crossed his bronzed chest and back. He paused to stroke Iron's chin, and he restored the filigree screen to its original position.

"I was looking for my brother," I answered, refusing to feel intimidated. My overall legal standing remained stronger than Andrew's, despite my current intrusion. I rested my hand on my philter purse.

Andrew's mouth curled in a thin and humorless smile. Hard muscles and cold green eyes promised nothing but unpleasantness. There was nothing flirtatious about his mood now. He murmured with saccharine irony, "You should have tried the public forum again. Benedict seldom stays at home when he can preach."

"I must tell him that you were a poor escort. You abandoned my uncle's dinner party very prematurely."

"So did you."

He must have tarried near the Stone Palace long enough to watch me leave, and I had sensed nothing, just as I had failed to detect him in my search spell last night. I could not sense any Mystic presence about him now. I lacked the nerve to level specific accusations against him, especially in the present, awkward surroundings. I waved toward the room. "Is this yours?"

He did not answer immediately. He strode to one of the ebony cabinets and opened its uppermost compartment with a touch. He draped his battered shirt across the raised lid. One by one, he slid his gold bracelets over his hands and into the cabinet's black velvet recess.

When Andrew turned to face me again, he extended his bared arms, palms upward. Though his skin beneath the gold was nearly as pale as mine, the triangles of silver lotus marks contrasted starkly, the twelfth pair gleaming prominently at the wrists. He turned his arms downward, closing

his fists in a subtle Mage's warning. Matched ten-shell triangles painted their bright designs against his powerful forearms. The twin scarabs atop each wrist shone more brightly
still. My voice caught in my throat.

"Tangaroa school," he commented evenly, lifting from another cabinet an aqua silk ceremonial robe and inserting his
marked arms into the wide, gold-embroidered sleeves. He
stepped away from the cabinet, permitting me to see the layers of rich violet folded inside the drawer. Iron leaped from
her cushion and began to weave around his legs, cloaking
herself gracefully in the aqua robe. Andrew knelt and let her
rub against his hands. "Iron could have advised you against
the perils of curiosity, Mage Marita. Cats have considerable
experience in that area."

"Have you a fondness for the color scarlet?" I asked, although my mouth tasted dry with fear.

He replied sharply, "As should be evident to any Mystic,
I am not a Kinebahan to employ symbolic crimson. Nor
have I ever exploited shades of blood magic." While I tried
to find a benevolent interpretation for the second part of his
answer, he switched topics and left me floundering. "You
have created an ethical quandary for yourself by this intemperate visit, since your meddlesome uncle undoubtedly inspired it. If you continue to spy on me for Dom Toby, you
will be betraying a fellow Mystic to an Affirmist, which is
not legal by either party's standards. If you report me to
Mastermage Lar, you will be forced to confess that your
Affirmist family has more control over you than your Mystic
vows. That is not an admission that any Mastermage can dismiss uncorrected."

I tried to resynchronize myself to the rapid pace of the
previous night's conversation. "The Mastermage and the
Dom share a joint obligation to ensure the welfare of Rit.
Neither would condemn me for actions against a known privateer."

"Known to whom?" demanded Andrew, but he gave me
no chance to answer. "Can you actually be more naive than
your brother was when I first met him? Assuming that your
hypothesis about me is correct, whom do you suppose my
privateering serves? Do you imagine that there is any act of
trade, legal or illegal, that does not bring profit to some
member of your inescapable family? Don't ponder my queries too long. Disillusionment is a terrible yoke."

"I have never had any illusions about your honesty, Mage Andrew of Tangaroa."

He laughed at me, startling Iron into a nervous hop away from him. "Such is the price of being a forthright pirate instead of a duplicitous politician. Very well. Distrust me. But weigh my lies against the truth that I have saved your brother's life repeatedly, and I have already helped you more than you appreciate."

"Concealment of Mage marks is a crime that clears my conscience."

"It is a crime only when concurrent with the use of magic, and that is something you will not prove against me, Mage Marita of Avalon." He extended his hand, and Iron bounded to his caress. "I am simply a collector, sentimentally attached to the symbols of my childhood folly." He smiled. "Prove otherwise."

He knew I could not meet his challenge. I was a ten-lotus potion maker, no match for a rogue Mage who wore scarab marks, a Mage who had quite possibly initiated two attacks against me as warning. Any hesitation about my forthcoming meeting with Lar vanished. I needed my fellow Mages. I needed the Mystic insight of a Mastermage.

My immediate need was a safe departure. I shrugged, as if defeated. "I am grateful for the help you have given Benedict." I tried to extract myself from the clinging cushions with some dignity.

"Propitiation is unnecessary, Mage Marita." Andrew offered me the same hand that had enticed Iron. I did not imitate her eager response, but I did accept his assistance. The hard set of his gray-green eyes softened, and he continued gently, "I am no more a threat to you than you are to me. I have given you more honesty than I would customarily offer to an intruder because your brother is my friend. I would, however, advise you to return to your lovelorn clients instead of dabbling in matters that you do not understand. I do *not* like blood magic, especially at the cost of someone I know."

I nodded, propitiating again. "Grow in wisdom, Mage Andrew."

He matched my formality but added a sardonic edge, "Good journey, Mage Marita."

I retreated the way I had come. Though Andrew had already discovered my "secret" entry, I pushed my brother's cupboard back into place and hurriedly restored most of the contents. I had intended to write a message, but Andrew's free access to my brother's apartment made that method seem suddenly vulnerable to compromise; Scribes could be hired easily enough, even by a privateering Mage. I left a pair of crossed spoons on the table, a childhood code that I hoped Benedict would remember and honor. I relocked his front door as I left.

I had planned to visit the Stone Palace before going to my office, but I abandoned both goals. I could offer little value to my clients in my present anxious state, and I could no longer make use of the formal contractual seals that I had demanded of Uncle Toby. My recalcitrance would displease Toby, but Andrew—Mage Andrew—was right: I could not legally accept an Affirmist commission against a fellow Mage. If Toby and Talitha actually tried to hold me responsible for Andrew's thievery, I would have no choice but to ask Lar to intervene. A Mystic had every right to expect the support of her Mastermage in a matter that pitted Mystics against Affirmists.

I returned to the Mage Center beneath the strong light of full morning, a favorable time of day for Avalon affiliates. I sealed myself in one of the communal E-units and let a simulated world coddle me. Phantom lovers are much more reliable than their physical counterparts. Unfortunately, both varieties tantalize more often than they satisfy.

The image of my phantom was a stock design that I had selected from previous experiments, but he insisted on adopting Lar's mannerisms. The E-units create a mental reality by supplying a basic situation and stimulating our minds to interpolate with details. My imagination is usually stronger than my memories, but I was tired. When I finally ousted Lar from my simulated encounter, the phantom lover began to assume an unmistakable resemblance to Andrew. I left the entertainment room more frustrated than when I entered.

I met Kurt in the baths reserved for Avalon. "Abandoning your clients today?" he asked, as I slipped into the water's cool embrace.

"I'm testing your recommendations regarding the advantages of an evening practice."

"Following my example?" he cooed cheerfully. "'Rita, dear, your wisdom grows daily. I may even forgive you for abandoning *me* at breakfast and leaving me with only my unbaked rolls to gnaw."

"Surely you could connive some crumbs from Lilith in my absence."

"Taking advantage of Miss Mouse is too easy to give pleasure to my jaded senses. How fared your epicurean feast with the Dom?" Kurt perched on the pool's stone edge and scratched at his freckled back.

I threw my soap at him. He dove beneath the water, reappearing cautiously with the amber soap in his hand. "You're in a good mood," he observed, offering me the soap. As I reached for it, he squeezed the slippery bar so that it flew at me, forcing me to duck in turn. I retrieved the soap just before it disappeared into the outlet for the circulating water.

"Did submersion clear your head?" asked Kurt, as I broke the surface, "Or do you need some more help from your friends?" He redirected a stream of incoming water with the heel of his hand, pushing it upward into a glistening arc that splashed my face. I dove for his ankles. In the pool, I can hold my own against Kurt, because he cannot take full advantage of his greater strength. One of the many beauties of water is that it helps equalize physical odds for an adept swimmer.

We churned the Avalon pool to waves, flooding the room, until Janine arrived. "Children," she sighed, "should be neither seen nor heard." Kurt and I were both breathing too heavily to answer her, but we grinned at each other. He had revived me far more effectively than the E-unit. "Are the two of you quite finished?" asked Janine. "Or must I wait until tonight for my bath?" She kicked a sodden towel away from the room's floor drain, and the flood began to subside.

Kurt climbed from the pool, wringing water from his dark hair. He nudged Janine and pointed to me. "Don't ask about last night's dinner," he said. He shivered dramatically, wrapped himself in a thick white towel, and left the baths.

I settled to my original purpose, scrubbing my skin with a sponge and my much diminished soap. Janine joined me in the water, but she simply closed her eyes and leaned against the jets of incoming water. She did not speak until I had finished my bath and pulled myself onto the pool's edge. "I made some quiet inquiries about your privateer," she said in a deep, sober tone that restored all my tension.

I dropped back into the water and joined her near the inlets. The heated stream pounded against my skin. "What did you learn?" I asked, trying to sound calm.

"Enough to stop me from inquiring further. Stay away from him, 'Rita. Stay away from a brother who keeps such company." She was earnest, and she was worried.

"What did you learn, Janine?"

She whispered, "He works for an Empire Prince."

The last Empire Prince was a bogeyman who had lived in rumors ever since the final war. Without conviction, I retorted, "You're becoming gullible, Janine."

Her blazing blue eyes snapped open. She hissed, "Little fool, listen to me. Just because you were born into 'the Family' doesn't make you invincible. Your privateer's employer has rebuilt one of the abandoned factories. He's producing new designs. You can't handle that kind of trouble, 'Rita. You've mastered a few spells that I lack, but we're not that different. We're both lesser Mages."

The knowledge of the Empire lords has passed away, Aunt Nan had taught me, *and we are well rid of it.* But Uncle Toby had a bright new toy that flew, and who but an Empire Prince could have created it? Andrew, the privateer, rogue Mage, and bogeyman's henchman? My brother had odd taste in friends. "Which factory?"

"I was not stupid enough to ask," snapped Janine, obviously wishing she had not confided in me. She shook her head at me, her flaming hair swirling across the pool.

"Janine, I need to know."

"It's Affirmist business."

"No. It isn't."

"Then it's the business of the Mastermage."

"I have an appointment with Lar this evening."

Janine looked at me grimly. "I'll see what else I can learn, but if I'm warned to keep my distance, I won't push. I'm not that generous with my life."

"Thank you, Janine." I hoisted myself out of the pool and tied my soggy towel around my waist.

Bitterly, as if she regretted her own concern, Janine cautioned, "Be careful, Marita. Your wrists wear more lotus marks than mine, but you don't know how to play outside the rules."

"I know. I'm naive." Perhaps Janine and Andrew were both right about me, but I did not see that I had much choice about withdrawing from the game now. I could only be a player or a pawn, and Benedict had already taken the latter role. I went to my room, rubbed my hair dry, and devoted myself to selecting the proper jewelry to accompany my best Avalon gown. Externals had always impressed Lar.

Andrew

Most Excellent Hiroshi,

I encountered a few items of interest in the Stone Palace, and I have included them in this shipment. The antique weapons are in poor condition, and the other tidbits may be equally worthless to us, but you have uncovered treasure in less likely receptacles. Before you protest my means of obtaining these dubious prizes, let me assure you that Dom Toby will not miss them. Talitha and he are too busy ruing the damage that I inflicted on their pitiful arsenal. The Protectors have ceased to obey their own rules, which adds a certain piquancy to the contest. Instead of encouraging them, the pressure of receiving the World Parliament's open approval seems to have made them desperate to achieve some visible success against us.

I met Benedict's fair, fabled sister yesterday—and rescued her twice from Ch'ango, although Mage Marita does not recognize my unintentional help. The electromagnetic shielding device that you designed for me intercepted and weakened the spells. (Yes, I did recognize the attacks unaided by your strict science, but a man's Mystic senses do not dissipate simply because he ceases to exploit his Mage marks. I have not abrogated my vows.) Ch'ango employs blood magic in its most callous form, but it is Lar as intermediary who transforms her coldness into careless brutality. That man is the poorest excuse for a Mastermage that I have ever met. Does he even know that Ch'ango wields him simply as an insult to me?

The attacks against Mage Marita do constitute an unexpected move on Ch'ango's part, because the spilling of Family blood would disrupt the Protectorate more than it would aid Ch'ango's spells. If Ch'ango believes that our devout friend, Benedict, would urge me to employ Mage skills for

any cause—even for his sister's safety—Ch'ango's wits are
slipping. Lar may have initiated the move without consulting
her, which would explain its clumsiness, but I doubt that he
could master the ice wind spell alone. The attacks may signal an ominous new aspect of Ch'ango's specialized Mage
marks, or they may represent Ch'ango's intention to control
Mage Marita by depicting *me* as the instigator. They could
even represent the commencement of a Mystic challenge,
except Ch'ango knows that I have renounced my Mage status, and Mage Marita lacks sufficient rank to be bound by a
challenge from Ch'ango. In any case, Benedict has due
cause for concern regarding his sister. Ch'ango's pawns tend
to lose more than a few drops of sacrificial blood.

Mage Marita has already taken injudicious steps toward a
deepened involvement. She searched one of my more revealing retreats. I would not have offered her the glimpse of my
scarred past, but I respected her courage enough to concede
a few snippets of honesty. She does share something of Benedict's character, despite their philosophical differences: a
yielding exterior that conceals unbreakable girders of determination. I would prefer not to see anyone else damaged by
Ch'ango's schemes or by the misguided Protectorate, but the
Family's rebellious siblings do not accept advice easily. If
she were a little less bound by her own views of righteousness, or if Benedict would tolerate some persuasive efforts
on my part, Mage Marita could contribute invaluably to our
cause. (Fear not, Anavai: I have few scruples regarding emotional manipulation, but I would not willingly misuse my
friend's sister.)

Ch'ango could make *much* more dangerous use of a malleable, literate Mage than augmenting a blood spell. If I discern any activity toward that end, I may be forced to
intervene in ways that neither Benedict nor Anavai would
approve. We must hope that the Scribes' Guild (i.e., the
doughty Talitha) continues to wield strong influence over the
Protectorate, which Ch'ango still needs if she is to constrain
our efforts worldwide.

Empire-inspired observation techniques provide a reasonable substitute for Mage discernment, but the temptation to
perform a Mage's seeking never leaves me. There is no
magic that I miss more than a good watching spell. If you
can identify the present character of Ch'ango's schemes,

please share your insights with me summarily. You know that I hate ignorance above *all* else.

A.

Marita

Lar looked smug. Though I had dressed in my best emerald gown and silver-and-moonstone girdle to keep my official appointment with my Mastermage, Lar wore an informal, thigh-length robe of violet silk, belted with a sash of the same glossy material. A platinum chain supported an enameled pendant, the peach of immortality, that rested on his bared chest. I had given him the pendant, an old Lung-Wang icon that had cost me the last of my allowance from my family.

Sleek, dark, and barely visible except for the slits of her eyes, Spider sprawled on a couch of indigo velvet. In an intimate corner of the ornately carved room, a mahogany table was set with violet linens, silver chafing dishes, and ivory chopsticks for two, and Lar offered me warm wine as I entered. I accepted the wine. I needed the reinforcement.

"This reunion is long overdue, Marita," he greeted me, a complacent smile lurking on his full lips. "I rejoice that you reconsidered my offer, albeit a day late." He touched the table's candles, and green-tipped fire sprouted from the wicks. It was another of those simple tricks that only Lar's arrogant style could make impressive. He raised his elaborately cut crystal goblet to mine. "A tribute to Avalon and her Mages."

I shared the toast. The wine was sweeter than I liked. I swirled it in its glass, seeking wisdom in the ruby depths. I did not know how to deal with Lar's apparent misunderstanding of my reason for coming to him. His interpretation was not unexpected, but it was discomfitting. "I need to talk to you, Lar, as my Mastermage."

"I know, Marita. Please, hear me first." He set aside our goblets and clasped my hands. "I cannot erase the past, as if it never occurred." I could not help comparing the softness of Lar's pampered skin to Andrew's hard grip. "I realize that

I hurt you. I've never done anything that I regretted more. I want to make amends, if only you will tell me how."

He might have lifted his apology from one of my phantom lovers, but I doubted that he had needed such a cheat. After all, the simulated lovers were patterned after Lar. I had almost programmed my response, as well, after so many sessions in the E-units: the reconciliation, the futile resistance of a long-neglected passion, the abandonment of doubts, and the lovers' reunion. Lar's intentions were undoubtedly more direct than my pretty script, since he had never had much patience for preliminaries.

"I should not have left without giving you a chance to explain," I began. "I overreacted."

Lar's deep eyes, which I had always admired, brightened with emotion. "We were good for each other, 'Rita."

We had often stood in such close familiarity. I had often simulated the smooth warmth of Lar's skin, his passionate voice and his expressive face filling me with the confidence of being loved. My words stumbled, "You made me believe in myself. Before you, I only echoed the life that my family expected of me." I did not add the rest, though my Mage marks ached with the pain of the past; I did not cry that Lar had then proceeded to shred my frail faith in self, family, and personal relationships. To hear kindness from Lar, after so long, was almost unbearable. If this was a healing type of pain, it was nonetheless difficult.

"I should not have stayed away from you so long. My only excuse is pride. I have never stopped thinking of you."

Spider streaked across the room. I turned away from Lar, my script interrupted, my emotions restored to the awkward present. "I didn't know Spider could still move that fast," I said stiltedly.

"Something must have frightened her." The statement emerged almost as an accusation, but Lar touched my shoulder with gentleness. Lar had formulated his own plans for the evening, and he seldom brooked interference with his personal agendas. "Powerful emotions can be very frightening." Lar maneuvered himself back into his position of conquest.

With a determined lurch of mind and heart, I escaped the self-inflicted spell of memory. I stared at the touches of silver in Lar's hair, the new creases around his eyes, reminding myself of how much time had passed. I stepped away from him again and declared with some asperity, "Mastermage Lar, I did not come here to keep a tryst. I need your help. Twice yesterday, an unidentified Mage of tremendous power attacked me. First, he or she interrupted a seeking in my office. My uncle and I faced a second attack together."

The expression of Lar's clear caramel eyes and sensitive mouth, all caring and reassuring, gripped me immediately. His hands kneaded my shoulders with tender strength. Lar donned concern without a pause, but where was shock, and where was outrage? "Dearest Marita, you must feel terrified. Have you kept silent all night and day for fear of disturbing me? Did you think that I would want you to face such a trial alone? If you had come to me last night, I would gladly have set aside all other business. I would always support you as your Mastermage, even if you were not so dear to me personally. Please, share this burden now."

He led me to Spider's velvet couch and sat beside me. I shared eagerly, talking freely of the past day's events. Lar expressed such persuasive sounds of sympathy. He touched me often, gently and fondly. He swore to find the miscreants himself and ensure justice. He promised to protect me from all forms of harm or grief. He vowed to confront Dom Toby and Scribe Talitha and vouch for my innocence.

I described Andrew circumspectly as my brother's unnamed friend. I intended to offer my discovery of Andrew and his scarab marks as my denouement. However, near the end of my recital, I realized that Lar was barely listening to me. At first, I wondered if he were simply upset at having his evening's plans disrupted.

I hesitated, remembering Andrew's comment about my naivete. Uncle Toby had openly tried to use me to learn about Andrew's privateering. Lar had a worse record than Toby for exploiting friends and lovers.

In the moment that suspicion stirred in me, I *knew* with the unswerving Mystic certainty that a lesser Mage like me only rarely experiences: Lar already knew what I had to say about the attacks. His only interest was Andrew. Yesterday's attacks against me concerned Lar only to the extent that they had driven me to confide in him, as of old. When I needed the help of my Mastermage, he offered nothing but schemes to his own advantage—as always.

I had almost believed his lovely apology. Lar still knew how to sway me. My credulity disgusted me.

Anger roiled in me, but I did not show it. I had gained a
little wisdom over the years since my intemperate affair
with Lar. My fellow Avalon Mages would support me better
than the self-serving schemer who was my Mastermage—
and never was the lover that my imagination craved. I
wished that we of Avalon were not so few, but at least we
knew each other's skills and limitations. We quarreled more
often than we cooperated, but the vows we swore to our
Mystic school bound us together. Even to ambitious, envious Janine, I mattered more as a Mage than as the daughter
of a Dom. To four Mages of Avalon, my true family was
only Benedict, honorably mad and unimportant, except to
me.

Lar hugged me and assured me that he would handle all
of my problems, past, present, or future, real or imagined.
He wore the handsome face and lean body of my lost love,
but he had needed only an evening to rcharden the wall that
he had built long ago around my heart. I ate with him and
enjoyed the food, and my emotions remained sterile. I flirted
with him outrageously, coldly satisfied that I could tease him
into impatience for our next meeting. Deceivers truly are the
most vulnerable to deceit.

If he had taken the trouble to use his Mage skills, which
certainly exceeded mine, he would have recognized my bitter insincerity. He was supremely confident. In his mind, I
had never stopped waiting for him. In a sense, he was right.

I did not feel triumphant over Lar. I felt sickened by the
years that I had wasted, pining for what I had imagined him
to be. I felt sicker, realizing that no Mastermage would defend me from an enemy's crimson tide or an icy wind of
Mage illusion.

Late in the evening, I escaped to my own room. I
slammed the door, then reopened it sheepishly. I scanned the
starlit courtyard for any witnesses to my childish burst of
temper. I saw none.

I did not change from my emerald robe, though I crumpled the skirt to sit cross-legged on my bed. With care, I
spread the contents of my philter purse in front of me. The
purse was cunningly designed to hold more than it appeared,
and I had a good assortment of Mage tools for the normal
circumstances of my profession. Tonight, the display of
vials, capsules, and powder packets discouraged me. Love

philters and sleeping draughts seemed woefully inadequate at the moment.

I lifted the wall panel that concealed the Avalon bell plate, a painted image of multicolored Mage bells that is one of a set of five. Now that we are so few, each Avalon Mage in Rit has a bell plate, Lilith having received mine when I moved into Dory's room. As far as I know, Avalon is the only school in Rit to own such devices.

By touching the painted bells, I rang the four sequences that would summon my fellow Avalon Mages to my room. We reserve the bells for official conferences. The members of my Mystic School would respond promptly, if possible, even if I were not their senior.

Lilith entered first, her water-colored eyes drooping from sleep. Lines of worry puckered her cherubic face, and she tripped on her long nightgown. "Is something wrong?" she asked with a panicky tremor in her soft voice.

I smiled and breathed a spell to calm her. Ever susceptible, Lilith curled contentedly on my pillow even before I answered, "Wait. The others will be here momentarily."

Kurt and Rodolfo arrived together, followed closely by Janine, and all three of them grumbled at the lateness of my summons. Kurt was still fumbling to secure the drawstring of his pants, and Rodolfo wore a loose green sleep-robe. Janine had wrapped a white quilt over her brief nightshirt.

"It's important," I declared and reestablished my protective pentacle from the previous night. At my direction, we gathered on my bed, though the mattress sagged and creaked from our joint weight. With flint and sulfur stick, I lit a black guardian candle and handed it to Lilith. "Keep a very careful watch," I told her solemnly. "Tell me immediately if anyone approaches, even if it's the Mastermage himself." I extinguished all lights except Lilith's single glow. Lilith made a competent guard, and she was the most expendable from the discussion. I needed the concentrated wits of my strongest Mages.

"Is this about your brother's friend, the privateer?" asked Janine, no longer grumbling. She raked her fingers nervously through her tangled red hair.

"In part." I took a deep breath, wishing that I had taken time to ingest a calming draught. "Andrew is more than a privateer," I answered crisply. "He is a Mage, complete with twelve lotus marks, ten shells, and scarabs. He keeps a Mastermage's violet robe, which he may well have earned."

Lilith's fretful expression reappeared with deepened furrows. Kurt gaped ridiculously, Rodolfo pursed his well-formed mouth in shock, and Janine's pale skin faded further. "This is the same privateer we discussed earlier?" asked Janine, as if I needed the reminder of what she had told me. I nodded. Twin splotches of crimson, as fiery as her hair, burned her cheeks.

"Mage Andrew is involved in something that I cannot name and do not want to understand. Whatever he is doing, he has attracted the attention of Mastermage Lar, as well as that of Dom Toby. Mage Andrew may be endangering all of Rit—or more. And he is using my brother."

"Was this the reason for your appointment with Lar this evening?" asked Rodolfo. Like Janine, he used his fingers to comb order into his straying blond hair, but his gesture spoke as much of vanity as of disquiet. Rodolfo would be intolerable if he were not so solid and diligent in his Mage work.

"No. There is more." I recounted my story of the attacks once again. This audience listened attentively. I was doubly glad that I had assigned Lilith to guardian's duty, because her eyes shed nervous tears even with that disciplined Mage task to distract her.

"A spell of ice," muttered Kurt, "could be particularly effective when used against an Avalon Mage, whose symbol is Ice."

"Other schools do not share our card symbolisms," argued Rodolfo, "and none of *us* cast that spell against Marita."

"What Mage school but Avalon uses ice in its common imagery?" countered Kurt. "The ice wind must have been tailored specifically for the attack against Marita."

"The Mastermage must resolve matters of illegal magic," declared Janine with firm insistence, halting the men's futile debate. She did not speak again of the rumored Empire Prince, but she added pointedly, "We are five lesser Mages who are out of our depth."

"Yes," I sighed and hesitated only a moment before adding, "but I do not trust Lar." I could have made the same comment about Uncle Toby, but that would have led to a description of Toby's flying toy, the one subject that I had entirely omitted with my fellow Mages, as well as with Lar. I shared Janine's reluctance to discuss forbidden Empire knowledge. "Lar may have initiated the Mage attacks against me."

"I thought you were the injured lover of the pair," remarked Rodolfo, craning his neck in an effort to see his image in my wall mirror.

I restrained my inclination to snap at him and replied calmly, "I left Lar because he could not confine himself to one bed, but that subject is irrelevant to my current suspicions." That old betrayal had, however, contributed to my present assessment of Lar's selfish motives. "If Lar initiated the attacks, he acted independent of any personal feelings toward me. I believe that Lar wants a share of Mage Andrew's illicit enterprises, and he hopes to use me and my brother toward that end. Lar quite naturally expected me to give a full report of the attacks to him, my Mastermage. I did report, and Lar listened—to every word that he could coax from me regarding Andrew. Lar had interest in nothing else."

"I have always considered Lar an overrated egotist, but you can hardly blame him for being suspicious of a privateering Mage," grunted Janine with a frown.

"I did not tell Lar about Andrew's Mage marks. The direction of Lar's questions began to trouble me before I reached that point of the story."

"Why don't *you* blame your mysterious Andrew for the attacks, 'Rita?" asked Rodolfo with a sly grin that annoyed me.

"They were abortive attacks. If Mage Andrew had wanted to eliminate me, I think he would have finished the job. Manipulative terrorism is Lar's style."

Lilith raised a cautioning finger, and we all fell silent. Her candle's flame flickered, but it brightened again. She shrugged, "False alarm. Someone approached, but he bypassed us."

"We would do anything to help you, 'Rita," said Kurt slowly, "but we are limited in our resources. What do you want of us?"

"I intend to meet with my brother tomorrow. I shall ask him to leave Rit, but I expect him to refuse. If I cannot persuade him by reason, I shall use magic to take him away from here. I anticipate interference from Andrew and possibly from Lar. I need protection and backup."

"What makes you think that this privateer places such importance on your brother?" scoffed Janine. "Benedict offers political embarrassment to Dom Toby and a weak point in your personal armor, but a scarab-marked Mage does not require such uncertain tools."

"Andrew has taken a great deal of trouble to cultivate Benedict. I don't know why."

"Then you're still missing something important, 'Rita. I don't like fighting unprepared."

"I wish I had that choice."

Kurt put one arm around me, the other around Rodolfo. "We won't abandon you, Marita." Kurt squeezed me gently, until I smiled at him. No one has ever known how to encourage me as well as Kurt. No one but Kurt is so entirely oblivious to my position in the Family.

Lilith whispered, "Marita." The black candle flickered and went dark. In silence, I set the extinguished candle in a holder at the foot of the bed. I groped for Lilith's hand. I felt her reach for Janine. When Janine touched Rodolfo, the power of our unity surged through the circle.

Something examined us. It was cold, impersonal, and painful, dissecting us with dispassionate curiosity. The pressure made my ears ring and my head throb. There was nothing tangible to fight, so we held to each other, presenting only our oneness as defense. The probe faded, but we had no opportunity to relax.

Lilith, our weakest, cried aloud when the next attack began, and I had to dig my nails into her hand to hold her with us. All of us shuddered, as the ice wind swept through my room. Rodolfo shouted a counterspell, but the wind barely slowed. The black guardian candle tumbled to the floor. My closet door swung open, and the wind lifted robes and gowns into ghostly shapes.

Visions of ourselves freezing and shriveling into husks beset us. I saw the withering of our hands. I felt the ice permeate and kill my flesh. Lilith wailed and tried to pull free of me.

My Mage marks tightened against my arms, and I struggled to feel them. I had rarely practiced any advanced Mystic disciplines outside of the standard routines that had earned me my marks. I had never had cause enough—or faith enough—to pursue the greater spells, but terror inspired me to new efforts. The silver film of all ten lotus pairs, entwined with my nervous system, throbbed more than at their original application. A cord of restraint snapped inside me, laying me bare to the cutting force of the Mage wind, but Janine sustained me until I could resume my counterattack. As I screamed incoherent defiance, the Mage wind recoiled from me. White Avalon Ice shimmered into fiery Lung-Wang Brass, and I recognized Lar in its midst.

"Lar, you fraud," snapped Janine staunchly, though I felt her fear, "we are not impressed by your tricks."

"There's a Mastermage in Rit," sang Kurt in an off-key, uneven voice, "who thinks himself quite fit." The wind redoubled and seemed to drive directly at Kurt, striving to tear him from me. Rodolfo's grip on Kurt's hand tightened visibly. I summoned as much Mage strength as my lotus array could grant. The wind peeled every dark strand of hair away from Kurt's face and caused his flesh to ripple, but Rodolfo and I held him fast. Kurt gulped at a blast of burning ice that scraped his skin raw, but he persevered with his poor, irreverent limerick. "He fails at his job, being only a snob, who has never been more than a twit." Kurt's words were an absurdity, but his stubborn act of completing them was a triumph.

Abruptly, the wind stopped. Five battered, lesser Mages sat again alone on a sagging bed in a dark room. Rodolfo began to laugh, although it was a tremulous sound, "Your psychology is better than your poetry, dear Kurt. Lar shares that common flaw of persons of power. Wound his pride, and he bleeds."

No one disputed the placement of blame now. Our unity had made us strong enough to recognize Lar's distinctive force in the attack. Lar had undoubtedly been able to sense us with equal clarity.

I flicked the switch beside my bed to restore the lights. Lilith sagged against me as soon as I released her hand. Tears streamed down her pale cheeks. "I've failed you. I disgrace Avalon," she gasped. "I'm sorry. You can't know how sorry I am, 'Rita."

I started to reassure her, but she had lost consciousness. Janine, our best practical healer, examined her and sighed, "She'll recover, but she's badly injured. I'm afraid she's right: She's not strong enough to be a warrior."

"Which of us is?" asked Kurt with unusual acerbity. He

touched Lilith gently. "I'd like to strangle Lar for causing this. What does he think he's proving by tormenting his own Mages? Mastermage violet is meant to proclaim impartiality to the petty rivalries of lesser Mages."

"Do you want us to stay here tonight, Marita?" asked Rodolfo. His generosity touched me deeply, because it was so unexpected from him. We both knew that he wanted only to distance himself from me and all the troubles that afflicted me.

I shook my head. "I've told you what I thought you needed to hear. I wish I had more wisdom to share."

Kurt gathered Lilith in his arms, and Rodolfo opened the door for him. The two men carried Lilith into the dark, quiet courtyard. Starlight showed me Rodolfo's pale hair, as the three faint figures disappeared toward Lilith's room.

Janine climbed to her bare feet, rearranging her quilt around her shoulders. She met my eyes. "That spell was more than Lar could manage unaided," she said grimly.

"He has more skill than we realized. He does wear scarab marks."

"So does your privateer."

"Lar was here," I argued. "He withdrew because we recognized him. We took away his reason for attack."

"He was not alone," countered Janine.

"Maybe not," I conceded, thinking of the initial probe. That cold inspection had not felt like Lar. "But I don't believe we'll be attacked again tonight, and we all need sleep." I hesitated, lacking confidence in my Mage instincts. Maybe we should have stayed together, just in case the attacker decided to retaliate against us individually. . . . "Do you?"

Janine had confidence enough for both of us. "No. You were right. It was a warning, meant only to frighten us." Janine walked to the door and added wryly, "It succeeded." She closed the door behind her.

I collected the black guardian candle from the floor. It had broken in two places, though the wick remained intact. I fused the pieces together with a few drops of fire oil rather than melt the wax conventionally. The resulting bond was cleaner, and the guardian spell needed all the strength I could instill.

I did not sleep well. Ravening monsters invaded my dreams. In the morning, Lilith looked healthier than any of us, for she was the only Mage of Avalon without dark circles beneath her eyes. She was fresh and awake. She was simply too weak to stand without Kurt's supporting arm.

Feti'a greeted the morning. Lar was nowhere to be seen.

Ch'ango

4 Fepuara, 510

Scribe Talitha, Rit:

You disappoint me, Scribe, in your failure to detain the villain, Aroha. You require my help and my guidance. Are we not united in our desire to protect our world from Aroha and his vile Prince? Admit your Affirmist pride and your weakness, and let the Protectorate succeed, unfettered by these inane and artificial restrictions.

Mastermage Ch'ango,
by the hand of Scribe Gavilan, Tathagata

Marita

Benedict and I discovered the isolated beach beneath the
bluff when we were, respectively, six and five years old. It
lay below the great, breezy expanse of sea grass that fronted
our childhood home. There existed only one access by land,
a twisting tunnel that descended through an ancient lava
flow. The tunnel entrance was an inconspicuous cave, accessible from a ledge just below the cliff's brink.

The black sand beach became our private haven, a place
for exchanging solemn secrets with only the pounding waves
as witness. Others in our household surely knew about our
"hidden" place, but they were kind enough to leave it for
our exclusive use. My brother and I had considerable freedom, as long as we remained apart from unauthorized human contacts. Treacherous fangs of rock guarded our beach
from oceanborne trespassers.

The dark tunnel seemed narrower to me now, but I was
still slim enough to fit through the tightest passage. I
climbed down the ladder of rock that led into the last cave.
I paused at the bottom to adjust the bubble vial that I had
tied on a silver cord around my neck. I had prepared the
philter before I came, certain that Benedict would not listen
to me. I would be ready to persuade him.

I removed my white sandals when I emerged from the
cave, and I crossed the damp sand to the flat rock where
Benedict awaited me. The rock jutted father from the sand
than I had remembered, but green top shells beaded nearly
all of the algae-slick base. The rock would still be a solitary
island at high tide.

Benedict watched me come to him. He had been swimming, and his gray robe was folded neatly beside him. Like
me, he had learned to swim almost before he could walk,
and he knew all the tricks of the local currents. Seeing his
bony, pale-skinned frame unrobed, I was astonished that he

still had the strength to contend with turbulent waters. There was a weariness in the fine lines around his eyes, but his breathing was light and even. He was far more emaciated than I had realized, despite Andrew's illegal largesse.

"I'd almost forgotten about the crossed spoons," he said, as I scrambled onto the slippery rock, choosing my footing with care.

I answered with a wan smile, "The 'X' that marked the hidden site of our treasure."

"It's still there." He nodded toward a sandy alcove, where we had buried an assortment of glass beads and plastcel coins, along with a cracked Hangseng figurine that Benedict had refused to submit for destruction. The Hangseng had been fashioned of white glazed clay, shaped as an improbably round man with a smiling face that looked little like the terrible princes of legend. An elderly servant had given it to us before he died, forgetting in his senility that world law forbade the keeping of such an overt Empire memento. Benedict had made the stubborn decision to preserve the figurine, but I had abetted him in his crime. I had always been too easily influenced by the people who touched my emotions; it was a common flaw among those Mages who eventually chose the specialty marks of crescents.

"We were rebels even then," I murmured, the memory of childhood disobedience compounding my present guilt. I could not allow Benedict to exert such influence over me now. My brother was legally irrational, and he was in danger.

"We were children, too innocent to understand the power of fear over reason." His thin mouth curled in a half smile, reminding me fleetingly of our father. Our parents would have hated to see what had become of Benedict, who might have been Dom instead of Toby. "We use the Empires' products every day, but a kindly Hangseng image terrifies us, and we rush to destroy it."

If I continued to listen to him, I would lose my hard resolve. I did not want to hurt him; I could not bear to see him hurt by others. I wanted him to be my brother, my friend, but *my* Benedict had left Rit years ago and never returned. I sighed regretfully, "Why did you return to Rit, Ben?"

"It is where I need to be now. I wish I could explain my reasons to you, but you would misinterpret them."

"You think I would disapprove because your *friend,* Andrew, brought you here?"

"What gave you the idea that Andrew brought me?" countered Benedict, widening his eyes in surprise tinged with dismay.

"Knowing that he extricated you from the Malawi prison, should I consider his arrival in Rit a coincidence?"

"No," admitted Benedict slowly. "Andrew came to Rit because I chose to come. He developed the habit of watching over me years ago—for reasons that no longer matter." Benedict shrugged. "He saved my poor life once and became chronically protective of me. He seems to imagine that I require his constant supervision in order to survive even among my own kindred."

Where would he get such a notion? I wondered wryly. "For a reluctant visitor he seems to have settled here quite thoroughly."

"Once he realized that I would not leave until the Intercessor guided me to depart, Andrew resolved to establish himself here for the duration of my stay. Naturally, he prepared a local base from which to continue his work. Andrew dislikes being idle."

I pried a slow-moving water snail from the rock and watched it curl tightly into its shell. "Do you approve of Andrew's 'work' as a privateer?"

Benedict weighed his answer carefully. "You should not make judgments without understanding. Andrew is not an evil man. He is a troubled soul in need of much guidance."

That was not the description I would have given to a prosperous privateer with scarab marks. "Your friend Andrew is a rogue Mage and a thorough scoundrel."

"If you had met him seventeen years ago," grimaced my brother, "your assessment would have come much nearer to the truth, though he was at that time considered a law-abiding citizen."

"You have known him that long?"

"When you found Lar and Mysticism," said Benedict gently, "I found other friends."

I cringed from the unspoken condemnation. For a brief time, Lar had blinded me to everything and everyone else. I knew that I had hurt Benedict. I did not want to believe that I had driven him to his Intercessor, his madness, and his privateering friend. I retained too many of my own hurts from that bitter year. "When I became a Mystic, you denounced me, Ben. You did not want a lawful Mage for a sister, yet you choose a lawless Mage as your friend."

"I wronged you," admitted Benedict with a frown, "as you now wrong Andrew. He has forsworn his magic. He is learning wisdom slowly."

"From you?" I asked with heavy irony. To have accused me of being more gullible than my brother, Andrew's opinion of *me* must be low indeed.

"I do my best to teach him, though I am only an instrument of the Intercessor's will." My brother paused for the duration of a crashing wave. "You will not believe me because my arms are bare of Mage silver, but I do have a gift of knowledge. I *know* that the Intercessor has a special purpose for Andrew. The Intercessor has not revealed the fullness of that purpose, but He has made me aware of my own responsibilities to guide Andrew. Our lives are linked, Marita. Andrew has *known* this since we met, and so have I."

I returned the snail to its damp, rocky bed. I did not reply immediately because my mind had leaped to a frightening conclusion. It was Janine's missing piece, so large and blazing that I wondered why I had not seen it earlier. "You taught Andrew to read, didn't you?"

Benedict did not seem to recognize my words as an accusation. He took pride in his unlawful achievement. "Andrew had never seen a printed book before I met him. It was wonderful to see his delight in the Holy Word. Do you know that he had developed his own form of writing? It let him preserve his own ideas, but he could not use it to communicate with anyone else, for the code was his alone, and he had no one with whom he dared to share it. You and I are so blessed, Marita, to have always had each other to trust."

I did not feel blessed at the moment, and my brother was doing his best to demolish any trust that remained between us. "How many people have you taught to read, Ben?"

He answered without compunction, "As many as I have found who were willing to learn. I copy passages of the Holy Word for them, so that they may have comfort and guidance after I am gone. They, in turn, teach others. The faithful are not as few as you think, Marita. Among our society's shunned and impoverished underclasses—who do exist despite official denial—the Intercessor's words represent the first hope of their lives. Fixers make particularly eager disciples."

The ocean stretched to the foot of our rock, stained the sand with ocher foam, and retreated. I swayed with the rhythm of the waves, wishing that I could stop caring for my brother. "Are there any laws or vows that you have not broken?" I asked bitterly.

"I uphold every law and vow that does not offend the Holy Word. My life belongs to the Divine Intercessor." Benedict's eyes became sad. "I cannot preach effectively to my own sister. I can only pray that you will come to understand eventually."

"Like your prize pupil, Andrew," I asked dryly, "who has used you to gain the knowledge of the Scribes?" I tried to console myself that such knowledge must have lessened Andrew's Mage skills, explaining why he no longer displayed his Mage marks openly. He must have considered the trade worthwhile, but that thought was terrible in itself.

"Andrew hungers to learn," said Benedict without apology. "I offered him a path to wisdom. He gained his cherished knowledge, and I gained his attention. We both gained more than either of us predicted when first we met."

"He's a privateer, not a philosopher," I countered, shrill with frustration. "Where do you think he obtains the chocolate, the furniture, and the gold? He's not interested in your Holy Word. He's interested in himself."

"You have become so sad and cynical, Marita. Is this what your Mystic practices have done to you?"

Conversion to cynicism was what my Mastermage had done to me, but I was too ashamed of my past with Lar to confess the whole of it to Benedict, even if it had been relevant to the immediate problem of my brother. "You must leave Rit, Ben, and you must not allow Andrew to 'follow' you again. You are in grave danger, which grows greater each moment that you stay." The silver crescents embedded in my skin grew icy to confirm my warning.

Benedict smiled broadly, suddenly looking more like the young brother I remembered. "Uncle Toby fusses loudly about my inconvenient behavior, but he will not hurt me. I am not that important to him."

"Uncle Toby is not the danger," I said, as if I actually knew.

The smile vanished. Benedict gathered his folded robe

into his lap. "That is true," agreed Benedict, regarding me thoughtfully. "Worldly evil works through Toby, because he disregards the Holy Word that is written on his heart. Do not become like him, Marita. You are vulnerable to the same forces that have corrupted him. They already maneuver to use you."

Benedict's preaching had always annoyed me, but I did not let myself react to it now. My wrists had begun to ache from the coldness of my Mage marks. "Ben, let me help you. We can travel together, as we once planned. Please, trust me. We must leave Rit." I could hardly believe that I had made the offer to accompany him. The words were weeping through me: We must leave Rit which I love because I love my mad brother more.

Benedict hung his head. His hair had begun to dry, but it still clung tightly against his skull. "I trust your heart, Marita, but your judgment is in error. A vision brought me back to Rit, and that vision keeps me here now. As a Mage, you should understand the force of a strong vision. Two of your Mage Schools have left Rit because of such a vision."

"Inianga and Kinebahan," I agreed, bothered by the confirmation of my unsettled dream as a form of vision. I wondered if Andrew had provided my brother with the rumors about Mage Shamba's prophecy. If so, which Mage of Rit spread the rumors so freely outside the Mage Center? "A philosophical disagreement with the Mastermage inspired *that* vision, Ben. A specious rumor makes a poor justification for stupidity."

"This sort of argument is precisely why I avoided contacting you when I arrived. You refuse to understand *my* reasons, and I *dare* not give you reasons that you might believe. I cannot leave Rit now," retorted Benedict with quiet stubbornness. "I have prayed on the subject, and this is where I am meant to be." He shifted position, preparing to rise.

I held my breath, as I popped my bubble vial, spraying its contents in my brother's direction. He coughed, inhaling Mage smoke. The ocean breeze dispersed the green residue quickly, and I breathed again. "Come with me, Ben." I climbed down from the rock, and he followed me obediently. I held his robe for him, and he dressed himself at my command. We crossed the beach, the sand squeaking beneath us, and we entered the cave.

Benedict resumed coughing. A powerful spasm doubled

him over, frightening me, though my persuasion philter was a simple and dependable formula. His face contorted, and his eyes bulged. I reached for him, but his flailing arms drove me back against the cave's black stone. I watched him helplessly. This was not a reaction that I had ever seen. I fumbled with my philter purse, trying to invent a remedy for an utterly unexpected ailment.

The spasm passed within moments, and Benedict stood straight and tall. His head brushed the cave's low ceiling. I stared at him in astonishment because his blue eyes were clear and all too aware of what I had done to him. He informed me quietly, "It is wrong to take away another person's will, Marita. The Intercessor protects me, but that does not mitigate your sin." He squeezed into the tunnel. I followed him, relieved that he had recovered, but bewildered by the failure of my philter. I always took care to verify the potency of my supplies. The aberrant reaction made me queasy with concern, but I could not let it thwart my intentions. I would simply have to create a stronger blend.

I had mentally formulated the new philter by the time I climbed to the top of the tunnel. I lifted myself from the last dusty ledge to the grassy headland and crawled away from the cliff, blinking at the brightness of the sunlight. My Mage marks tightened with bruising pain, an unusually severe and ominous reaction.

Andrew sat cross-legged on the sea grass in front of me. "Your groveling entrance lacks something of dignity, Mage Marita," he observed. He had braided his shining black hair without adornment, but all of the gold bracelets were in place. Gold embossed his sandals, and gold belted him and bound tan-colored silk against his legs. Even his supple vest seemed to be woven of that precious metal. Benedict stood a short distance away, dangerously near the cliff's edge, studying the white-crested ocean while his gray robe whipped around his thin frame.

"I was not expecting company," I replied. My voice creaked with nervousness. The sun was hot enough to counteract the wind, but a deep chill settled inside of me. I sensed a raw, potent energy about Andrew that did not uphold my recent theory of his diminished Mage skills.

"Didn't it occur to you that I would follow your brother? The spoons were effectively cryptic, but they were obviously a signal." Andrew sighed, "I had hoped you would stop meddling after you broke into my home, but you seem to feel compelled to continue your involvement. I must warn you again: This is not an exercise for novices."

My breath felt ragged from more than the exertion of the climb. "Janine," I whispered, hoping she was alert and in place with the others of my School.

The Mage's force surged in me, and I knew that I would not fight alone. I smiled, my confidence bolstered. We gathered our strength from our unity. Even Lilith, despite her injuries, enhanced the whole beyond her individual measure. We might none of us have more than ten lotus marks, but together, prepared and partially rested, we had mastered a twelve-lotus warding spell. I cast the powder that would seal the spell over Andrew and mitigate his ability to direct magic against us.

Andrew watched my philter dust settle around him. He made no effort to avoid it. "You are being unreasonable," he said, and he vanished.

My Avalon fellows shared my disappointment. We let go of our tenuous contact to save our energy, and I felt alone again. The sea grass, where Andrew had appeared to sit, waved tall, unbruised blades. Mage illusions, especially of an image as complex as a living man, are not usually so solid to the senses of a trained observer. Clearly, Andrew deserved his scarabs, despite my brother's illegal teachings. My wasted philter powder sparkled briefly and faded into the blue-green grass in wind-scattered streaks. I grasped a slender seed-stalk to confirm its reality. The stalk was moist, and its scent was sweet.

I brushed the dirt from my shirt and pants, wishing that proper moral neutrality were connected with more practical colors than beige and white. Andrew blinked back into view in front of me, wagging a scolding finger. Even knowing that his presence was the product of a Mage spell, I could not find a flaw in the visual illusion. I reached toward him experimentally. My hand passed through the image of his bronzed chest.

He grinned wickedly, "Sorry I can't be more physical at the moment."

"I don't mind." Distance would dilute his magic as well as mine. I left the image of him and joined my brother. The sunlight danced briefly off a white ship near the horizon.

"It's time to go, Ben. I *can* force you, but I would much prefer to avoid distressing you with Mage methods."

"Have you been to the house, Marita?" he asked, as if I had not spoken.

"No." I looked toward the tangle of straggly weeds and barren twigs that had been our father's attempt at an orchard. Our old house, a two-story white box crowned in stolid Affirmist brown, was nearly hidden. No one had lived there since our parents died. Without a Dom's staff of servants to carry supplies from the central city, a pre-automation house had little appeal. I had stopped visiting it after the first time vandals wounded it.

"One of the trees has survived. It produced a blossom this year." Benedict sighed, "Father was right."

"He hoped for fruit, not flowers."

"He hoped. That is what mattered."

"Show me the tree, Ben." If he would not follow me, I would convince him to lead me in my choice of directions. The orchard was a reasonable start.

We crossed the expanse of sea grass, bare now of any Mage images or other intruders on its serenity. The broad gravel path that sloped down to the main beach remained clear, despite long neglect. The path's upper stretch led us to the iron gate of our childhood home. The lock had broken long ago. The gate creaked from disuse.

Mildew stained the white plaster of the house, and several of the shutter boards had split. Most of the brown tiles were missing from the porch, and only diamondlike splinters remained of the frosted glass panels that had bordered the front entry. From the little I could see through the broken entry, the interior had been stripped to the bare walls.

The single living tree stood beneath the arched window that had been mine. The tree's leaves were sparse and curled, but they were green. Tears stung my eyes.

"Andrew says it will produce fruit in time," said my brother.

I did not want to hear Andrew's name spoken in this hallowed place, but I could not dismiss the present by ignoring it. "Andrew is an authority on everything, isn't he?"

"Knowledge is his obsession. He solves problems compulsively."

I rubbed a tear from my cheek. If Benedict cared nothing about his own life, perhaps he cared something about mine.

"Problems like me?" I asked bitterly. My tactic was unkind, but it was not entirely dishonest.

"Is *Andrew* what you fear, Marita?"

"I have become one of Andrew's problems, Ben, and I'm afraid that his solution may not be merciful. I have been attacked twice since I followed you from the forum. I cannot leave Rit without you, knowing that this man dominates you, but I will not survive long if I stay. I am only a lesser Mage. Andrew wears *scarabs*. Come with me for my sake, Ben, if not to save yourself."

Benedict cocked his head to study me. The gate creaked behind us, a prosaic sound that made my raw nerves shriek. The skin surrounding my Mage marks tingled and became numb.

Three brown-trousered, brown-shirted, brown-cowled figures with shadowed faces entered the yard. Every privateer has supporters, but I had not predicted this shape of attack, and chestnut brown was not a color for a Mage's servants. *I am still missing some vital part of understanding,* I thought frantically, recalling Janine's words to me. Nonetheless, I whispered to Janine, and my fellows readied themselves. A prepared Mage is not helpless against physical assault, though a physical attack aided by magic is both illegal and exceedingly dangerous to all parties.

The same cold probe that had challenged our midnight pentacle swept through the yard. My lotus marks tightened in response to the anticipated clash of magic. We of Avalon met and tried to block the probe. The coldness flowed away from us like water, deflected but quite intact.

I rubbed a preblended powder between my fingers and moved to cast it into the air. Benedict grabbed my hand before I could complete the spell. "Do not defile this precious place with violence," he censured me sternly.

I had no opportunity to argue with my brother. Two more cowled figures tore through the weeds and stopped beside their fellows. The tallest of the original three figures grunted in what must have been a prearranged signal. The small troop spread out, moving silently to surround my brother and me. They were so covered, gloved, and booted that they hardly seemed human except in basic structure. They held Empire-vintage stunners, which I recognized only from secret family texts.

"As I have informed your counterparts, good sirs," said

Benedict mildly, "I am not prepared to accompany you." He seemed unconcerned by the weapons, though he and I had read all the same texts as children.

The five cowled strangers did not answer. With matched and measured strides, they tightened their circle around us. I reached again for my philter purse, but the orange flash of a stunner beam deadened my hand. The cold probe, surging anew, seemed to create a similar effect in my head. My Avalon fellows sent me the strength to retain awareness, but the probe's sudden strike had dulled our contact. My brother took my arm and led me as the five dictated, and I could not demur.

One captor marched at either side of us, two marched ahead, and one marched behind. The leader grunted, directing every step and turn. They drove us from the yard, herding us toward the cliff. Each time I tried to stop, turn, or defy them in any way, the cold probe and a stunner thwarted my efforts. My Avalon fellows were reaching for me, trying to help, but our contact thinned to a futile wisp. A bleak, icy shell divided us.

Benedict marched in perfect obedience to our five captors. The path to the main beach lay before us, but I feared that the five, cruelly silent, armed men would force us across the land's edge and onto the deadly, watery rocks below. Benedict murmured, "The Intercessor is with us. Do not fear."

Perhaps he meant only to bolster his own confidence, but his sanctimonious certainty succeeded in rousing my earlier anger. Benedict's preaching had landed me in this predicament. I snatched energy from my irritation. I threw it into the reestablishment of my Avalon link.

My comrades were ready for me. Kurt fed me with encouragement, as Janine rebuilt our bond. Rodolfo's peculiarly intermittent gift surged, and the nearest of the five warriors staggered to his knees. I managed to snatch a vial of fire oil from my purse and flung the contents across another of the cowled figures. The man broke his silence with a very human shriek of pain and outrage.

Benedict pulled me with him to the ground, as stunner beams oppressed the air with their humming force. Bitter sea grass filled my mouth. My brother shielded me, a generous act that only caused me frustration because it prevented me from reaching my philter purse again. Benedict's strength surprised me. He held me quite immobile.

The humming ceased, and the five began to mutter. They cursed and accused, and I knew that my brother and I had been hidden from them. Avalon had no such hiding spell in its lore, but I could not afford to question the gift at this point. I stopped fighting my brother and joined him in stillness.

The five abandoned their mysteriousness with their common talk of sore feet and thirst, becoming only working men interrupted in an assigned task. Already, their initial agitation had passed. They said nothing to indicate what master they served. They grumbled against the heat, but not one of them removed his cowl.

The five thwarted captors made only an abortive effort to search for us, an oddity that suggested powerful magic being wielded against them. In a ragged line, they departed down the path to the main beach, where autoboats still visit the old pier occasionally. Benedict released me and climbed to his feet.

"I shall consider what you have asked of me, Marita," he said, "but I fear that it is your misguided attempt to help me that has revitalized our enemy. You have placed me in a very difficult position, where I must accept either personal sacrifice or a form of rescue that can only lead to catastrophe. You should not have let Uncle Toby involve you." He began to walk thoughtfully toward the house.

I tried to quiet my breathing and regain my Avalon bond. Andrew's golden apparition reappeared beside me, but his expression had become grim. "Don't follow Benedict," ordered Andrew with crisp arrogance. "Go back to the city, while you have the chance. I shall defend him, as I defended you both just now. Go to his flat. Cris will guide you to a place of safety."

Janine whispered in my mind, "Don't trust him, 'Rita."

Andrew snapped, "She has no alternative—and no reason to distrust me. I do not send servants to fight my wars, and I would never arm myself with inadequate pre-Empire peacekeeping trinkets that have been corroding in a storeroom for a few centuries. If I *were* your attacker, you would all be dead by now." My Avalon fellows recoiled from the powerful voice that had invaded us. Far more intense than the whisper-sense of ordinary Mage speech, Andrew took hold of our link, used it for his own purpose, then shredded its remnants. To me—unable now even to sense Janine's bright essence—Andrew added quietly, "Your friends may join you, if they wish, but my hospitality to them has a price."

I was badly shaken and no more eager than Janine to trust Andrew, but I asked him sharply, "What do you expect *me* to pay?"

"No more than Benedict has already paid on your behalf." He was gone again.

Benedict had disappeared into the old orchard. I had never expected reason to hold sway with my brother, and I had stretched my Mage's energy—as well as my Mage's Luck—as thin as I dared. Andrew's advice was probably sound up to a point. I would not be able to help my brother by letting myself be trapped with him.

Alone, I began the long walk back to the city. I did not intend obedience to Andrew. I almost believed that his counterspell had stopped the probe and discouraged the five, but his motives remained highly questionable. As I neared Rit proper, I managed to rebuild a trace of contact with Janine. It was a feeble link, but it renewed my courage. Feeling defiant, I arranged a meeting, using a private code that I hoped would defeat even a scarab-marked Mage.

Benedict

Dear Anavai,

Pray for us. The enemy uses temptation too well. Andrew is weakening in his resolve.

Throughout the night I heard him pacing among his old Mage tools, which is his habit when he torments himself with the possibilities that he has forsworn. Before dawn, he ordered Cris to go to the docks, while he prepared himself to exercise a Mage spell, if the "necessity" arose. By the Intercessor's mercy, Hiroshi's devices again sufficed to save us, but the enemy will not cease to threaten those of us whom Andrew defends.

Andrew must learn that he is not solely responsible for our survival. Pray that he may grow in wisdom, lest our enemy reclaim him through his pride. As several of the faithful have observed, Andrew could fulfill the prophecy too easily—and disastrously. Those who have once walked in evil must maintain exceptional vigilance, for the relapse is far more difficult to cure than the original ailment.

Pray, also, that I may receive the Intercessor's guidance. It was I who brought Andrew to Rit, though I did not anticipate that he would actually abandon his larger undertakings to follow me. Do I unconsciously force fulfillment of my own vision? Or has the Intercessor indeed guided me here at this time, as I have long believed? My coming has brought fear into my sister's life, and I am helpless to comfort her, for she has no faith.

The prophecy remains my terror and my hope. *From Rit will rise destruction. The condemned will gain release by righteousness, and those who obey the law of sin will be enslaved.* I trust in the Intercessor's merciful wisdom, but my imperfect faith makes me regret my prophetic gift. As once I prayed for deeper understanding, I now pray that this bur-

den of knowledge may be lifted from me. How I miss the
company of the faithful!

The Intercessor's grace be with you,
Benedict

Marita

Janine's office suits her, though she often grumbles about its inadequacies. It is at once arcane and flashy. The exterior is ominous, a sagging plasteel door at the end of an obscure, trash-filled alley. The visitor enters through a cobwebbed curtain, passing through a dark hall. Beyond a series of black velvet hangings, the visitor's eyes are shocked by a blaze of shining emerald-glass beads and mirrors. Janine burns enough candles to torch the island.

A few villainous wretches always loiter in the neighborhood. Janine pays them to assure the safety of her customers and friends. I suspected that her hirelings would earn their pay today.

Janine and Lilith were sitting facing each other across a silver-draped table when I arrived. They both wore neutral street clothes, although Lilith had tied her brown hair with a green silk scarf. Lilith had spread the cards. The two women were arguing over the interpretation.

Kurt grabbed me from behind and nearly scared my remaining wits out of me. "You should always be prepared for surprises," he told me solemnly. Like Janine and Lilith, he was dressed for travel.

"And a good journey to you, too," I retorted. "Where is Rodolfo?"

Janine answered without raising her eyes from the cards, "He's prying information from a Lung-Wang friend about the Ice Wind spell."

We did need help, but betrayal hovered as an uncomfortable specter. "Rodolfo does recall that Lar is a Lung-Wang, despite wearing Mastermage violet? *Lar* reaffirmed Ao Jun as the official Lung-Wang senior in Rit, after Ch'ango retired to Tathagata."

"Rodolfo is always careful of his own skin," said Kurt,

massaging my shoulders. "This Lung-Wang has an intimate interest in Rodolfo's welfare."

"Lovers do not carry warranties of reliability."

Janine could not resist the opportunity to jeer, "Rodolfo has better luck with his lovers than you, Marita. He doesn't share your unfortunate talent for collecting the attention of power-hungry men." I would have retorted, but Kurt pinched me, and my riposte deteriorated into a yelp. Janine continued, "Do you think you've evaded your predatory privateer?"

I did not know what to think about Andrew, but I wished that Janine would not discuss him in the context of my failed relationships. I tried to relax into Kurt's gentle ministry. "Andrew will find us if he sets his mind to it, but I think he's occupied with larger matters for now."

"This morning's attack?" asked Kurt.

I nodded. "And Benedict."

"You've learned something," said Kurt, and his hands grew still.

"I've made some deductions." These were my friends, but I chose my words carefully. I had made a solemn vow to my family, and I meant to keep it. "The Family expected my brother to become a Dom and trained him accordingly." They had trained me, likewise, and that implicit addendum was not lost on my listeners. Janine no longer split her attention between me and the Mage cards. She distrusted my family—with some cause, I had to admit—and all of her suspicions, resentments, and doubts had surfaced in her taut expression. I continued determinedly, "Benedict will share certain *privileged* knowledge with anyone who pretends an interest in his 'Divine Intercessor.' Such teaching is illegal because of the potential dangers, but my brother does not recognize social law. Benedict seems to consider Andrew a disciple."

"Thus, the Mystic privateer cultivates the madman," muttered Janine. "Because the Family may disown the madman, but they cannot eradicate his knowledge."

"Andrew has been using my brother for some time. We cannot be the first to wonder why Mage Andrew shows such prolonged generosity to a religious zealot."

"When did anything but trouble come from your Family?" asked Rodolfo.

I did not let myself feel the insult, which I had heard painfully often in Mage Center whispers. "Benedict has broken his family connections too thoroughly to offer much value for his origins alone," I countered, then resumed my original theme "A man of Andrew's lawless form of success obviously develops enemies, who would use any opportunity to act against him. We reaped some of Andrew's self-serving charity this morning because Andrew was the real focus of this morning's attack. When we fought, we were helping *him.*" I clasped Kurt's hands for reassurance, but even he had stiffened with resistance to my words. Just as he has always been least envious of my peculiar birthright, so he is also the most reluctant to acknowledge it. He did not move away from me, but neither would he face me, even by reflection in the mirror. Like Lilith, he bowed his head rather than meet my eyes.

Only Janine held her brightly crowned head upright and undaunted. "Dom Toby?" she asked crisply.

"Or Lar. Or both. They are both aware of Andrew. I think that *someone* else has recognized Andrew's reason for tolerating Benedict and covets the prize. Evidently, Andrew has not yet finished with Benedict, but now Andrew is in much the same position as Uncle Toby: reluctant to dispose of Benedict but frantic to control him. At some point, both Andrew and Uncle Toby will decide that my brother brings more trouble than worth, and my brother's life expectancy will plummet dramatically."

"Lar doesn't need your brother," said Kurt softly. "Lar had you, even if he didn't have the sense to keep you."

Kurt was making amends for Janine's barb and his own ambivalence regarding me and my family. Ordinarily, I would have welcomed the kindness, but I could not leave Kurt's underlying assumption unchallenged. "I have never betrayed my family oaths for Lar or anyone else," I retorted. Kurt did not try to tease or to smile away my indignation. He tightened his grip on my shoulder briefly, then nodded.

"There is more at stake than Marita's pestilential brother," grumbled Janine.

Lilith enunciated clearly, "The Prince."

Having shocked me, Lilith continued to sit scowling, hunched over her cards, the pale green fringe of her scarf tickling her neck. I could not believe that Janine had confided in Lilith about the Empire Prince. The idea of sharing

such a sensitive rumor with hapless, ineffectual Lilith appalled me. I looked accusingly at Janine, who shook her
head in vehement denial. I realized somewhat guiltily that I
distrusted Lilith because of perceived weaknesses in spirit
and Mystic skills—a very incorrect attitude, as any Affirmist
would avow.

Kurt, blithely uninformed about Janine's ghastly rumor,
snatched a white silk handkerchief from his vest pocket,
reached past Lilith, and used his bit of silk to collect one of
her Mage cards from the table. He waved the card above his
dark head, reclaiming his clownish habits. "Marita missed
the lively part of the discussion." He grinned at me sheepishly, "Lilith and Janine have been debating the significance
of the card of the Sable Prince in the reading. Janine says
the card represents the powerful force that has been used
against us. Lilith insists that he's actually a man who opposes us." Kurt replaced the card respectfully.

I could easily imagine why Janine preferred a symbolic
interpretation. Each of the five Prince cards had originally
depicted a Nikkei or Hangseng figure, and the Empire influence remained implicit in the cards' meanings. Most Avalon
Mages viewed the black-robed Prince of Sable as the most
intimidating of the lot, though we seldom admitted the
gloomy undercurrents to our clients. In the customary symbolism, Sable could indicate the earth element and its power,
wisdom or artistry—or simply dark coloring. Any Prince
card suggested the characteristics associated with the Empires, but a "powerful force" did not necessarily connote aggression. I had frequently interpreted the card quite
favorably for my clients.

I also knew better than to augur from another Mage's layout. I pushed aside my rationalizations and asked Lilith
bluntly, "Do you see the Sable Prince as Andrew?"

Lilith raised solemn eyes to me, and their watery sheen
impressed me. Only the most intense readings bring tears.
She pointed a stubby, beringed finger at another card. "Andrew is the Blood Mage."

" 'Rita said he wore Tangaroa colors," argued Janine tes-
tily, "which would suggest the suit of Shadow. Blood is the
suit of Inianga." She continued under her breath, "A one-
lotus initiate could produce a more plausible reading."

Showing unusual spirit, Lilith snapped back at her, "And
Sable is the intrinsic suit of the Kinebahan school, but that

does not make every Sable spirit an Amerind. The Sable Prince is also the purest symbol of Empire power, an earth power in its most intense form." Lilith shook her head primly, rebuking Janine with a dry recital of basic Mystic lessons: "Every card's meaning must be evaluated in context. Blood is also the representation of either blood magic or a vivid life, as well as the emblem of spirituality."

"Andrew does not strike me as particularly spiritual," I mused. But he certainly made a vivid impression. I could not bring myself to contemplate the possibilities that "blood magic" raised, despite *his* unsolicited disclaimer.

Kurt dragged a third chair to the table and rested his chin in his hands to study our subject of controversy. I stood behind him and forced myself to look at the rest of the reading. Lilith had used a simple layout of five cards, with one face to represent each suit. The Blood Mage and Sable Prince occupied the two dominant positions, with the Brass Dom, the Ice Dreamer, and the Shadow Cat as the three secondaries. By classic interpretations, that foundation signified an uncomfortable triumvirate of stern law, disciplined sacrifice, and changeable mystery. To find Prince, Mage, and Dom in a single reading was grim enough, but the Sable Prince and Blood Mage made a particularly ominous pair for joint dominance: the respective essences of cold Empire power and Mystic life force. The conjunction of strong, contradictory cards typically resulted in the least reliable prediction of the most inescapable events. It was not a helpful reading, but at least it contained no Mixies.

The four of us stared at the cards longer than necessary. All of us were professionals. All of us knew how easily a reading could be adapted to fit an existing set of circumstances. From personal bias, I sided with Janine in minimizing the Sable Prince, but both of us would have preferred to see another card in that position.

We heard Rodolfo's identifying whistle in the alley and awaited his arrival in silence. "Grow in wisdom," he greeted us cheerfully. Like the rest of us, he wore neutral colors of cream and beige for shirt and trousers, but an old Mystic necklace brightened his ensemble. Enameled patterns of Mystic beasts plated the wide necklace with the colors of the five surviving Mage Schools, as well as rare Aleut burgundy and a deep rose that I could not even identify. It was expensive jewelry for an uncertain time. I hoped that Rodolfo's Lung-Wang friend appreciated the attractive extravagance.

"Good journey," answered Kurt. "What did you learn from Yin Hsi?"

"He's heard of the ice wind. It was one of Ch'ango's last inventions before she left Rit entirely. He doesn't know of anyone now in Rit who's ever mastered it, including the current Mastermage. Whoever is using that spell is working without official Lung-Wang permission: no surprise, there. More surprising: The Lung-Wangs know that someone is using illegal magic. Several Lung-Wang spells have been compromised and taken out of circulation as a result. Traps have been laid, but no one has landed in them."

"The Lung-Wangs might have had the courtesy to alert the other Schools," snarled Janine.

"And risk a claim of criminal neglect? They've just begun to talk of it among themselves. Can you imagine how this Affirmist city would react to the knowledge that spells are being stolen and used uncontrollably?" Rodolfo slouched elegantly onto the black velvet couch, entwining his fingers behind his fair head. "Every Mage in Rit would be open to lawsuit."

Thoughtfully, Kurt ran his left hand—the hand best suited for receiving Mystic impressions—above the card of the Blood Mage. "I wonder," mused Kurt, "if the Iniangas and Kinebahans had more than Shamba's insubstantial prophecy to inspire their abandonment of Rit."

I whispered in reluctant acknowledgment, "Our troubles may not be as isolated as we believed." Kurt's speculation disturbed me because it was both plausible and consistent with my disturbing dream/vision. The leaders of the other Schools might have confided in Dory, who had led Avalon with quiet capability for so many years, but I was too young and inexperienced to be trusted with the confidences of Feti'a of Tangaroa or Ao Jun of Lung-Wang. Shamba of Inianga and Pachacamac of Kinebahan had both left Rit less than a month after Dory's unexpected death, and Avalon had still been officially leaderless at the time.

Janine confirmed my bitter thought, "The other leaders might have talked to Dory, but they don't quite trust a Mage whose uncle is the Dom."

"I'd like to hear what the Tangaroa Mages have been discussing recently," I muttered.

Kurt asked quietly, "Do you trust Feti'a?"

"Feti'a serves her Mastermage with unquestioning loyalty," replied Lilith, vaguely wistful. She gathered her cards into their silken pouch.

As one, we heard the padding of feet in Janine's entry hall. Janine raised her hand in readiness, and I realized that she held a smoky vial filled with an oily, unpleasant-looking potion. Kurt and Rodolfo moved swiftly to either side of the door, as if by prearrangement. Lilith pressed her fingers into the soft wax of a crimson tower candle that she had lifted from a hanging lamp. I reached for my philter purse.

A hound parted the drapery, but none of us relaxed our guard. The hound, a brindle monster, trotted directly to me. She settled her hindquarters on the floor in front of me, watching me with bright black eyes that seemed neither friendly nor inviting. She wore a fine gold chain around her thick neck.

"Sand," I tried, tentatively offering my hand for her approval. She granted me a very cursory inspection, as if humoring me.

"The mixio boy's dog?" asked Janine softly.

"I think so."

"Your brother's piratical friend didn't take long to find us," observed Kurt. The hound ambled to the door, stopped and looked at me expectantly. "You're being summoned."

"A gentle reminder from Mage Andrew."

The hound growled. Rodolfo remarked, "The next request may be less friendly."

A sound like distant chimes trickled over us. "Mage spell," whispered Lilith, gathering her cards with nervous fingers. The hound growled again.

The chimes became louder, filling the room and shaking the beads and mirror strings. A candle toppled, and Janine crushed the fire hurriedly. The hound growled a third time.

My Mage marks burned, and I gasped, "We can't stay here." Janine snatched her darkest cloak from the rack. Rodolfo cast a powder to extinguish the candle flames. The hound ran ahead of us, as we emerged into the noisome alley.

The air had the sulfurous taint of pyromancy. A dirty, gnarled man, one of Janine's hirelings, rested among a pile of rags beside the sagging door. His eyes were closed. When

Janine prodded him with her foot, he did not stir. "Sleep spell," muttered Kurt.

In desperate haste, Janine bent to shake the man. Before she could touch him, he tumbled sideways to the ground. Blood trickled from his mouth.

"He was alive when I arrived," protested Rodolfo shrilly, as if we had accused him of enacting the sacrifice. "He asked me for a ten-piece."

"Someone works quickly," I said, feeling sick. I could see no wound on the man. No *physical* hand had touched him. I could taste the cruel power of the spell that had taken him, though it was a spell far beyond my experience.

"And ruthlessly," added Janine. Her face was pale. Harsh, metallic chimes continued to clamor ominously. Some vicious distortion of Mystic teaching still hunted us, but not one of us seemed able to escape the presence of the nameless, fallen man. "What sort of spell demands the blood sacrifice of a *man?*"

The remote spell that detains us here to meet a similar fate, I thought, but awareness did not free me from the magic's deadly, numbing grip. The hound barked from the far end of the alley. I moved with the stiffness of a rusted, pre-Empire wheel. I could still hear the chimes, but they had softened into a more melodious pattern. I stepped forward slowly and felt Janine shift beside me.

Kurt slapped Lilith's face until she lost her glazed expression, though her color remained wan. Rodolfo growled several eloquent epithets. The sound of the chimes faded as we left the alley.

"Are we following the hound?" asked Lilith nervously. She really did not look well, though her movements seemed strong enough.

"Yes."

"I don't think I can walk all the way to the wharfs," said Lilith, "if that's where we're headed. I'm sorry, Marita. Last night was hard on me."

I had almost forgotten her internal injuries. She stumbled, as if to justify her sad reminder. We could hardly force her to continue in such a state, but we could not leave her here alone.

"I'll stay with her," offered Kurt without much enthusiasm. Dirty, dilapidated buildings blocked our view and offered no hope of hospitality. Such miserable districts seldom housed anyone more benign than mindless E-unit addicts.

"You're almost as helpless in this neighborhood as Lilith," argued Rodolfo gruffly, showing as much altruistic concern as he knew how to muster. "Janine is the only one of us who knows these people."

"Loki's mischief," cursed Janine, because Rodolfo was so obviously correct. Janine had much the best chance of protecting our injured Mage. Lilith shook her head miserably and moaned, but Janine waved at us impatiently. "Go on, before you lose your guide. I'll take Lilith to a friend and try to meet you later." She added sardonically, "Unless I decide that I'm safer without you."

The hound paced and snarled a block ahead of us. I felt an atavistic resistance to the idea of proceeding without Janine, but we had little choice. Kurt, Rodolfo, and I continued our lonely parade down the desolate street. I wondered absently what sort of friend Janine could find among these broken and abandoned houses. Janine's resources usually surprise me, because she is so adept at making use of assets that I overlook. I had long thought that I should train myself to match her aptitude, but I had never had any particular incentive prior to these last few days.

Within minutes, I doubly regretted leaving Janine, as I concluded that we did not really need the hound's guidance. I knew the way to my brother's apartment, even starting from Janine's dismal home district. Even injured, Lilith should have been able to walk *that* far.

The hound did seem to know the most direct route, darting through alleys that I would not have noticed. She always waited long enough to ensure that we followed her. Sand was either exceptionally well trained or bespelled. We left the chimes behind us entirely when we approached the wharfs.

Sand galloped from view as we reached the row where my brother lived. The mixie boy stood directly in front of my brother's apartment house, his florid, pock-marked arms crossed defensively. Only the white puppy, Milk, accompanied him. The boy glowered equally at Kurt and Rodolfo.

"You're paying for them?" he asked me, nodding at my fellow Mages. "I don't guide without pay."

"What's your price?" I asked.

Cris pointed his ruddy finger at my philter purse. "Spells. One for me, one for Lillie."

I forced myself to answer patiently, because Cris could only be a pawn, as helpless as my brother. "I'd have thought your friend Andrew could keep you supplied with Mages' wares."

"Andrew's no Mage."

Kurt and I exchanged a pitying glance. Rodolfo asked archly, "What sort of spells do you want, boy? We can pay our way."

"Don't want them from you," spat Cris. "She pays, or there's no deal. Andrew told me she's a specialist."

"You want a reciprocal pair of love philters?" I asked gently, "For you and your friend, Lillie?" Part of my professional expertise is an ability to make shy clients comfortable with their requests. The process is always more difficult with witnesses, and Rodolfo's contemptuous snicker did not help.

"You laughing at me, pretty man?" demanded Cris, his mixie face puckered in anger that made him even uglier than usual.

"Forgive me," replied Rodolfo smoothly. "You seem young to be requesting love philters. I mean no insult. You are wise to insist on Marita's skills for such a delicate matter. Her love philters are unsurpassed."

Cris appeared slightly mollified but still suspicious. Kurt grinned winningly and put his arm around Rodolfo, which seemed to make Cris relax a trifle more. I offered Cris two ampoules of a stock blend that I kept in my purse. "I shall tailor a more precise formula for you later, if you come to my office for a consultation."

The boy's laugh was disquieting, because he no longer resembled a hesitant, lovesick youth pleading for a favor. He was a dangerous privateer's worldly-wise runner. He knew something that I did *not* know, and he relished his secret. He snatched the ampoules from my hand and thrust them into a pocket of his rumpled linen jacket. "I'll take you to Andrew," he said curtly. "Then you can figure how you'll pay *him*."

Cris led us into the house adjoining my brother's home. The stark entry was similar to the neighboring building, and the blank apartment doors provided an equal dearth of enlightenment. Cris opened a low door beneath the stairway and ducked inside. The white puppy bounded after him.

Kurt bowed gallantly in my direction. "An old Avalon custom states that ladies should have the privilege of entering first."

"Thank you so much," I muttered, resigned to the duties of my seniority, if not to Kurt's false chivalry. I bent low to follow Cris, feeling my way with slow caution. Cris lit a pair of dusty glass sconces, which helped. A plasteel stairway spiraled down to a damp basement. Cris bypassed most of the steps in his descent to the lower level. He knelt to scratch the puppy's floppy ears.

Rodolfo and Kurt joined me in the crowded alcove. Rodolfo whispered to me, "I'm leaving a trail for Janine." He nodded toward the faint halo of powder that he had scattered over the threshold.

"Glad you thought of it," I commended him, although I was not sure that Andrew would tolerate an unescorted visitor, even if Janine managed to track us this far.

Our escort growled impatiently, "Come on. The tide'll be rising soon." Cris pointed into a tunnel, dark but for the intermittent glint of flowing water.

"I hate boats," groaned Rodolfo. Kurt cuffed his arm in sympathy.

A battered, shallow skiff in an underground channel was enough to warrant dislike even from me, and I normally enjoyed anything that moved on or in the water. The channel's overhead clearance barely sufficed for the boat, leaving no room for passengers to sit upright on the benches. Cris crouched with the puppy beside the motor. Kurt, Rodolfo, and I folded ourselves into the dripping hold. The skiff heaved forward in silence but for the slap of the wake against the channel walls.

We must have paralleled the shore for a kilometer. In a rush of sloshing current, we emerged from the tunnel beneath a busy wharf and hurtled alarmingly between two gray transport ships a hundred times our size. Once I had caught my breath, I contrasted these crowded waters to the desolation of Rit's main wharf and reached an unsettling conclusion. Someone had learned how to redirect the automatic routing of the supply ships. If this was Andrew's domain, Rit was receiving more supplies from privateers than from legitimate sources.

Cris maneuvered the skiff deftly, but Rodolfo cringed
from several narrow misses. A few wharf workers hailed
Cris, and he responded with an absent wave. The mixie did
not seem capable of forming a pleasant expression, but his
squint lessened, and his scowl eased. The puppy yapped de-
lightedly. If our journey was a secret one, then these wharf
workers could only be fellow conspirators.

I did not recognize the wharf from this sea-level angle,
but I memorized small details for future reference: a bloated
Mage lotus scratched on the piling, a broken pulley abandoned near the shore, the uneven planks that formed the
wharf shack's siding. My study was interrupted when we
slipped between another pair of looming ships. Cris stopped
the engine of the skiff. A plasteel lading basket settled just
above us.

Cris collected the puppy in his arms and climbed into the
basket. "You come," he said, pointing at me with his encumbered hands. "They can wait for the next basket."

Kurt patted me on the back as I clambered out of the hold.
I rejoiced to be able to stand, but I was not happy to leave
my allies behind, even temporarily. As the swaying basket
rose above the skiff, my expression must have been forlorn,
because Kurt mimed a figure of grand tragedy. Rodolfo,
looking slightly green and completely miserable, had closed
his eyes to the entire spectacle.

Andrew himself, all golden and magnificent, lifted me
from the basket to the ship. Except for Cris and Milk, there
seemed to be no one else on the ship's polished deck. "You
certainly know how to show a girl a good time," I said with
a grimace.

"I'm glad you begin to appreciate me, Mage Marita." His
tone was as wry as mine. Andrew told Cris, "Watch the pair
in the skiff. Mage Marita and I need to negotiate their fate."

"If you harm them, Mage Andrew, not even your formidable skills will save you." Threats are not generally my style,
but I wanted Andrew to understand that my Avalon fellows
mattered to me almost as much as my brother.

He laughed brusquely, "Must I keep telling you? I am not
a practicing Mage, or even a registered Mystic, and I bear no
ill will toward you or your friends." I responded with a suitably scornful expression, and Andrew's smile thinned. "I
am, however, a businessman, and I expect to be paid accordingly." He commanded like one accustomed to unquestion-

ing obedience, "Please, join me in my office, where we can discuss these matters like professionals."

Wishing I dared to contradict the master of the ship, I glanced wistfully toward Kurt and Rodolfo before I accompanied Andrew to a solitary plastiglass enclosure. It was the original technician's post, well preserved and accordingly uncomfortable for a discussion. No apparent effort had been made to renovate it as a personal cabin. As a result, there was only a single chair, which Andrew offered to me. He perched on the hard console.

"I expected a more sumptuous office, Mage Andrew, since your tastes seem to run toward such extravagance in other respects."

"This is a working transport ship, not a passenger cruiser."

I gestured toward a display of flickering lights. "What purpose is served by a console that only a Nikkei could have interpreted?" Any discussion of the Empires was delicate, but I was pleased with my inspired approach. I had introduced a difficult subject daintily enough to have satisfied the most ardent Affirmist.

"I am not a Dom, who can choose to abandon expensive resources because of trivial technical failures."

"You imply that this is a functioning technician's post, and you are the technician."

The accusation seemed to amuse him. "I admit my guilt freely. I study Empire devices and engines. I do my best to understand them. I value Empire science, and I apply it as frequently as possible. I like to solve problems and make things work."

His smiling confession chilled me, though I had expected it. "Use of the Empires' methods is a serious crime against world society."

"So is privateering. Come, Mage Marita, you have surely realized that I have my own ideas of justice."

I swallowed my fear of what such *justice* might entail. "Where did you learn the Empire skills?"

"I taught myself some of them through experimentation. Others, I have gleaned during my travels."

"As you gleaned a skill with letters by deceiving my brother?"

"Your brother is a friend, and I do not deceive my friends."

"I think you are deceiving me."

"My friend's sister is not necessarily my friend."

I was not sure that Andrew was a friend to anyone but himself, but I had to acknowledge—privately—a reluctant admiration for his obvious talents. "Where is my brother?"

"Preaching in the forum, as is his custom at this time of day."

"You said that you would protect him!"

"He is still alive, healthy, and free. Did you expect me to lock him in a cage?"

"It might help," I muttered, but I could not muster too much indignation against Andrew. My own approach for defending Benedict had failed miserably. "My brother and I were attacked this morning by five armed soldiers. I think you know who sent those soldiers and why."

"I have a few ideas on the subject." The console emitted a series of clicks. Andrew touched a switch, and the sounds stopped. His gray-green eyes, remarkably light for a man of such dark coloring, turned back to me. "But I am not inclined to share my suppositions. You already have enough to report to your dear Uncle Toby. Tell him, if you wish, that his flying toy is only what it seems: a toy. He uses more sophisticated Empire products daily. The only legal distinction is age, which is a thoroughly artificial and irrational gauge of 'correctness.' "

"The distinction is the knowledge that produced the toy. There is too much power in that sort of knowledge, and it nearly destroyed our world. The Empire sciences must not be resurrected." I recited the law frantically, wondering if Andrew were as mad as Benedict—or simply indifferent to anything but his own convenience. "You are a Mage. How can you be so blind to the dangers of what you are doing?"

He tapped a rapid pattern on the console keys, before he gave any sign of having heard me. He responded circumspectly, "Ignorance, not knowledge, leads to such destruction as war epitomizes." Andrew raised his forearm with its weight of embossed gold. "Knowledge does not disappear simply because it is hidden. It is *ignorance* that breeds abuse. I wear scarab marks, and I am quite capable of using the power that they imply, but I understand the repercussions too well to employ such magic carelessly. I study Mysticism, as I study everything within my reach, but I have used no active magic in fourteen years."

"You are almost convincing until you lie so blatantly. You projected an image of yourself this morning that could only have been generated by a scarab-marked Mage."

"The image was the product of an Empire device, as was the defense that I created for you and Benedict." He leaned forward suddenly, gripping my wrists and pressing his fingers against my Mage marks, bruising every nerve beneath the sensitive film. "You imagine that you are protecting yourself by gathering your fellow Mages and uniting your magic to thwart your invisible foe. You are wrong, Mage Marita. You are making yourself increasingly vulnerable. You are not defending your brother. He is defending you."

Andrew released me, crossed his arms, and rested against the console. A procession of red lights, orderly reflections of the Empire past, marched across his bright bracelets. Beyond the plastiglass wall, I could see Kurt and Rodolfo watching me. Cris stood defensively between them and the technician's post, but the mixie boy was a small enough obstacle if I truly needed help. If Andrew had spoken truly about his Mystic skills, three lesser Mages of Avalon might yet have a chance to stand up to him, though the prospect daunted me. Kurt smiled at me, as if he could sense my uncertainty even from afar.

Andrew continued, "Because he lacks formal Mystic training, Benedict's personal resources of energy are limited, and you have nearly drained him. I am willing to protect you, Mage Marita, for your brother's sake. For a price, I will extend that protection to your friends, despite my doubts about their worthiness. However, I will not try to protect any of you from self-destruction. If you want my help, you must renounce the practice of magic for as long as you are in my care."

I swallowed my outrage and answered coolly, "You do not stint on your demands, sir."

"I make an offer which you may accept or reject."

His bluntness seemed to demand a reply in kind. "How can I decide intelligently? You decry ignorance, but you refuse to enlighten me even about the names of my attackers. You guard your secrets too well for a man who professes that knowledge should not be hidden."

"Do not confuse thoughts of a personal nature with knowledge in the general sense. The former are subjective and deserving of privacy. The latter is truth, at least as far as truth can be understood by our finite minds."

"The name of my enemy, if you know it, is not subjective."

"Even the designation 'enemy' is subjective."

"You twist your definitions to suit your purpose of the moment. Your philosophy is built on conceit." I heard my own words, openly disrespectful and incorrect, and I realized my error, but the damage was done. Andrew had goaded me with such seemingly rational conviction that I had not even noticed my descent to a privateer's level of argument. He had perverted my lawful outrage into hypocrisy.

Andrew smiled sardonically. "Like most people, you hear what you already believe, rather than what is said. You choose not to understand your brother, and you choose not to understand me." With unstudied grace, he slid from the console and crossed the narrow cabin to the door. He swung the door open with a clean, strong gesture. "I had hoped there might be more of your brother in you, since he told me that you were close at one time. That shows how wrong *my* subjective thoughts can be. I cannot help you, Mage Marita. Cris will take you and your companions back to town."

I did not like being censured by an arrogant criminal, but I had already made enough mistakes in regard to Andrew. I held my pride in check. Andrew's help was a two-edged blade that I would happily avoid. Andrew's information, however, was something that I wanted and badly needed. I did not expect him to offer me another chance at it.

Could three lesser Mages withstand him? Possibly. Could we safely work with him to our advantage? Only with a hefty dose of Mages' Luck.

I would have used any spell in my repertoire against him, if I had thought I could achieve a positive result. I weighed the strength of Kurt and Rodolfo united against Andrew and Cris, but my Mage brothers were not brawlers to be used so coarsely. I remained seated, hoping that Andrew would hesitate to evict me bodily, while I struggled to regain the advantage that I had lost before I recognized its existence. "You said that you would help my friends for a price. Do you rescind that offer as well, Mage Andrew?"

"I have few scruples that cannot be overcome by enough gold, but the price for this particular service has risen sharply. I seriously doubt that you or your friends can still afford me."

"Would the price be equally high to protect a Mage who agreed to your terms? If she promised to use no magic, to remain in your sight, and to obey all reasonable commands, would you help her for an affordable fee?"

Andrew let the door swing closed. "You speak of the Mage who was injured last night."

I was not surprised that Andrew knew about the Mage attack that I attributed to Lar. Such knowledge could have indicated guilt, but it did not prejudice my prior opinions. I had already accepted the unpleasant fact that Andrew seemed to know about everything. I did not bother to question his source of information, since I was sure he would not answer me. "Her name is Lilith. She will not survive another onslaught. Her Mage skills are limited at best." But she had ears to listen and eyes to observe. And she was sweet and sympathetic, where I was cynical, too quick to speak my mind, and too impressed by Andrew as a man.

"Lilith," murmured Andrew, as if seeking knowledge from the name. He frowned. "Mage Lilith will learn nothing more from me than I have told you, Mage Marita."

Silently, I cursed him for discerning my motives. However, he had not refused me outright. "How much will her protection cost?"

He shrugged, "Twenty pounds of gold. In any form."

"You call that affordable?"

"I call it a moderate price for a life."

"If I traded everything I own, I could not raise more than five pounds."

"Then I suppose you will be indebted to me for a very long time."

It was an unnerving thought: being under obligation to a rogue, scarab-marked Mage who dabbled in Empire science. Andrew was not likely to make a legal claim against me, but I felt quite sure that he intended to make me pay. Between Andrew and my family, I was establishing an uncomfortable conflict of interest against my Mystic vows. "Extortion is an odd way of expressing your friendship for my brother."

"It is what you expect of me. Hence, you imagine that you understand me after all, and we are able to reach an agreement. Let me know when and where to collect your damaged friend."

"I assume that my brother knows how to contact you."

"He does, but I'd rather spare him from the unappreciated role of messenger. If you look for me, I'll find you."

"You do seem to have an aptitude for spying on me, Mage Andrew."

"Don't strike the hand that saves you."

I stared at the banks of lights, buttons, and switches that monitored and controlled the ship. I could not read the markings or instructions. They were written in Empire characters. I murmured to myself, "Perhaps he is the Sable Prince as well as the Blood Mage."

Andrew spun my chair away from the console, leaned over me, and whispered, "I am neither Prince nor Mage, Marita. I am the Shadow Cat." He smiled as enigmatically as the image that he claimed, defying me to question his source of information.

I did not accommodate him, because I did not want to know what spell or Empire trick he had used to watch us. Neither did I trouble to question why he, a Tangaroa Mage, knew the symbolisms of Avalon's cards so fluently. I had heard of other Mages—usually the most powerful Mages— who explored the lore of multiple Mage Schools, and Andrew had admitted to a voracious appetite for knowledge. I concentrated instead on assessing his interpretation.

Shadow signified Tangaroa, air, magic, and changeability. The cat represented mystery, uncertainty, and beauty. I had to admit that all of the descriptions fit him. My crescents also shivered with the satisfaction of a true reading, a reaction that none of our Avalon speculations had inspired. The idea of a Tangaroa Mage making better use of our cards than Avalon stung my pride, and I challenged him, "Interpret the rest of the reading, if you know so much about it."

He crouched beside the chair. "The Ice Dreamer is your brother. Your Uncle Toby is the Brass Dom. The Blood Mage is Scribe Talitha."

"And the Sable Prince?" I asked, pondering Talitha as a key player instead of a subordinate. Andrew could be lying again, but he spun an interesting yarn, and my crescents whispered that I should believe him. Just when I had abandoned hope of learning anything more from him, he tantalized me with new ideas.

"The Sable Prince is the source of the attacks against you," said Andrew, "including the indirect attack that precluded you from interpreting the Mage cards accurately for yourself."

To compromise a card reading without the advantage of physical proximity was difficult and unethical but not unprecedented. "Mastermage Lar?"

"He contributes one element of the attacking force, but he is a puppet ruler, inconsequential except as a relay and a recruiter of new elements."

"The Sable Prince is a composite?"

"There is a dominant element."

"He's your employer."

Andrew's smile could have signified confirmation—or amusement at an outlandish guess. His answer proved equally unenlightening, "I work for many people."

"How many of them are Empire Princes?"

"The remaining Nikkei and Hangseng are rare. Those who survived the war were hunted, along with anyone suspected of Empire allegiance."

"But they do exist?"

"A few families hid successfully and still maintain the old traditions. For obvious reasons, the descendants of the Empire rulers seldom advertise their origins to members of their former subject races."

"But they acknowledge themselves to a privateer?"

"I respect them and their skills. They reciprocate. Are you sure you won't let me help you? Consider how much information you could coax from me if we spent days together instead of moments. I think we could both benefit from the experience. At the least, we might enjoy it."

He was cunning, baiting me with the knowledge that I needed, teasing me with snippets of truth. He certainly did not hurt his case by including pleasure as an inducement. But I had my own price to extract: "Name my enemy."

"Marita of Avalon," he said.

If he had given me a forthright answer, I might have reconsidered his offer, even on his arrogant terms. "The enjoyable aspects almost persuaded me, Mage Andrew."

"They are the reason I gave you a second chance to reject me."

"Don't take the rejection personally."

"I don't." He rose to his feet, and this time I accompanied him to the door. Kurt and Rodolfo both seemed to relax at my return.

Kurt asked dryly, "Did you decide our fates?"

"We're going home," I answered. "I've arranged for Lilith's protection. The rest of us are on our own."

"You made the choice, Mage Marita," retorted Andrew. "Your prices are too high."

"I shall see that you return safely to your brother's home," said Andrew, as Cris steadied the lading basket for me. "After that, you will indeed be on your own. Remember my advice."

"I shall remember every word." The basket dropped away from the deck.

Talitha

4 Fepuara, 510

Mastermage Ch'ango, via Scribe Gavilan, Tathagata:

How dare you usurp control, Ch'ango! We had an agreement, approved by the privy council of the World Parliament: No blood magic, no magic at all without concurrence of the full leadership of the Protectorate. The death of the Avalon Mage's servant is inexcusable. Lar's unhappy confession of it only heightens my shame. Our patrols could have tracked the mixie eventually, and I would have told Marita a thousand lies rather than let you subject her to your blood spell. I have pleaded with Lar to abandon the remainder of your appalling plan. No one yearns to see Aroha destroyed more than I, but I will not condone the murder of innocents.

We shall both know the outcome of your unconscionable scheme by the time you read this letter. If Lar fails to halt the process that he described to me, I shall make every vile detail known to the other Protectors. Lar and Toby may obey you blindly now, but I shall disable them with doubt. I *can* cripple you, because you cannot wield your distant magic without another Mage's help, and your remote spells cannot greatly exceed the capacity of your servant. Lar is not Aroha, either in power or in corruption.

I know what Pachacamac learned: I know why you dare not show yourself to any responsible Mystic. I know what Shamba taught me: A Mage mark is more than a sign of status. An unfinished Mage mark steals Mystic power as surely as a completed set creates it, and you are caught halfway. You trusted Aroha to finish the job for you, but *he* would not create a power greater than himself.

I care nothing for your self-proclaimed status as Mastermage of Mastermages. The Protectorate *can* succeed without you. You are not above the law, and I will not continue to respect the secrecy of your involvement. Press me further, and I shall shout your guilt from Rit to Tathagata.

Scribe Talitha, Rit

Marita

Cris deposited us in the basement where we had first entered the skiff. The mixie boy did not wait to see us climb the stairway. He and his wriggling puppy took their skiff and disappeared back into the shadow-wrapped tunnel. Kurt scattered Mage light to aid the sconces.

"So much for Andrew's protection," said Rodolfo, watching the boy's retreat. Rodolfo's color had begun to return to normal.

"Andrew promised to see us safely to my brother's home," I replied. "We're not quite there yet."

"You think he's still with us?" asked Kurt. He whispered a spell of magic detection, but it went unanswered.

"I don't know his method, but Andrew is watching us." Whether by magic or Empire trickery, Andrew would keep his promise. I might not understand his lawless philosophy, but I fancied that I had begun to know when he was telling me the truth. I did not credit him with many honest moments.

"Suppose we don't go to your brother's apartment at all," suggested Kurt. "You think your privateer will maintain his guarantee of our safety?"

"I think his guarantee was also a recommendation. If we decline to accept his advice, he will consider his obligation to us ended."

Rodolfo put his arm around me and murmured, "Marita, dear, I think you're reading too much into this privateer's words. I can appreciate why he fascinates you, but I wouldn't trust him. It's the same mistake you made with Lar."

I snapped at Rodolfo, "Are you taking rudeness lessons from Janine?"

Kurt sighed loudly. "I don't like damp basements. I don't

like standing in them, sitting in them, or arguing in them. I want to go home, Mom. Please, can we go home now?"

"Shall I punch him in the nose?" asked Rodolfo.

"I think I'll punch both of you," I answered, but my flare of anger was gone. As we climbed out of the basement, I kissed Kurt on the cheek. He grinned at me. I would have felt nearly cheerful, if Rodolfo had not observed that the trail we had left for Janine had been eradicated.

Benedict was sitting on the tide-wall, undisturbed by the foul smells of rottenness. This morning's trial had not marked him visibly. "I never tire of watching the ocean," he told me. He gave me a crooked smile. "I am sorry I was angry with you earlier." I could feel the sincerity of his regret; arguments had always upset my brother. "I disagree with what you tried to do, but I know that you meant to help. I hope you now realize that I truly am protected."

After all my worrying about him, finding Benedict so calm and relatively carefree made *me* feel tired. He craved reconciliation and understanding, but I would not pacify him with pretense. "You remember Kurt and Rodolfo?" I asked brusquely. Benedict had met them after our parents' memorial service. I doubted that he would remember, since he paid little attention to my friends, but he nodded.

My coolness hurt him, and he retaliated by embarrassing me. "You have gained very little wisdom, Kurt," declared my brother solemnly, "despite your inherent sensitivity and kindness. You let physical appetites impede your journey. You could progress so easily if you learned self-restraint." Benedict shook his head, as if deeply embedded in mournful thoughts. "I regret that you, Rodolfo, have strayed even further from the ways of the Holy Word than when last we met. You are far too consumed by your vanity. It makes you shallow. You must repent, or you will lose everything that you value."

Rodolfo's fair skin became flushed. Even amiable Kurt struggled to hold his temper. I scolded my brother, "Your rudeness is inexcusable, Ben."

He raised his face to me and squinted. He wore a puzzled expression, which seemed somehow unconvincing, as if he *knew* his offense but chose to pretend innocence. "You should not feel insulted by the truth, Marita. We are all flawed and sometimes need a detached perspective to enlighten us. Insincerity does not help anyone."

At such moments, I wondered why I cared about my brother's troubles at all. Consciously or unconsciously, Benedict had molded himself into someone uncivilized, socially oblivious, and devoid of common sense. Judging from behavioral evidence, he had not matured with age; he had regressed. I asked him, "Are you this offensive with your criminal friend, Andrew?"

"I am honest with Andrew, as with everyone. I am sorry that you and he have been unable to reach an understanding."

"Why should I understand him, when I cannot even understand you?"

"Andrew's manners are better than mine," answered Benedict with equanimity, "and he generally knows what people want to hear. I had hoped he would take the trouble to persuade you to remain in his care. You do not know the magnitude of the danger you face." Before I could demand elaboration, Benedict shifted into incongruous social propriety, "Would you and your friends join me for tea?"

"We'd be charmed," replied Kurt dryly.

The three of us followed Benedict to his apartment. Crossing the threshold, I heard a whisper, "Stay no longer than an hour, Mage Marita, or your enemy will find you again, and I shall not be there to help." No one else seemed to hear the quiet words, which had come to me in Andrew's unmistakable voice.

"We can't stay long," I said.

Benedict only hummed an ancient praise-song, as he filled a blue porcelain pot with steaming water and fragrant herbs. Kurt and Rodolfo inspected the apartment with unabashed suspicion and a liberal use of magic. Each Mage touched the cupboard, and I almost expected them to push it away from the hidden stair. They continued to prowl even after Benedict poured weak tea for them. Only Benedict and I sat at the table.

I demanded, "Ben, who were the men at the beach this morning?"

"Confused, misguided souls. Violence is always terrible, but violence without emotion or thought is bestial."

"Who were they, Ben?"

"I don't know," replied Benedict, almost gruffly. For one moment, I suspected him of lying, but I reminded myself that this was my brother, honest to the point of irrationality.

"You should have asked Andrew. He's quite knowledgeable about such worldly matters. Indeed, he has almost a fanatical hunger for such knowledge. It is his greatest weakness."

"Andrew refused to answer me."

"Did he?" Benedict sipped his tea thoughtfully. "He must have had a good reason. The danger may be more imminent than I expected."

I explained with care, as if to a child, "That is why I want you to leave Rit, Ben."

Porcelain clattered and tea sloshed on the table, as Benedict impatiently replaced the cup in its saucer. "And I must repeat: This is where I am meant to be at present. Stop worrying about *me*, Marita. I know you mean well, but you are only creating trouble for us both."

As Benedict criticized me, Kurt tapped his cup of tea in an odd cadence. Rodolfo echoed the tapping briefly. Neither Mage had the Mystic strength to signal me more clearly without Janine's help, but I understood the odd maneuvers of my Mage brothers. Kurt and Rodolfo had readied themselves with force of strength and force of magic. They would take Benedict at my command. My mind whispered acknowledgment, accepting their improvised plan and their aid without weighing its wisdom. I was far too relieved that someone had lifted the burden of decision-making from me.

Rodolfo blocked the door and built a warding spell, as Kurt cast a paralyzing powder over my brother. Benedict's movements became sluggish, and he pushed himself away from the table with agonizing slowness. His eyes reproached me.

"Where do we take him?" asked Kurt.

"Away from here," I answered, cautioning him to silence with a Mage word. Our chances of escape were slim enough without advertising which of the dozen ports would be our point of departure. I thought that the Westwind Port might serve best, because private autoboats could be leased there by a fully automated exchange. If Westwind proved too difficult to reach, I would reevaluate.

Kurt's powder had lost its glow, meaning that we could now touch Benedict without being affected by the spell of paralysis. "The spell is temporary, Ben," I assured him. I felt horribly guilty, though I had attempted a very similar form of coercion against my stubborn brother. My Mage brothers had only completed the job that I had begun.

Kurt and Rodolfo carried Benedict, each Mage supporting one arm. I opened the door into the hallway. The cat, Iron, streaked past me into Benedict's apartment. I knew she had other means of egress, but I left the door ajar for her. I kept waiting for Andrew to make a move to thwart us, but he seemed to have abandoned my brother as well as me.

"We need a cart," said Rodolfo, when we had walked only a few steps away from the apartment house.

"A boat would be better," I countered. I hoisted myself onto the tide-wall and continued to walk along its top. The plastone was cracked in spots, and it was slippery, but I moved carefully and watched the sand. "There is bound to be some sort of boat tied along here. We don't need anything sophisticated."

"Haven't you had enough boat trips for one day?" asked Rodolfo.

He did not expect an answer, and I gave none. After a few minutes, I found my boat. It was a sorry thing that was little more than a raft, but it sufficed for my purpose. I slipped down to the sand and pried years' worth of dry seaweed from the plastiwood hull. I dragged the boat to the shallow water of the bay to test for leaks. Wet sand wedged itself into my sandals and dragged at my feet. I flung my sandals into the boat's storage box, as soon as I had assured myself that the craft was sound. The Empires made their products to last.

The boat's engine, however, had been cannibalized and did not function. I unfolded the oars, as Kurt positioned Benedict in the bow. Rodolfo had returned to the land side of the tide-wall as soon as Benedict had been placed in the boat.

"I'll find Janine," announced Rodolfo, defying contradiction, "and we'll deliver Lilith to that privateer, if you're sure that's the wisest course."

I hesitated, because I was sure of nothing, and my Mage brothers had just altered my own vague plans considerably. I mouthed my earlier reasoning, less as an answer than as an offering for Rodolfo's use, "Andrew can keep her safe from other enemies. She might learn something helpful."

Rodolfo nodded, interpreting my words as agreement. "Contact me when you reach your destination," Rodolfo said, though none of us knew whether we would all meet again. It was a perfunctory farewell, but it suited Rodolfo's style.

The boat would not have held him. It was barely large enough for three. Kurt and I took turns with the oars until we were far enough from shore to catch the Rit Stream's current. Once in the current, we could relax and let it carry us all the way to Westwind.

The ocean was clean where the Rit Stream swept it. I could see the brown tops of the kelp forest a little farther from shore, but beneath us swirled clear water, a hundred meters deep and as blue as a Hangseng banner. I trailed my hand in the water's coolness. The reflected sun felt hot against my arms and face. My skin had acquired a rosy flush.

"Where will you go?" asked Kurt, squinting against the dazzle of light.

"I don't know." It seemed absurd to worry about unwelcome listeners out here on the bay's swaying breast, but too much had occurred that I had not expected. I had a few ideas about possible destinations, cities that Benedict and I had visited with our parents. I wanted a city large enough to allow anonymity, small enough (or decayed enough) to be unsophisticated in its census techniques.

Kurt understood my non-answer and did not pursue the subject. Nodding at Benedict, he said, "He may not forgive you."

"Forgiveness is necessary to Benedict's creed," I replied, but I could not meet my brother's eyes.

After several minutes of silence, Kurt paused in his rowing and added, "I'll miss you, Marita." He resumed rowing immediately, as if to distance himself from his own regret.

I would have hugged him, but I did not trust the boat's stability that far. I squeezed his hand when we next exchanged the oars, and I said feelingly, "You're a good friend, Kurt." Rodolfo's terse leave-taking had been much easier, both for its brevity and for the lesser pain that it would cost me. I felt much closer to Kurt than to Rodolfo, and I would miss Kurt much more keenly. I rowed for a dozen strokes in silence. "I've never had many friends, Kurt."

He scratched absently at his bare arm, then winced because the skin had begun to sunburn. "Friendlessness is the price of belonging to the Family. It's hard for the rest of us not to let envy get in the way."

"Do you envy me?" I asked, startled and a little hurt.

"Gods, no!" Kurt started to grin at his own vehemence but abandoned the attempt. "But it is hard to forget what you could be, if you wanted."

"I'm a lesser Mage, no different from any other."

"Tell that to Lar—or to Andrew the Omniscient."

"Or to that poor man who died outside Janine's office?" I asked bitterly. "I don't even know what his sacrifice achieved."

"When a major blood spell achieves its purpose, I'd rather not see the results." Kurt nodded again at my brother. "Are you sure that is the best answer?"

How could Kurt imagine that I was sure of anything? "I'm tired. I feel defeated. Retreat is the cleanest answer." My arms ached. Though I had not rowed far, I handed the oars to Kurt. Even my head was beginning to hurt; all I needed was a dose of heatstroke to compound my other woes. "I hope the attacks against Avalon will stop when Benedict and I are gone, but if not, accept as much of Andrew's help as he will give. He has agreed to take care of Lilith. She has a way of generating sympathy that may persuade Andrew to help the rest of you. If you continue to have trouble, I'll try to return, once I've found a safe place for Benedict."

"I'm sorry I can't offer to go with you."

"You have obligations here." I had never tried to count Kurt's lovers. I did not want to know about that aspect of his life. I had always feared that I could become jealous and spoil our simple, precious camaraderie.

A plastiglass toll bubble rose from the water in front of us. It bobbed quietly until the current drove us against it and triggered its speech mechanism: "Record credit identity for Rit Stream usage fee."

Twisting his mobile face into comical disgust, Kurt pushed at the bubble with the oar. The bubble sank briefly, only to reappear a moment later. The toll units were obsolete and powerless to enforce their demands, but some of them were annoyingly persistent once they had locked onto a target.

The unit whined at us, "Illegal traffic will be reported to

Empire representatives. Unauthorized vehicles will be confiscated."

Kurt raised the oar in order to hit the toll unit more emphatically. My brother ordered sharply, "Don't touch it again!" Kurt ignored him.

I had no time for surprise at Benedict's recovery of speech. Kurt's blow fell. With a sharp popping sound, the bubble spit a fountain of bronze philter powder over us.

Sections of our little boat began to crumble around us, the structure riddled with pinholes wherever the powder touched it. I tried to think of a counterspell, but my head felt muddled with two much sun and too much fear. My view of Kurt was hazy, and I could not seem to focus on Benedict at all.

The boat foundered quickly, as the powder ate through the buoyancy pockets. Water chilled my hot skin. I pushed myself away from the wreckage and swam free of the downward draft, as the broken boat sank out of sight.

Coils of bright color drifted snakelike away from my philter purse, though most of my vials were sealed and would remain intact. I watched Kurt trying to tread in place, but he was not a strong enough swimmer to resist the Rit Stream. He shouted at me, but he had drifted too far and I could not hear him.

Benedict was nowhere to be seen. I began to search for him, panicked at the thought of my brother drowning in the grip of a paralyzing spell. I need not have worried about him. When I finally spotted my brother, he was swimming strongly toward the shore, his robe tied at his waist so as to free his legs.

I could have followed Benedict, but I would not have caught him before he reached the land. Unless he waited for me—and why would he wait, after what I had done to him?—he would escape me. I was not sure that Kurt could even swim free of the Rit Stream's powerful grip. There was no choice to make. I swam with the current, following Kurt.

Part of me felt glad that Benedict had regained his freedom. All of me wondered who had equipped an antiquated toll unit with an active Mage spell. I did not believe that the unit had located us by chance.

The bronze stain of the destructive philter drifted with me and did not dissipate. I avoided swallowing any of the salt-sweet, tainted water, but it stung my eyes. For a few meters, I tried to swim beneath the floating residue of the spell, but my clothing hampered me and deep currents began to pull me farther from shore. By the time I reached Kurt's side, the stinging philter had spread through my sinuses. Even that slight ingestion made me queasy.

Kurt was floating on his back, singing loudly about drunken sailors. I started to laugh at him, until I recognized the glazed expression on his face. He was euphoric from be-spelling. If he had gulped the tainted water, its poison would spread through him as quickly as it had through our van-quished craft.

"Come along, son," I told him, masking my dread with a wheedling smile. "It's time to swim to shore."

Kurt batted innocent blue eyes. He made a fist and used it to squirt water in my face. I reached toward him. He som-ersaulted, grabbed my feet, and tugged me underwater.

It was our old game from the baths, but I found no humor in it now. This water was deep. These currents were strong. And Kurt, my dearest friend, was a poison-riddled madman trying to drown us both.

I had always felt evenly matched with Kurt in the pools, but this was not a teasing frolic. Kurt crooked his arm around my neck, and I might have been chained with iron. He dove, pulling me with him into the cold, dim depths. My lungs ached for want of air.

We struck the bottom and scraped along the sand. I strug-gled, but I could not escape Kurt, and my lungs felt ready to burst. All the images of a Mage's worst fears writhed through me: dragons and demons and serpents and Mystic power turned deadly against itself. Avalon images inverted into bleakness: Blood of life became Blood of death; Brass energy became fiery destruction; Ice made water deadly; Shadow darkened the air; and Sable ravaged the earth.

I do not know when my hand found the stone. I do not know how I used it, but a demon's blood was in the water, and I had freed myself from the monster's grasp. I kicked against the sand to hurl myself to the surface. I gasped and choked. My head pounded, and for several seconds I was blind.

I swam toward the shore, hand over hand in a mechanical rhythm that was almost effortless and unconscious. I dragged myself through the stinking debris from a drainage channel. The beach before me was narrow and black with oil. The tide-wall loomed ten meters above me. I crawled from the water and sat on the fouled sand with my head bowed against my knees.

Evening had come to Rit. The silver crescents above my wrists glowed briefly in salutation. In their light, I saw the brown strands of Kurt's hair snagged by my philter purse. I became violently sick.

Talitha

Scribe Gavilan, Tathagata:

In the past hours, I have discovered how little I knew of the Protectorate's intentions in Rit, and I see the sham of our unity. You have read my letter to Ch'ango. Toby has enlightened me further, and I am ashamed that he divined more than I about Ch'ango's plans. His vision is narrow, but Lar confides in him. They have a common bond of weakness. They have both aided Ch'ango, but human sacrifice frightens them as much as the threat of Aroha. Now they vacillate with their own guilt, and they crawl back to me for guidance.

I do not want a leader's role. I have never yearned for personal power. The Protectorate should be more than the instrument of any one person's will, but if I do not lead it, Ch'ango will dominate our every act.

Ch'ango has abused our trust. She does not represent the Protectorate, but I stand alone when I condemn her methods openly. None of the others will risk offending her, because she is likeliest to succeed against Aroha and his prince. Thus, I must aid Ch'ango, even as I attempt to restrain her. We serve the same cause, and we hate the same man.

Perhaps it is the only way, as Ch'ango claims. Aroha was, after all, her protégé. She knows his weaknesses. She shares his arrogance.

I shall use what Ch'ango has given me. I shall not waste the innocent blood that we have spilled. But *I* shall direct any future sacrifices. I shall extract blood from the *guilty*.

So be it. This dark time will pass, and the Protectorate will proceed against the true enemy of our society, this self-styled Empire Prince whom Aroha abets. Then, I shall no longer suffer these doubts.

Make it known to the Protectors, Gavilan, what Ch'ango has caused to be done. They will know soon enough whether I achieve as much by lawful measures. Let them judge us both.

Scribe Talitha, Rit

Marita

For much of the night, I walked back and forth along the narrow strand that encircled Rit's main bay, wading through muck. My shoes were lost, and I can only imagine how bedraggled and begrimed I looked. Dimly, I felt Janine's search spell, but I did not respond to it. I did not try to block it either. I did not care.

When Janine's spell finally found me, I had wandered almost five kilometers beyond the bay. Another kilometer would have taken me back to the family home, where I had walked with Benedict that morning, but I had no interest in completing the journey. I was standing within the tidal bounds, letting the waves slowly bury me in coarse sand.

Janine asked me (in impolite terms) what I thought I was doing. She demanded that I return to the Mage Center immediately because she certainly had no intention of trekking into the wilderness to meet me. From Janine's perspective, "wilderness" meant anything with more than a square kilometer of unconstructed land.

Compliance was the easiest course. I knew this area well. Benedict and I had explored every path between the shore cliffs and the sere hills that ringed the town of Rit. By cutting inland, I would reach the Mage Center in time for the dawn greeting. It seemed a worthy enough goal.

I ducked beneath the next wave, letting it rinse the last of the bay's debris from my hair. The remnants of Mage spell may have left me with that ocean cleansing, because my numbness began to dissipate. My skin felt tight and raw. I resumed thinking, albeit sluggishly.

Aching truth, torn from my lips in a whispered confession, forced me to remember fear. I informed the sea grass, "I killed Kurt." A breeze bowed the blades disinterestedly.

The warnings, the spells that teased with mordant imagery, the attacks: To someone, Kurt's murder, like the murder of Janine's hireling, meant no more than another gesture of the same perverse cruelty. The warnings had escalated in severity, but they left me still untouched by physical injury. I wished I could believe that Kurt's death was no more real than the shattering of Uncle Toby's great table. I felt sick and numb and terrified, and my entire universe seemed to have shattered in that spell-thick ocean current.

I had tried to save my brother. I had instead destroyed my friend. Andrew had accused me of being the enemy whom I feared. If *he* was that enemy, he had chosen a brutal way to make his point seem prophetic.

I reached for my sodden philter purse, as if a potion might restore my world to what I wanted it to be. I sliced my finger on the smashed remnants of an emptied vial. I watched my blood bemusedly, then cried aloud a spell to steal the magic from my own life fluid. I could conjure no clearer words than, "Help me," and I formed my spell by Mystic instinct rather than any trained intent. I had never practiced blood magic, even in its most minor forms.

Though the spell was meagerly endowed, the signal heat of blood magic scorched my nerves. Numbness spread from my crescents. The emotional perceptions that crescents generally enhanced became the receptors of my spell of denial. I did not usually endorse the deliberate abandonment of conscious functions, because the practice suggested the cultivated mindlessness of an E-unit addict, but I reacted instinctively to a grief that I could not face.

I moved. I reasoned. I did not feel, except for a remote awareness of my bodily aches. I had successfully bespelled myself beyond pain of mind or heart.

The minor spell would not last, but it might sustain me until I could reinforce it with a philter. My first order of business on reaching the Mage Center would be to replenish crucial philter supplies. This was not a time to be ill-equipped.

My leg muscles throbbed by the time I climbed the last hill to the Center. I had beaten the dawn, but the race was closer than I had hoped. I squandered one of my remaining philters in order to enter undetected, even by Janine.

As soon as I had completed my raid on the supply room, I visited the baths and sloughed sand, grit, and oily refuse from abraded skin. I did not welcome the privilege of having the pools to myself. I would gladly have exchanged my peace and privacy for Kurt's boisterous companionship.

I spent the remaining hour of night in my room with mortar and pestle, blending philters and sealing them into ampoules and vials. The Mage Center's supply room could not provide the more unusual ingredients, since Feti'a refused to distribute the expensive items without prepayment. To avoid Feti'a's questions, I would have to augment my purchases elsewhere, though I kept a few choice blends hidden in my office.

When my blood spell began to fade, I ingested a tranquilizing draught that I had frequently prescribed for distraught clients. With my second-best purse filled and secured at my waist, I felt as well equipped as I could expect under the circumstances. Not even my full panoply of spells and philters had sufficed to save Kurt.

I reached the pentacle before the sun could banish the gray of night. Only one Lung-Wang and a pair of Tangaroa Mages had preceded me, but each of us maintained a silent vigil as we awaited the dawn greeting. Without the sun to color us, our robes appeared indistinguishable.

When Janine joined me, she stared at my purse thoughtfully. Her curiosity beat upon my Mage marks, but neither of us broke custom by speaking in voice or mind before the dawn greeting. Rodolfo arrived barely before the ceremony began. Only the three of us stood for Avalon. I wondered about Lilith, as Janine and Rodolfo presumably wondered about Kurt. As the sun cast its first rays above the horizon, our three, frayed emerald robes seemed to become lost amid an aqua and citron sea.

Lar arrived with his customary dramatic flair, showering violet-colored fire and plumes of a sugary scented smoke. The spectacle struck me as shabby and affected, though it was one of Lar's more elaborate performances. I awaited the finale with impatience, unable to delude myself into a reverential attitude. Despite spells and tranquilizing philters, my entire body ached; my eyes burned with tears that hurt too much to shed.

"I did not expect to see you today," whispered Rodolfo, as soon as Lar's staff descended resoundingly to complete the dawn ritual. Rodolfo's pretty face wore a pucker of concern. "Where is Kurt?"

"I don't know," I answered with literal truthfulness. I

could not talk about Kurt. I could not think about him. "Where is Lilith? Did you take her?" I would not name Andrew.

"No," replied Janine, regarding me oddly. "Lilith refused. She's understandably frightened of your privateer. She spent the night at her office, I think." By common consent, the three of us moved away from the crowds of other Mages. Our fellow Mages of Rit had evidently accustomed themselves to Lar's presence, because the formal order of procession was sporadic this morning. "I tried to persuade Lilith to stay with a friend of mine, but she insisted that she would feel safer in familiar surroundings. I can't pinpoint her injuries, and she's too nervous to be an easy patient, but she seemed to have recovered some strength when I left her. At least, she had enough sense to stay away from *here* for the moment."

Rodolfo persisted with the painful questions, "Did you leave your brother in Kurt's care?"

"No," I replied brusquely. "Benedict escaped me."

"Is that why you stood alone on a desolate beach, screaming for help?" demanded Janine. She had applied rice powder liberally, but her eyes still had the bruised look of fatigue. I had not thought to examine my own reflection for evidence of the guilt and horror that churned inside me. I added cosmetic repair to my list of morning goals.

"I did not scream," I argued. The minor issue seemed important at the time.

"You did," she insisted. "You had me thinking something had gone seriously wrong." She paused, but I offered her no excuse or confirmation. "If you ever mislead me like that again, 'Rita, I'll rip those crescents from your arms to keep you from bombarding me with your mind spells."

I rubbed the silver crescents. Shared feelings were listed as a gift of the crescent marks, but I had never known such spells to occur spontaneously. The crescent spells generally required a great deal of effort, considerable planning, and large doses of entrancement oil. A ten-lotus Mage could not bombard anyone. I might well have screamed all night; I did not remember; but I would not believe that my lesser Mystic skills could have transmitted my desperation. "I don't know what you sensed, Janine, but I could not have initiated it."

A young Tangaroa Mage pressed close to us. We smiled at him politely and discussed the cracked expanse of tile on which we stood. When the Tangaroa Mage disappeared into the commons, Rodolfo asked me, "What do you plan to do now?"

I shook my head, struggling to formulate a clear response. "Visit my uncle. Try to persuade Lilith to go to Andrew and hope that she can learn something useful about him. Talk to Lar."

"That's a full list," said Rodolfo.

"But it's a little short on specifics," added Janine.

"What would you suggest?" I retorted.

Janine shrugged. "Breakfast. If we dawdle any longer, someone will become curious."

Janine's grimly set expression was curious enough for me. I sensed distinctly that she wanted to tell me something but had decided to hold her tongue—and not because of temper's bite or possible eavesdroppers. Quandaries of judgment assaulted me regularly, but Janine's straightforward nature seldom allowed for hesitation.

Rodolfo headed for the commons. Janine and I matched stares, each waiting for the other to speak first. Neither of us relented. With a sigh of disgust, Janine turned and left me.

I was light-headed from hunger, as well as from fatigue, self-inflicted spells, and abysmal depression, but Janine and I had built a wall with our silence. Dismantling that barrier would require energy and understanding. I had a shortage of both at the moment.

Instead of following Rodolfo and Janine to the commons, I locked myself in my room. I constructed my protective pentacle, though I had little faith in its efficacy. I draped my emerald robe across a chair and slid between the bed sheets. I closed my eyes in exhaustion.

I did not sleep. My mind spun with images of Andrew's gold and Lilith's Mage cards. My senses swayed with the ocean's rhythm, and I tasted salt. I imagined Lar: viciously sacrificing sad, old Spider and the gray cat, Iron; turning his ceremonial knife against Kurt; drawing power from their thick, crimson blood.

After an hour, I accepted the inevitability of insomnia. I dressed in a silky white blouse and skirt, and I topped the neutral colors with the emerald tunic that had been my first Avalon garment. The tightly woven blouse was kinder to my sunburned skin than any other clothing I owned. The tunic partially hid my philter purse, which might make my second-best accoutrement less obvious. I added a neutral cape for public correctness, because I intended to go first to my office, next to the Stone Palace.

I had nearly readied myself to leave, when I heard the click of my door's latch. I could not sense my visitor's identity, but I could make a confident guess based on that lack. A Mage with stronger magic than mine was coming to me surreptitiously. I braced myself for confrontation.

Like a thief stealing into a victim's home, Lar slipped into my tiny room. He wore a hooded citron robe that draped across his face, an adequate disguise amid the morning throngs. He leaned against my door, guarding it. He stood only centimeters away from me, because the cramped floor space allowed me no retreat. He threw back the hood with a dramatic grace and accused me earnestly, "You reduce me to a beggar, Marita."

"That was never my intention." The years since our closeness had made him, if anything, more handsome, but the only quickening I felt now was of a cautionary nature. My tranquilizing oil seemed to have sharpened my Mystic awareness, even as it dulled my emotions. I *saw* my suspicion of Lar, as if it formed a tangible barrier of smoky gauze between us.

"I waited for you last night." He swallowed heavily, and I wondered what caused his nervousness.

"I'm sorry, Lar. I did not realize that we had an appointment."

His deep eyes narrowed at my sarcasm. "Let me help you, Marita. Let us help each other."

"I'd like that." It would have been true, if I had trusted him.

"You're safe now."

"Am I?"

Lar answered slowly, "I've ensured that you won't be attacked again."

"That was clever of you." I sounded too cynical. Lar had cared for me once, after his own fickle fashion. He would not have humbled himself to come to my room unless he valued me in some respect. I tried for a more appreciative tone and succeeded only in sounding pathetic. "Who attacked me, Lar?" I asked, pleading despite myself. *Who attacked Kurt?* I thought, but could not voice. "I have never made enemies. I am a simple seller of innocuous potions."

"Toby should never have involved you," said Lar gruffly, and his regret felt real to my crescents. "There is so much that you do not know, Marita." He passed his gaudily beringed hand across his eyes. I did not doubt that it was a practiced gesture, but he *was* troubled. I knew him well enough to recognize an echo of my own uncertainty, and my Mage marks affirmed my reasoning.

I laid my hand on his chest, needing to share his hurt as a substitute for my own deliberate void. "Lar, tell me, please."

For a brief moment, we were both younger, closer, and more honest. "I don't want to talk, 'Rita. I want to be near you."

"You used to confide in me, Lar. You know that I can guard your secrets." He touched me, but he stopped as soon I shook my head. My suspicions revived accordingly, but I listened with no less attentiveness when he began to speak.

"I am not a cruel man, 'Rita. I derive no pleasure from the spilling of blood." He added with alarming earnestness, "But there is so much at stake."

"Does any cause merit human sacrifice?" I demanded with the raggedness of the intolerable pain that existed in me, though I had disconnected that pain from any conscious emotion.

Lar seemed to understand me, which was frightening. "A crime against society outweighs any offense against an individual. It is a war that we fight."

"A war?" I echoed helplessly.

"Sometimes in war, mistakes are made. Bystanders are hurt."

I snapped at his contemptible excuse, "I have been more than a bystander, Lar. I have been a focus of direct attack." My body refused to know that I had severed it from emotion. My voice cracked, as I wept, "Kurt is dead because of an attack against me."

"The extremists do not care whom their revolution hurts," responded Lar in cold disgust. My terse announcement of Kurt's death did not seem to startle the Mastermage. "Many of us within the World Parliament agree that change is necessary. Most of us—like your uncle and myself—favor sane, orderly reform. An impatient few want a radical, dangerous upheaval of our entire social structure."

"What revolution, Lar?" I twined my fingers in his citron

robe. I willed him to answer, praying that I could actually make my crescents serve me actively, as Janine had accused. "Help me to understand!"

Lar replied, "Our world is old. It suffers and withers with all the diseases of its age."

"I have seen the decay of Rit," I replied, impatient with his condescending slowness to give a meaningful answer.

My urgency seemed to displease him, but he continued, "Rit is only a lesser example of a growing crisis."

I prodded again, risking a runic persuasion spell that my fingers drew in the folds of his robe, "The World Parliament surely has addressed this issue."

By a twitch of his jaw, he showed his reaction to my spell. I expected him to denounce me for insubordination, but Lar conceded reluctantly, "For too long, inept members of the World Parliament refused to accept reality, and they kept the rest of us floundering helplessly." He was trying to justify himself, but he lacked conviction. "We have dawdled, allowing ruthless opportunists to flourish. They intend to change our world into their own private dominion."

I tried not to sound frantic, but I failed. "I still do not understand why Kurt is dead. Make me understand, Lar!"

"Because your uncle and I care about you," he muttered, unkindly sharing with Toby the guilt that he obviously felt, "our enemies made you a target. The cowards deceived us. We expected to assault them, but they turned our assault against you."

Lar's explanation contained just enough indignant conceit to sound credible. It made his side of the "war" sound like a group of fools, although Lar's pride appeared impervious to that humbling fact. I hesitated to believe him only because I knew Lar too well, and he had said too much too willingly for a Mastermage influenced by a mere ten-lotus spell. He might offer me harmless tidbits, but he would not tell me secrets of high politics—unless he thought he had something significant to gain.

"Has my brother been used similarly?" I asked. I would not waste my present opportunity, whatever Lar's motives might be. Every Mystic sense wailed inside me: Kurt was gone, and I had helped to kill him. I needed to identify a reason for his sacrifice—desperately.

Lar shaped his expressive mouth into regret, and he sighed, "I wish I did not need to tell you of your brother's part." Lar placed his hands on my shoulders. His caramel eyes held all the sincerity of a well-fed hound pleading for table scraps. "Benedict is one of the radicals. He has allied himself with our enemies."

I could believe my brother to be a pawn, a fool, or a madman, but I would *not* accept that he could become a deliberate enemy of humanity. I snapped at Lar, "Who are these enemies, and why are they in Rit?"

A frown flickered across Lar's face, and I realized that he was beginning to question his ability to win my confidence. Perhaps I was not alone in feeling helpless before an unknown antagonist. Sensing the unexpected weakness in him, my fingers traced a second rune to reinforce my spell of persuasion. Lar answered my second question, "Your uncle and I have been the strongest proponents of gradual reform. By bringing the war to Rit, our enemies force us to miss critical Parliament meetings, for it is our duty to tend our own people first. In our absence, seditious voices will speak against us, portraying these radicals as harmless eccentrics, deserving of legal tolerance. This is why it is so vital that we quickly restore the peace in Rit. We must return to the larger battle. You can help us, Marlia."

We had migrated from "helping me" to "helping each other." Now we had reached the point where I helped my Mastermage. The progression was inevitable with Lar. It cured me of any impulse to trust him. "How?" I asked, expecting lies and connivance.

"You have met some of your brother's friends."

I replied cautiously, "A few."

"You met a man named Andrew."

"Yes." I extracted my hand from Lar's clinging robe, using the moment to weave my fingers in another augmentation of my tentative spell. I formulated a careful response, "He was my brother's delegate at Uncle Toby's dinner. I told you about him yesterday. I believe he arranged my brother's release from the Malawi prison. Uncle Toby said that Andrew is a privateer." Andrew was inescapable even when he left me alone. "Is Andrew involved in your 'war'?"

With every word I spoke regarding Andrew, Lar's mouth twisted more definitively into loathing. "*Andrew* is the war."

I could not answer such hyperbole—typical of our Parliament's vociferous members—without irony. " 'War' seems a large definition for any one man to uphold."

"Several years before my election to Parliament," Lar informed me crisply, "an arrogant youth named Aroha became the Mastermage of an insignificant island called Purotu. He was the first House member to be converted to the extremist movement. He converted that feeble movement into a major threat to the entire Mystic/Affirmist social contract. He renamed himself 'Andrew.' "

Andrew of Purotu, Talitha had called him, mocking the name with an emphasis that I had not understood. Both she and Uncle Toby must surely have recognized even an *insignificant* Mastermage. "Who converted him?"

"The rebellious son of a wealthy family. The family has always been reclusive and correct in their attitudes, but the son claims Nikkei descent. He calls himself Prince Hiroshi." Lar paused, but I offered no reaction. "We believe that Hiroshi is the leader of the extremist movement, and we believe that Andrew can lead us to him. If you could talk to your brother or his friends, discover Hiroshi's whereabouts and purpose, and tell me what you learn, I would be deeply grateful to you." Lar's hands traveled to my wrists. "It is only Feti'a's jealousy that has kept you from advancing beyond ten lotus marks. You should wear scarab marks, Marita. You could earn them if you tried."

Lar's meaning was sufficiently clear: I could wear scarabs if I pleased my Mastermage. "Neither my brother nor my brother's friends are likely to confide in me."

"You are overly modest. You have skill enough to enchant the Mastermage of Rit."

Lar undoubtedly imagined that he was flattering me. Encouraging his conceit disgusted me, but I did not dare offend him. As long as he thought of me as the besotted girl who had once been willing to do anything for his approval, he would treat me as fairly as his nature allowed.

He would also expect to use me freely, beginning now. I yielded enough to make me feel degraded, but I had no intention of resuming our old relationship. When his lust had befuddled him, I managed to feed him a delusion potion that would leave him sated, if a little vague about details. The spell worked brilliantly, which confirmed my suspicions about the dubious worth of his scarab marks.

I wiped the remaining delusion potion from my skin and applied a fresh supply to vulnerable regions of my anatomy. I did not expect to be ravished twice in one day, but it did not hurt to be prepared. I left Lar snoring in my bed. I placed one of my business cards, an indefinite sketch of lovers, on the pillow beside him. I hoped he would interpret the card as an innocent, affectionate message that I had gone to meet a client.

I had not even considered keeping my morning appointments until I arrived at my office. Llewella, my stern disciplinarian, expressed her disapproval of my recent absences in very forceful terms. She had already deposited the first client in my office, and helping him was the fastest means of evicting him. As soon as he had departed, Llewella handed me another desperate supplicant. I did not manage to raid my own supplies until noon, when Llewella graciously allowed me a lunch break.

It was humiliating to be manipulated so easily by my own receptionist. How could I expect to contend with brutal blood magic, high politics, and Empire technologists, when I could not even say *no* to the plain, pudgy woman who organized the tokens on my calendar? I made sure that I completed all of my private office work before Llewella returned from her own lunch. I removed the colored pins from my afternoon schedule board and laid them in a dainty pile on Llewella's immaculate desk.

I ate a soggy cheese sandwich from a public supply unit, because I thought that eating would be wise. I felt neither better nor worse as a result of the meal. Nervous energy, fear, and shock were carrying me. Whenever I began to *feel* more than physical sensations, I ingested another Mystic draught. At odd intervals, tears tumbled from my eyes, but my self-bespelling denied the tears any meaning.

I kept expecting some form of attack or confrontation. Walking the relatively busy streets near my office, I glanced suspiciously at everyone I passed. Hurrying professionals, philter-dazed vagrants, or decorous ladies who sipped lemon water on the shady stoops of their own homes: All received equal attention from me. I did not try any spells of protection or detection, for such spells might awaken my crescents from numbness. I had already taken more than the recommended dosage of tranquilizing draught.

My Mystic skills keened in rebellion against the abuse that I inflicted on myself. They united inside me insidiously with an echo of Andrew's warnings against the use of magic. His bizarre injunction signified one more mystery that I had not yet begun to unravel. Lar's unlikely confidences, extracted by spells that ought not to have worked against him, only compounded my bewilderment.

The guard at the Stone Palace admitted me with a careless nod. I barged into the courtyard and stopped. The dolphin fountain was filled to its rim with clean, clear water. The dolphins splashed merrily, a cascading tune trickling from their endless romp. At the fountain's edge sat Nan.

Nan's Affirmist brown pantsuit had the detailed cut and stitching of an expensive antique, but it was Nan herself who looked ancient. She had become as thin as Benedict, and her coiled hair had turned from auburn to white. Her fingers were gnarled, and her chin sagged. She was older than Toby by a dozen years, but she seemed to have doubled her age since last I saw her. "I always loved this fountain," she murmured, her voice still as vibrant as I remembered. "I'm glad it's working properly again." She turned her bright, dark gaze on me quizzically. "Your friend came and fixed it for me this morning."

"My friend?"

"The young gentlemen who escorted you the other night, when Toby invited you for dinner."

"Andrew," I replied, too numb to feel surprised.

"Yes, that was his name. He is a very polite young man. I like him. I have always liked fixers. They work and create, even though their efforts deprive them of ordinary legal rights. They have their own society to sustain them, but they *are* outcasts."

"Andrew is somewhat more than a common fixer."

"Fixers have been uncommon in Rit for several years. Your friend is a distinct improvement over that self-important Mystic you used to see."

"Lar," I interpreted quietly.

"That one, yes. He visits Toby sometimes."

"Where is Uncle Toby?"

"Gone. He left yesterday, along with that rather terrifying woman who accompanies him everywhere." Nan smiled at me, crinkling her face into a lacework. "You know that I never sit in the courtyard when Toby is home. I watch, though, from my windows. That's how I recognized your friend when he arrived today."

"How long ago did Andrew leave?"

"No. I didn't say that, I'm quite sure. You misunderstood

me, my dear. You were a better listener as a child. Or perhaps that was your brother. I don't always remember things clearly these days." She tilted her head like one of her birds. "No, your friend is still here. He asked if he might wait for you. He's repairing Calli's cage. She gnawed through two of the wires, the naughty girl, and I'm afraid she'll hurt herself. She's just a bit of yellow fluff and feather, scarcely any substance at all. You remember Calli."

"She's your best singer, isn't she?"

"I'm glad you remember, my dear." Tears welled in Nan's eyes. She shook her head and turned back to the fountain. "You go along and visit with your friend now. Offer him some lemon water and vanilla cake. He is such a polite, helpful young man. I don't know why people are so distrustful of fixers."

I nodded, for there seemed to be no point in trying to shatter Nan's illusions about Andrew. "Thank you, Aunt Nan."

I climbed the iron courtyard stairs to Nan's suite, thinking that the rusted metal had more need of repair than Calli's cage. I entered Nan's suite diffidently, not sure what might greet me, but the rooms had not aged as visibly as Nan had. The brown sofa and chairs were clean and orderly beneath their woven beige throws. A few sturdy orchids danced like variegated butterflies on the low table and on plastone blocks in the room's dappled corners. I proceeded through the tightly shuttered doors into the hall that led to the greenhouse, where Nan's birds lived among the majority of the orchids.

Opening the plastiglass door at the end of the hall was like stepping into Rit's prewar past. A diligent ancestress had gathered most of the surviving species of birds and flowers, and here Nan cherished and sustained the legacy. The greenhouse air had the rich, wet aroma that had fascinated me as a child. The birds chattered endlessly, their melodies a vital part of the texture of Nan's domain. Everywhere there was color, for it was color that Nan cultivated first in her floral specimens. She valued the form of the flowers, but she tolerated no pallid children among them, no unadorned whites or browns or creams.

Bars of light crossed me as I moved through the greenhouse. A lattice of tarnished copper supported the plastiglass ceiling, casting the intermittent shadows. Orchids and odd, trailing vines potted in yellow moss hung from chains that had been hooked into the latticework. Plasteel shelves and benches, all covered with pots, formed walls and narrow aisles in what was actually a single room. In the center, beneath the hexagonal dome, a great cage held dozens of tiny birds, brown and black and white, fluttering among the leaves and branches of an artificial, saffron-blossomed tree. Smaller, individual cages held the colorful birds, Nan's protected pets.

Andrew was seated at Nan's littered workbench, hunched over the damaged bird cage. The vest and bracelets were as golden as ever, but their color seemed muted by the greenhouse shadows and the pale contrast of his short-sleeved workshirt. As I watched him, he touched a thin metal wand to the broken silver wires, stretching and fusing the pieces into solid lines. He laid the wand across the lid of a stone jar. "The cage needs replating to do justice to Calli," he remarked without looking at me, "but I don't have the equipment here to complete the job."

A man who could concern himself over a canary's cage seemed perfectly harmless, although I knew better. "Uncle Toby would be horrified if he knew that Nan was encouraging you," I said.

The corners of Andrew's mouth twitched into a brief smile. "He'd be glad enough to enjoy the products of my labor, as long as he could remain ignorant of their origin. Such is the hypocrisy of our society."

He was proselytizing again, and I had neither my dear Kurt nor Rodolfo waiting nearby to support me. "Have you rebuilt any aquatic toll units lately?" I asked grimly.

"Not lately. Not ever, that I recall." He selected a tool from an assortment laid before him, and he applied it to the hinge of the bird cage door. "It seems a rather eccentric interest on your part."

"I take after my aunt. We have odd hobbies."

Andrew smiled openly. "She likes me better than you do." He glanced at me. "I hope you haven't doused yourself in delusion oil for my sake. I didn't plan to take such intimate liberties."

I retorted dryly, "A woman can't be too careful." I would have liked to ask how he had identified the clear, odorless oil, but I distrusted his brand of knowledge. Where Andrew was concerned, curiosity could spread too easily into the forbidden arts of the Empires. I had already learned too much from him.

Andrew intended that I learn more. "Delusion oil is not a very efficient defense," he informed me. "It reacts with half a dozen common substances to leave that characteristic ocher stain." I looked at my fingers. They were indeed tinted around the nails, although the coloring was so slight that I could barely discern it. "The oil is too obvious to an educated observer," continued Andrew, "which makes it equally easy to circumvent."

I grumbled, "I'm glad you're not my Mastermage." It was a heartfelt sentiment. Knowledge of Lar's weaknesses had always given me a sense of freedom, despite my solemn vows as Mage and Mystic. A Mastermage like Andrew could make such halfway fealty impossible.

Andrew laughed heartily. "You didn't use delusion oil against Lar? He's less astute than I realized."

"You know Lar?" I asked with care.

"I know him well enough to say he deserves the oil's end results but not the pleasurable preliminaries."

I moved a potted orchid and sat on its plastone stand. "Lar told me that you were once a member of the House of Mastermages."

"Using your Mystic arts to gain Mage Lar's confidence," clucked Andrew, "is a severe breach of oath. You *should* be glad that I'm not your Mastermage. I would never have tolerated such disloyal behavior from one of my Mages."

In view of Andrew's blatant lawlessness, I did not dignify his remark with a reply. "Lar said that you become a follower of a radical named Hiroshi."

Andrew did not hesitate to respond, "I proposed that the Parliament should listen to what Prince Hiroshi wished to say before condemning him. For my heretical suggestion, I was banished from the House of Mastermages with several unofficial death threats on my head. The experience persuaded me to question our government's wisdom in other areas as well." He shrugged. "I have adapted accordingly."

"You now use magic and Empire science indiscriminately."

"Untrue. I am very discriminating in my tools, my methods, and my applications."

"I dispute your ethics, but you have successfully impressed

me with your skills. I don't know of anyone but you who could have adapted a toll unit to deliver a Mage spell."

With care, Andrew stored his tools in the pockets of a canvas case, rolled the case tightly, and tied it. He turned toward me, but he bowed his head, so I could see little of his face. "What sort of spell was used?" he asked softly.

"A spell that resulted in the death of a good friend," I answered, sternly denying myself the salve of tears.

"One of your fellow Avalon Mages?"

My throat had tightened. My crescents tingled with a hint of returning sensation. I would have swallowed another spell draught immediately, though repeated use was decreasing the potion's efficacy, but I would not allow Andrew to see my weakness. I could barely answer, "Yes."

"I'm sorry, Marita."

I muttered bitterly, "In a war, a few mistakes are made."

"I was expressing sympathy for you, not making a confession. I did not create the spell that killed your friend. The rules of Empire science are not secrets known to me alone, and they can be imitated by Mage illusion as well as employed directly. I would prefer that Empire science were not a secret at all, precisely because of such abuses as you have just recounted. The most benign knowledge, when possessed by only a few, can acquire the power to corrupt." He raised his gray-green eyes to look at me. "I cannot restore your friend, but I could teach you how to prevent a recurrence of such tragedy."

"I want no part of what you teach."

"I think you do, but you're afraid to admit it. Our society has conditioned you to value ignorance—with a few well rationalized exceptions."

He had a devil's talent for temptation. "You offered to protect Lilith," I said. "I assume that's why you're here."

"I don't think she wants to accept that offer from either of us. She is not quite as passive and helpless as you imagine."

"When did you meet her?" I demanded, suddenly unsure of the wisdom of my assignment to Lilith. She was no better equipped than I to deal with Andrew, and I had failed miserably. Having lost Kurt, was I also risking Lilith?

"Never. But I know her better than you, it seems."

"You promised to protect her," I repeated.

Again, he declined to confirm his pledge. "I'd still prefer to help you," he told me, "even at the sacrifice of my twenty pounds of gold." Some Mage sense tingled a warning in me that Andrew was sidling deliberately away from the subject of Lilith. "Do you have any idea how you tantalize me, Marita, professionally as well as personally? You are a literate Mage, indeed a rare combination of talents in this uninformed age. I could teach you so much, so easily."

"I'll take you to Lilith." The longer I spent in his company, the more enticing his ideas became. If I had not scorned his help yesterday, would Kurt still be alive? I could not know. I could not bear to wonder.

I could not simply hand the problem to Lilith, but I might feel braver in her presence. I hoped she really would accept the agreement that I had arranged for her. I hoped that I could locate her.

Andrew tucked his roll of tools into a pocket beneath his golden vest. He restored the bird cage to its customary hook. He opened a smaller cage, and Calli hopped obediently onto his finger. He murmured nonsense to her as he transferred her back to her home. She sang beautifully in reply.

Benedict

5 Fepuara, 510

Dear Hiroshi,

I hope that this letter reaches you. I will leave it in the wall crack, where my disciple, Tyna, should find it. I have taught her to take such letters to Andrew's autoboat at the old wharf.

I have grim news. The Protectors have taken Cris. His friend, Lillie, betrayed him to them. I have not seen Andrew this morning, but I sense that he already knows what has happened. He will be furious, and I dread what he may do.

They are coming for me now. I hear them on the stairs. The Intercessor defends us. Pray that my faith remains strong.

Benedict

Marita

Andrew stopped me just short of reentering the living room. An instant later, I heard Nan greeting her orchids by name. She did not seem to recall that she had guests, although it was difficult to tell with Nan. She might have been well aware of us.

Facing Andrew behind the concealment of the shutters, I wondered what he expected to learn from Aunt Nan. She had cultivated her vague, scatterbrained demeanor for many years, and few people recognized anything deeper about her. I had good reason to want to know my aunt's thoughts: I remembered her shrewdness, and I knew how much she observed from her windows. Spying on my own aunt did not seem very courteous, but I listened no less carefully than Andrew. He was a corrupting influence.

Nan sighed, "Don't be troubled, Odonto, but Toby has returned already, and that woman is with him. I know how she upsets you, but you must believe that she won't hurt us. We're not important to her."

I could hear Nan moving through the room. She hummed and fussed before resuming her odd monologue, "I wish Toby would not bring her here. She has such extraordinary ideas, and Toby simply cannot see it. They complement each other, as Toby and I never did, but Toby flatters himself that they share a common vision. Toby never has had that much imagination. The vision is all hers. Cattley, you need more light. I shall move you back to the greenhouse. Phaela is nearly ready for a turn in here."

Andrew motioned to me to stay. Apparently confident of my compliance, he opened one shuttered door and slipped into the living room. He moved with the easy stealth of experience. I heard Andrew ask, "What is Talitha's vision?"

Nan did not sound surprised by either his presence or his query. "The Protectorate," she answered.

"Does Dom Toby know what Talitha expects from the Protectorate?"

"He thinks he understands it," said Nan, "but her plans are much more powerful than Toby grasps. She is such a dominant, willful woman."

The conversation was not enlightening me, but Andrew seemed to know what Nan meant. He told Nan, "Talitha's true enemies realize the power of her vision. They are using her, as she imagines that she uses Toby."

"That is what the Inianga Mage said to her," observed Nan mildly. She clucked with concern, "Laelia, you have dropped a petal."

"Did Mage Shamba meet Talitha here?"

"They always met here, except when Toby was home. The Inianga Mage was a close friend of hers until that argument."

"I presume that none of the servants or guards ever mentioned these meetings to Dom Toby."

"Dear me, no," Nan said. "You do understand about the servants, don't you?"

"I think so. Yes."

"You wouldn't think it from watching them work, would you? All these dutiful, inconspicuous young men and women with their neutral colors and their inoffensive ways—they are all her supporters. They come and they go. They are the Protectorate's agents, and this is one of their bases."

"It is a lesser base, I think," commented Andrew. "I have seen no more than ten workers here at any given time, and the armory is small."

In the warm greenhouse, I shivered. Could Nan and Andrew be correct about armories and secret meetings with a senior Inianga Mage? By ignoring the Family politics, could I have blinded myself to so much? I could, of course; I had worked hard to sustain such ignorance. I had thought Aunt Nan shared my distaste for such matters, but now I wondered. Talitha's schemes seemed as plausible as the evident rapport between my reclusive aunt and a privateer.

As a child, I had always known our family's servants well, but I could not remember noticing an individual among the Stone Palace staff since my parents died. The faces seemed to change with every visit, but I had not stopped to considered the reasons for that curious fact. Neither had I focused much attention on Mage Shamba's abrupt withdrawal from Rit, and I would never have correlated the Mage Center dissension with my own family's machinations. I had thought too highly of Mage Shamba's ethics. Yet, the events fit together with a horrible consistency.

Nan said, "Toby has always been so fond of her, ever since he became a Dom. She is so unlike me. I was his wife, but I could never be a rival to a woman like her. When she sets a goal, she achieves it. She is frighteningly capable."

"The Protectorate will consume her," commented Andrew. His quiet prediction made me reach instinctively toward my philter purse for defense. I restrained my hand, reminding myself that his words held no power in themselves.

"The Protectors mean well," replied Nan, "but they will become tyrants like the rest. We don't mind, do we, Laelia, as long as they leave us in peace? Did Calli return to her cage without a fuss?"

Andrew answered, "Calli's manners were impeccable."

The canary's manners were better than mine. I pushed through the doors and nodded a greeting to my aunt. She chided me, "You should have served the lemon water to your young man."

Lemon water had not contributed to my sense of guilt, but I apologized automatically, "I'm sorry, Aunt Nan. I forgot about it."

Fussing with the placement of her orchid, Nan persisted, "Your young man will think you don't appreciate him."

Andrew grinned impudently, which made me decide to share my discomfort. There also seemed to be some advantages in being mistaken as Andrew's friend. I went to him and smoothed the collar of his shirt with mock affection. "Andrew already knows how I feel about him, and we haven't time for cake and lemon water now. Andrew has a promise to keep. I'm sorry we can't stay longer, Aunt Nan."

"I could meet you later, Marita," offered Andrew, as unperturbed as ever. "You might want to spend some more time here, since your uncle has just arrived."

I could not decide if he was making a recommendation or hoping for an easy excuse to disappear once more. I declined to accept either option. I wanted to see him confront Uncle Toby again—and Talitha. "I have obligations of my own to keep, Andrew."

Ignoring both of us, Nan collected one of her orchids and

carried it past us into the greenhouse. I was left feeling ridiculous and ashamed of my behavior. My crescents had begun to shift between hot and cold; my spell draught had not dissipated, but it faltered. Andrew snatched my hand from his collar and kissed my palm, which compounded my confusion of reviving emotions.

Whatever unusual mix of racial types had produced him, the effect from a close vantage point was particularly striking. The idea of exploring his strangeness held the sort of appeal that could become addictive. "Stop complicating matters," I complained.

"Why? You're not wearing delusion oil on your hands. You're too cautious of your own safety."

"That's not the point."

"A few grains from your purse could nullify the delusion oil entirely."

"You're just seeking a convert to your cause."

"Think of the pleasures of discovery."

"You've already introduced me to your cause, and I don't care for it." I did, however, enjoy his present method of persuasion more than I would have liked to admit. I might distrust everything he believed, but I discovered that I felt abundantly ready for a detailed introduction to Andrew on a personal level.

Being less ready, more rational or both, Andrew stopped what he had begun and murmured, "You've benumbed yourself into witlessness. You don't know what you want, do you?"

He successfully destroyed my momentary haze of blissful insanity. I might have known that Andrew would recognize the effects of a common Mystic potion, since he identified delusion oil so easily. I felt humiliated and sick with grief, but I answered glibly, "I've had a difficult week. What's your excuse?"

"You," he responded flippantly. He tilted my chin upward. "I'd rather not see you caught between Talitha and me. She is ready for me now, which was not the case when last I came here. She will do her best to prevent me from leaving."

"Talitha knows about you. Aunt Nan knows about Talitha. You know about everyone. Am I the only one who's ignorant?"

"You're caught in the fringes, my dear. I'd welcome you to my side, if I were sure that's where you'd choose to stay.

Otherwise, I'd advise you to maintain your present neutrality. A fringe position is uncomfortable, but it's far safer than most of the other options."

"You're completely unbiased, of course."

"I'm opinionated about virtually everything, but that's not a reason to disbelieve me."

I craved only ignorance and oblivion, but I *needed* to understand. "What is the Protectorate?"

"It is a union of some of the noblest and the most corrupt of the World Parliament's influential forces. The noblest consider themselves the necessary defenders of our present civilization. The corrupt have recognized an opportunity to make a new empire for themselves. The corrupt, being ruthless, will dominate."

"You're being opinionated again."

"It's a chronic flaw." He walked to the door, opened it, and paused on the balcony, watching the courtyard. When he began to descend the stairs, I followed, but I maintained a steady distance between us.

Talitha, draped in an orange and umber striped caftan, entered the courtyard, as Andrew reached the fountain. He waited, and she strode proudly to meet him. Her hair was braided into fine rows, sculpted against her finely shaped head and woven with a cascade of carnelian beads that hung down her back. She wore long earrings of gold filigree. Talitha and Andrew made an impressive, visibly powerful couple. Seeing them together, I felt very small, pallid, and insignificant. I wanted nothing more than to let one of them—either of them—take away all the troublesome decisions from my life.

Talitha said to me, "Your taste in friends is deteriorating, Marita. Bringing this criminal here once was bad enough, but I could forgive that first occasion on the basis of your ignorance. Bringing him here again is inexcusable."

I would not have bothered to argue against her point, but Andrew answered, "She did not bring me, Talitha. You know that I go nowhere except by my own choice."

"I know what was true of Mastermage Aroha," replied Talitha with a smirk, "but he was a proud man, respected even by his enemies. I see before me only a common privateer."

"And I see a woman who has too much honor for the part she has chosen," replied Andrew. "Can you continue to believe in your Protectorate when even Shamba leaves you? What is the worth of your vision, when the most visible Protectors are merely weak opportunists such as Toby and Lar? You are creating the nemesis that you believe me to represent, and you are making all of us vulnerable to the true enemy, whose ambitions you persistently deny."

Talitha's strong hand struck Andrew's face. "You have broken many women and men with your cunning lies," she snapped, "but you will not break the Protectorate. We are stronger than your deceptions."

Andrew barely flinched. "I am only a messenger," he said. "I did not create the truth that frightens you."

"You chose to become Prince Hiroshi's military strategist," replied Talitha contemptuously, "instead of fulfilling your responsibilities to your fellow humans. You sell the world to sate your greed." Her dark gaze did not leave him as she addressed me, "Marita, child, you should leave us. You have no idea of the evil of this man. He corrupts anyone who makes the mistake of trusting him."

From Benedict, I might have expected such a blanket judgment—and given it accordingly little attention. From Talitha, the forthright condemnation had a startling impact. I recited the legal doctrine, "Things and situations, not people, may be inherently evil. Between people, there are only differences of perspective."

"Do not preach to me, child," retorted Talitha. "You do not understand what you are defending."

I jumped when Uncle Toby spoke from behind me. "Be kind to her, Talitha. Marita has served the family well. From her limited awareness, she is quite right," said Toby. "Intolerance is the greatest crime."

Andrew demanded, "Is that why you have arrested Benedict?" I stared at him, but I was the only one surprised.

"You have heard already?" asked Toby. His face was glistening from exertion or from nervousness. "I commend your sources for their efficiency." Toby patted my arm. Revulsion, empowered by awakening despair, made me shrink from him. Toby shrugged. "I am sorry, Marita, but I had no choice. Benedict earned his punishment. We shall arrest all of Prince Hiroshi's local allies, now that they have led us to their organizer." Toby nodded to Andrew. "You have been a clever opponent, Mage Aroha, but you became too confident. You will not escape us this time."

Talitha scolded Toby, "Do not gloat, Dom Toby. This criminal is not even worth our scorn." Then she made the official declaration of arrest, "Andrew, legally known as Mage Aroha, you are guilty of using and spreading forbidden knowledge, employing Empire techniques for personal ambition, creating objects that jeopardize the human species and the world peace, inciting rebellion and aggression, privateering, tampering with social stability. . . ." She continued naming crimes. At every exit, a guard had appeared. I made a point of studying the guards instead of their brown uniforms and stunners: a tall young man with earnest black eyes, a thick-waisted woman with a pretty face, a man with a solid build and curly hair of ashen blond. All of them looked at Andrew with loathing.

Andrew did not stop smiling, until Toby pointed toward a high window opposite Nan's rooms. A dimly visible servant pressed an orange, misshapen face against the plastiglass. It was the face of the mixie boy, Cris. Released by the servant, the boy drooped as if he were drugged or bespelled.

"We do not want to hurt the boy," apologized Toby sanctimoniously, "but you must understand our position. You threaten all civilization. We must do whatever is necessary to protect the people of the world."

Andrew said quietly, "I understand Talitha's position, although I disagree with it. Your only position, Dom Toby, is cowardice, based on ignorance, fear, and greed." Andrew looked at Talitha and shook his head. "I expected better of you." A line of brown-robed figures, armed and indistinguishable from the troop that had accosted Benedict and me, filed into the courtyard. "I see that you have gathered your assets in preparation for me," remarked Andrew. "I am flattered that you consider me worthy of so much trouble."

Talitha gestured sharply toward the fountain. "Throw the tools, the bracelets, and the vest into the water," she ordered.

With a glance at the window where Cris had been displayed, Andrew began to strip the bracelets from his arms. His Mage marks looked white against his strong wrists. He dropped the golden bands, one by one, into the sparkling water. He murmured, "I'm sorry, Mage Marita, but I shall not be able to accede to your request after all." He removed the vest and let it sink to the bottom of the pool. He showed reluctance only in releasing the canvas roll of tools. He held the tools, weighing them and frowning.

Toby growled, "The boy will pay, if you continue to resist."

With a humorless laugh, Andrew threw the tools into the fountain. The tools jangled together as they fell, and the echo seemed to linger like distant chimes. The dolphins splashed obliviously. Talitha pointed toward the water. She commanded Andrew tersely, "Destroy them."

"You credit me with too much skill," answered Andrew. His voice had tightened, but his expression remained calm and mildly insolent. My crescents began to burn in reflection of a seething anger. Andrew's emotions had never registered before on my Mage senses, but I suspected that the anger came—at least in part—from him.

"When you made the water burn in the White Lotus Pool at the Tangaroa temple in Tathagata," said Talitha tensely, "you turned the sand to glass." She glanced at me, as if to assure herself that she had impressed me with the deadliness of Andrew's skills; she had succeeded. "Use the same method to melt your own foul devices."

"You have taken my tools," countered Andrew. "I am helpless."

"No," argued Toby. "Your son is helpless."

Andrew shook his head once more. "Cris is a friend. My son died two years ago. Mixies don't live long." Andrew looked toward one of the shadow-faced troop members. "Your stunner is whining, sir. Don't you know a safety alarm when you hear it?" Andrew turned back to Talitha. "If you want to see my tools destroyed spectacularly, throw that failing stunner into the fountain. The result should satisfy you."

At first, I had expected to see Andrew enact another of his impossibilities and disappear from our midst. The subtleties of this war eluded me. I did not know how to measure the strength of the weapons or the warriors. I could not see why Andrew, who had walked freely through so much, should succumb to Talitha and Toby without any evident struggle.

Yet, as I watched him, it began to seem inevitable to me that I should witness Andrew's defeat. He was a criminal, as he had freely admitted. My uncle was the Dom of Rit, and it was right that he should enforce justice. I could easily blame Kurt's death, Benedict's incarceration, and all of the turmoil of the last few dreadful days on Andrew. I could not rationalize my sympathy for Andrew, whom I had no reason to trust above Talitha and Uncle Toby. Andrew's reference to a mixie son only reaffirmed how little I knew about him.

When Talitha snatched the whining stunner and cast it into the fountain, blue lightning shot through the water. I recoiled and bumped into Uncle Toby. The water boiled. Gold vest and bracelets lost their form, fusing into lumps. The roll of tools exploded, creating a spout of water that shot five meters into the air and splattered us, as well as darkening a wide circle of the courtyard cobbles. The water-shrouded lightning struck two dolphins, melting them from the ring, and then the lightning died.

The remaining dolphins sank to the bottom of the pool. The water drained rapidly through new, wide cracks. The melody of the fountain died.

"Can't you see," murmured Andrew, "the pointlessness of such waste?"

Talitha gestured, and two soldiers emerged from the circle that now surrounded us. Andrew did not resist as they chained his wrists. Talitha said, "We shall not hurt the boy. We shall only correct him."

Andrew smiled mirthlessly. "Cris has little enough life to lose, but I'd prefer to let him live it as he wishes." Andrew whistled a strange, atonal sequence of notes.

At each of the three exits, the guards stumbled aside from their posts. A furred streak of gray appeared first, cut through the line of soldiers and raced across the courtyard. It leaped onto Talitha. The cat, Iron, raked her claws through Talitha's caftan, eliciting a startled cry from Talitha. Iron dropped to the ground and dashed back between the soldiers.

Milk snapped at the feet of the soldiers, who were reluctant to squander their weapons' limited energies on the animals. Sand was smeared with blood, but she broke free from the agitated guard who had tried to hold her by the tail. With a growl, the brindle hound hurled herself at Uncle Toby and locked her jaws around his arm. My uncle shouted at me, "Get this beast off of me, Marita."

I had my hand on the philter that would deter a dog's attack, but I hesitated to cast the powder. I looked at Andrew, still chained and held by the two determined guards. As if he had been waiting for my attention, Andrew clapped his wrists together.

White light burst from his scarab marks, and the chains clattered to the ground. The air flickered above the heads of his guards, and both men reeled drunkenly away from their captive. Five more soldiers who tried to approach Andrew met the spell with the same abrupt effect.

The powerful Mage spell spread and brightened into a rainbow aura. Cautious soldiers, who sought to avoid the shimmery spell-cloud, began to move leadenly. The spell seemed to shun the fountain, sparing those of us who stood beside it. I might have attempted a counterspell, if I could have identified any element of Andrew's rainbow cloud.

Within less than a minute, all of Talitha's grim supporters had succumbed. They had become a milling, glassy-eyed troop, abandoning their hoods and their discipline. They began to drift and stumble out the various doors that opened onto the courtyard.

Andrew reached into the fountain and withdrew his charred packet of tools. Talitha struck at his arm, but her blow seemed to slide off him. He retrieved one bracelet that had somehow remained intact. He held it warningly before Talitha's eyes, saying, "You should know better than to force my hand." Talitha retreated one pace and stopped still.

Toby was pleading with me to free him from Sand's relentless grip. Sand seemed determined to imprison him with her jaws rather than to injure him, although her fangs had certainly pierced my uncle's skin deeply. I opened my vial.

With terrible calm, Andrew cautioned me, "Please, Marita, don't mix your spells with mine. Sand, release." Sand dropped Toby's arm. Blood began to gush from the rents in Toby's beige shirt. Toby whimpered like a child, and I helped him tear and twist his sleeves into bandages. I had healing powders, but I did not try to use them in front of Andrew.

Watching Talitha closely, Andrew unfolded his battered tool case and extracted a slim wand, a little larger than the device he had used in mending Calli's bird cage. He pointed the tool at the window where Cris had been visible earlier, and the window shattered. Andrew ordered loudly, "Milk, get Cris."

The puppy trotted up Nan's stairway and leaped between balconies to reach the broken window. Milk stepped carefully through the plastiglass, although plastiglass shards are seldom sharp, and then hopped through the window's opening. Moments later, Cris appeared at the ground-level door with Milk at his heels. The boy wobbled slightly, but he wasted no time in crossing the courtyard. "I'm sorry, Andrew," pleaded the boy. His puckered face conveyed his shame and abject misery.

"Next time you want a Mage spell," answered Andrew with a sharp glance at me, "consult me first, even if it's 'only' a love philter."

To my bewilderment, Cris gave me a look of pure hatred. "She turned Lillie against us," he growled, nodding in my direction.

"Enough, Cris," snapped Andrew. "Hers were not the major spells at fault." Holding the bracelet before him like a warding talisman, Andrew circled Talitha and backed through the bespelled troop with Cris, Milk, and Sand at his side. Iron darted from under a bench and joined them. Andrew's odd allies disappeared through the main gate. Before following them, Andrew shouted a final, fierce taunt, "I was never as ambitious as Ch'ango claimed, Talitha. You have forced me to become what you feared." He turned and left, slamming the iron gates closed behind him.

Talitha came and stood over me, watching me try to ease Toby's injuries. "I have some healing salve inside," she said. She looked at her defeated army, her expression alternating between grief and disgust. She marched toward the main salon. Toby limped after her, as if injured in his leg as well as in his arm. I saw Nan retreat from her window.

Alone in the courtyard, I sat on the fountain's edge. The water was nearly gone now. Most of the gold had fused into an unmovable mass, but one band still formed a circle, although the floral pattern of the surface had been damaged. I collected the bracelet gingerly. I could see nothing unusual about it, nothing that could suggest Talitha's concern about its kindred. I slipped it over my arm under my sleeve, pushing the bracelet nearly to my shoulder. Thus uncertainly prepared, I pursued Talitha and Uncle Toby by pressing through the doors to the main salon.

A young man, one of Talitha's defeated guards, sat cradling his head and moaning. I paused beside him and touched his shoulder. He raised his black eyes to me, but he could not acknowledge me more directly. I forced an ampoule of headache powder into his mouth and ordered him to swallow it. Using my philter on the victim of Andrew's Mage spell might have been unwise, but I could not simply leave the youth in his misery.

I discovered and treated three more such victims before locating Talitha and Uncle Toby. Each victim, very young and very broken, made me angrier at Andrew, Talitha, Toby, and Lar—angrier at this war of theirs, wasteful and cruel like every war of our species' wretched history. Their war had killed Kurt. I had sympathized with Andrew when he seemed defeated. Now, I felt some understanding of why Talitha fought him so bitterly, though she damaged her own cause each time she battled him. The old, forbidden knowledge still inspired destruction, whether by those who sought it or by those who feared it.

In the room that had once been a hotel kitchen, Talitha was wrapping a bandage around Toby's arm. Blood and healing salve splattered the white marble table where she worked. Toby was hunched in a captain's chair that creaked from his weight. Both Toby and Talitha ignored me as I entered.

I offered timidly, "May I help?"

Toby roused himself. Sounding entirely like the Dom of Rit, he demanded, "I gave you a commission. Have you completed it?"

"I'm not sure," I replied, trying not to feel offended by my uncle's cold inquiry. The commission that he and Talitha had forced seemed unreal to me now, when so much had occurred to outweigh an Empire toy and the opening of an old vault. "I know more about Andrew of Purotu than I ever wanted to learn, but you seem to have known a great deal about him all along. I don't know where he obtains his merchandise, if that's what you expected me to discover. If you want to hold me responsible for whatever he stole from the Stone Palace, I can't stop you or make amends. I don't know what you want of me." I was almost in tears.

Talitha murmured, "We asked too much of you, child, without warning you of what you confronted. Having witnessed his destructiveness, you understand why we must stop him, even at a terrible cost to ourselves."

I nodded, steeling myself against a surge of wistfulness for that moment alone with Andrew, minutes ago. "You could have told me directly. I could have prepared myself." Perhaps I could have protected Kurt and Janine's hired man.

Toby sighed heavily. Talitha said, "We could not trust you without testing you, child. Your brother made the choice of betrayal. You might have done the same. As you have seen, our foe has too many advantages already."

Had I been tested? Had I made a choice? I could not think that clearly. "Andrew abused my brother's guilelessness. Benedict made no choice."

"You're wrong, Marita," grunted Toby. "I wish I could tell you otherwise." He winced with pain, as Talitha applied stinging salve to a lesser souvenir of Sand's attack. "Benedict is not an injured innocent. He has worked directly for Andrew for at least seven years. We have hard evidence."

"I don't believe it," I lied.

"Benedict has already confessed to many crimes in support of Andrew," said Talitha. She sounded exasperated, with my brother or with me. "If you condemn Andrew, you must condemn Benedict equally. You cannot continue to waver in the middle, Marita. You must choose either to support your world or to see it destroyed by Andrew and his kind. You have seen what we confront. There can be no compromise."

Talitha made everything seem so clear and absolute. Her confidence was comforting. I did not share her vision, but I could easily let it dominate me. At that moment, I was far too tired and nauseated by excess spells and potions to want to think for myself.

Uncle Toby supported me, "Marita knows what is correct. She will stand by her family." His warm smile seemed more genuine, tinged with pain.

"Are you loyal, child?" demanded Talitha.

"I suppose I must be." My answer was weak, but it seemed to satisfy Talitha and Toby.

"Then go and see to the servants' injuries," ordered Talitha. "I shall talk to them later."

Marita

Nearly three months have passed since Benedict's arrest. During most of that time, I have felt too weary to think for myself. It is so much easier to let Talitha take charge. If I had turned to her sooner, Kurt might not have died. That, at least, is the needle that has jabbed me into continued obedience.

My business has prospered, delighting Llewella. She presses me to hire an assistant, but she has not usurped the task of interviewing as she would have done a few months ago. Her respect for me has increased recently. Even Janine has stopped calling me a fool. Both Talitha and Lar have suggested that I apply for a parliamentary staff position. Lar has awarded me an eleventh lotus. I am successful, and I am miserable.

I testified reluctantly, but my testimony formed a major factor in the case against my brother. If my conscience had not been troubled enough, both Lar and Toby sent me gifts after the jury's verdict. Talitha, at least, did not embarrass me with her thanks.

Benedict will die tomorrow. He has been tried and convicted of crimes against civilization. Dom Toby sentenced him to death. Mastermage Lar decreed the method of execution. Benedict will die, and Kurt has died, and I am lonely beyond endurance.

Each day, I have waited to hear that Andrew has freed my brother. I was so sure, at first, that Andrew would retrieve Benedict, as Andrew retrieved the mixie, Cris. Despite Uncle Toby's brave words about arresting "all" of Prince Hiroshi's local followers, I have seen evidence only of Benedict, Andrew, and Cris.

Throughout the trial, I pretended to myself that it was a farce we played, meaningless because Andrew moved beyond the reach of social law. All of us expected Andrew to make *some* effort to rescue Benedict. Toby could have had no other reason for pressing such serious charges against my brother, just as he had no other reason for capturing Cris as hostage. Both traps have failed, and my farcical play has acquired a tragic ending.

Benedict can no longer be considered a valuable lead to Andrew, but Uncle Toby has committed himself to my brother's destruction, and the Dom must not be seen as indecisive. My uncle's rote reelection is more significant than my brother's life. The second trap has not closed upon its target, but it will not injure the private ambitions of a Dom.

The trap that used Cris as bait failed more disastrously. Talitha does not talk about it, but Lar has made disparaging remarks about that plan's naïveté. Evidently, Talitha did not believe that Andrew would—or could—mix his Mage skills with Empire science. Despite her taunts against him, even she had not realized how far he had descended into villainy. So, at least, Lar has led me to believe.

Talitha tells me where to go and what to do and say, but she does not confide her own thoughts to me. She speaks to me as to a child. Toby is a little freer with his words, simply because he is less reticent by nature. Uncle Toby admits that Andrew has won this skirmish and escaped. After Benedict's execution, Toby plans to return to the Site of Parliament, where the governing Houses will again debate the problem of Andrew and Prince Hiroshi. I do not know what Talitha and Lar intend, but I presume that they will also take ship to Tathagata.

I have searched for Andrew, not knowing what I would do if I found him. The hidden room above my brother's apartment is vacant, stripped of wealth and magic. I located the wharf where Cris took me with Rodolfo and dear, lost Kurt, but the ships and workers were gone. Only an empty, half-drowned derelict, a rusty transport boat that must have been abandoned for years, floated on the bay. The main wharf seems to have regained some of its former level of activity. Janine has made some grudging inquiries on my behalf. All of the reports are the same: The major privateers have left Rit.

I even tried to talk to Feti'a and Ao Jun, but the effort merely confirmed that they distrust me, despite my elevated status with the Mastermage. If anyone at the Mage Center has heard from Mages Shamba or Pachacamac about the departed Mage Schools and the infamous prophecy of disaster, no one has seen fit to inform me.

Rodolfo blames me for Kurt's disappearance, even though I have confessed nothing. Lilith has become strange and distant. Janine is my only remaining friend, and she has never been much of a comfort.

Lar granted me permission to visit Benedict yesterday, but I lost my courage and did not go beyond the prison's admission room. My brother told me at the end of the trial that he forgave me. Benedict has not spoken in my presence since uttering those words.

I am being childish, hiding beneath this fine, soft quilt that Uncle Toby gave to me. I am too late for the dawn greeting, but I should go to the city and try once more to visit my brother. Perhaps, even now, Andrew will come. I have felt reluctant to see him, even when I searched for him. This morning, however, I want to see Andrew again, almost as much as I want my brother to be saved. I wish I had my brother's faith—in anyone.

The routine of rising, bathing, and dressing does not make me feel better, but it helps me to stop thinking for a little while. I take a crusty roll from the commons, but I do not stay to eat it. No one speaks to me as I leave the Mage Center.

I walk rapidly to the base of the hill, slipping once on a piece of gravel. I have just regained my stride, when I hear my name spoken. I think that I have resumed a dream, but he speaks my name again. I turn toward the voice.

In the shadow between two empty apartment houses, I see Andrew, all golden and composed. His new bracelets have more complexity of form and color than their predecessors. Each bracelet seems to represent a creature out of Oceanic myth or history. Most incorporate fantastic forms of fish, birds, or serpents. Several are jeweled, chiefly with amethysts and aquamarines.

"You should not be alone this morning," he tells me, when I reach him.

"Why didn't you help Benedict?" I cry, and Andrew shakes his head at me. He has shorn his thick hair. It hangs no further than the base of his neck. Cut and unbound, his hair is wavier than I would have expected.

"You still don't understand, Marita. I have not helped your brother because he does not want my help."

"He does not want to die!"

"Death does not frighten Benedict. His merciful Intercessor will carry him gently to peace."

"You don't believe my brother's foolishness. You are using his words to excuse your refusal to help."

"I'm not sure what I believe where your brother is concerned. I sometimes think his madness makes more sense than our civilized standards of sanity."

Andrew is still compelling, but I will not submit to his influence. "You once indicated that you would sell anything for enough gold," I say accusingly. "What will you charge to save my brother's life?"

"I could ask you for anything, and you would give it for Benedict's sake, wouldn't you?" Andrew touches the floral bracelet, which has slipped down to my wrist, and I feel suddenly shackled by his gold. "You would leave Rit on your brother's behalf. You would agree to leave Rit as my ally, following me and learning from me, though you consider me a criminal against all humanity. You would even stay with me, if I asked it now."

"If that is your price," I answer, but I vow inwardly that Andrew will never own my soul.

Andrew stares past me, as if I have become a sight that is painful to him. "You love your brother so much, but you understand so little about him. Do you think he would willingly let you pay for his life with your own? He is not as helpless as you think. He would fight us both to prevent you from making such a sacrifice, and he might win. His weapons are intangible and difficult to counter."

"Grant me the right to make my own choice, Mage Andrew."

"Marita, you do not know what you are asking of me. You certainly have no idea of what you offer in payment."

"I know that you would not have met me here this morning unless you expected to make such a trade."

He does not deny my accusation. "If I were a better man, I would not have come."

"Save my brother," I plead. "I will forswear Mysticism, if that is what you require."

Bitterness twists his smile. "Your generous offer to abandon Mysticism comes too late," he replies with derision. My crescent marks sting very little, suggesting that he aims his mockery at himself. "I have already unleashed calamity," he admits, confirming my Mage sense of his guilt, "by compromising my own skills, commanding Empire science and scarab skills in unison. I have betrayed myself and the cause I serve, and we shall all pay the price of my weakness."

"I see only my brother suffering for your guilt."

Andrew removes one of his bracelets, a ruby-eyed lizard, closely braided from three shades of gold. A gap separates the head from the tail. Andrew slides the bracelet onto my right arm. He squeezes the bracelet together, fitting it near my wrist on top of my Mage marks. The gold does not hide my crescents, but it distorts the symmetry of the lotus blossoms.

Andrew declares, "You are mine, Marita, and I shall not free you, though the bargain costs us both too much."

I touch the lizard bracelet. Its metal seems unyielding now, though Andrew bent it easily. "Save my brother," I repeat.

Andrew nods. "I shall save him."

II.

MAGE CARDS:

Shadow Prince

Brass Mage

Ice Cat

Blood Ghost

Sable Mixie

Marita

I saw neither Talitha nor Toby that morning, and I faced Lar only across the Mage Center's crowded courtyard. I came late to the morning greeting, but not even Janine commented on my tardiness. Lar left the pentacle without a glance in my direction. Only a dismal puff of violet smoke marked his departure. Damp weather had thwarted his usual exhibition.

I stood alone, as the rest of the Mages vanished into the commons. I studied the blue tile pentacle that was slick with a night's rain, and I wondered why I could not care that I might never see it again. Neither Janine nor Rodolfo spoke to interrupt my brooding.

My fingers found Andrew's lizard bracelet beneath my robe's long sleeve. The imprisonment was real, whether magic or Empire science chained that inescapable bracelet to Andrew's control. Eleven lotus blossoms crowded around the golden emblem of my bondage, but my Mage marks could not free me. When a Mystic surrendered to a Mage of Andrew's skills, the captor could easily lay spell-claim to the captive's entire complement of Mystic power. Only the captor could ever dissolve such Mystic shackles.

I had valued the first ten symbols of my Mystic progress, ridiculously satisfied by my ability to perform the simplest Mage arts, because I thought such tricks gave me stature outside my family. I had taken pride in my crescents, but now I had come to hate them because they seemed to make me susceptible to the influence of anyone who believed deeply in his or her cause. I followed Andrew or Talitha or Lar or Toby, until I could not even imagine what *Marita* wanted, except to save her brother's life.

The depression that had clouded my reason since Kurt's death had thinned, squeezed aside by a quietly seething, universal anger. I hated myself for conceding to lawlessness, still wishing feebly that someone else would pay the price of

Benedict's freedom. I resented the cost of Andrew's help, which had escalated far beyond mere gold. My family behaved no better, squandering Benedict as a blood sacrifice, even if their Affirmist words denied the truth. Lar, who would sanctimoniously execute my brother and expect my devotion, disgusted me almost as much as I disgusted myself.

Repeatedly in the past three months, Lar had troubled to explain to me why, for political appearance, we should refrain from intimacy until after the expiation of my brother's crimes. I had listened dutifully, declining to comment. As far as I could tell, Lar still did not know how I had deceived him. He thought he dictated my life, both as lover and as Mastermage. He thought I would serve him as he wished, and he seemed to believe that I longed for him to summon me. He may have been fond of me in his own way, but he already fretted that I might again expect fidelity of him. He did not realize that *he* was now clinging to *me*, and I no longer cared.

With Benedict under his control, Lar had little use for me except to bolster his ego—which Andrew seemed to have shaken badly. Lar's political assessment of me was correct, of course: I *was* weak and unimportant, except as a symbol of the Family to which I belonged, and I had deliberately dismantled my value to him in that regard. I understood why Lar dismissed me, even as he deceived himself that I remained besotted by him. His ambition had always driven his desires. Once, such rejection had hurt me. I could, at least, be grateful that the past few months had freed me of that burden: Lar no longer owned my heart. No one, including Andrew with his bonds of Empire gold, would ever claim such mindless devotion from me again.

I raised my eyes from the polished pentacle. Bloated clouds thickened darkly in the sky. Their turmoil caught my attention and kept me standing blindly in the misty dawn, though the courtyard had emptied completely but for me.

Detachedly, I listened when soft footfalls approached from behind me, but I did not turn, even when Rodolfo made a pointed issue of clearing his throat. He spoke curtly, uncomfortable at being with me on the morning of my brother's execution, "A messenger brought this for you, 'Rita." Without facing me, he thrust a brown velvet armband of Affirmist mourning into my unresisting hand. "From Dom Toby."

"How exceedingly proper of him," I murmured. "But social correctness is the first requirement of a Dom's profession, isn't it?"

"He's your uncle, not mine." Rodolfo sounded irritable. "And it's your brother who carries the death curse."

I steeled myself to look at Rodolfo's fair, familiar beauty, and I wished for the thousandth time that he was Kurt. "A death sentence is not a death curse."

"It is a curse against all past and future incarnations, when a Mastermage acts as the executioner. Ch'ango enacted that spell twenty years ago to quiet some rumblings of Mystic insurrection. You're old enough to remember," he added with the scorn of a Mystic-by-birth for a converted Affirmist.

"Twenty years ago, I was a child and an Affirmist," I reminded him unnecessarily, "and Ch'ango is no longer Rit's Mastermage."

"Only because she wanted more than Rit could give her. Do you think Lar would even try to counter one of Ch'ango's curses?"

"No," I acknowledged easily. A death curse meant nothing, until the death occurred. "Even my grandfather feared to contradict Ch'ango." I slid the soft velvet onto my left wrist, where the fabric dangled with the band of gold that I had taken from the fountain. "Thank you for bringing the armband, Rodolfo." He resented being a messenger, but he was not Janine to refuse outright to carry a token to the senior member of his pathetically small school. I touched his fine hair, where it curled to his shoulders. I would not miss him deeply, but we had both loved Kurt. "I'm sorry, Rodolfo. I have not brought much good to our Mage School."

His pretty face softened into a contrite smile. "The guilt's not yours. You're not your brother. I know all this waiting through the trial and verdict has been hard on you, but it will end soon."

I am not Benedict, and you are not Kurt, who would encourage me with honest caring instead of trite condolences. My friend is gone, and my family betrays me. For the sake of a brother whom I do not understand, I have bartered myself to a man I do not trust.

"I expect to leave Rit for a time," I said.

"Janine predicted that you'd be bound for Tathagata," answered Rodolfo with a smirk. His comment surprised me, until he pursued it, "Better luck handling Lar this time, 'Rita. Remember to keep your perspective. Lovers come and go. Enjoy them, but never regret them."

"Thank you, Rodolfo," I answered dryly. A droplet of rain caught him on the nose. I watched him dash to the commons, feeling no temptation to follow him and offer my farewells to Janine or anyone else. On returning to my room, I dressed simply and packed nothing. I smoothed the soft comforter across my bed and left.

Talitha, from her own perspective, had prepared for Andrew. She anticipated another of his audacious personal visits, because she attributed too much arrogance to him and underestimated his cunning form of practicality. She did not believe that he would trust anyone else to perform his work. She certainly did not expect *me* to serve as Andrew's agent. She did not credit me with either that much initiative or that much duplicity.

I may forever remember Benedict's prison as a lightless monolith, brooding and diabolic. I may never be able to walk past the building and see it from a clearer perspective, though I know that the descriptions given by others, who are less prejudiced by events, would belie the ominous image. It is a relatively small, plastone building with a narrow stoop and generous windows. The roof is flat, and the plastiwood eaves sag. The windows are striped by unobtrusive silver bars embedded with the plastiglass. Otherwise, the prison resembles any public building of early Empire vintage.

In my mind, every aspect of the day was dark and bleak: the sky, the streets, the people. Walking from the Mage Center, I saw no smiles, no children, no hope. Darkest of all was Andrew in his gold, because he accompanied me only in my haunted imagination.

I could not name the Face that signified him—Cat or Mage or Prince—but I knew that Andrew's Suit was Shadow in every sense of symbolic truth. He was changeable and unpredictable and saturated with magics of both Mystic and Empire kinds. In his formidable presence, I could almost imagine trusting him. Alone, I knew better.

I did not try to excuse him for trapping me. I judged harshly all of those who had used and manipulated me with guilt and grief and fear. I knew little about their war: far less than Andrew or Talitha; less even than Aunt Nan. With no greater mercy, I judged myself. If I had long ago accepted the obligations implicit in my privileged upbringing, my family might have confided in me instead of treating me like the invalid twin of my mad brother. Unhampered by ignorance, I might have feared Andrew and his Prince too much to sell my loyalties, even for the sake of Benedict.

The result, however, would probably have been the same. Andrew had such Mage skills that I doubted anyone less powerful than Ch'ango herself could have resisted his direct attentions.

He met me not far from the Mage Center, halting me with a whisper from a shadowed alleyway. Fine gray wool, hauntingly like Benedict's customary robe, cloaked him and his gold. He wasted no instant on false cordiality. I was grateful for his cold efficiency, because it demanded nothing of me.

Andrew equipped me with devices that I did not understand but recognized as products of his Empire. Most of the devices were fashioned as toys: tiny painted cats, hounds, birds, boats, and wagons. The entire panoply fit easily alongside the largest vials within my philter purse. Andrew provided rapid, baffling explanations regarding the origins of the objects he gave me. I followed little of what he said, and I requested no elucidation.

I listened more attentively when he instructed me as to where I should place the toys, once I entered the prison building. Andrew gave other explicit instructions as to my actions. I accepted all that he offered in the way of practical advice. It was for Benedict.

Andrew adjusted the sleeves of my cream linen jacket to hide both gold bracelets: the ruby-eyed lizard that he had bound on me and the etched floral band that I had taken from the Stone Palace fountain. Andrew also fastened new gold posts through my ears, replacing my jade lotus earrings with gold shells that spiraled upward from the lobe. "The earrings will facilitate my communication with you," he said tersely. "The lizard contains electronic devices that I shall activate remotely. The floral bracelet is too damaged for direct use, but it may serve as a psychological deterrent to those who recognize it as mine." I did not ask him to explain his Empire mechanisms further. We had little time, and I was already too aware of my guilt.

I had set aside all Mystic vows and social conscience. Except for my philter purse, I wore only neutral colors, but I could not cling to the illusion of my impartial role. Accepting Andrew's help and Andrew's rules made me an active part of the destructive Empire past that my family had spent generations trying to heal. It also proved to me how easily I could adopt the worst aspects of my ruthless, manipulative family.

With Andrew's dangerous toys, we would save Benedict from the trap in which I had helped to place him. I believed Talitha: Benedict was guilty of abetting Andrew, and Andrew's crimes were terrible and far-reaching. I had testified honestly. I had done as law and family demanded, but I was not as strong as Talitha. I could not finish the job.

I would think of nothing but my brother's survival. I would hold the image of him alive and well in my mind and in my spells. I would not let him die. I had failed Kurt; I refused to relinquish my brother.

I walked to the prison alone and presented myself in the prison's cheerless admission room. A single plasteel desk rested before the barred, opaque plastiglass door. The ocher boards of the plastiwood floor squeaked as I crossed the narrow expanse that seemed endless. The receptionist, an elderly Amerind man in a charcoal gray uniform, whispered into a small, silver speaker box mounted on his desk.

I could not hear his words, but the barred plastiglass cleared to transparency. Uncle Toby and Talitha conferred in the corridor beyond it. Both of them wore grim expressions and the full, unadorned white robes of execution. I was unsurprised to see them standing alone in the unfriendly corridor, because the prison was empty except for my brother. Lesser criminals, guilty only of infractions against individuals instead of against society, occupy a cluster of buildings on the neighboring island of Halmand. Society's condemned, like Benedict, spend little time in prison, since they always receive sentences of death. Such executions are private, intimate events, quickly carried out.

"Please," I requested quietly, "let me see my brother once more, even if he does not wish to speak to me."

The receptionist pursed his thin, wrinkled lips, but he spoke again into his mouthpiece. Talitha nodded with slow dignity, and Uncle Toby gestured toward someone beyond my view. The barred door slid upward silently. "Go ahead," said the receptionist, inclining his gray-streaked head. He sounded like a kindly man, pitying me.

I entered the prison. The door behind me creaked back into place, rushing the last few centimeters to a final crash of closure. With a muffling spell and the sound of the door to aid my secretive movement, I dropped Andrew's first set of toys, five gray mice, and surreptitiously kicked them against the wall.

Silently, Talitha handed me a white taffeta robe. The sleeves were too long for me, but I folded the stiff fabric away from my hands. I needed the mobility, as well as all my Mage skills, in order to enact Andrew's orders. Like the receptionist, Talitha pitied me.

"You may visit Benedict for five minutes," conceded Toby, "but no more." His perpetually genial face made his words seem like mockery.

"Thank you," I answered, hating him for his indifference.

"Benedict is in the last room," said Talitha, pointing down an empty hallway with a white-gloved hand.

The prison's defenses appeared meager to me, but I concluded that entry did not make the extent of them evident. In his quick summary of the prison's equipment, Andrew had indicated that all of the precautions were designed to retain a captive, not to preclude a harmless visitor's arrival. If Andrew had entered the building, I did not doubt that strong barricades would have risen quickly and securely behind him. I restrained a backward glance on considering that such defenses might be closing behind me more extensively than I realized.

With a Mage's legerdemain to shield my actions, I dropped the next set of Andrew's toys along the hallway, as he had instructed. These toys were small blocks, colored to match the plastiwood floor and padded enough to fall soundlessly.

Lar stood with folded arms, waiting outside the room where Benedict was to die. Even Lar wore a robe of white, which made the matching streaks in his hair more prominent. He, of course, was the actual executioner, a role that took precedence over his normal functions as Mastermage. Only the collar of amethysts at his throat betokened his Mystic status.

Lar beckoned to me peremptorily. No bracelets hid *his* scarabs. His smile struck my critical eye as condescending instead of sympathetic. He opened the door to admit me to my brother's cell.

At the door to Benedict's cell, I brought tears to my eyes, embarrassing Lar enough to make him look elsewhere for a critical moment. I used Lar's inattention to scatter the third set of soft toys. "May I speak to my brother privately?" I asked, when Lar seemed inclined to enter with me. I made my voice break. Lar hates emotional scenes that do not center on him.

"No more than five minutes," decreed Lar, repeating Toby's injunction. He allowed me to enter alone.

I did not look at Benedict until I heard the door seal behind me. He knelt in the center of the room, away from the bed that was intended as his bier. His eyes were closed, and his hands were folded. He was dressed again in his own gray robe, for the beige clothing worn during his trial would be cleaned and given to the court's next prisoner.

I placed the final set of toys carefully, three against the door, three against each of the other three walls. Triplets carried potent influence from many mythologies, and the perfect Mystic number, twelve, traditionally fed powerful spells. I sat on the edge of the bed, squandering my few, precious minutes in watching my brother and remembering our childhood. We had grown together in our own delightful unreality, fashioned equally of our imaginations, Nan's eccentric teachings and the Family's protective power. Neither of us had learned how to contend with the true world. "Benedict," I murmured, "forgive me."

My brother raised his head, and he smiled. He was at peace. I knew that Andrew was right: Benedict did not want this rescue that Andrew had contrived at my behest.

"Your death will serve no purpose," I said. "You will only be a dead fool, not a gallant martyr."

Benedict's smile became a frown. "I am cowardly, not gallant, but the Intercessor grants mercy even to me."

"Then He will not want you to die without a struggle."

I thought at first that my ironic words had reached my brother, but he seemed to glean my intentions from them. He jumped to his feet, swept across the room and stood over me. He grabbed my left hand and pushed the sleeve above the golden lizard bracelet. "Marita," he sighed raggedly, "you do not know what you have done."

"Tell him," whispered Andrew's voice in my ear, "that his prophecy will be fulfilled."

"Your prophecy will be fulfilled, Ben."

Benedict stared at me keenly. "Those words are not yours," he accused.

"Do not speak my name," ordered Andrew softly, "but tell Benedict that I will not violate his beliefs. He will know whose words you repeat."

I obeyed, "He will not violate your beliefs."

"He violates his own, and yours," replied my brother urgently. His thin fingers clutched at my prison robe. "You must not let him complete this betrayal, Marita. Leave me, *now.* Let this calamity remain undone!"

"He is your friend, not mine," I retorted.

"This is not the act of a friend," declared Benedict. He backed away from me, as if in revulsion. He lifted his pale hands with his palms turned upward nearly to the low ceiling. "Great, merciful Intercessor," he prayed in a shuddering voice, "do not condemn them for the weakness of my faith. If my sin must be atoned, let me suffer it alone. Have mercy on us, Intercessor. Have mercy!"

Lar flung open the door in his grandiose style and announced, "You've had your five minutes, Marita. Go and await me in the admission room. I'll accompany you back to the Center when I've finished here."

I disregarded both Lar's unfeeling commands and Benedict's passionate pleas. As Andrew had instructed, I raised the arm that wore the lizard bracelet and shielded my face with my other gold-encircled arm. The lizard bracelet pulsed with blistering heat. The room began to shake, as if Gaia herself struggled to propel us from her skin.

I felt the tingling dust of Lar's retaliatory philter settle over me, felt the weakness begin to creep into my muscles. I bit the ampoule that I held between my teeth and inner cheek, the ampoule that Andrew had provided. Strength surged into me.

I lowered my arms. The lizard bracelet still pulsed, beating with the rhythm of the shuddering room. Each of Andrew's scattered toys glowed as brightly as candle flame. Benedict stood apart, pressed against the wall, mouthing prayers that I could not hear. He watched me with an expression of terrible sorrow.

Lar had contorted his handsome face with righteous fury,

but I sensed fear in him, as well. He did not try to approach me, settling for alchemical Mage spells that a five-lotus Mage could have wielded. The spells were no less dangerous for their simplicity, however, and Lar used them deftly. His fist hurtled forward, and he threw fire oil at me, singeing the floor and the bed. His quickness caught me unprepared, and the white robe that I wore caught fire. I shed the garment hurriedly. My own clothes and skin remained impervious to Lar's spell, though the scent of the watery potion that Andrew had strewn on me became sharp and bitter.

Talitha and three armed men had appeared at the door. They all raised weapons, but I met this threat with the calm of expectation. They could not defeat Andrew with devices that he understood much better than they. Andrew's spell had taken hold, and none of their weapons functioned. I stepped beyond Benedict and cast Andrew's rainbow philter.

"I will strike every lotus from your treacherous arms," shouted Lar, countering my spell with a powder of his own. I cringed for a moment, accosted by my own guilt, but the rainbow cloud merely parted around Lar's flailing figure and drifted into the hallway. Talitha and one well-prepared guard covered their noses and mouths with Inianga-orange scarves. The other two guards did not move swiftly enough, and the spell reached them before they could place the oiled Mage silk across their faces. The bespelled guards acquired the glazed expressions that now seemed wickedly familiar to me, and they wandered down the hallway with a clumsy, aimless gait.

"Marita, child," cried Talitha through the muffling fabric, "how can you betray your people?" I could see little of her face, but her black eyes were filled with bitter loathing.

"How could you condemn my brother?" I shouted in return. Again, I raised the lizard bracelet, and its eyes shot ruby fire. Talitha stiffened, stumbled, and sprawled upon the cold floor among a dainty menagerie of Andrew's toys. Lar and the guardsman ran toward her, but both men slumped to the floor before reaching her side.

The prison was quiet but for the shuffle of bespelled guards. The white-shrouded figures of Lar and Talitha, two people who had for years loomed as dominant forces in my life, lay crumpled and defeated before me. I stared at the lizard bracelet, horrified by the effects of Andrew's perverse gifts.

Andrew whispered to me, "Tell Benedict that they are only unconscious, but I am prepared to make their sleep permanent if he does not accompany you promptly." In a leaden voice, I repeated Andrew's words.

Benedict nodded. He now seemed resigned and unsurprised. My brother was evidently more familiar than I with Andrew's methods.

In my ear, Andrew ordered, "Leave immediately, Marita. The disabling gas has dissipated, and the 'toys' will prevent the prison mechanisms from functioning for only a few minutes."

"We need to leave now," I told my brother numbly. I walked past Lar with only a slight qualm, but stepping across Talitha made me feel thoroughly traitorous. When I saw Uncle Toby wandering in the hallway with a vacuous smile, I averted my eyes, unable to confront more guilt.

"What did you expect, Marita?" asked Benedict gently. "You have defied your own conscience. Such choices entail cruel consequences."

"I'm not the one who was sentenced to death for crimes against society," I muttered. We had reached the barred door to the admission room. The door rose automatically before us.

The stocky, elderly receptionist stood beyond the door, waving us forward urgently. His broad jawline, cleanly defined despite his age, was set with determination. His eyes were narrowed into slits. Andrew whispered, "The receptionist is an ally. His name is Chaac."

My brother and I entered the admission room. The barred door crashed into place. Chaac thrust a small crimson bag, woven with a pattern of yellow wheat, into my hand. "My debts to Aroha are paid," he said, his wrinkled face solemn. "I serve Prince Hiroshi now by choice."

"Confirm that his debts to me are paid," answered Andrew, and I relayed the message mechanically.

Chaac nodded. His eyes were kind, but I could not meet them. "The bag is yours," he told me. "You will have need of comfort." To Benedict, he spoke cryptically, "Righteousness frees the condemned."

The words seemed to trouble my brother, but he agreed, "So says the prophecy."

Chaac touched the sleeve of my brother's robe almost with reverence. "Will you grant me a blessing, wise one?"

"It is not for me either to fulfill your prayer or to refuse. It is the Intercessor who blesses the faithful, who ask His help. What is it that you wish?"

"Heal my grandson, who was bespelled and is near death."

Briefly, a remoteness akin to Mage seeking blanketed my brother's long face. Benedict nodded slowly. "By the Intercessor's mercy, your grandson will be healed."

Andrew said softly in my ear, "And it will be so, though I do not know how Benedict, a man of no Mage marks, exercises such a gift." I did not repeat Andrew's odd comment. The exchange between Benedict and Chaac troubled me, for it recalled what I had dreamed of Mage Shamba's prophecy: *From Rit will rise destruction. The condemned will walk free, and the lawful will be enslaved.*

"Thank you, wise one," answered Chaac.

Chaac showed a respect for my brother that seemed incongruous from an old man to a young. Chaac still seemed to regard me with pity. His attitude, like his words, disturbed me. The Kinebahan tell of animal spirits, disguised in human form, who see beyond human range. When we left Chaac and the prison building, my mind carried an image of the Amerind as a great bear of legend instead of a man.

Rain was falling, and the street was empty and slick. Even in foul weather, a few signs of life are generally visible in the heart of Rit, but now I saw no one. "Those who mourn do not show their faces to their neighbors," said Benedict, though I had not voiced my uneasy observation.

"It's a wretched neighborhood and a wretched day for a walk," I mumbled, hurrying my brother toward the street corner where Andrew had told me to wait. The corner was desolate and depressing. It held the hollow, black shell of a building that had burned years ago, but there was a sheltered bench, an old bus stop, where we could escape the rain.

Benedict and I huddled together on that crudely carved and painted bench, where so many idle, uncaring hands had scrawled their pitiful statements. The individual drawings had little artistry, and most had been overwritten many times, but the whole collage made an eloquent cry of frustration. A stream of dirty water ran past our feet and trickled down to the channel where the plasteel busrails gleamed.

The ground rumbled. A bus, one of the boxy, battered vehicles that had lain abandoned in its garage for a century, emerged clumsily from the shroud of rain. The gray bus did not glide smoothly on its rails, but it moved, and it stopped before us. Its door folded open.

Benedict sighed, but he climbed into the bus while I still stared at it doubtfully. Rit's buses did not function. At least, they had not functioned before Andrew's intervention. This was not a toy, a bird cage or a fountain. By its relatively massive size, the bus seemed to represent a more threatening application of Andrew's Empire methods than I had yet seen.

I tried to comfort myself. The principle of restoring an automated bus was neither worse nor better than tending the smaller objects, and Andrew's Mage skills seemed more obviously dangerous than his science. Even fixers could sometimes repair an autobus. I joined my brother inside the bus, seating myself beside him on a molded bench that was distinctly uncomfortable. I jumped nervously when the door clattered shut.

"Are you listening to me, Andrew?" asked my brother, but he did not await a response from any obvious source. "What you have done is wrong, as you know. You made an informed choice for personal gain, and you will suffer for it. You have taken advantage of a holy prophecy. You have entrapped my sister through her misguided concern for me. Do not compound your sin by destroying her. Let her go now, or the enemy will gain that much more power over you. If you care nothing for your soul, consider Hiroshi. His cause will fail without you."

The bus squealed and jostled us. The rain, becoming heavier, streamed down the windows. We turned a corner, heading toward the wharves. A dim, wet figure ran from the path of the bus. Benedict sighed.

I told him, "I'm not entirely ignorant of Andrew's crimes, Ben."

He shook his head, but he laid his hand on mine. "Thank you, Marita, for caring so much about me."

"You are my brother."

Benedict touched the lizard bracelet that Andrew had fastened on me. "This was a gift to Andrew from Prince Hiroshi. It was crafted by a master goldsmith in the last year of the Empires. It's actually a puzzle, as well as an elaborate device for self-defense. It is extremely rare."

"Do you know how to release it?" I asked anxiously.

"No. Andrew never told me how to work the puzzle."

I had expected nothing else. Andrew guarded his secrets too closely. "You know him better than I do."

"I have known him for seventeen years. I thought I knew him well. I did not think he would use me this way." The bus jostled, and Benedict braced himself to keep from bumping me. "I never imagined that the prophecy would unfold with such violence."

"What was the prophecy?" I asked slowly, fearful of the reply.

Benedict drew his thin body straight. He stared unseeingly through the window of the bus. "From Rit, destruction rises. The law of sin enslaves the free, as righteousness frees the condemned." His voice rang with power, as in my dream, but he slumped back into sorrow and continued quietly, "When the vision came to me, I went to Andrew. I told him that I must go to Rit. He agreed, and he accompanied me."

"Mage Shamba of Inianga prophesied almost the same words," I said hollowly. I did not believe that Benedict could have heard Shamba's words and made them his own. I had never weighed my brother's potential as a Mage, but we shared the same heritage. Prophets are rare, even among Mages, but Mystic history suggests that prophets *did* exist before Mage marks.

Benedict shrugged. "True prophecy is often given to several voices."

"Then what has occurred was inevitable," I murmured. I did not feel consoled.

"A prophecy should never be forced," answered my brother fretfully, reciting a Mystic dictum to me. "Andrew has tried to control the future's shape, but he only makes himself its pawn."

Andrew, a pawn? I scoffed inwardly. From my view, it seemed that Andrew had trapped me neatly in the trap designed to take him. "But for Andrew, you would never have been arrested, Ben. He uses you, uses me, uses untold others in this 'war' he fights against the world. He *is* destruction, and it is our entire society that he enslaves." I did not want to believe my own claims, but a hard, golden lizard gripped my arm too tightly to be ignored. "And I must serve him."

"Do not elevate Andrew to godhood. He is only a man, Marita, as misguided and confused as anyone who refuses the Intercessor's wisdom."

"If *you* are wise, Ben," I said with bitter irony, "tell me: What have I done?"

My brother sighed, "You made a judgment. I cannot call it wise, but it was mercifully intended. We must proceed from where we are, not from where we might have been. Andrew is right in saying that we cannot hide from what we know."

I hunched into the uncomfortable bus seat. "I feel miserably ignorant."

"Andrew will cure you of that regret, at least. He will not let you remain ignorant much longer." Musingly, Benedict continued, "You have rare knowledge, and Andrew will expect you to share it. Hiroshi always needs more teachers, and so few of us are qualified. The need will become even greater now that the enemy has forced Andrew out of hiding." My brother turned to face me, and tears flowed down his cheeks. "None of us is innocent, Marita. But for *me,* Andrew could not have used *you.* I was prepared to die, but that death was not the Intercessor's will, after all. I am not prepared, as yet, to live with what I must face instead. None of us are ready for direct war. Andrew alone cannot fight all the battles, and he has weakened himself by recruiting you against your will. I have served as the voice of prophecy, but I can interpret only a little of what we must face."

"Was Talitha right? Do you serve Andrew's cause?"

"Andrew and I serve the same cause, Marita, in our very different ways. You will understand better when you meet Hiroshi." After a slight pause, Benedict added, "You will also come to understand that it is not Talitha's Protectorate we fight. It is the blindness of the *other* Protectorate."

The bus shuddered to a halt. The doors folded open, and Benedict ducked through them without hesitation. We were at the pier in Rit's desolate Petra district, not far from the wharf where a mixie boy had once guided three Avalon Mages in a life that seemed centuries removed. The rain continued to fall, but Benedict seemed oblivious to it. He was walking toward the end of the pier, his arms folded in front of him, and his head upright. The rain darkened his robe in streaks.

I could not force myself to move. The bus did not resume its course, and the doors remained open, apparently waiting for me. Salty wind blew the rain through the doors, chilling me with the spray. There was an autoboat tied at the farthest dock, a small craft such as I might once have leased to escape from Rit with my brother. The autoboat was painted gray, making it nearly invisible against the gloomy sky and swelling ocean. If other ships occupied the nearby waters, I could not see them.

To excuse my hesitation, I opened the crimson bag that Chaac had given me. It contained an ampoule filled with a common luck philter. A few months ago, such a philter might have sufficed to comfort me. Contemptuously, I dropped the ampoule and the purse on the bus bench. I had sold hundreds of such ampoules, and I knew how little they were worth. I had accepted too much from Andrew; I wanted nothing, not even symbolic sympathy, from his ally.

"Please, Marita, don't make me fetch you," snapped Andrew's voice in my ear. I glanced around me, half expecting to see him, but I was still alone. Irritably, I removed the earrings that he had placed on me and thrust them in my jacket pocket. I climbed out of the bus. Its doors closed behind me, but it did not move further. The whir of its engine stopped.

I walked slowly, though the rain soaked my clothes and pasted my hair against my head. I stared between the slats of the pier, hypnotizing myself with the swirl of water around the mussel-encrusted pilings. Several stairways led to the lower docks, but I continued to the pier's end.

The stair that slanted down to the last dock was gated, but the plasteel barrier opened for me like the doors of the bus. When the gate clattered shut behind me, I said my silent farewell to Rit, not knowing where I was headed or whether I might return. The autoboat bobbed, as the ocean tossed it against the rubbery edge of the dock. These waters received partial protection from a stone jetty, but they were much rougher than Rit's main bay. The autoboat seemed to stabilize at my approach, and I stepped easily onto its sandpaper deck.

The autoboat resumed its tossing, and I grasped the cold plasteel railing for support. The docking mechanism released its hold with a vehement splash, and the autoboat pulled swiftly away from the pier. I remained on the deck, stiffly clinging to the icy rail, until the autoboat passed the jetty and settled into a constant, gentle undulation that skipped across the waves. The autoboat displayed far more speed and maneuverability than any vessel I had ever leased.

Through the cabin windows, I could see Andrew and Benedict, each apparently oblivious of the other—and of me. The cabin was luxuriously apportioned with polished brass and wood. Except for a small, enclosed area aft, the cabin was surrounded by windows that curved from the deck's height to a narrow rectangle of light panels that ran the room's length.

I descended the three steps to the cabin's door. The door slid open to admit me, and I stepped forward into a gust of warmth. Neither the rain nor the damp outside air seemed able to reach inside the cabin. The door closed.

Padded red benches, the hinged type that unfold into cots, occupied most of the solid wall space. Beneath the benches were storage cupboards, each labeled in meticulous script, engraved in brass. The floor was likewise labeled, indicating holds and retractable devices. Colored display panels, indecipherable to me, lined the forward section. Every device and piece of furniture fitted together seamlessly. There was nothing extraneous and no space unused.

Benedict sat on a bench opposite me. His eyes were closed, but his posture was not relaxed. Andrew occupied the forward position, his chair integrated into the console of controls and displays that evidently consumed his attention. He had exchanged his neutral clothing for a loose shirt and trousers of Tangaroa aqua.

Andrew swiveled his chair toward me, but he watched me in silence. I asked him, "Where are we headed?"

"To a larger ship," he answered. "We have a lengthy journey ahead of us. You won't be aware of most of the trip because I am not ready to entrust you with the location of Prince Hiroshi's community."

"I suppose I should thank you for saving my brother's life."

"Don't bother. I neither require nor expect your gratitude." He looked at Benedict. "Your brother certainly does not intend to thank me, although he will forgive me. By tomorrow, he will behave as if his imprisonment never occurred."

Still Benedict did not react. "Have you bespelled him?" I demanded angrily.

"No. He's deep in prayer. I've seen him maintain that state for days at a time." Andrew smiled bleakly. "He's not too pleased with me at the moment, and he's repenting for his anger."

Stifling a harsh retort, I opened a cupboard market "blankets" and rummaged through the neatly folded contents. Andrew returned his attention to his variegated displays. I selected a beige thermal and wrapped it around my drenched shoulders.

I crossed to Benedict and touched his hand. He squeezed my fingers, but he did not respond otherwise. Even if Andrew had bespelled him, I was powerless to help. My eleven lotus marks did not make me Andrew's equal. I sat on one of the corduroy-cushioned benches near my brother and tucked my feet beneath me.

When I began to feel thawed, I trusted myself to speak: "Benedict says that you expect me to teach."

"At present, there are only five of us in the community who are fully literate," answered Andrew distractedly, "and we have a population of seven hundred. Since you are intelligent and were trained with your brother, I assume that your Scribe skills match his."

"I made a vow to my family . . ." I began.

Andrew did not allow me to present my argument. "That was before you indentured yourself to me," he retorted. He glared at me across his shoulder, his gray-green eyes fierce. "I know that you're an unwilling recruit. I do not need to hear you reminding me of your sorry plight. You made your choice, and you will live with it. I do not expect your devotion, although I hope that your feelings toward me will become more rational as you realize that my 'evil' Empire methods have not converted you into a monster. I *do* expect you to behave like a mature, intelligent woman who fulfills the responsibilities that she accepts."

I swallowed my anger. "You have not defined those responsibilities very clearly."

"If I ask you to teach someone how to read or how to concoct a Mage philter, you will teach. If I tell you to abide by the laws of Prince Hiroshi's community, you will be a model citizen. I shall not abuse my authority over you, but I will enforce it."

"You are the tyrant that Talitha claims," I muttered.

"You have been so sheltered and pampered by the 'Family' all your life, you would consider anyone a tyrant who contradicted you. You are spoiled, lazy, and undeserving of the gifts that you waste."

"I can't believe I actually respected you for a time."

He hesitated for an instant before responding, "You thought you could enjoy making love to me, which is the shallowest sort of admiration. A woman with your professional credentials should know the difference between respect and lust, but I suppose you design love philters to eliminate the need for deep emotions. You are certainly not overburdened with strong personal relationships."

"And what deep emotions do you feel, Mage Andrew?" He had a quicker temper than he had shown me in Rit, or his mood was as raw as my own, but I was past caring about the dangers he presented. "Do you delight in your avarice? Do you take pride in your contempt for others? Or are you so blinded by ambition that you feel nothing for anyone? What did you feel for your *son?*"

Andrew remained silent so long, I thought he would not answer. When he did reply, his voice was almost inaudible. "I grieved for the waste," he said tonelessly, "and I learned how to repair the supply factory that distorted my son and killed his mother." He adjusted one of the autoboat's controls, as if to prove his mastery of it. "There will be no more children condemned to be mixies, if I can prevent it. I shall reverse the decay of our world, even if I must dismantle our society in the process. If destruction rises from my actions in Rit, then let it destroy ignorance." He added crisply, "All the hatred you can throw at me, Marita, can cause me no more than a moment's qualm, because I need what you can provide."

I had achieved more than Talitha, Toby, or Lar with all of their machinations. I had successfully hurt Andrew, but I felt no triumph. I had spent all of my fury against him. The respect that he mocked was rising dangerously back into my view, and that was not a prospect I either welcomed or trusted.

I shivered and clutched the blanket more tightly. I asked Andrew, "What spell will you use to keep me 'unaware' of our route?"

"No spell," he answered quietly. He, too, seemed to have exhausted his anger. "I shall give you a chemical cocktail that will keep you pleasantly hazy for a few days. I'm told it tastes like the synthetic guava juice from the exotic food supply units. It has no significant side effects."

"May I have it now?" Oblivion was the coward's path, but

I was too tired to match wits with Andrew. I had already conceded too much to him.

"As you wish." Whether from Mystic skills or natural astuteness, Andrew seemed to divine my reasoning. "In a fair battle, you could hold your own against me, Marita, but I have better resources, more experience, and the advantages of a prepared strategy. A judicious retreat is probably your wisest course at present. You and my temper both need the rest."

"Am I a prisoner of war?"

"You are an extremely precious commodity, and I do not intend to waste you." He reached beneath his console and withdrew a small plastiglass bottle, filled with a pale green liquid. He tossed the bottle to me. I grabbed for it nervously as it tumbled into my lap. "Drink it freely," he said. "When you've had enough, you'll lose interest in it."

My brother's eyes were still closed. I pried free the bottle cap. The fragrance of the liquid was sweet. I raised the bottle to my lips, and I let its contents delude me into peace.

Talitha

Mastermage Ch'ango, via Scribe Gavilan, Tathagata:

Benedict, the condemned, has walked free. Disaster, whose name is Aroha, has risen out of Rit and moves against us, as we have dreaded. We who uphold the law are enslaved by our fear of what Aroha and Prince Hiroshi may do, now that Aroha has cast aside pretense and shown his destructive ambitions clearly.

I shall continue to denounce your blood magic, but I admit that you predict Aroha's actions better than I. You were right, Ch'ango, and I was wrong. His spells have become more lethal with the years. The Protectorate cannot defeat Aroha by the old methods. Such methods *have* served for centuries to deter Prince Hiroshi's forebears from similar efforts to revive the Empires, but those feeble, sporadic rebellions had no advocate like Aroha. A halfhearted war cannot succeed against an enemy of such pitiless cunning and savagery. Choose whatever weapons you deem best. I shall not deter you from fighting *Aroha*.

Toby and Lar will leave for Tathagata by the next autoboat, as I presume you already know. I shall remain in Rit a little longer, so as to bring the local operation to a decent end. Aroha has closed his base here. We shall leave a skeletal staff, but I doubt that Aroha will return to Rit. Tathagata is where this war must eventually end, and it is Tathagata that we must fortify. We have waited long for Aroha to emerge and fight us openly, but we are no better prepared to deal with Aroha now that when first he espoused Prince Hiroshi's disastrous ideas of social reform.

Is this what you wanted, Ch'ango? A battle with Aroha the Mastermage? I am not blind to what you and Lar have done. You maneuvered me to taunt Aroha in order to goad him back into his Mystic ways. Was he not sufficiently dangerous with his Empire learning and Empire tools?

I do not comprehend the minds and methods of Mages. I yield to you in dealing further with Aroha. Destroy him, Ch'ango, for the sake of us all.

Scribe Talitha, Rit

Marita

Hiroshi's island belonged to a primordial era. A single mountain, riven through its crown, drove twin black fragments into the sky. Thick, verdant life tangled all the surrounding lands. The trees grew tall and strong, their trunks expanded by thirsty aerial roots that had merged into veils. Graceful, arching palms lined the white beach, craning toward the turquoise and sapphire water. Twisting vines sprawled across every surface, spiraling up the larger trunks with green and flaxen leaves a meter in diameter. Looking closely, I located the dark scars and distorted growth rings of the war, but this island had healed itself. I could see bright fish darting through the living reef beneath us.

There was no pier on Hiroshi's island. I assumed that we had left the autoboat anchored beyond the reef, although I could not remember clearly how we had come to this place and moment. Andrew transported us to the island by canoe, rowing with deft, powerful strokes through the narrow channels between coral towers. He seemed to know every current.

Benedict sat in the bow of the canoe, watching the water with a contemplative smile, and I sat in the stern, facing Andrew's gleaming back. My Rit clothing felt sticky and miserable in the tropical humidity, although I had lost my linen jacket. The men were dressed more appropriately in aqua trunks. Even Andrew's gold had yielded to the heat. His arms were bare except for his striking array of Mage marks.

My senses remained foggy. I had only a dim recollection of the ship that we had left minutes ago, and I had no accurate concept of the time that had elapsed since our departure from Rit. Benedict's skin had acquired a light tan since leaving the prison. I knew that we were approaching Prince Hiroshi's island, Ha'aparari, but I did not remember being given that information.

"Does anyone live here?" I asked, because we were near the shore, and I had yet to see any sign of human habitation.

Benedict replied with surprising animation, "This part of the island is a coral atoll, and Hiroshi keeps it as a natural preserve. When we reach the volcanic portions of the island along Roa Bay, you'll see a few homes, if you watch carefully. The community lies near the base of the mountain. It's almost impossible to discern until you're within it."

As he spoke, the sandy shoreline seemed to rush upon us, then melt away from us on either side. A canopy of jungle growth enveloped us and spewed us forth. What seemed to be the wide center of the atoll stretched toward the sundered mountain. Ahead of us, the shores of coral sands gave way to dark rock, where lava had evidently buried the old coral base.

"Watch now," said Benedict. He sounded as excited as a child, thoroughly unlike the subdued brother I had escorted from the Rit prison. "There's a house on your left just beyond this bend. A tree grows from the center of it. The walls are plastiglass, interspersed with supports that resemble aerial roots. Do you see it?"

Even with my brother's description to guide me, we had almost passed the structure before I recognized it. Unlike the obtrusive buildings of Rit, this followed the soft lines of the landscape. It blended almost indistinguishably with the tree that supported it. "Someone doesn't want visitors," I remarked.

"Nothing is hidden here," countered Benedict, "except from those whose eyes do not see. Anavai designs for harmony. Her buildings encourage peacefulness of spirit."

"Who is Anavai?" I asked.

"Hiroshi's wife. She is an architect, as well as a gifted artist in several other media. I think you will like her."

Andrew inserted dryly, "Your sister is disinclined to like anyone at the moment." Having dampened the conversation with truth, Andrew resumed his quiet rowing.

A bubbling ring of clouds spilled across the mountain. Benedict said, "It rains on this island almost every afternoon."

Andrew grunted between strokes of the oar, "Clouds form when the sun heats the ocean's surface. The air cools as it rises, and the rain falls. Each day, the cycle repeats."

Benedict glanced back at me. His smile was almost mischievous, which made him seem years younger and impossible to equate with a man who carried a sentence of death. "Andrew insists on finding a reason for everything."

Andrew replied emphatically, "If I understand the process of the rain, I can apply it to distill water or to power an engine. Science is built on observation, fueled by the question 'why?' and defined by the answers. Science approximates physical reality. As the approximation improves, science advances."

"Is listening to this sort of lecture a requirement of my indentured status?" I demanded, fascinated by Andrew's stern passion, despite myself.

Andrew answered very seriously, "Yes. Despising Empire science is like closing your eyes to stop a fire. The reality does not change simply because you choose to ignore it."

Curious, I asked my brother, "Do you agree with him?"

"In this case, yes. Truth exists, and pretending otherwise is purest folly."

"How long have you lived here, Ben?" I asked, because it was obvious that he knew the island intimately.

"Andrew introduced me to Hiroshi almost ten years ago. For the last seven years, I've spent nearly every winter and spring on this island, teaching and learning." Benedict pointed ahead of us, where a waterfall tumbled down the mountain to the distant end of the bay. "That's the Nui River. Most of us live along the gentler Iti. Like the island, the mountain is called Ha'aparari, which means broken."

We continued in silence, until Andrew veered toward a stretch of sandy shore amid the rocky outcroppings. With long, powerful strokes, he propelled us onto the narrow beach. Both Andrew and Benedict hopped out of the canoe and began to drag the boat from the water. I followed their example, although I contributed little to the effort. Andrew appeared quite capable of carrying the canoe's weight by himself. Benedict and I only complicated his task.

We left the canoe and headed inland. The trees bowed over us gracefully. I could see no clear path, but Andrew marched into the daunting jungle without hesitation. The overwhelming life-sense stunned me. Everything was overgrown with emerald moss and delicate ferns. Vivid flowers clung to the trees, forming mosaics of crimson, yellow, and fuschia that would have delighted Aunt Nan. The irregular lines and light, so much more intense than any history book

could portray, might have bewildered me completely if I had
not experienced Nan's greenhouse. I could hear the tumbling
of water, and I almost forgot the grim circumstances of my
coming to this disturbing, lovely place.

A distant chiming wrenched through my reverie, reviving
both my memories and my fears. I had heard such a sound
in Janine's office in Rit, and her hired man had died. Benedict spoke before I could form my concern into words: "Can
the wind chimes be heard from here, Andrew?"

Andrew answered tersely, "No."

"It's a Magc spell," I informed them. Reaching for my
philter purse, I realized that it was gone, and I felt crippled.

"Philters won't help," grunted Andrew without looking at
me. "At the moment, we're only receiving a reminder that
there is no escape. The destruction born in Rit now spills
across the world."

Benedict's mood swung back to sorrow, as he murmured,
"You freed it, Andrew."

"Did you think that I could win every battle indefinitely?"
snapped Andrew.

"You defeated yourself," replied my brother calmly.

"Such is the nature of most defeats."

Frustrated by their endlessly cryptic talk of battles and defeats, I stopped walking and waited for the pair of them to
notice. Benedict turned back to me almost immediately. He
frowned in concern.

Andrew paused only long enough to remark, "Tell her
what you wish, Ben. She's too embroiled now to escape by
innocence. Prince Hiroshi wants to meet her, after you've
shown her to Tiare House." The chimes followed Andrew,
fading as his muscular frame disappeared among the trees.

The air felt thick with moisture, scented by the heady
sweetness of the flowers. Standing still among the thick tangle of growth, where the breeze from the ocean did not
reach, the heat became oppressive. I unfastened the top button of my linen shirt, but the fabric still clung uncomfor-
tably.

"We can talk at the house," offered Benedict. "It's not
much farther."

"Where has Andrew gone?"

Benedict sighed, "To wrestle with demons."

"Ben," I grumbled, "I am so tired of clever answers that
tell me nothing."

"Perhaps you're hearing what you expect to instead of listening to what is said. You must open your mind and heart to grow, Marita. Change is seldom easy, but truth overtakes us all eventually."

At that moment, trying to coax sense out of my brother seemed like an impossible undertaking. I could follow even Andrew's rapidly darting trains-of-thought more easily, because Andrew's logic, however ruthless, remained generally cohesive. "You were cheerfulness incarnate a few minutes ago, and now you're gloomier than ever. Are you glad to have been rescued from execution, or do you hate me for my part in freeing you? How long have I been bespelled or otherwise blinded to the world? What Mage haunts Andrew?"

Benedict responded in crisp sequence to all three of my questions: "I accept the Intercessor's will. Two weeks. I shall try to explain, but let us go to Tiare House, where we shall be more comfortable."

"I don't have the energy to understand you, Ben. Lead me where you wish, or leave me here. Give me rational explanations, or grant me the dignity of honest isolation from your secrets."

Benedict took me by the elbow and coaxed me forward in gentle silence. After a few minutes, we emerged into a small, flower-encircled clearing beside the river. Before us stood a hexagonal plastiglass house, similar in design to the tree-supported structure we had seen from the bay. The glass was smoky, concealing the interior. Blossoming vines covered the entire roof and dangled from it like living garlands. The star-shaped ivory flowers emitted an intoxicating perfume. Stone steps led down to the river, where the water turned a wooden wheel, connected by mysterious shifting pipes to the base of the house.

"This is Tiare House," said Benedict. "Anavai designed it for me, but I usually stay at the chapel. The house is yours, if you like, for as long as you wish." He slid aside the door and gestured for me to enter.

The interior was cool and fresh, surprisingly unlike the usual compromise between stagnant heat and stale air-conditioning. An oval pond occupied the center of the room, its midnight-blue water clear and rippling. The plastiglass walls and ceiling seemed entirely transparent from here, giving the impression that the blossoming vines floated overhead. The simple furnishings consisted of a few low tables and cushions colored like variegated leaves. The floor was made of polished black stone.

Benedict gave me a cursory tour. Translucent celadon screens divided the house into four segments, none of which was large, but the design conveyed an overall impression of spaciousness. Only the living room and one bedroom contained any significant furnishings. The house, surrounded by a flowering jungle, resembled a fabulous garden more than a human dwelling.

"It's lovely," I acknowledged. "Mage Andrew treats his prisoners well."

"We are not prisoners," countered Benedict mildly, "and Andrew is not a Mage." My brother displayed the most consistency when his rationality seemed most questionable. He seated himself amid the cushions beside the inviting pool, removed his sandals, and dangled his feet in the water.

I joined him quietly, resisting the temptation to argue. I had learned little by demanding answers. As a child, Benedict had always worked best without pressure. I would let him speak freely, and I would try to withhold judgment. By the architect's design or by the island's natural beauty, there was a peacefulness at work in this place.

Benedict swung his scarred legs with childlike energy, but he bowed his fair head like an old man. "When Aroha renounced Mysticism," said my brother with solemn care, "he took the name Andrew after his father, an outspokenly independent man who disapproved equally of Mystics and Affirmists. It was Aroha's way of conceding to his father's belief in the inadequacy of both official philosophies, though the reconciliation came several years after his father's death. *Aroha* was the Mastermage of Purotu. *Andrew* is neither Mage nor Mystic."

"The man who calls himself Andrew wears scarab marks, and he wields scarab spells."

Without raising his head, Benedict frowned. "Aroha has revived and is resuming dominance."

"Being a Mage is not a crime."

"Not in itself," agreed Benedict, surprising me for once by expressing lawful tolerance instead of condemnation. "Aroha was always an extraordinary Mage. For him, there is no middle path. He is Andrew, who uses no magic, or he is Mastermage Aroha, whose magic is too vast to be controlled safely. I do not know if Andrew can subdue Aroha again.

Banishing a demon is hard, but letting it return makes the second battle infinitely more difficult." My brother glanced at me sidelong from blue eyes so like my own. "I fear that the worst elements of the Protectorate involved you for this purpose and have succeeded. The temptation to use such power as Aroha commands is strong, even without external pressure. How could Aroha remain passive, watching you fight an enemy greater than yourself with such an imbalance of Mystic naïveté and Affirmist knowledge to hamper you? Mastermage Aroha could not resist showing you how such battles *should* be fought, according to *his* Mystic training."

"Do not blame me for Andrew's 'lapse' into old habits," I protested, having already accepted more guilt than my conscience could handle. "I asked for his help to free you, but he had already used Mage spells to escape Talitha and Toby."

Benedict stirred the pond with his finger. "Andrew used his spells to rescue Cris after a Mage of your School trapped the boy—with your assistance." I began to protest again, but Benedict shook his head. "I know that you acted unwittingly, Marita. Andrew knows it also, but he blames himself for failing to protect Cris from such a simple Mage trick. In retaliation, I'm afraid Andrew yielded to the combined pressures of pride, anger, and a desire to impress an attractive ten-lotus Mage of Avalon, whose father was a Dom. The Protectorate set the trap against him cunningly. Aroha's spells provided a pyrrhic victory, because such methods serve our enemy."

"What Mage trapped Cris?" I asked hollowly, grasping at the claim that troubled me most, because I understood it best.

"Do not be angry at her," said my brother before answering. "She was weak, and her Mastermage used her, as the enemy uses him. Lar had placed her in Cris' path months before you met the boy. Andrew says that Lar originated the idea of obtaining the disastrous love philters from you."

I interrupted, "How long were you and Andrew in Rit?"

"Almost a year," replied Benedict. "For several months, I accepted Andrew's advice and avoided attention, but I needed to share the Intercessor's Word." He continued smoothly, "Lar used a blood sacrifice to weaken Cris' resistance to the idea of approaching you. When the boy tried to use your philters, he made himself vulnerable, because he was defying his own conscience." Benedict washed both his hands in the swirling pool, as if to cleanse himself of the crimes of others. "The enemy works through guilt and weakness. The enemy reached Cris, and the enemy reached Andrew, because both of them betrayed themselves." Almost as an afterthought, Benedict added, "Cris called her Lillie, but I believe you know her as Lilith. She is not a cruel young woman, but she is terribly weak. Lar used her hatred of Affirmists to prevent her from confiding in you, a member of the Family."

"Did Andrew tell you this fable?" I demanded. Benedict's description fit Lilith well, but I did not want to believe the rest.

"He told me the facts as he knows them. Andrew does not lie to me. He cannot deceive those whom the Intercessor guides."

I will not believe that Lilith could betray her own Mage sister, I cried inwardly, but I could not stop myself from remembering those few, terrible days last Fepuara. Lilith's controversial layout of the Avalon cards had warned me about the Sable Prince, whom Andrew would not name to me: not Prince Hiroshi—Andrew spoke freely enough of *him*—but a powerful opposing force that wielded a scarlet Kinebahan spell. Did Lilith spread her Mage cards in a coward's obscure effort to rationalize her duplicity? Or was it another of those abortive attacks, compounding fear? It was Lilith who had faded—or retreated—from the Mage battle waged against our circle; we had believed her claim of injuries, though neither Janine nor I had been able to identify specific damage. It was Lilith who had kept Janine, my strongest ally, away from the confrontation with Andrew and the dreadful aftermath. If Janine instead of Kurt had accompanied me, perhaps no Avalon Mage would have died. I asked in a whisper, "Who is this all-powerful 'enemy'?"

"Her name is Ch'ango. She was the Mastermage of Rit before Lar," Benedict replied.

"Ch'ango retired years ago," I countered, but every Mage mark on my arms had turned cold, confronting a terrible truth.

"She developed ambitions beyond the position of Mastermage. Lar serves her, as do many others, including Uncle Toby in his own indirect fashion. Unintentionally, Talitha serves her also because Talitha serves the Protectorate, which Ch'ango actually leads. Talitha considers Ch'ango simply a fellow Protector, 'nobly' devoted to the extermination of Empire technology."

"There was a Protectorate with that goal after the Great War."

Benedict nodded. "And similar Protectorates have arisen to meet each challenge to the World Parliament's social contract. Mage Ch'ango created the latest Protectorate as an artifice to eliminate her only serious rival."

"Andrew?" I asked, wishing that I could dismiss Benedict's claims as madness.

"Mastermage Aroha," corrected Benedict. "There is much more to that rivalry than anyone but Ch'ango or Andrew can explain to you, but I can tell you what Ch'ango fails to recognize: Prince Hiroshi is the rival that Ch'ango *should* fear, though she does not understand him or his cause. She does not see that Hiroshi succeeds because, unlike most of his predecessors, he wants to share his knowledge, and our society needs that knowledge desperately. Andrew is simply Hiroshi's champion, and Hiroshi's cause will outlast us all, Intercessor willing." Benedict climbed to his feet. "We should go to meet Hiroshi before the rains start."

I looked forlornly at my short-sleeved shirt and pants. My rumpled state seemed inadequate for a meeting with a prince, even if his royal line had been condemned for centuries. The inability to do something as trivial as change my clothes made me feel like curling into a huddle of despair. Such small concerns grow overwhelming, when magnified by the vastness of problems beyond reach or hope. I pushed helplessly at the lizard bracelet that Andrew had clasped around my arm. I could barely shift it.

I followed my brother at a leaden pace, weighted by my discouragement. He did not try to hurry me, and he had apparently told me all that he intended to say. He hummed a joyous praise-song, as we walked along the path beside the river, climbing gradually up the mountain's broad base.

We passed several homes, all of similar construction. Some were designed around individual trees. One seemed to merge with a low waterfall, another with a grotto that delved into a cliff. We encountered no people, until we came to an isolated building larger and more conventionally boxy than the rest.

"This is Hiroshi's research center," said Benedict, and he led me inside.

The interior was as bright as the sunlit beaches, although trees shaded the plastiglass building and I could not locate the source of light. The room contained a myriad of silver consoles, their appearance not unlike E-units bereft of their upper enclosures. The room would have horrified any member of the Scribes' Guild. Unconcealed books, bound in crisp, new paper or ancient leather, filled rows of tall shelves, and tables were spread with fresh documents covered with annotated diagrams.

Half a dozen persons worked diligently at the consoles and desks, giving us no more notice than a distracted glance. Few pale, neutral colors garbed the employees here. Every shirt and pareu was bright with a flowering pattern of large or small dimensions.

An exceptionally pretty Polynesian woman, her black hair pinned neatly atop her head, looked up at us and smiled. Her face and tiny, slender figure belonged to youth, but her eyes had a depth of wisdom that seemed much older. She wore a yellow-flowered pareu, tucked and knotted to fit her smoothly. Creamy seed pearls hung in strands around her neck.

She arose, elegant and dignified in her motions. She shook my hand firmly, though I had not offered it for her grasp. "My name is Anavai," she said crisply. "You must be Marita. Your brother has always spoken highly of you. I am so glad you have joined us."

I could not give a cynical reply about the reason for my coming. Anavai's welcome seemed too genuine. I answered simply, "Thank you."

Anavai nodded and took me by the arm, as if we were old friends. "My husband is in the back room with Andrew. We'll try to interrupt them, although it's never easy to get their attention when the two of them are together. They become even worse when Andrew's been away for any length of time. They are like children, consumed by the world of their imaginations."

She led me through the maze of furniture. I glanced behind me, seeking Benedict. "Your brother has gone to the chapel," explained Anavai, "to give thanks for his safe return to us."

Anavai's arms were bare of Mage marks, but I knew practicing seers who showed less indication of natural psi talents than Anavai. I reached instinctively for my philter purse. I felt helpless without it.

"I'll ask Andrew to return your purse to you," offered Anavai, "and I'll see that you receive new clothes. Andrew can be so single-minded about his work. He forgets about the trivial things that matter to the rest of us."

"He did not take my philter purse out of forgetfulness," I responded.

"No. He was concerned about you. He tends to be overly protective of all of us. We have forced him into that habit, I'm afraid. We do rely on him for our survival."

Anavai was so quietly matter-of-fact about her rebellious lifestyle. I had difficulty equating her with the Empire rulers of legend or the terrible revolutionaries of Talitha's descriptions. When we entered the back room and I saw the short, plain, and pensive man who was the dreaded Prince Hiroshi, I felt almost cheated. Hiroshi looked more like Benedict's round-faced porcelain figure than a man who had challenged the World Parliament for control of human destiny. Andrew was far more obviously impressive and intimidating than the man he served, and even Andrew appeared less threatening in this odd environment.

The two men, dressed alike in denim shirts and trousers, were huddled together over a table, strewn with bits of metal, plastic, and wire. Hiroshi held a plastiglass panel, dotted with silver and crossed with thin, colored lines. "It works just as the text scribed it," he was saying as we entered, "until I install it in the case. Look at it! Nothing protrudes. Nothing is exposed. What can be causing the interference?"

"If you can't locate the problem, Most Excellent Hiroshi," said Andrew, "I am not likely to succeed." Andrew was smiling, more relaxed than I had ever seen him. I understood the larger change after only a moment's Mystic sensing: Andrew regarded the man beside him as a superior. I had never expected to see Andrew defer to anyone.

"Your eyes are better than mine," answered Hiroshi, "even with my lenses to help me. Here, take it." He offered the panel to Andrew.

"You need to complete that diagnostic base, so you'll have a better method than my visual examination," replied Andrew. He reached for the panel, but he stopped suddenly and jerked his attention to Anavai and me. He became as alert and deadly as some coiled serpent from a Kinebahan legend.

Anavai remained composed. "Husband, this is Marita," she announced.

Hiroshi raised his solemn, smoothly lidded eyes to me. His smile was gentle, almost shy. He laid the panel carefully on the table and covered it with a silver paper. He wiped his hands on a snowy kerchief, taken from the pocket of his equally pristine shirt. He stood, and Andrew rose instantly beside him like a guardsman at attention. Andrew was a head taller than Hiroshi, but there could be no question that Hiroshi held the position of authority between them; Andrew would abide no such doubts.

"We are pleased to have you here, Mage Marita," said Hiroshi politely. His voice had a soft lilt. "I am sorry that the circumstances have been so difficult for you. I hope that we can make amends." He nodded to his wife. "Thank you for bringing her, Anavai. Please, forgive the interruption of your work."

"I share your gladness at her coming, husband," responded Anavai with odd formality. To me, she added, "I look forward to our next conversation, Marita." She bowed gracefully and left the room.

"Andrew will you please bring us tea in the garden?" asked Hiroshi mildly.

"Of course, Prince Hiroshi," replied Andrew, and he followed Anavai.

Hiroshi slid aside a plastiglass wall panel and beckoned to me. I would not have dared to argue with him. A man who could command Andrew with such calm assurance—and receive obedience—deserved a significant measure of respect.

We crossed the river via an arched bridge and climbed a stone stairway to a small plateau. The broken mountain's sheer, jagged sides towered over us, but we were high enough to have a view of much of the bay, as well as the shining ocean beyond it. The plateau seemed to hover between a froth of stormy clouds and hot sunlight. All of the rich blues, grays, and greens of water, sky, and jungle existed only to provide a serene backdrop for the simplicity of the plateau garden.

Hiroshi's garden consisted of three dwarf pine trees, a few strategically placed lava rocks, and a wide expanse of coral sand. Sections of the sand had been raked into rippling designs. Other areas were smooth. A pebbled pathway wound through the garden, ending at a volcanic glass bench where Hiroshi stopped.

"This garden is my sanctuary," said Hiroshi, his manner at once formal and familiar. With no pomp or self-acclaim, he made his status clear. Whatever the World Parliament—and my family—might decree, Hiroshi accepted himself as a royal prince of a worldwide Empire.

I was raised among the most powerful leaders of our world. I would not allow myself to feel inferior to Andrew's rebel prince. "Doesn't the rain disturb the sand patterns?"

"The patterns are not intended to be permanent. They must be appreciated like a single flower, perfect in its moment."

I admitted, "Flowers are uncommon in Rit."

"Because no one has chosen to reintroduce appropriate species. Most of this island was desolate until we came here and cultivated it intelligently."

"You do sound like Andrew."

"He has learned to share my vision." Hiroshi knelt at the edge of the sand and removed a curled leaf that had blown onto the garden. "You disapprove of us, because you do not understand the importance of what we are trying to achieve. The Empires built well. They did not build for eternity. We have already lost most of what they knew, and our society despises the 'fixers' who remember best. We still have time to recover, but if we wait much longer, there will be too few human survivors to reestablish any form of organized industry. The Empire factories and devices are failing, and the Doms and Mastermages are doing nothing to prevent the coming disaster."

Hiroshi managed to impress without intimidating. I felt free to talk openly and honestly, as I had not felt since Kurt's death, possibly because I had already lost almost everything I valued. "Do you intend to rule in the place of the World Parliament?" I asked with a forthrightness that would have horrified me a few months ago.

"That is not my intention, but if I must rule in order to restore sanity, I shall accept the responsibility. My ancestors did contribute to the downfall of the great civilization that they helped create. I would like to redeem some of their honor."

"The Hangseng and Nikkei dynasties destroyed most of the Earth through their rivalry."

Hiroshi did not deny my accusation. "Their greatest crime was the means by which they held power," said Hiroshi solemnly. "They monopolized knowledge. The subject cultures shared the blame, for they did not think that knowledge was worth defending."

"Knowledge has not disappeared from society."

"Science has virtually disappeared, except for a few fixer techniques and the misunderstood chemistry practiced by the Mages. Mathematics is reduced to the arithmetic of monetary exchanges. The ability to read and write is the legal privilege only of the Scribes' Guild members, and they use their skills nonproductively in the service of political intrigue. Art is practiced in guilty secrecy. Of history, our children are taught only to hate the past and to exploit its remnants. Geography consists of knowing which automated craft will travel to a desired destination."

A raindrop trickled across my face. Hiroshi's reasonableness disturbed me because it seemed inarguable. There were sound reasons for the laws that proscribed the use or teaching of Empire knowledge, but Hiroshi seemed to have erased my ability to argue intelligently. I made a weak attempt, "I did not choose to come here. You may have some ideas worth considering, but I do not like your methods of recruiting supporters."

"Andrew becomes overly zealous at times, especially when Mage Ch'ango presses him. As I understand it, however, you did agree to come here in exchange for a comparable service from him." Hiroshi raised his eyes to the sky. "The rain is beginning early today. We shall have our tea inside the pavilion."

He led me back down the stairs, but we turned away from the river instead of returning to the research center. A short distance into the trees, we came upon the pavilion, a latticework of tightly woven palm fronds and living vines. It was an open-sided structure with a single low table on a white mat. Andrew sat on a plaited mat at one side of the table, pouring tea from a white porcelain pot into each of three clear cups.

Hiroshi seated himself beside Andrew. As I took my place opposite Hiroshi, the rain began to flood from the sky in torrents. Not a drop entered the pavilion.

As Andrew placed a cup in my hand, he quirked one eloquent brow, his expression a tantalizing mix of wry amusement and challenge. He seemed freed of the tension that had met my arrival in Hiroshi's office. If I had sensed such a change in a client, I would have concluded that a critical decision had occurred in the past few minutes. With Andrew, I was not sure that common perceptions applied. "Did you wrestle your demons successfully?" I asked him.

Andrew did not reply because Hiroshi condemned my inquiry, "We do not speak of such matters at tea."

Andrew gave me an odd half smile, maintaining solemnity with the side of his face that Hiroshi could see. "The tea is jasmine," said Andrew, and launched into a dissertation on the history of tea, the cultivation of diverse herbs for infusion, and the optimum methods of blending new buds with aromatic oils. Into each pause that Andrew made, Hiroshi wove some piece of lore regarding the formal tea ceremonies of his own ancestors. Between them, they wasted not an instant on silence. I could not have interjected a comment if I had known anything pertinent to contribute.

Their rapid voices united with the rain to lull me into a dreamy state. The teacup in my hands became my focal point, the jasmine fragrance carrying me like a Mage's incense. I knew that I was drifting into a vision, but I felt confident that I could break it with a thought.

I had performed no true seekings since Benedict's arrest. This place and moment seemed to demand such magic. The tea and talk stimulated and soothed at once. If Andrew wove a spell to inspire me, he performed it so skillfully that I could sense nothing but my own new peace. Reaching outward from myself, I felt such warmth of camaraderie and understanding between Andrew and Hiroshi, I wanted only to be part of what they shared. My anger against Andrew dissolved into wistfulness.

Hounds, the symbols of certainty and continuity, bounded gracefully through my mind, but these Hounds wore none of the neutral shades of their card images. Their colors belonged to all the Mage Schools, intermingled with sapphire and violet. In the oldest Avalon tradition, such deep, clear blue represented the Empires. A single Cat traveled side-by-side with the Hounds, and its colors were silver and gold.

As it transpired, my vision seemed clear and rich and important, but it resembled an elusive dream too closely to be grasped. It faded utterly as Andrew and Prince Hiroshi let their dialogue lapse into silence. By the time Hiroshi arose, signifying the end of the tea service, the rain had stopped. Andrew gathered the dishes into a woven palm basket.

During that hour in Hiroshi's pavilion, my sense of isolation began to fade. When I let Talitha and Toby use me against my brother, I had lost my meager self-respect. When I entered Benedict's prison, I had abandoned family, home, friends, and hope. I could not recall the days that had actually elapsed since leaving Rit, but my seeking vision had inspired a healing worthy of years. I did retain enough self-doubt to ponder the level of Andrew's meddling, but I cherished no resentment. I had been too effectively entranced.

My feelings toward both Andrew and his Prince had undergone a softening process. Despite the vast differences between the two men in outward manner and appearance, they spoke with a single voice. Their thoughts meshed nearly as easily as those of psychic twins. Beneath his serene, civilized demeanor, Hiroshi admired Andrew's roguery, and Andrew believed as passionately in his cause as the Nikkei Prince did.

They were even more dangerous than Talitha imagined. Together, they could make anyone feel inferior, while conveying the impression that the observer had only to ask to be raised to their level. They flaunted their cherished knowledge with absolute delight. They made it almost irresistible.

Sensitivity to external influence is the gift and curse of the Mage's crescents that I wear. Abetted (as I suspected even at the time) by a philter in the tea, my susceptibility made me helpless. An afternoon with Prince Hiroshi and Andrew left me feeling that all of my precepts of social correctness were founded on sand, as impermanent as Hiroshi's garden and significantly less beautiful. As soon as we left the pavilion, I returned to myself enough to remember my own vulnerability. I might have gone to Talitha, if she had been accessible, to seek a balancing perspective.

Solitude was a poor second choice, but even that was denied to me. When Hiroshi and Andrew finished with me for the afternoon, they returned me to Anavai. She took me from house to house, introducing me to the people of Hiroshi's community by describing their individual contributions to the unified vision. I met at least twenty children, a surprisingly large number for a small, predominately male community. All of the children charmed me, even as I tried to keep myself detached from them.

Many of the adults worked in the factories, producing the goods that Andrew sold in his privateering. Others practiced independent trades for local use, openly utilizing Empire techniques to enhance their crafts. Many of them admitted their origins as fixers. None of them displayed any shame about their fixer status or their descent into lawless professions, although several seemed suspicious of me and my Mage marks. I met no one whose arms wore so much as a single lotus.

Anavai did not allow anyone to treat me unkindly. To those who seemed reluctant to welcome me, she made her displeasure clear in her gentle, dignified way. She introduced me as the new teacher, a title that seemed to command respect from even the most recalcitrant citizens.

Prince Hiroshi's community was no utopian ideal. Many of the people were little better educated than the citizens of Rit, though they all studied according to a regular schedule when they were not working at their chosen labors. Anavai's architectural designs were beautiful, but these people had no supply units to feed or clothe them, no E-units to entertain them. They worked to survive, as much as to fulfill their leader's vision. The men outnumbered the women by a factor of five, and Hiroshi's peculiar insistence on monogamous relationships struck me as a sure means of creating interpersonal tensions. Nonetheless, the people of Hiroshi's island were a community, united by their goals.

When the stars blazed in the darkness, Anavai led me to a sandy beach lit by yellow paper lanterns, scented with a protective Mage smoke that I attributed to Andrew. The water of the bay mirrored the lights, and insects danced across the reflections, never approaching the Mage-defended light spheres of the lanterns. Over a hundred people gathered on that beach, spreading their individually patterned blankets across the sand. Both Hiroshi and Andrew moved constantly among the various small groups. I could hear many welcomes given to Andrew.

I sat with Anavai and a shy man named Evien, who was introduced to me as the community's physician. Evien looked enough like Kurt to dispel some of the insidious

charm of Hiroshi's community, but I could not hold long to
bitter memory. Anavai coaxed me to talk of Rit.

We shared a communal supper of broiled fish and fresh
vegetables, a meal that all of my family's wealth could not
have provided. Two young men, a talented guitarist of mixed
ethnicity and a handsome African with a magnificent singing
voice, performed during the supper. We ended the evening
with a formal blessing, pronounced by my brother to a surprisingly receptive audience.

The people gathered their woven blankets and cleaned up
every trace of their joint supper from the beach. Groups began to disperse, vanishing into the trees and darkness. Benedict left before I could speak to him. Anavai bade me good
night and disappeared with her husband, leaving me with
Evien as my guide back to Tiare House.

The physician might look like Kurt, but the resemblance
did not extend to personality. I could not imagine Evien
teasing, joking, or wielding a Mage spell. However, Evien
was courteous, kind, and eager to please. He seemed intelligent, but he did not display his superiority like Andrew and
Hiroshi. He said little, leaving me to fill an uncomfortable
void with mindless chatter about the supper. After dealing
with so many dominating personalities, Evien seemed childlike. Part of me relaxed because I finally felt in control of
my immediate situation. Part of me longed to reach Tiare
House and see Evien leave.

I did not fault Evien for the awkward aspect of his company. Anavai had made it clear that one of her many roles in
the community included matchmaking. She had informed me
that her husband expected the community's relatively few
women to choose husbands and contribute to the expansion
of Hiroshi's supporters. She had introduced me proudly to
her own son, a six-year-old who looked astonishingly like
his father.

I might admire aspects of Hiroshi's community, but I did
not plan to become accepted as a part of it, either now or
later. I certainly did not intend to select a husband to satisfy
the island's leader. If I *had* wanted a husband, Evien would
not have been my choice.

Evien left me to enter Tiare House alone. I waited at the
threshold until he had gone. I had no philters left, but I was
still a Mage. I might be indentured, but I was not owned.

I raised my arms to the white moon. My silver crescents

grew warm, and the lotus marks glowed even beneath Andrew's relentless bracelet. I reached toward Janine, but I could not find a sense of her or any Avalon Mage. Deliberately, I wept for Rit and all the damage that I had done to my family and friends on behalf of a brother I no longer knew. I had made a long journey, and I might not return, but I could send what power I had to those I had left behind me.

The sound of distant surf could have belonged to my home. I let my spell fade. I turned to enter the house where I would dwell for now.

The pool of water glowed from lights beneath its surface. The rest of the house was dark. I grumbled to myself about my brother's impracticality. I presumed that the house contained basic living supplies, but Benedict had shown me nothing of the sort. The erratic light of the central pool was artistic but not particularly useful for rummaging through a strange house.

I nearly tripped over Andrew before I realized that he was present, lounging against a stack of cushions near the door. In the watery light from the pool, I could see little more than a faint gleam of the gold that again covered his arms. That limited view sufficed. The serenity of my moon greeting abandoned me. I mumbled nervously, "Please, go. I cannot handle a private conversation with you tonight."

"I brought you a parcel from Anavai," said Andrew, ignoring my remark. "It's on the bed in the next room."

"Thank you." When Andrew did not move, I regretted that I had not invited Evien to stay. I had an idea that finding me with another man might have flustered even Andrew. He deserved to have his ego slapped, making himself so at home in the house that had purportedly been offered for my personal use.

"At Anavai's request," he informed me, "I have returned your philter purse. However, I must insist that you refrain from using it until we have discussed our current situation. Even your little spell session a few minutes ago was injudicious and should not be repeated."

I had not wanted an argument, but Andrew did not intend to let me avoid it. "If I am to be a member of this community," I demanded, "does my allegiance belong to Prince Hiroshi or to you?"

"Effectively, Prince Hiroshi is your Dom, and I am your

Mastermage. Obey him in secular matters. Obey me where magic is concerned."

"I promise not to use any more spells tonight. I assume you know how to find me in the morning."

"I'm leaving in the morning."

The idea that Andrew would not remain on Hiroshi's island stunned me, although I should have realized that his privateering was more than a temporary phase. In many ways, Andrew seemed like the bane of my life, but he was my only sane contact with Rit and the world beyond this insular community of lawlessness. Benedict was totally undependable.

"Where are you going?" I asked, as if I had a right to expect an answer.

"To confront a demon."

I groaned and clenched my hands into fists of frustration, "Couldn't you give me a simple, direct response?"

"If you want to understand my answers, invest some time and effort in learning how to interpret them. Stop worrying so much about whether I'm corrupting you with Empire knowledge."

His peremptory attitude annoyed me. I shook my right arm, which wore his inescapable lizard bracelet. "Stop trying to convert me. I already conceded to you. At the moment, I am exhausted, and I intend to sleep for a week. If you want to tell me something, write me a letter. We're both literate."

"Stop babbling and sit down," ordered Andrew. He grabbed my arm and pulled me onto the feathery cushions beside him. "Listen to me, Marita. I am not and never have been your enemy. Benedict told me about you and your abilities years ago, but I did not travel to Rit with any intention of exploiting you. I share your distress over the events that terminated my stay in Rit, as my reprehensible temper this morning probably demonstrated."

"You gave a poor introduction to your prince's cause."

"I trust that your intelligence will enable you to judge Prince Hiroshi's cause irrespective of my limitations. I am not a particularly honorable man, Marita, as I am the first to admit. I do, however, have sense enough to recognize reality. The entire Mystic/Affirmist social contract is a sham built by the World Parliament's egotists, deluding themselves that their 'government' matters to a passive society of E-unit addicts. We live off the past, more truly enslaved to the Empires than our ancestors were. Unless a substantial percentage of humanity reeducates itself as Prince Hiroshi proposes, our society is doomed. I do not like the escalation of war that occurred in Rit, nor do I rejoice at making you a reluctant recruit, but I intend to adapt to circumstances that were inflicted on us both. It is time that you did the same."

As always, when he exerted the effort, Andrew was persuasive. His proximity did not make the situation any easier. The faint aroma of Mage incense from his skin had a dizzying effect. "Give me clear explanations, Mage Andrew, and I will listen to you."

He complied with terrible precision, "You were attacked in Rit. Your friend died. Talitha interceded to spare you, but she has never been as influential in the Protectorate as she thinks she is. You owe your life to me, to Prince Hiroshi's ingenuity, and to Lar's private conflicts about you. By freeing Benedict, you humiliated Lar, which is an offense that he will not forgive. Lar's hesitation no longer protects you, and I cannot continue to shield you except by telling you something of what you face."

"Ch'ango?" I asked, shaken by his urgent words and by his means of emphasizing them. He had opened himself, and for the first time I could sense him clearly as a Mage. I had never sensed anyone more powerfully in my life.

Andrew gave an oblique confirmation, speaking even more quickly than usual. "Benedict understands the personalities, but he takes little interest in the methods or the reasons. When Prince Hiroshi first approached the World Parliament, I was the only member to support him openly. I was not the only Mastermage to listen to him privately. Ch'ango went to Prince Hiroshi in secret and learned from him by pretending to be torn by an internal debate regarding his cause. Prince Hiroshi tends toward idealism, and he has had little firsthand experience with the type of treachery that your average Tathagatan would recognize instantly. By the time Prince Hiroshi realized that Ch'ango had ulterior motives, she had acquired most of what she sought. She had deceived him into reading for her a few words of a Mystic scroll. Those words sufficed to enable her to interpret an ancient Lung-Wang manuscript that described the method of creating Mage marks."

The ramifications of his words penetrated slowly, but I did

not hesitate to argue, "Any apprentice Mystic learns to make a lotus." I felt a little smug, pleased that I had matched Andrew's accelerated pace well enough to reply at all.

"I don't mean the process of applying the silver film that binds to the nervous system. Ch'ango's manuscript shows how to create and modify the film. It also depicts the techniques of designing a mark to convey a particular power." He paused, and I frowned, beginning to understand. "Many of us have the capability of using more powerful marks than scarabs, but we have never had the option to tackle anything stronger. Ch'ango has created her own Mage marks, which enable her to wield spells that cannot be countered by any less-marked Mage. To hide her unique marks, she lives in seclusion, manipulating from afar." Andrew extended his own gold-plated arm. "She does not hide her marks in denial of them but in defense. Seeing the shape and placement of her marks, another Mage could duplicate them."

"If she has made herself so powerful, why hasn't she defeated all of her rivals already?"

"She still hungers for the knowledge that Prince Hiroshi did not give her."

He barely paused, but my laggardly thoughts managed to catch up to his conversation. "And that is the knowledge that you are trying to disseminate to the world?" I asked, horrified by the plausibility of Andrew's accusations. They seemed to justify all of the traditional injunctions against Empire science.

"No. I don't think either Prince Hiroshi or I have what Ch'ango wants, but we're still alive because she's not sure what we know, and we're not sure what she thinks she needs from us."

He had appeased my conscience slightly, but he was creating grim questions faster than comforting answers. "Where does that leave the rest of us?"

"Ch'ango's powers are not infinite. She often uses Lar as a relay. She also uses Affirmists like Talitha and Dom Toby because she can't directly reach someone who has never worn Mage marks. Ch'ango's remote spells cannot exceed the capacity of the recipient." His fingers brushed my right arm's triangular array of Mage marks. "Lar did you no favors by granting you an eleventh lotus set, though the eleventh pair is hardly more than a preparation for twelve. Be glad he didn't inflict you with scarabs."

"I don't have the natural ability to wear scarabs."

Andrew's laughter contradicted me. "You have trusted the judgment of envious Mages who dread the thought of a scarab-marked member of the Family. Dear, naive Marita, you have abundant ability. I could give you twelve lotus marks, shells, and scarabs now, if I wanted to subject you to that burden." His touch alit briefly on one of my crescents. "A ten-lotus Mage with crescents has the potential to create a few strong illusions, but the actual destructive ability is small. As your capabilities have increased, so has your vulnerability."

"Even illusions can destroy," I said slowly.

"Yes. They killed your friend, Kurt." My eyes stung. Andrew added with unexpected gentleness, "You have no reason to feel guilty about his death."

Denying tears, I grumbled, "How do you know what I feel?"

"I have not exploited my psi skills to delve into your soul, if that's what worries you. I have merely observed you and drawn the obvious conclusions. I know enough Empire science to adopt existing technology for my own purposes. Every major empire city had a widespread network of surveillance monitors."

"You've used your vaunted science to spy on me?" I demanded, snatching at indignation to combat an embarrassment of grief.

"Isn't that less invasive than observing you by Mystic methods?"

"I do not suppose that courtesy motivated you."

This laugh came softly, an inexpressibly warm sound that made me glad to hear it and doubly glad that Evien *had* left. "You malign me, Mage Marita."

"With the truth?"

"I confess my ulterior motives." The humor lingered enticingly in his voice, but it ebbed as he continued, "I avoid the active use of Mage spells because every spell provides another possible route for Ch'ango, as well as contributing to her education about the mingling of Mysticism and Empire science. I'd advise you to exercise similar caution. You rely heavily on Mystical alchemy, most of which is relatively harmless with respect to Ch'ango's remote efforts. However, until you know how to distinguish chemistry from susceptible magic, please take no chances. I'll teach you if I have the opportunity."

"Do you ever stay in one place long enough to teach anything?"

"Occasionally. When I'm not replenishing Prince Hiroshi's finances, distributing his products and ideas, or chasing prophecies."

"Which is your current reason?"

"None of the above. I'm paying for my sins, as Benedict would say. Ch'ango had lost of track of me while I abstained from magic, and I had dodged mundane searches for several years. I became . . ." He smiled self-mockingly before completing the sentence. ". . . careless in Rit. So far, Ch'ango hasn't reached me with anything but the chimes, and that's a scarab spell that I can counter with moderate effort. However, she *will* reach me—dangerously. Until I've reassembled some better self-protection, I don't want to be near anyone or anything I value." His fingers traveled to my cheek and curled around my chin. "That's why I'm leaving here in the morning."

He might have feigned the regret in his voice, but I did not imagine the responsive shivering of my Mage marks. "If you stay away too long," I murmured, "Anavai will have me married to her pet physician."

"Evien is a good man. He's fine genetic stock, and that is what interests Anavai."

"Is it legal to marry one man, when I'm indentured to another?"

"I don't own your personal life."

"Do I still have one?"

In reply, he kissed my throat. "If I stay here much longer, I won't choose to leave in the morning," he whispered, "and that course would jeopardize us both."

"I don't know how to deal with you, Andrew. I don't know if you're the worst thing that's ever happened to me or the best."

He repeated the kiss. "If Anavai tries to match you with Evien or anyone else, tell her you're previously committed."

"Am I?"

"It's your choice. I made mine."

"I'll bear that in mind." He could have persuaded me to decide anything at that point. Instead, he rolled to his feet and trotted into the night, whistling.

Andrew

8 Me, 510

Most Excellent Hiroshi,

I expect to leave before dawn, so I shall not see you until I return. I shall make the deliveries, as we discussed. Beyond that, I do not know where I shall go, but it will be an isolated place, possibly near the Deadlands. I doubt that I will communicate with you for some time, unless our enemy alters my plans.

Why do I cling to that vague term, "our enemy"? I have relied so long on secretiveness that it has become instinctive in me. We both know our enemy's name. All the world will know her soon.

Inevitably, I must face Ch'ango, or she will continue to undermine all of our progress. If I had not used Mage skills in Rit, I would have revealed myself to her eventually by some other slip of pride or need. Do not blame Benedict or Marita. He was only obeying his faith, and she only tried to save him as best she could in her ignorance. If Marita tempts me, it is my weakness and not hers.

I shall keep Ch'ango from you, even if I must storm her Tathagata citadel and steal her own twisted magic. I am the prize she covets most because she thinks that I can give her all the rest of what she desires. We must be grateful that she still does not appreciate your talents fully. Scribe Talitha has a better understanding, but she is blinded by her hatred of me. I fear that I have brought more pain than worth to your cause, my friend. All of us will pay for my sins if the Mages' Luck fails us again.

Ask Benedict and Anavai to continue praying for me. I do not understand their faith, but I respect its intent in Mystic terms. I need whatever help or good will I can amass, even if it is unearned. I am feeling very alone these days, and that is an unaccustomed and unwelcome sensation.

Those last three months in Rit took a toll on me. I nearly

lost Cris through my inattention to him. If Marita had not come to me, I do not know whether I would have tried to rescue Benedict. Either by saving him or allowing him to die, I would have given Ch'ango another victory over me. Waiting for the next attack has been hard, as Ch'ango undoubtedly realizes. She is tormenting me as much by her inaction as by her intermittent taunts.

I am honestly afraid of Ch'ango. I am afraid of what she might have made of me, if not for you and that unwise, unfortunate Tathagatan girl who bore me a mixie son. You have long advised me to stay away from Ch'ango, to be patient with the progress of your cause, and to let time defeat the Protectorate. I am not sure how long I can continue to comply with your advice. I want to be rid of this war. I want to be free to stay in one place, to walk through a city without searching every crowd for enemies, or to love a woman without worrying that she will become a blood sacrifice against me. I want to be free to tell the truth to those who matter to me.

It is late, I am tired. I apologize for my self-pitying mood. It is always hard for me to leave Ha'aparari. If I return again, I fear that it will only be to bring grief to one whom I would rather not hurt. Using people to my advantage, even those I value, is too much a part of how I survive.

I have annotated the roster of trusted privateers in the file. A few of our old contacts have become unreliable, and I have added a few names based on recent information. The network is reasonably solid with or without me to coordinate it.

Grow in wisdom,
A.

Marita

The people of Hiroshi's community did not need me to teach them. Most of my students already knew their letters and struggled only to master the sophisticated, antique texts that Hiroshi and Andrew had gathered. Andrew had acknowledged five fully literate teachers, excluding me—himself, Hiroshi, Anavai, Benedict, and a former Scribe named Doreena, whom I had not met—but Andrew defined literacy more stringently than the Scribes' Guild. According to other islanders, Hiroshi had commissioned at least thirty traveling teachers like my brother, all of whom visited the island with some regularity. By Andrew's standards, most of those teachers were pathetically under-educated, but I was told that he held an even more severe opinion of most official Scribes. Regarding other members of my family, especially those Doms who guarded their secret learning too well to ever employ it, Andrew (I was told) applied terms that ranged in nature from contemptuous to virulent.

The education of Hiroshi's people would continue with or without my participation. On that basis, I rationalized my position in the island community. It was also difficult for me to condemn these people, who seemed so diligent and productive, for wanting what I had been given as a birthright. I had broken so many laws by now and betrayed my family in so many respects, one more vow to my family could make little real difference to me. I spent most of each day at the school, a building much like the research center, and I did not complain.

If Benedict approved of my cooperation, he did not express his opinion to me. He taught his Intercessor's Holy Word, while I worked to enable the advanced students to read manuscripts that I could barely interpret myself. Benedict had drifted deeply into his serene form of madness. He was kind, but he maintained a remote, impersonal relationship with anyone who did not accept his Intercessor as divine. Benedict did not distinguish between me and any other disbelieving islander. He had a surprisingly large following on the island, and he devoted his time to them.

Benedict made no further references to his Rit imprisonment or to his prophecy. Each time we met, he invited me to attend his worship service. Each time I declined, he looked at me with pity and said no more. No aspect of Ha'aparari life made me more aware of my lonely state.

I had experienced loneliness long before my unlikely recruitment by an Empire Prince. Even in Rit, I had few real relationships. Whether bespelled or mad with panic, I *had* slain my best friend, Kurt. I was not sure that I wanted my isolation breached. At that point in my life, Ha'aparari suited me expressly because I did *not* fit.

Anavai acted as the ubiquitous organizer of island life. While Hiroshi worked toward the restoration of Empire knowledge on a global scale, Anavai ensured that Hiroshi's followers lived well in the present. She was architect, arbiter, and administrator of everything from marriages to evening meals. She was tireless, efficient, and mildly tyrannical. I admired her energy and talents, but I did not feel comfortable with her. She was too determined to organize me, especially with regard to the men she considered suitable for my consideration. I did not have the nerve to repeat Andrew's suggestion to her, even as a diversionary tactic.

The island was beautiful. The life was peaceful and comfortable. The people were as considerate as I could wish, although their standards of diligence exceeded those of the most arduous Mage School. Their island was a seductive paradise, but the islanders resisted its tempting offers. They were intolerant of laziness. They had worked too hard to establish their lovely home, and they would not rest until they had extended it across the world.

In many ways, I enjoyed Hiroshi's island and community, but I missed my dilapidated, imperfect Rit. I could not return to Rit now, even if the means presented itself, but I mourned what I had sacrificed. If Andrew had not left, or if Benedict had been more accessible, I might have felt differently.

I greeted each dawn alone and silent in front of Tiare House. I obeyed Andrew's advice and refrained from casting any active spells. Obedience was easy since none of Hiroshi's people wanted the services of a Mage. They certainly did not need my love philters with Anavai arranging their lives so efficiently. The only spell that might have benefitted me on a personal level would have been directed at Andrew, who was unavailable and undoubtedly capable of a counterspell.

When Andrew returned after an absence of more than a month, he did not come to see me. Irrationally, I felt disappointed. I heard of his arrival from my students, who reported that Andrew and Hiroshi had been conferring seriously for the past two days. My students did not express any surprise or concern over the lengthy meeting between their leaders. They did remark that Andrew had returned prematurely. They had expected him to remain absent for at least six months.

Evien, who was one of my students, confided to me that Andrew's actions never truly astonished the islanders, because Andrew made a point of being unpredictable. Only Evien seemed to realize that the news of Andrew's return had upset me. As Andrew had said, Evien was a good man. Evien did not make a similar claim about Andrew.

Within an hour after learning that Andrew had returned to Ha'aparari, my crescent marks had puckered and tightened the adjoining skin visibly. I could explain emotional uncertainty in regard to Andrew, but the sense conveyed by my Mage marks was more akin to a warning. Andrew had returned, and I knew that he had brought his battles with him.

As soon as I completed my last class of the day, I hurried to find Benedict. I had no clear idea of what to say to him. My compulsion to seek him was akin to a panicky rush to collect my dearest possession from a burning house.

The chapel refused to serve as focus for my imaginary catastrophe. The building represented one of Anavai's finest works. Three gnarled trees formed the only visible support for a structure that seemed to be composed of sheets of water. The actual construction material was a form of plastiglass invented by Hiroshi, but the illusion of liquidity was as perfect as a powerful Mage spell made permanent. Inside the chapel, three pillar lamps glowed like underwater fire. The floor was blue nacre. The mountain framed the chapel, the great waterfall visible in the distance.

I found Benedict kneeling on one of the blue silk prayer cushions. His gray robe was made of a lightweight fiber developed by the islanders, but it looked as bulky and mis-

placed as its woolen cousin. Benedict seemed immune to
such external concerns. He raised his head from his meditation and nodded at me. "It is as you perceive," he said.

"What do you mean, Ben?"

"Andrew has returned because the reprieve has ended. He
has come for you."

"For me?" I demanded although I felt the truth of what
my brother told me. It kindled my anxiety—and a restless
anticipation that was not altogether unpleasant. Whether
Benedict relied on his well-connected followers or an unorthodox application of psi skills, his sources of information
generally seemed to be reliable.

"I hoped that you would be safe here among us," he
sighed, "but you are too much like Andrew at his worst.
Both of you cling to your Mystic heresies, even when you
use no active magic. Andrew fuels the unhealthy dichotomy
between Mystics and non-Mystics by taking you with him."

"The dichotomy is real."

"It is as unnatural as your Mage marks. Ch'ango will
reach you through your Mystic misconceptions. Andrew understands to a limited extent, though he lacks the wisdom to
repent. At least he tries not to jeopardize those of us who
have resisted the Mystic course."

Trying to distinguish reason from my brother's personal
beliefs invariably frustrated me. His religion had become in-
separable from his perspective on every subject. He could
only be viewed as rational if one accepted the unique divin-
ity of his Intercessor.

I almost wished that I could share his faith, if only to regain the brother I still loved. Since I disbelieved, I tried to
draw my conclusions from the few hard facts that Benedict
offered. "What is Andrew discussing with Hiroshi?"

"Andrew proposes to go to Tathagata."

"To the Site of Parliament?"

"The Houses will soon convene to discuss a 'solution' to
Prince Hiroshi since the Protectorate's plan failed in Rit. Andrew wishes to be present. Hiroshi hesitates to take such a
risk. He fears that it is a trap set by Ch'ango."

"The risk would be Andrew's."

"An injury to Andrew hurts all of us." Benedict folded his
thin hands and stared at them. "Andrew proposes to con-
found Ch'ango by taking you with him. He intends to use
you to split her Protectorate."

"I thought he wanted me to teach the islanders."

"He would prefer to be a teacher here himself, but he recognizes when other obligations take precedence. He fights this war with swords of knowledge and cunning, and he will expect the same of you."

"I don't suppose he plans to ask for my opinion."

"Would you expect your Mastermage to consult you on a question of governance? If you cling to Mysticism, you have no right to complain about its laws."

"Andrew is not my Mastermage."

"Are you obedient to Lar?"

"No," I muttered.

"If you are a Mystic, you must be under the authority of a Mastermage. Do you renounce Mysticism?" asked Benedict, gesturing to the philter purse that I wore over a long, flowered green pareu.

"No," I grumbled. "Ben, stop haranguing me."

"I'm sorry that the truth upsets you," replied my brother with maddening calm. "I need to prepare for the evening service. I shall pray for you, Marita."

"Thanks," I answered curtly. Resigned to Benedict's obsession, I left the chapel. The day would end soon with the abruptness typical of equatorial latitudes, and supper would be served again on the beach to which Anavai had first taken me. Other groups of Hiroshi's people would gather on other beaches around the bay. I did not belong with any of them.

I began to follow the river path toward the mountain with a vague intention of locating the infamous factories. I had explored very little of the island although no one had curtailed my movements. I stopped after a few minutes, realizing that I was only likely to become lost in the darkness, long before reaching the factories. If I never saw the factories, the lack would not impair my life.

I started back toward Tiare House, but I changed my mind again. I turned aside near Hiroshi's research center and stood outside the building, contemplating it silently. I could see one worker still hunched at his desk. Andrew and Hiroshi might well be locked in debate in the back room, but I had already discovered that the windows of Hiroshi's office appeared opaque from the exterior. Even using my best spells and philters, I doubted my ability to detect Andrew without his cooperation. Any attempt to sense Hiroshi would probably gain me Andrew's attention in its most painful guise.

I did not leave until the solitary worker showed signs of imminent departure, which would lead to discovery of my futile watch. In the dark, I walked cautiously, although the paths between the buildings were relatively smooth and well-defined. The footing became more difficult near the bay, where the paths were deliberately hidden by jungle growth, but I had learned to follow the sound of singing to locate the beach gathering.

Anavai was not present. Her friendly domination often grated, but I had accustomed myself to it. I did not know any of the islanders well enough to feel comfortable about joining them uninvited. Evien smiled at me, but I did not want to raise his expectations. I returned the smile but declined to sit with him and his friends. I accepted my basket of fish, bread, and vegetables from the servers and took it to the farthest point of the beach.

I leaned against a rocky ledge, far enough from the lanterns to let me sit unnoticed. I scattered my own philter to repel the swarms of insects. I ate alone, listening to an ancient folk song about betrayed lovers. It was an unusually sad theme for these gatherings.

Hiroshi and Anavai arrived together after most of their people had finished eating. Both of them made their rounds of the groups. No one looked in my direction.

"We doomed ourselves to be outsiders in such a gathering," observed Andrew from the volcanic outcrop behind me, "when we accepted our first Mage marks." He jumped down to the sand beside me. He was dressed in neutral breeches and a gold vest like the one that he had worn in Rit. He extended his braceleted arms. "We can hide the marks and refuse to exercise them, but we cannot remove them."

"You never stay in one place long enough to become part of a community."

"*You* never become part of a community, even when you live within it." He sat next to me, taking the supper basket that I had laid aside. "Finished?" he asked.

"Yes."

He began to attack the dinner that I had barely touched. After several minutes, he returned to the subject of my earlier comment, "I lived at the Purotu Mage Center from my twelfth year to my twenty-third, and I was a member of Parliament for six years after that. I never planned to become a nomad, a privateer, or a revolutionary. I feel about Purotu as you feel about Rit: It's home. Unfortunately, it's no longer mine."

"Do you have a home?"

"I have a semi-permanent dwelling on the other side of the bay. It's more a home for my adopted sons than for me."

"Cris?"

"Among others. I collect mixies since no one else wants them. The girls are too fragile for travel, but I've gathered over a dozen boys. Prince Hiroshi and Benedict visit them periodically, but the boys tend to be shy of 'normals,' and they're well able to care for themselves in this benign climate. Cris was the best adjusted until your friend Lilith broke his limited faith. I doubt that he'll leave this island again."

"I'm sorry if I contributed to his pain."

Andrew shrugged. "Cris has survived better than most of Ch'ango's victims. He'll probably outlast me."

Andrew's quiet fatalism sent a dagger of pain through my heart. Such candor was not the form of intimacy I wanted from him, although it made me feel more tightly bound to him than any threat or physical enticement. "Has Ch'ango reached you?"

"She has come closer. She learns a little more about me each time she tries. She will reach me soon."

"What will you do?"

"If her contact leaves me capable of deciding for myself, I shall give her a choice: to leave me alone or to see her attacks against me rebound on Tathagata and the World Parliament. Ch'ango wants to establish herself as lone Empress, but she wants to rule the undemanding world that currently exists. To achieve that ambition, she still needs the help of the existing leadership. As a governing body, the Parliament is helpless and hopeless, but its members hold real economic power on an individual basis. The Doms control the factories, the Mastermages control the distribution of services, and seventy percent of the world's legal supplies originate in Tathagata's inland valleys. Destroy Tathagata without replacing the supply network, and what's left of civilization will disappear into chaos and famine faster than even Prince Hiroshi predicts."

"Ch'ango hasn't tried to reach me since I've been here."

"I think she has tried and succeeded. From the nature of

her attacks on me recently, I would guess that she has been studying you to learn about me. She does not always rely on such obvious spells as the scarlet tide that she stole from the Kinebahans. She is capable of great subtlety in her magic."

"She won't benefit from the little I know about you."

"You know enough." He laid the empty supper basket on the sand and turned toward me.

I fingered the knotted fabric of the pareu beneath my philter purse, but I was not planning any spells. The pareu was a perfectly practical item of clothing, but it seemed insecure with a man who affected me like Andrew. In the shadowy light, I could see Andrew smile at my fussing. I said stiffly, "Your former fellows in Parliament must know just as much about you as I do, or more."

"They knew the recklessly ambitious Mastermage Aroha, and that is why they continually misinterpret and mispredict my actions. They judge me by the past. At the risk of sounding like your brother, I have 'repented.' "

"Benedict says that you refuse to repent."

"He says the same about you, but you've laid aside a great many prejudices since I met you. Ben's judgment is remarkably astute, but it's not infallible."

"I don't think you and he share the same interpretation of penitence."

"I'm a heathen," he admitted, touching my Mage marks and evoking a decidedly carnal sensation. With a snap, he released the lizard bracelet. He performed no accompanying ritual for relinquishing his claim over my Mystic self, but the rush of freedom dizzied me. Andrew proceeded to stimulate reactions from my Mage marks that I had not known were possible.

"Are you bespelling me?" I asked, trying to remain lucid despite the provocative feel of Andrew's mouth and hands.

"I told you that I never found a need for love philters."

"That's not an answer."

"It's a matter of semantics, which I'm not inclined to debate at the moment."

The music from the supper gathering had stopped, but a stronger melody beat through me. I never did discover whether Andrew enhanced that night with Mage spells. I used every spell and philter in my repertoire to seal him to me. Andrew did not complain.

Gavilan

Scribe Talitha:

I have just been informed of your decision to accept an official post as record keeper for Parliament. I congratulate you although I confess that I am puzzled as to why you have reversed your original stance. While I realize that you and Dom Toby have been at odds since the unfortunate business in Rit, I did not expect you to resign from your position as his aide. You already had control of significant parliamentary records, and Dom Toby's status has long enhanced your own power. I cannot believe that he is pleased by your choice, since he relies on you heavily, although I can believe that he would sacrifice you for his own protection.

I shall be blunt: Were you pressured to resign because of the Rit fiasco? I have heard Mastermage Lar try to place the blame on you, but he is a notorious self-promoter with little credibility. Everyone knows that he is Ch'ango's pawn. Many Protectors will stand by you if you wish to denounce his lies.

Many of us share your distrust of Mastermage Ch'ango. We would be loath to see you yield control of the Protectorate to her and her extreme methods. I would rather see the Protectorate dissolved than obey that bloodthirsty witch. Personally, I fear her much more than Prince Hiroshi, who alarms me chiefly as a tool of Aroha's ambitions. When we formed the Protectorate, I did not expect it to become an instrument of violence. At least half of the membership now consists of women and men who joined from dread of the consequences of refusal. This is Ch'ango's work.

After Mastermage Lar and Dom Toby describe Aroha's actions in Rit, I am confident that Parliament will stop dithering and take formal action to thwart Aroha. Let the Parliament do its job, and let us do ours. We are Scribes, Talitha, and we understand the past better than those outside the

Guild. We must consider the possibility that Prince Hiroshi is right about the factory failures and the need to consider repairs. We must not let Ch'ango overpower our reason. She is no better than Aroha. It was she who trained him in ruthlessness.

Forgive me for expressing myself so bluntly. I am concerned about you as a friend. Hasn't Aroha hurt you enough?

Scribe Gavilan

Marita

Waking next to Andrew was pleasantly disconcerting. We had found our way to Tiare House during some giddy moment of the night. The bed, not much more substantial than a thick floor mat, was narrow enough to have provided us with a shared hilarity that conquered my last doubt about loving him. I could sense Andrew's Mage marks against my skin before I opened my eyes. I had given my heart, mind, and body to this lawless scoundrel, and I refused to look back at my distrust of him.

Andrew was already awake and watching me, his gray-green eyes unreadable. He returned my smile and my kiss, but he was obviously preoccupied. "If you tell me you're leaving me again," I said, "I'll resign from the love philter business."

"Don't resign," he whispered against my ear.

I was quite willing to abandon the discussion, but that enigmatic gaze of his refused to disappear. "Then why do you keep looking at me so seriously?"

He pressed his Mage marks against mine to delightful effect. The physical contact pleased me much more than his words, "Because you may not like what I'm about to tell you, my Marita."

The blossoming roof of Tiare House above us seemed to hover just beyond his dark, heavy hair. The dawn light outlined his strong, beautiful body, and I wanted nothing more than to know him with all my senses. The night had assured me of his desire, but the crescents on my arms would not let me ignore the change effected by daybreak. His ardor had not diminished, but his calculating mind was back in full action. I sighed, "Couldn't you wait until after breakfast to spoil a wonderful morning?"

"I'm taking advantage of your present receptive mood." He helped his case, applying more of his uniquely tactile

skill with Mage marks before continuing, "We're leaving for
Tathagata tomorrow."

Andrew's war would not stop for my convenience, and I
would have to learn to live with that discouraging fact.
"Benedict told me about the parliamentary debate over
Hiroshi," I answered.

"You're going to make peace with your family."

"That would take more magic than either of us can produce."

"Not if you approach them with an irresistible offering."

Andrew had predicted accurately, as usual: I did not like
the trend of the discussion, even with his creatively seductive presentation. "What offering did you have in mind?" I
asked, restraining his hands from their distracting work.

"Me."

"I'm no good at subterfuge, Andrew."

"If not, you're the only member of your extensive, influential family to lack such talent."

"You forget Benedict."

"Hardly. Your brother is a champion at the art. He even
has you convinced that he's crazy."

"Because he is crazy."

Andrew's tilted smile created a single, endearing dimple.
His indefatigable brain hurled forward with its daunting
craftiness, "By having the courage to let himself be declared
irrational, Ben acquired a freedom denied to those of us who
are officially sane and responsible for our actions. His ideas
are more radical than Prince Hiroshi's and mine, but Benedict Linden of Rit is condemned only for his association
with us."

"He was condemned to death."

"But he didn't die. He's surviving quite comfortably,
spreading his ideas, while Prince Hiroshi and I fight for our
lives. I don't call that a sign of insanity."

"Maybe I'm the one who's crazy," I sighed, releasing Andrew's hands.

He traced my Mage crescents lightly. "Not crazy. A little
too dominated by the external emotions that your crescents
inflict on you. I can teach you to protect yourself from the
normal level of influence."

"By Mage spell?"

"No. By mental discipline. I learned the technique from
Prince Hiroshi. It takes some practice to perfect, but it builds

a better barrier against invasive magic than any Mystic School's teaching."

"It's a little late to protect myself against you, isn't it?"

"I hope so." He grinned. "But I also know how to circumvent the mental defense with a physical approach." He proved his point. He did not let me enjoy his argument for long, however. "I need to visit the factories before we leave," he said, kissing me once more before gathering his scattered fortune in bracelets from the polished stone floor of the bedroom. "I'll be back before evening."

"You could invite me to come with you."

He threw my pareu at me. "You have classes to teach."

"Aren't today's classes rather meaningless, if we're leaving tomorrow?"

"The spread of knowledge is never meaningless, Marita."

"You don't want me to see the factories."

"Not until I have time to explain them at leisure. They deserve better than a hasty tour."

"Do they look so unimpressive?"

"Very. Unless you know what you're seeing." He finished dressing and knelt beside me. "Tathagata won't be easy for either of us. Ch'ango will be watching us closely, ready to pounce on any slip we make."

"I don't even know what you expect me to do."

"Prince Hiroshi and I are still negotiating the details."

"That's reassuring. I don't suppose you'd let me contribute to the discussion of my own fate?"

"Prince Hiroshi does not share my confidence in you."

"I like this less and less."

"Don't worry about Prince Hiroshi. I'm very persuasive."

"I've noticed. But I'm not entirely helpless in that area."

"Anavai wouldn't approve, and neither would I."

"I didn't plan to seduce Hiroshi."

"Good. Try not to seduce anyone until I return."

"What do you think of me?"

"Too much," he answered, which delayed his departure considerably.

After he had gone, I spent an hour in the pool, letting my euphoria dissipate gradually. I had embraced Andrew, not necessarily his ideas, and the distinction presented definite problems. He *was* persuasive, as long as he was present. Away from him, Talitha's logic still seemed disturbingly sound. The more I pondered the consequences of committing myself to Andrew, the more I terrified myself.

Right or wrong, Andrew fought for the overthrow of the society I knew and accepted. Nearly every person of authority in the world wanted to eliminate him. Even without the specter of Mage Ch'ango, Andrew's enemies were numerous and powerful. They had already killed Kurt, who had only offended by being my friend, at a time when I was at best a peripheral element of this strange war.

Now, Andrew intended to place me squarely in the battle lines. I suspected that he had been positioning me for that role since before we met. He may have included our personal involvement in his original plan as a means to secure his hold over me, or he may have considered private intimacy unrelated to his larger goals. He acknowledged his reputation as an ambitious man, and I was still the daughter of a Dom.

I did not doubt the sincerity of Andrew's feelings for me. I did question whether he would have acted on those feelings if I had been less valuable to his cause.

I did not regret loving Andrew, but I did not need the prophecies of Benedict or Mage Shamba to foresee a painful outcome of such love. Could I yield Andrew as a peace offering to my family, even at his own request? The possibility of seeing him condemned like Benedict—but without hope of rescue—made my lotus marks turn cold. At the same time, I could not let Andrew destroy Uncle Toby, Talitha, or even the distant cousins, uncles, and aunts who were members of the House of Doms. I had fewer reservations about injuring Lar, but I did owe some loyalty to the House of Mastermages.

Clouds arrived early to cover the island that day. Their shade stole the Iti River's shine and made Roa Bay almost as dark as Ha'aparari Mountain. Even the brilliant flowers looked gray with shadows, but the entire island seemed more beautiful to me than I had ever seen it. The future, not so far away, might bring disaster. Today, I loved and was loved.

I taught my classes with enthusiasm instead of bitter endurance. Some of my students regarded me dubiously. Most of them became friendlier. Evien spoke freely instead of stammering, for the first time sounding like an intelligent man, but he watched me with a sadness in those blue eyes

that reminded me so poignantly of Kurt. Evien thanked me
at the end of class, as if he expected never to see me again.

I went to the chapel to visit Benedict, because I wanted
my brother to know my happiness, but Benedict was not
there. A lone worshiper knelt on a prayer cushion, his dark
head bowed. He wore the gaudy flowered shirt and shorts
that were the most common attire of the male islanders. I
started to retreat in silence, but the worshiper rose and
turned toward me. He was Prince Hiroshi.

I felt like a voyeur, caught in my improper spying. I said
awkwardly, "I didn't mean to interrupt."

"I was finished, thank you," answered Hiroshi politely.

"I didn't know you shared my brother's beliefs."

"Your brother and I have much in common. We both express unpopular philosophies." Hiroshi sighed, "I do not
have Benedict's depth of faith. He does not share my commitment to the recovery of ancient knowledge. We compromise by remaining open to each other's views, until we have
tested them fully according to our individual guidelines."

"I understand." Oddly enough, it was true.

Hiroshi nodded. Even in flowered shirt and shorts, he
managed to convey a sense of formality. "I am glad that you
came here. I had hoped to have an opportunity to talk with
you before your departure from us."

"Has Andrew spoken with you today?"

"Yes. We visited the factories together." He gestured toward a stone bench in the clearing that formed the chapel
yard. I sat, expecting him to join me, but he remained standing. There was a sternness in his black, tilted eyes. "I value
Andrew as my friend," said Hiroshi, "as well as my ally. I
do not think that you are good for him. He has become reckless again. He has sacrificed too much to win you."

"I have made a few sacrifices on his behalf, as well."

"You are useful to my cause, Mage Marita. Andrew is vital. You do not understand the importance of what we are
working to achieve. Empire devices are failing worldwide at
an accelerating pace. They were never designed to last for
multiple centuries without maintenance, and fixers only
know how to perform the minimal *legal* repairs. Virtually no
effort has been made to restore natural ecologies to war-
ravaged islands, and the continents are still largely uninhab-
itable. When the Empire automatons cease to function, most
of humanity will have no food, medicine, or transportation,

and they will have neither the necessary knowledge nor the strength to sustain the species."

"There are other resources," I said, unable to accept his gloomy prognostication.

"Mage spells? Without tools, philters, and the neural implants that you call 'Mage marks,' Mysticism becomes only a muddle of ancient superstitions. Your Mastermages charge dearly for your supplies because the last factory that produced Mage tools failed thirty years ago."

"Mysticism is more than tools and superstition," I said coldly. I did not expect lawful social tolerance on this island, but Prince Hiroshi would not keep my uncertain respect by criticizing my personal beliefs.

"Even if elements of 'true magic' exist, they are neither reliable nor sufficient. Humanity is in danger of extinction, unless the course of decay is reversed rapidly. My followers are few, and the required work is vast." As he became agitated, some of his words became tangled as if his mind ran too fast for his tongue. "The members of the Protectorate do not realize that they will soon have nothing left to protect, unless world laws and attitudes change fundamentally. The original Protectorate orchestrated the execution of Empire 'criminals' by exploiting the frustration and confusion of the war's struggling survivors. The ineptitude of the current Parliament serves this Protectorate's goals. Ch'ango cares only for her personal power. She is entirely willing to let the world die with her." His arms waved in a gesture of disgust.

"I do not defend Ch'ango, if that is who attacked me in Rit."

Hiroshi folded his arms, resuming his quiet, formal dignity. "She attacks all of us in different ways, but she is always brutal, because she has no foundation of either personal understanding or formal ethics to constrain her. This island, the knowledge we have gathered here, and the progress we have made in the last few years can make the difference between survival and destruction for our species, if we are allowed to continue." Hiroshi almost smiled. "My family told me that my vision was hopeless, but they are wrong. Change is difficult but possible."

"Change can occur without revolution. If you offered to make a few repairs to the factories, I can't believe that anyone would object. But when you condemn the social contract and all of its legal principles, you must expect resistance."

"My ancestors ruled the Nikkei Empire," said Hiroshi almost humbly. "The knowledge I wish to share is all that my family salvaged during the years of persecution. I made peaceful offers to the Parliament, but they saw and heard only an Empire threat."

"The laws of personal tolerance were extended long ago to include any surviving Nikkei and Hangseng people. You imagine that others view you as a threat, because your family has never chosen to release the past. Only Empire images and methods, the actual yokes and symbols of Empire authority, remain illegal."

"The barrier of prejudice is no less terrible when it goes unacknowledged by its perpetrators. Neither logic nor a lawful plea for tolerance can combat a thing that does not officially exist. Intangible prejudice can hurt in the small ways that damage individual lives, or it can produce disastrous consequences, such as Ch'ango's ruthless ambitions. She defies the world in a misguided effort to validate her Hangseng heritage."

In a wisp of Mystic vision, I heard my parents whispering that Ch'ango had Hangseng blood. I responded as if that memory had rested always in my consciousness, "Ch'ango has spent her life cultivating personal power by intimidation. Perhaps you have revived the old antagonisms equally by styling yourself as an Empire Prince."

"My husband," declared Anavai, coming upon us in the chapel yard, "*is* an Empire Prince, and there is no reason why he should hide the truth. If not for the efforts of his family, we would have no Empire texts from which to relearn the ancient sciences. The vision that can restore us is his alone."

I had not appreciated the depth of Anavai's commitment to her husband's goals. She was not recounting loving anecdotes of his private foibles now. She spoke with almost the same impassioned fervor that my brother applied to his Divine Intercessor. Hiroshi inclined his head toward her, and she broke off her proud verbal defense immediately. For such a harmless looking man, Hiroshi commanded some remarkably strong people with astonishing effect.

"Mage Marita," murmured Hiroshi, "I have reluctantly authorized Andrew to take you with him to Tathagata. He and I have rarely disagreed more strongly about a significant issue, but he insists that he needs your help, and he is willing to gamble his life on your cooperation. I ask only this: Be honest with him. If you do not trust him enough to obey his commands in the battles he must face, let him know the limitations of your support. Do not wait until all of our lives are in jeopardy."

I could not answer. I wanted to shout that I loved Andrew and would never let harm reach him, but I could not make that promise. Hiroshi and Anavai left me there in the chapel yard with my happiness shadowed by fear.

The gray clouds were collecting overhead again, though they had already produced the usual afternoon downpour. The air felt thick, and even my pareu seemed too heavy and warm. I resolved to locate Andrew and coax him into joining me for an evening swim in the bay.

Thinking of Andrew's return revived my spirits. The flowers became bright again. The emerald moss that crawled over the chapel grounds became a wondrous patchwork quilt, instead of a poor effort to cover the black soil. The magnificent trees shed droplets of hoarded rain instead of tears.

I cast away the gloom of my conversation with Hiroshi and Anavai. Two swollen clouds separated, and a crescent moon peered between them. My Mage marks tightened briefly. I had no other warning. I stood alone before the chapel of glowing water, and then I saw only Ch'ango.

Marita

I knew that Ch'ango did not really stand in front of me, but her spell was compelling. I had seen her when she was Mastermage of Rit, though I had never met her. At that time, I had not yet become a senior Mage, and Ch'ango's bitter antagonism toward my grandfather had precluded social exchanges.

I remembered her eyes. Even before I matured into cynicism, Ch'ango's black eyes had impressed me as arrogant. She narrowed them perpetually in suspicion or contempt.

She was not a tall woman, but she stood so straight and rigid that she seemed imposing. She looked the part of some dowager Empress of an autocratic dynasty. She was far more regal in appearance than Hiroshi. She wore her silver hair braided atop her head like a crown. Her cheeks were hollow, her lips were taut, and her thin neck was shriveled but adorned with a blazing collar of topaz and ruby. She was not young, but she conveyed a sense of burning energy.

The silk jacquard of her citron jacket and black trousers hung loosely on her. She wore a scarf of Kinebahan crimson draped across one shoulder like a pennant of conquest. Silver bracelets, the feminine counterpart of Andrew's gold, concealed her Mage marks from my view.

She studied me. I wanted to speak, but my voice did not function. Rainwater dripped from the eaves of the chapel, breaking the silence with its erratic beat.

And I was seated in my own office, but I occupied the client's chair, and it was Lilith who sat behind my desk. Over a long-sleeved Avalon robe, she wore the violet armbands of service to the Mastermage. A sheer yellow veil covered her head. In her small hands were a deck of emerald cards edged in silver. Lilith fanned through the deck, allowing me to see the familiar Avalon suits and faces.

She selected the card of the Ice Mage and placed it as significator. "This represents you, a Mage of Avalon," she told me, as if I did not know the meaning.

Lilith shuffled the cards before me, and cut them three times. "The Shadow Prince," she said solemnly, pointing to the first primary, "is the enemy. His name is Aroha."

She laid the second primary on the green silk mat that covered the desk. "The Brass Mage opposes the Shadow Prince. His name is Lar, and he is your Mastermage, to whom you swore obedience and love."

She placed the secondaries: Ice Cat, Blood Ghost, and Sable Mixie. "The Sable Mixie is Hiroshi," she said, "who brings misery to the Earth and calls it wisdom. The Blood Ghost is Talitha, whom you betrayed and hurt mortally. The Ice Cat is the uncertainty of what you may become if you persist in your lawless journey."

My office began to swirl around me in waves of scarlet. Like a tide of blood, the color drowned my senses. I was sinking into a great, bottomless spirit jar. Beyond my reach was another victim, flailing helplessly against the current.

Kurt, the left side of his skull broken, looked at me with sad, accusing eyes. "Why, 'Rita?" he asked.

"You killed him," accused Ch'ango, "your fellow Mage."

I raised my arms to strike her, not caring that she could destroy me. She had killed Kurt. I hated her.

She laughed cruelly. "You will not grow in wisdom by that route, Mage Marita." She pointed her bony fourth finger at me. A tight beam of fire poured into me, charring my heart.

The fire was silver. The water that extinguished it was gold. The hands that shook me from the horrible vision were Andrew's.

"Marita," he chanted repeatedly, spreading each syllable upon my heart as a healing salve.

When I whispered his name in response, he gathered me in his arms and held me. We clung together in the mud of the chapel yard, warm torrents of rain soaking us both. "I saw Ch'ango," I told him.

He touched my eleventh lotus gently, but I shuddered from the raw pain that throbbed through my Mage marks. "Her sendings have gained force," said Andrew, "because you have more power for her to tap."

I whispered, "What does she hope to achieve with such cruel visions?" Leaning into Andrew's strength was at once joy and torment. Both sensations spun dizzily from the nerve centers created by my Mage marks.

Andrew's voice sounded hard and angry. "She hopes to wear us down, so we shall be weak when she finally launches her true attack."

"Did she reach you?" I asked, my concern suddenly expanding beyond myself. The pain within me eased.

"Not this time," replied Andrew soothingly.

I sighed as the last traces of Ch'ango's vicious sending against me stopped. The immediate conflict had passed, and I could delight in the feel of Andrew's wet skin against mine. "Is this the price I pay for loving you?" I asked him.

He gave me no answer. "Let's return to Tiare House, before we're washed out to sea." He spoke lightly, but he led me in haste from the chapel yard.

The paths were slippery, yet Andrew wasted no time seeking careful footing. In several places, he left the river's winding course and cut directly through the jungle. We reached Tiare House without passing close to any other dwelling. I did not ask him to explain his sense of urgency because I shared it.

Once inside the house, he ordered me curtly, "Get in the pool." Already drenched, I complied without even untying my pareu. Standing in the pool, the water reached my shoulders. I held my philter purse above my head, though I had sealed all of the philters safely in glass or plastic vials.

Andrew disappeared into the bedroom and returned moments later with two sky-blue candles and a square silver box that had decorated one of the tables. "Hand me your philter purse."

I hesitated. A philter purse is as personal an object as a Mage possesses. Andrew had taken the purse from me once and returned it, and I did trust his Mage skills implicitly, but I could not make myself relinquish the soggy silk and canvas parcel, even to him.

He shook his head and did not repeat his request. "Well enough," he muttered to himself. "What else can I use that's available?" He cast his gaze around the room, bestowing keen attention on every insignificant meter.

He brought forth a pocket knife with a wickedly sharp blade and attacked one of the silk pillows. While I stood in the pool, clutching my purse with guilty relief, Andrew gathered the pillow's fibrous stuffing into a pile in the middle of the stone floor. He laid the box atop the stuffing, flanked by the two candles.

He spent several minutes cutting the pillow's small square of silk into a spiraling pattern. When he had finished, he shook the fabric into a single ribbon loop more than his height in its length. He arranged the ribbon loop on the floor in an irregular circle surrounding his other collected tools. He removed all but two of his bracelets, selected five, and tossed the others among the floor pillows. He used the five bracelets as points of a pentacle, stretching the frayed ribbon loop to form the solid lines. He knelt within the pentacle and laid both hands on the box.

The room shuddered, jarring me and scattering petals from the overhead blossoms. Something fell with a crash in another room. I ducked beneath the water of the pool, dousing even my philter purse, as the floor surrounding Andrew's pentacle erupted into sheets of flame.

I held my breath tightly as I watched fire dance across the water's glassy surface. The pool began to bubble and swirl much faster than its usual current. A loud snap, distorted but undiminished by the water, reached my ears. The fire turned blindingly white. I closed my eyes instinctively. I reopened them to darkness.

I raised my head from the water and gulped hot, sulfurous air. The room was blacker than night, except for the golden halos of two candle flames. The candlelight did not reach beyond the pentacle, but I could see Andrew clearly. He held the open box in his left hand, while his right hand traced patterns of alabaster light on an invisible dome above his head. The two wide bracelets on his upper arms glowed with engraved runes. His scarab marks seemed to have acquired the dimensions and metallic green color of the true beetles.

With a quick, fluid motion, he emptied the box onto the mound of fiber stuffing between the candles. Broken leaves, dried petals, and spices spilled onto the floor. A rich fragrance, vivid with life, drove out the odor of sulfur. The air lightened visibly, and I could see the dim outline of the room.

Andrew held his hands above the candle flames. He began to chant a spell song, his resonant baritone achieving a hypnotic cadence without decipherable words. A sweetly scented breeze swept through Tiare House, cleansing it of the last trace of the sooty, malodorous Mage smoke. The lines of light faded from above Andrew's head, and the runes disappeared from his bracelets. His Mage marks pulsed, blurred, and returned to sleek silver.

He grasped the candles' wicks, extinguishing their fire. He rested his hands on his knees. He ended his spell song abruptly, finishing with a spoken phrase in a language that I had heard among advanced Tangaroa Mages. I comprehended only the name "Ch'ango."

I climbed the steps from the pool slowly. A sense of peace had returned, though it was the false peace of exhaustion. I crossed the room to stand before Andrew in his pentacle. The water dripping from me darkened the blue silk ribbon. "What did you say at the end?" I asked Andrew.

"A Tangaroa warding spell: aitea Ch'ango 'i haere mai," he murmured. He smiled and translated, "Ch'ango is not yet come."

He spun one of his five chosen bracelets in its place at the pentacle's foremost point. With a flash, the ribbon caught fire along its length. A trace of white steam arose from the dampened silk, but the moisture did not prevent the ribbon from burning rapidly to pale ash. With a breath, Andrew scattered one segment of the pentacle, breaking its power as a barrier.

I stepped through the ashen door. "Good journey, Mastermage," I said. Only that greeting accompanied a Mage's offering, for it was the act of giving that conveyed respect for an exceptional demonstration of Mage skills. I placed my philter purse atop the singed mound of leaves and spices.

Andrew shook his head slightly, but he laid his hands upon the purse and blessed it into my keeping, "Grow in wisdom, Mage Marita." He arose and restored the philter purse to me.

"Thank you," I whispered. "I'm sorry I withheld it from you when you needed it."

"I should not have asked for it. You were right to refuse." He sounded as remote as any Mastermage, defining Mystic policy to a lesser constituent.

"For a man who no longer practices Mysticism, you wield a powerful spell."

"It was the wrong answer," he replied, frowning at me, "but I trapped myself in Rit. Now, I have no choice but to fight Ch'ango as she dictates. If Ch'ango attacks me with re-

mote magic, then magic is the only weapon I can use to retaliate."

Andrew had not accused me of complicity in his Rit entrapment, but he had made enough cryptic comments at the
time to suggest that he shared Benedict's perspective. I
trusted Andrew's judgment about magic more than my
brother's. "You seem well equipped to combat her."

He dismissed his remarkable Mage skills with a shrug. "If
Ch'ango had wanted mortal combat, she could have killed
me just now. With such weaponry, she will eventually win."
He began to gather the burned herbs back into the silver
box. "I need to equalize the battle using Prince Hiroshi's
brand of knowledge if we are ever to succeed."

You knew the terms of sharing his life, I reminded myself,
trying to stanch resentment against the war that consumed
him. "You seem to be the sole warrior."

"Being a Mage, you recognize only the battles of magic.
Prince Hiroshi fights in his own patient way."

"Ch'ango is also a Mage," I observed pointedly.

"Which is why she would like nothing better than to restrict this war to her terms. Every Mage battle serves her because it weakens us. Time serves Prince Hiroshi. All he
needs for his victory is to be allowed to work without excessive interruptions. He has many more followers than you see
on this island, and each enclave is growing." Andrew carried
the box and candles back to the bedroom, and I followed
him.

"What does victory mean to you, Andrew? I know that
you want to spread Hiroshi's ideas, but that's a life's work.
Is victory the destruction of Ch'ango? Is it the legalization
of what you and Hiroshi are doing? Is it Hiroshi's ascen-
dancy to Emperor? How will you know when your war is
ended?"

He laughed, "Wars are not generally defined as neatly as
you seem to imagine, Marita. If I should manage to destroy
Ch'ango before she destroys me, the Protectorate will still
consider me their enemy. If we could dismantle the Protectorate, the rest of Parliament would fight to preserve their
control of world resources. If Prince Hiroshi managed to
claim his ancestral rights—and he can establish a legitimate
claim to the Hangseng throne as well as the Nikkei—he
could revise every law by decree, but an unsupported autocracy would be no better than what Ch'ango seeks. Even if

we eventually convince society that the teaching of Empire science is both necessary and wise, we shall still face the monumental task of educating a world that has forgotten nearly everything that it once knew."

"You're telling me that you can never win this war."

"True," acknowledged Andrew. Having restored the box and candles as slightly battered decor, he came to me. "However, I could lose the war today. Ch'ango could eradicate every hope. When Prince Hiroshi first approached the Parliament, Ch'ango thought she had discovered the key to world domination. We have frustrated her ambitions for much longer than she ever anticipated."

"What do you expect to achieve in Tathagata?"

"I expect to locate Ch'ango."

I wished that I could stop hearing my brother's words echo in my head: *Hiroshi thinks it is a trap set by Ch'ango.* "Won't you be fighting on her terms again?"

Andrew shook his head. "I only need one look at her Mage marks. I can record the image and re-create it. I'll be able to nullify any spell she can produce."

"And she can create new marks to give her even more power."

"Not before I can take the Mage book from her. Remember that I have Prince Hiroshi's talents to augment mine."

The battle he had just completed had apparently left him untouched, but it had frightened me more than any warning from Benedict or Hiroshi. *Be honest with him,* Hiroshi had told me. I did not know the truth to tell, except that I loved this gifted man in front of me, and I feared for him. He took enormous risks and had, so far, reaped accordingly large gains, but even the most successful gambler exhausts the Mages' Luck eventually. "Are you sure that you can use Ch'ango's Mage marks? You won't have much time to practice with them."

"I've always been a quick learner," answered Andrew, beginning to trace my lotus array. "I do not want to fight Ch'ango as a Mage, but I have planned for that inevitable confrontation. Once I have acquired Ch'ango's Mage book, we'll all be able to work to our potential. When that book's knowledge is available to all Mages, a balance can be restored, and the Mystic threat will be neutralized again. Prince Hiroshi will be free to win his own battles."

"Most Mages can't master the marks that exist now.

You're gambling that no one can exceed *your* Mystic skill level."

"I'm sufficiently egotistical to believe as you say, but I'm not depending solely on myself." He smiled reassuringly and added, "Or on you, dear Marita. Based on my own readings, I think there is a practical limit on Mage skills imposed by the human nervous system, and I believe that many Mages will be capable of attaining that maximum. We'll be balanced because we'll be reasonably numerous, just like scarab-marked Mages now." He gave me a moment to respond, but I did not want to elaborate on my doubts.

He continued, "I am also convinced that most Mages could use scarab marks, if they were educated properly. Even without active practice, I've mastered more spells since studying with Prince Hiroshi than I learned in all my years of intensive Mystic training—and I stopped trying to acquire new spells years ago. The myth that literacy negates Mage powers was obviously cultivated by clever Affirmists, preying on Mystic superstition to limit Mystic influence. With the incentive of extra Mage marks, I'll be better able to recruit Mystics to Prince Hiroshi's cause by appealing to their ambitions, and Affirmists will join us out of fear of Mystic supremacy. They will learn to fear ignorance, instead of cherishing it."

"Fear and ambition don't motivate many people to join you now. You may create new heights of power for a few Mages, but the results won't affect average citizens."

"Starvation will affect even the E-unit addicts. Prince Hiroshi can justify his grim projections."

"Is that another way by which you can lose the war?"

"Yes. There are too many ways and too many questions to answer all at once." With his familiar persuasiveness, he discouraged me from asking anything more for some time. That night, however, he was not alone in his preoccupation with his endless war.

Benedict

Dear Brother Den, Tathagata,

Please reassure our sisters and brothers. I have not forgotten any of you, who are so precious to me. Your prophecy of my return is not unexpected to me. If the Intercessor is willing, I shall come to you before the end of next month. Like you, I am troubled by the prospect of dealing with the Tathagata monastery, since the Mystics have always stood against us, but the Mages *are* my special ministry in this difficult endeavor.

I failed the Intercessor in Rit, but He is merciful. In the Intercessor's time, we may learn His purpose in testing us.

You are always in my prayers,
Benedict

Marita

I had not seen Tathagata since my father was Dom of Rit. It had impressed me as an ugly, frantic city, as decayed as Rit but too self-absorbed to recognize its own failings. Older now, I expected to discover it diminished even further from the tawdriness of my recollections.

Tathagata's plastone waterfront buildings did appear even smaller and dirtier, despite their ornate grilles and expensive window trimmings, but Tathagata was more than its ancient structures. The power of Tathagata, which had eluded me as a child, pounded against my Mage senses and demanded respect. This power was the heady wine that intoxicated my family into lives of ruthless scheming. This was the goad that had also driven the ambitious Mastermage Aroha.

Tathagata was exciting, especially with Andrew beside me. He might denigrate Tathagata and its denizens, but his undeniable position in the ruling city represented a major part of the vitality that I felt. The forces that ruled Tathagata feared Andrew, and they had good cause. He intended to become Tathagata's conqueror.

Andrew did not enter Tathagata by the public port. Reminding me unrepentantly that he *was* a privateer, he approached the city in that defiant guise. He knew Tathagata well. As he had told me, he had lived here as a member of Parliament for six years.

The island that boasted Tathagata as its ruling seat had several smaller cities scattered around its irregular coast, but those cities served mostly as occasional retreats for the dwellers of Tathagata proper. As I recalled from childhood visits, the interior of the island was more closely guarded than the actual Site of Parliament. The dry, guarded landscape contained hundreds of acres of supply factories, which produced most of the world's legal trade items. Automated vehicles traveled endlessly between the factories and ports.

Various members of my family owned the majority of the island.

The coastal regions consisted of wide sandy beaches, interrupted by artificial harbors with plastone jetties. The stalwart waterfront houses faced the sand directly. There were gaps between the houses, since rare but potent storms had conquered portions of Tathagata over the years, but most of the waterfront remained solid. Beyond the waterfront stood row after row of closely spaced buildings, each row rising a little taller than the last in an effort to capture some absurdly tiny ocean view. The wide, parallel streets of dense houses and offices continued all the way to the government district, where conflicting architectural designs from five centuries of human culture stood in uneasy proximity to one another.

After the primeval naturalism of Ha'aparari, the approach to Tathagata seemed like a voyage far forward in time. I belonged to that "future," but it struck me as sterile and harsh after island jungles, flower gardens, and living reefs. The disparity made me realize the magnitude of the task that Hiroshi had set for his people.

"Hideous, isn't it?" asked Andrew, as he maneuvered the sleek boat through a man-made bay choked by broken supply units and other massive forms of garbage.

"It's our history," I answered. Backed by a view of the city's distant, shining towers, the bay of wrecked Empire wonders evoked the full devastation of the Great War.

"That is a regrettable truth."

"Shouldn't there be an automaton to remove the garbage?"

"Yes," he replied cheerfully. "I disabled it a few years ago to keep this bay private. The decontamination and sewage filtration systems still function, so the bay isn't really as polluted as it appears."

Away from Ha'aparari, Andrew seemed more privateer than noble rebel. He had appropriated the autoboat we now used by sheer piracy, facilitated by a summoning device of Hiroshi's design. Everyone uses abandoned Empire buildings and their accoutrements, but Andrew seemed willing to take and remake any resource that was not at that moment in the hands of its owners. "Does Hiroshi approve of using your talents to cause this sort of damage?" I asked.

"He wouldn't like it, but he'd tolerate it, as I do."

"Did you learn to value expedience as a Mastermage?"

Andrew's laugh was not humorous. "Are you disapproving of me again, my Marita? I know how to play by the rules of Tathagata. I was very successful in my term as Mastermage."

"Until you met Hiroshi."

"Until my son was born," he answered brusquely. He summoned a rapid sequence of grids and gauges on the autoboat's monitor. He studied each display with apparent care, but I was sure that he did not need the data, except as an excuse to avoid my eyes. For two weeks, we had been confined together, alone except for the cat, Iron, and I had become accustomed to Andrew's methods of shunning topics he did not like.

I had also learned that he would talk, if encouraged carefully, about nearly anything. "I don't suppose there is any event that changes a life more than the birth of one's own child."

"A mixie's birth is not exactly a moment of joy."

"Didn't you already know that his mother had been contaminated?"

"The great Mastermage of Purotu," explained Andrew cynically, "was sure that he could overcome the effects of a mere factory failure. He discovered his error. If I hadn't become disenchanted with Mysticism before Prince Hiroshi arrived, I doubt that I would have listened to him. Trying to keep a mixie son alive, while watching his mother die, rearranged my priorities. I was ripe to receive Prince Hiroshi's ideas."

"Was she your wife?" I asked.

"No."

Andrew's jaw had acquired a hard, stubborn set, a warning that I should not delve too deeply. His brief answer had assuaged my jealous curiosity for the moment, although it only confirmed what I had already guessed. Andrew had not married her, just as he did not intend to make permanent his liaison with me.

Aside from hurting my professional pride, his legal independence did me no real injury, or so I kept telling myself. He was already mine. The world's social laws meant nothing to him. Hiroshi's laws meant little to me. Andrew was not Lar.

I relented and changed the subject, "Where do we go first in Tathagata?"

The jaw relaxed immediately. "First, we'll meet with a property broker who specializes in quiet exchanges. Tathagata is too crowded to have comfortable living accommodations sitting vacant, waiting for visitors to lay claim."

"Is this 'property broker' a privateer?"

"Yes, but don't say it to his face. He considers himself an honest man. Living in Tathagata tends to warp one's moral perspective." Andrew steered the boat beneath a collapsed pier and into a mountain of tilted pilings that had looked impenetrable. Hidden within the wreckage was an enclosed dock, slightly corroded but fully operational. The automated berth functioned more smoothly than most major port facilities. When he had completed docking, Andrew spun his console chair to face me. "In Tathagata, it's usually safest to assume that everyone is lying to you, until proven otherwise."

I could not help wondering if he applied his rule to himself. "I know my family's flaws."

Andrew smiled. My comment had amused him, as I had intended. "Many of them make Dom Toby look saintly."

Sometimes, my love, so do you, I thought. "Do you actually expect me to approach Uncle Toby?"

"Would you prefer to approach Lar?"

"No!"

"Poor Lar," clucked Andrew.

"Won't all the members of Parliament be too busy deciding *your* future to accept visits from a family reprobate like me?"

"Parliament's current debates about Prince Hiroshi have been in progress for two weeks, which means that senior members like Dom Toby will have grown disgusted with the lack of progress. They will display their disdain by arriving late and leaving early. All of the serious deliberations occur outside of the official sessions, even when a difference of opinion actually exists. Where Prince Hiroshi and I are concerned, the entire process of debate is a farce because the members of Parliament have already condemned us and yielded us to the Protectorate. Since Talitha failed to entrap me in Rit, the Protectorate is Ch'ango."

"I'd rather confront Toby *or* Lar than Talitha," I muttered. The thought of facing Talitha made me sick with nervousness, even with Andrew's confidence to brace me.

"You're not likely to encounter her. She's a little more diligent in her attendance of parliamentary sessions than your uncle. However, you should not fret about meeting her again. Astute members of Parliament don't hold personal grudges where political expediency is involved."

"Talitha is a Scribe."

"She is a slightly different breed," acknowledged Andrew. "A little nobler. A little more dangerous."

"More vengeful."

"Possibly. She has reason to hate us both. She also has reason to listen. Talitha believes in the Protectorate, and Ch'ango wants me alive."

"Until Ch'ango knows what you intend."

"I'm still too valuable to discard."

"Ch'ango could eliminate you and take Hiroshi."

"The former doesn't guarantee the latter."

"In Ch'ango's place, I think I'd prefer risking the loss of Hiroshi to the idea of keeping you as my enemy."

"Let's find Karam."

"Who?"

"The property broker. Acquiring goods is more time-consuming in Tathagata than elsewhere, and I'd like to make a reasonable start before nightfall."

I nodded toward Iron, sprawled indolently on an aqua silk cushion. "Does she go with us?"

"Of course. She excels at detecting unpleasantness before it starts. She's also a friend whom I would not abandon."

Iron was watching Andrew closely. I had not realized before how closely the cat's eye color matched Andrew's. "I was thinking of her safety."

"Iron and I are experienced at taking care of each other. She inherited the job from her mother, Ava'e, who came to me when I became Mastermage." Andrew extended his hand, and Iron bounded into his lap. "Iron is much like Ava'e: beautiful, strong, and intelligent."

Maybe I should have directed my jealousy toward Iron and Ava'e instead of Andrew's late mistress. He seemed to feel more devotion to the cats than to the woman. I had already concluded that Iron resented any attention Andrew gave to me. She was delighted to accept me as long as I did not interfere with her private property, Andrew.

Andrew draped Iron across his shoulder. I had never seen a cat willing to settle in such an unnatural position, but Iron latched her claws in the gold mesh vest as if she had traveled there frequently. While settling, she licked Andrew's neck to be sure he remembered her. He gestured for me to lead the way onto the deck, while he secured the autoboat with one of Hiroshi's devices. I collected the canvas bag of clothes and personal items that Anavai had provided for me. I did not try to move the larger bag that Andrew had brought. It was so weighted with gold and gadgetry, I could not lift it.

The interior of the dock enclosure was stark and stuffy. I climbed the narrow, worn plasteel stairs, and the white doors slid apart above me. Cool, fresh air rushed against my face. The sky was a cloudless blue. Around me were dilapidated warehouses, the plasteel siding bleached and cracked with age.

When Andrew joined me, I nodded toward the warehouses and asked him, "Did you arrange the abandonment of the buildings as well as the bay?"

"Once the autoboats stopped visiting the bay, the warehouses stopped receiving supplies. Sabotage is pathetically easy when no one is willing to make a minor repair."

"There are fixers, even in Tathagata."

Andrew's brusque laughter puzzled me, but he answered fairly, "Fixers have limits of skill, as well as legal scope of effort. Having some familiarity with those limits, I always adjust my sabotage accordingly."

We walked to Karam's office. The street just beyond the warehouses looked surprisingly respectable, lined with plastiglass-fronted shops that displayed more luxury goods than all of Rit contained. The autobuses functioned smoothly, collecting and delivering well-dressed passengers at every stop. Most of the shoppers wore classic, neutral colors like mine, but there were many touches of Mystic brightness and shades of Affirmist brown.

Even amid Tathagata's bold prosperity, Andrew and his gold were conspicuous. I asked him quietly, "Won't you be recognized?"

"Before the pertinent persons of power have debated whether I am actually here and why, I intend to address the assembled Houses of Parliament. In the meantime, let them speculate and gossip. Notoriety builds interest, and a world revolution deserves a large audience." He nodded toward a small, distinguished office suite, fronted with glass, gray marble, and bronze. "This is Karam's."

The interior proved equally impressive in its restrained, expensive style, though the orderly desks and guest chairs were empty. Our arrival did not go unnoticed, however. A stout, blustery man with curly black hair burst through a door at the back of the reception area. His face seemed too small for his body, until he grinned broadly, displaying chipped teeth. He flung wide his arms, embracing Andrew and Iron together. "My friend," he gushed, "it is a welcome day when you return to my humble establishment."

"Good journey, Karam," replied Andrew, permitting Karam's enthused greeting without reciprocating in kind.

Karam tilted his head in my direction. "You have not lost your taste for beauty."

"Nor have you lost your intemperate curiosity," answered Andrew.

"You cannot blame a man for trying." Karam smiled at me, but he did not inquire further about my identity. "How may I be of service to you, great Mastermage Aroha?"

"Are any of my buildings unoccupied?"

"Be assured, great Mage, I would not let your investments sit idle and unproductive. Your income grows each year in Karam's hands. I can give you a full, accurate accounting at a moment's notice. The records are not, of course, blessed by the Scribes, but the confidentiality of your ownership must be maintained."

Andrew seated himself in a plush, white chair. Iron leaped to the adjacent desk and preened. "I'm looking for a temporary residence," said Andrew.

"I have precisely what you seek," responded Karam, adapting immediately to Andrew's request, "an exceptional home near the Kinebahan temple of Viracocha. The price is a little high, but for you, my old friend, I shall waive my customary fee."

"I have neither the time nor the inclination to renovate some Viracocha ruin for you, old *friend*. What do you have in the Avalon district?"

Karam glanced surreptitiously at my emerald philter purse. "That is a difficult neighborhood, Mage Aroha. It offers little for a man of your excellent tastes."

"I know what it offers. What do you have available?"

"Nothing that is in good repair. The Viracocha house would require far less of your estimable talents."

"I am not interested in Viracocha," said Andrew coldly.

Karam shrugged, as if mystified by his customer's whims, but he did not press his point. "Along Danu Street, number ten is empty, but the last tenants destroyed the cooling unit. Number five has no water. Number sixteen is smaller than your closet at the Faremoni address."

Andrew stroked Iron's ears. "What about the unavailable houses?"

"Every owner and tenant in Tathagata is in residence. No one travels when the Parliament convenes a special session."

Andrew smiled. "What does Julia have?"

"Not even for you, Mage Aroha, does Julia allow anyone to use her houses for more than a single night at a time."

"As I recall, number thirteen was quite comfortable."

"Mage Aroha, number thirteen is reserved for Julia's most special customers."

"I am a member of that elect group."

"Great Mage, you know Julia has her rules. I would not even dare to ask her. Would you not consider something in a more respectable district? I have an excellent value near Lu Tung-pin."

"Perhaps I should go to Julia directly, if you feel incapable of making the arrangements."

"Great Mastermage, I will do whatever you ask. I want only to act in your best interests."

Andrew began stacking gold coins on the desk, while Iron stood guard, switching her fluffy tail. "Number thirteen," said Andrew. "Starting tonight."

Karam watched the gold covetously. "May I ask how long you plan to honor Tathagata with your presence, great Mastermage?"

"You'll know when I leave." Andrew started a second stack of gold. "There are two Mages in Tathagata whom I would like to visit while I'm here: Shamba of the Inianga and Pachacamac of the Kinebahan. Where are they staying, Karam?"

Karam slid both stacks of coins into his hands and rattled them appreciatively. "Where do senior Mages stay when they are in hiding in Tathagata?" he asked.

"The monastery," murmured Andrew. He whistled, and Iron again draped herself across his back and shoulder. "Thank you, Karam. As always, your service is impeccable."

I did not question Andrew until we were well away from

Karam's office and curious ears. "How did you know that Shamba and Pachacamac were here?" I whispered. "And why do you want to see them?"

"I want to hear their versions of the prophecy," said Andrew, ignoring my first question.

"Aren't they allies of the Protectorate?"

"Shamba was a founding member, but he left the Protectorate when he left Rit. Pachacamac never belonged, which is why Ch'ango vandalized his school." At the next bus stop, Andrew pressed a call button to signal that passengers waited. "I'm not sure that I do want to see them, but it's useful to let Karam know I'm interested."

The autobus stopped, and so did my questions. I did not need to ask why Andrew used a property broker, when he had already decided on his residence. Karam also sold information, and Andrew had just ensured that Karam had prime, new merchandise of Andrew's choosing.

I knew the methods. I liked them no better from Andrew than from my own family. The excitement of reaching Tathagata had begun to acquire a sour flavor.

Hiroshi

29 Tiunu, 510

My friend, Andrew,

I hope this letter reaches Tathagata before your arrival. I have transmitted it via the radio link that we established and tested last summer. I am entrusting the transcription and delivery to Bara, whose loyalty is absolute and whose ingenuity is significant. I have instructed him to monitor the offices of all your usual information brokers to locate you promptly. Reward him well for his trouble.

Yesterday, we received worrisome news from one of Benedict's disciples, a man named Den, who lives in a village north of Tathagata. Den writes that Ch'ango has declared herself Mastermage of Tathagata, a city that (as you know) has never had either Mastermage or Dom of its own, due to its unique status as Site of Parliament. This news has, according to Den, received none of the protest it deserves, even from the Affirmists. The parliamentary criers announced Ch'ango's new rank as a temporary measure in their "war" against us. No one has been named as Dom of Tathagata, which suggests to me that Ch'ango is feared even by the Family.

Lar continues to represent Ch'ango in front of Parliament, but there are many rumors about deaths and injuries attributed directly to her. The Tathagata monastery is purportedly bursting with Mages who have fled from her remote attacks. Those who do not flee are trying to propitiate her and secure their future positions in what they expect to become the next regime of world power. Talitha and the other moderates in the Protectorate have lost control, and ambitious Tathagatans are swarming to Ch'ango's support. She is being called the only hope of salvation from the evil Empire Prince, Hiroshi, and his master of destruction, Aroha.

It is clear to me that Ch'ango expects you. She has magnified rumors of the Rit conflict into a war between our "terrible army" and noble Rit citizens, defending their homes from us. With the aid of puppets like Mastermage Lar and Dom Toby, Ch'ango is preparing Tathagata to become the next battlefield. She creates the war and forces you to fight it as she wishes. You have told me often enough that you cannot defeat her on her terms. Have you forgotten what you have learned in these past years?

I cannot believe that you were ignorant of these events and rumors when you left us. Your sources of such information have always been better than mine. What do you intend, my friend, that is so terrible that you could not discuss it with me? Is it the nullification of Ch'ango's Mage marks? I hoped that I had dissuaded you from that course, which could destroy you more surely than all of Ch'ango's spells united. I have shown you the text regarding the early Mystics and their discovery of the nerve film. The standard forms of marking are limited for good reason. Other marks were tried, but their usage damaged the brain and nervous system irreparably. Ch'ango's recklessness does not excuse your own.

I should not berate you. I have placed too much of the burden of our cause on you. Until your last letter to me, I did not realize how much the effort had cost you. Whatever becomes of us, I shall always appreciate the blessing of the years you have given us of your genius, your courage, and your friendship. I shall not, however, allow you to pursue a course that can bring disaster on us all.

I hope that I am wrong in my suspicions about you. I have doubted Mage Marita since you first wrote of her, for I have worried that she represents the Family and uses you accordingly. I remain unsure of her, but I find myself questioning you equally. I have discovered too many indicators of your own deceptions since you left. I have distanced myself too long from the methods that you employ to serve me.

Benedict insists that you have urgent need of me, and I have found his advice on such matters to be wise. He intends to go to Tathagata, and I shall join him. Anavai is sufficiently troubled that she wishes to accompany us, though she has not left Ha'aparari since our son's birth. Both she and Benedict spend many hours in prayer for you.

You are not a lone warrior, Andrew, and you do not need to gather your allies by trickery. If you are using Marita, as I now suspect, you will hurt only yourself.

Be wise, my friend,
Hiroshi

Marita

Number thirteen, Danu Street, belonged to that class of beautifully preserved homes affordable only to members of Parliament and their intimates. From the stained glass window in the front door to the mahogany furniture, every detail represented a perfect example of pre-Empire craftsmanship. All of the appliances functioned. Every option for comfort or luxury was included, and all of them were operational. If Andrew had not repaired, restored, or rebuilt some percentage of the accoutrements, another of Hiroshi's talented followers had performed a similar service. Even expensive homes usually had a share of imperfections.

"Your friend Julia lives well," I remarked, admiring the floral paintings that covered one wall of the light, spacious living room. I had completed a self-guided tour of the ten-room house, and was duly impressed and uncomfortable. I was sure that Janine, with her worldly perspective, would have offered many pointed comments regarding this elegant establishment that rented exclusively for single nights, except to Andrew.

"Julia doesn't live here," replied Andrew. I found him seated at a finely carved desk, writing notes in his own indecipherable script. Iron occupied the windowsill facing the street, her gray fur rendered silver by the sheer curtains that cloaked her.

"Julia only spends single nights here with special friends?" I asked cynically.

His eyes acquired a piratical gleam. "You'll have a busy agenda if you plan to become jealous over every woman in my past."

"It's not your past that concerns me."

Andrew grimaced. Instead of humoring me with glib reassurances, he demanded, "Who concerns you? Julia or Ch'ango?"

"Both."

"You already have some idea of Ch'ango's unpleasant intentions toward me. Julia is a thoroughly Tathagatan businesswoman, willing to sell anything for the right price, unwilling to give anything for free. The only woman with me now is you." He laid aside his pen and sorted the papers on his desk. "Eliminate the past and disregard the present, and there's not much left. I'm doing my best to have a future, but it's a dubious prospect at the moment."

"You are in a depressing mood."

"I have just received some troubling information ..."

How? I wondered but did not ask.

"... which may force me to accelerate my plans. An anticipated fact was confirmed: Parliament has accepted Ch'ango as Mastermage of Tathagata. She has effectively held that position for many years, but the open declaration indicates the panicked state of the Parliament. No corresponding Dom has been named."

"That violates the entire balance of the social contract."

"It only proves how ineffectual the World Parliament has become," he answered. He offered me a letter that he had written in standard characters, and I accepted it dubiously. "This is a preliminary outline for your visit to Dom Toby tomorrow. You might wish to study it. Please, don't alter it too much without consulting me."

"Am I visiting Uncle Toby tomorrow?" The idea did not thrill me. A quick look at Andrew's outline did not improve my opinion.

"It would be helpful." He resumed his scribbling. "I'll be making calls on various acquaintances this evening. I should be back before midnight. Don't become concerned unless I fail to return by mid-morning."

"If you don't return, what would you suggest that I do?"

"Do *not* try anything heroic."

"You could tell me where you plan to go tonight, so I could make inquiries in case of a problem."

Andrew glanced at Iron. Since I could not detect Andrew scanning for unwanted observers, I assumed that he employed one of Hiroshi's subtle devices. I did not doubt that some precautionary tactic filled the moment of Andrew's silence. He had admitted that Tathagata made him paranoid about eavesdroppers.

Satisfied that no interloper was watching or listening, Andrew tapped the upper right drawer of the desk. "I have placed an envelope in here that contains a brief list of useful names and addresses, among other data. Everyone I plan to visit is named on the list."

"You entrust your list to an unlocked drawer but not to me?"

"Yes, for three reasons: A desk drawer cannot be held accountable for possession of illegal information, Mage techniques have disguised the envelope's contents as an innocuous set of furniture sketches, and none of my literate enemies are Mages."

"What about Ch'ango? If she countered the envelope's disguise, she could hire a Scribe easily enough to decipher the rest."

"The counterspell requires some insight regarding the nature of the contents. Ch'ango can interpret diagrams and a few Empire symbols, but she does not read because she's too afraid of lessening her power. You will need a blend of binding power, vision oil, and visualization spell to decipher the list. With your knowledge of philters, you should be able to create the right chemical reaction without much trouble. Don't resort to the envelope except in an emergency."

"I thought you believed in disseminating information whenever possible."

"I am trying to respect your preferences as far as possible. If you want to become a full conspirator, I'll accommodate you, but that decision will commit you even if I'm taken out of the battle. If I disappear and you prefer to avoid my associates thenceforth, you may ignore my list. I'm sure you can locate a sympathetic cousin somewhere in Tathagata."

"I don't think any of my cousins would feel sympathetic toward you."

He smiled, losing the austerity that had marked him since reaching Tathagata. "I'm sorry, Marita."

"For what?" I asked warily. I could imagine a large variety of answers.

"For leaving you here alone. For being unable to give you any guarantees of what the next few days will bring. For entangling you in my unpredictable life."

"It was not a one-sided decision." I repeatedly latched and unlatched the lizard bracelet that Andrew had given me. He had shown me how to solve the puzzle of its fastening. He had tried to explain the more sophisticated mechanisms embedded within it and its compatriot from the Stone Palace fountain, but I understood only the dangerous outcome of using them—and the magnitude of Andrew's gift in freeing me from the lizard's bondage. "Both Hiroshi and Benedict seem to believe that I should apologize to you," I murmured.

"I hope we have the leisure to make amends to each other."

I only nodded. Andrew returned to his writing. Reading the outline of lies that he expected me to tell Uncle Toby, I decided that Andrew's apology was merited on yet another score. To avoid starting an argument, I resumed my prowl through the house. Andrew departed while I was upstairs, and Iron disappeared with him.

Waiting alone in a strange house, however luxurious, did not improve my temper. Andrew imposed knowledge on me when I least wanted it. The rest of the time, Andrew enjoyed his secrets.

I respected his preoccupation with his mortal enemies, but I would not let them dictate the course of my relationship with Andrew. I had been unwilling to be Andrew's servant prior to becoming his lover. I was certainly not going to let our changed status make me submissive to his every whim. Lar had educated me about the folly of that course.

I would *consider* visiting Uncle Toby. I would *not* spend the evening worrying and waiting for Andrew's return.

I locked the door of the unknown Julia's elegant house. I secured the silver keycard within my philter purse. In my sadly wilted linen suit, I made my short pilgrimage to the great Avalon temple of Tathagata. I refused to believe that Ch'ango's avaricious influence could extend into the spiritual center of my Mage School. If Andrew had not wanted me to pay homage to my School, he should not have chosen a residence in the Avalon district.

The temple stood at the end of Danu Street, flanked by narrow, well-kept houses similar to Julia's. The sidewalks were quiet. A plasteel autobus trundled down the cul-de-sac and deposited four emerald-clad passengers in front of the temple. I watched them mount the front steps and enter the main sanctuary before I approached the building myself.

The limestone exterior of the Avalon temple owed more to ancient Greece than to the mythos of northern Europe that I knew best, but every remembered European legend had its representation inside. The inner columns and floors were cut of green marble years before the Empires reached their height of power. Massive murals depicted elves and dwarves, fairies of every bright or terrible description, armored knights and dragons, Norse gods, Russian rusalka, and Olympian heroes. The murals were colored with precious stones and metals that could have purchased all of Rit. In those early Empire years, the Avalon School was second only to the Lung-Wang in size and prosperity. We had declined more than the rest, because we had become a particular target of both Empires' rulers.

The Empires had not favored any Mystic organization, although some Hangseng members had tolerated Lung-Wang practices out of respect for ancient history. The Empires had likewise despised the anti-technology secularists who became known as Affirmists. From joint anger at the decades of Empire contempt, the postwar uniting of Mystics and Affirmists had altered the shape of world culture into a social contract that had endured unchanged for generations. The Avalon temple instilled a spirit of reverence in me for past Mystic glories, and it made me regret the inevitability of Prince Hiroshi's undertaking.

I knelt at the first empty shrine and lit a green candle for its patron, Merlin. The shrine depicted him as a younger man, commanding stone to fly into a great circle. His face was radiant and powerful.

I could not worship Merlin or any of the other Avalon saints. My brother was right in accusing me of a lack of faith in my own creed. Still, the Avalon traditions meant a great deal to me. I saw no reason why they could not coexist with Hiroshi's spirit of technology. If Benedict could teach Hiroshi's recruits, and Hiroshi could pray to Benedict's Intercessor, Andrew and I should be able to meld Mystic practices with a revival of the creative, industrious aspects of Empire lore. Ch'ango was only an obstacle. The ultimate goal had to be more than her defeat.

Meditating at Merlin's shrine in Tathagata, I attained my own understanding of Prince Hiroshi's vision. In an odd way, Benedict led me to the revelation of my personal beliefs. My brother was the most thoroughly single-minded religious devotee I had ever known, but he found no conflict in supporting Hiroshi's efforts to rebuild, replant, and revitalize a fading world. Andrew's vision, as far as I could discover it, seemed flawed to me because it made a war of something that should have been an evolution, as natural and as pleasant as Anavai's designs.

One of the shrine's spent candles sputtered, and its glass holder cracked explosively. I cringed from the ominous sign, and my pleasant meditation became a Mage vision in truth: images of furious scarlet, images of relentless ice, images of Ch'ango melting into the card of the Sable Prince. The war between Andrew and Ch'ango was real. I had not imagined the attacks against me. I recognized Andrew's intensity of effort merely to survive. My vision tossed like a stormy sea, threatening to capsize my fragile mind.

I squeezed my wrists, applying hard pressure to my crescent marks until I numbed them. I recited a litany of discipline that Andrew had taught me during our voyage, and I gripped my own vision and restored its balance. Instead of retreating immediately, as had too long been my habit, I forced the vision to resume at my behest.

I would *not* let Ch'ango consume me. I would look beyond her. I would formulate my own concept of the future, and Andrew could accept his place in it if he so chose. I would help Andrew to combat Ch'ango, but my vision would not be his. I tried to solidify an image of Andrew beside me, but my effort was still too new and incomplete to include specific individuals.

Opening my philter purse, I sprinkled a little prophets' oil into my hands and rubbed it into the skin of my arms. I held my wrists close to the flames of the shrine candles until my Mage marks burned. Relying on the power of the great temple to defend me from Ch'ango, I forced my focus to encompass all that I knew of Hiroshi's work, Mage skills, and my own family. From ice, I fashioned my vision, because Ice belonged to Avalon.

Perspiration streamed down my face from the exertion of a type of Mage spell that I had seldom exercised. I chiseled time away from my future truth, seeking perfection of form. When I erred in my mental creation, I discarded it and began anew from the present.

The ice sculpture began to assume a satisfying shape around the edges, although the deep blue core of its design continued to elude me. In the background, clear ice renditions of Aunt Nan's orchids bloomed amid a crystalline Ha'aparari jungle. Frost-white dolphins leaped joyfully in the water of the Stone Palace fountain. My father's tree bore a round, blood-red fruit on branches of frozen, brassy light. Carved from the northern snowfields of Avalon myth, legions of books and Empire toys spread to infinity. Instead of broken stones and refuse, the Rit forum became a larger, ice-rimed version of Anavai's walls-of-water chapel.

A face began to appear before me, and I moved cautiously, afraid of damaging the vision yet again. Though I had left my tainted, private Mage cards in Rit, I extended my Mystic senses by the regimen of the cards' images in my mind. I tested the *rightness* of each of the five suits, each of the nine faces, individually and in combination. When the Brass Prince asserted itself twice in sequence, I conjured that card's blazing figure from Merlin's candle flames.

Unlike the Brass Dom, whom the sun merely enhaloed, the Brass Prince *was* the sun, transfigured into human form. The rays of light, which the card's flat image portrayed as a few wavy lines of gold, flowed blindingly from the face and robe of my conjuring, and the ice of my larger vision reflected the light in a thousand dazzling motes. Though the vision had no physical presence, my eyes watered from the pain of so much beauty and energy. I tempered the vision in order to see it clearly.

The Brass Prince's androgynous features shifted, becoming Ch'ango as she might have been, Ch'ango as she should have been. She was strong, and she was gifted, but there was a *wrongness* in her. She raised a great, curved sacrificial knife and plunged it into a mass of squirming flesh that might have been a man. His crimson blood bespattered her, and the brightness of her dimmed to a perverted shade of Sable.

A crimson runnel flowed from the sacrifice, swirling around the feet of the Sable Prince, taunting, teasing, rising into its own Face as Prince of Blood. The Blood Prince was hazy and ill-formed, until a tall, proud woman took his Face, her dark hair bound in a smooth, cloth-of-gold turban that matched her golden robe. "Marita, child, you are too thin," chided Talitha fondly, and I felt the full, warm power of her personality engulf me. I became eager because there was *rightness* in the development of this vision.

Too quickly, I reached for another Face, darkly embedded in the ice, and I found a Dom. His color was black, the color of a Suitless Dom, a Dom who has betrayed his own essence. He was Toby.

His genial smile had become twisted and corrupt. Looming behind him was a figure of fear, a power that I did not want to see more clearly. I did not need to peel away the mask of time or imagination to recognize the Sable Prince in this cruel context. Ch'ango's gnarled hands gripped my uncle's shoulders.

I discarded the spoiled vision. Staring at the painting of Merlin with his flying stones, I recalled myself to the present. I clutched my own arms, letting my Mage marks cool gradually.

I needed my twelfth lotus pair to complete the future vision. Shells would have facilitated the effort, but I could function without them; it was raw Mystic power that I required, not dexterity. Andrew had a supply of the silver nerve film that I needed. If I could gird myself to accept the pain of insertion without a numbing philter, I could apply the marks myself. I could give myself scarab marks, as well. Kneeling at Merlin's shrine, I felt capable of anything.

Footsteps slowed behind me, and I realized that I had monopolized the Merlin shrine for more than an hour. I dropped one of Andrew's gold coins in the offering box. Bowing my head, as if in devotion, I left the shrine to the next supplicant.

I stopped briefly in the temple shop to purchase a new Avalon robe and veil. I selected a robe of the simple, classic style, V-necked and sleeveless, with a matching cloak and a veil that hung to my waist. The fabric was a tightly pleated emerald silk, woven with a thread of gold. Both items were finer than any of the tattered garments available in Rit. They were accordingly costly, but I considered them a worthwhile investment of Andrew's gold. If he intended to act as Mastermage of Ha'aparari, then as the sole Mage under his jurisdiction, I felt some obligation to uphold his prosperous image.

Persuading myself of my noble intentions, I also bought a new philter purse and a braided gold sash. I studied the crystal-guarded display of Mage cards, but in the arrogance of my vision's aftermath, I rejected all the fibron and plastic decks as props for an immature Mystic; my conjured images would serve a twelve-lotus Mage more reliably than vulnerable, physical cards. Andrew had a better supply of philter ingredients than anything the shop offered, or I might have spent the rest of what he had given me.

Ha'aparari had restored a part of myself. I regained another part in the great Avalon temple. It was a confidence that Lar had shaken from me, weakening everything that I had done since the day I learned of his faithlessness. It was also a cousin to ambition, that family trait that I had never acknowledged in myself.

My vision had exhilarated me into a state of rash defiance: *Beware, Ch'ango. Andrew is not the only Mage capable of fighting you. He has a consort now. Like him, she is both Mage and Scribe. She is also a legitimate member of the Family of Doms, and she may decide to take the seat of Rit away from her dear Uncle Toby.*

"As long as Prince Hiroshi intends to rewrite world law," I whispered laughingly to the sky, "let it be revised to *my* liking."

Andrew

9 Tiurai, 510

Most Excellent Hiroshi,

Bara did not fail you. I may not make the same boast of myself, if indeed you have resolved to leave Ha'aparari. How I wish that we had completed the restoration of the autoboat's radio, so that I could have received your message in time to prevent you from following me! I fear that I am too late, but if not, heed me: Stay away from Tathagata, from Parliament, from Ch'ango, and from me. If you sacrifice yourself for me, then all that we have achieved will be lost. Do not abandon your trust in me now, when I need it most.

You write as if you had just now realized that I have kept secrets from you. When have I ever claimed to be innocent of guile? Is it Benedict who has presented this as a revelation? He is not unbiased. He may have forgiven me for involving his sister in his release from Rit, but he has not forgotten.

You want honesty from me? Yes, I *am* using Marita, because my belief in your cause supersedes my personal preferences. I care for Marita more deeply than I ever intended, but I shall use her more ruthlessly than you can imagine, because Ch'ango has left me no alternative. If I am successful, Marita will never forgive me, and I shall spend the rest of my life regretting what I have done to her.

You have never demanded more of me than I was ready to bear. Please, do not force me to bear the guilt of causing your death.

A.

Marita

Andrew returned just before dawn. He slipped quietly into bed beside me, wrapping himself in the white silk sheet. I allowed him to sleep, wishing that I could do the same. Reaction from my powerful vision in the Avalon temple had plunged me from my initial euphoria into depression. My horde of questions for Andrew would wait.

I watched the plaster ceiling emerge from night's shadows, discovering shapes and faces in the erratic textures. Most of the images belonged to a nightmare's realm. A picture that appeared in every cluster of thick paint was the dreadful pairing of Toby and Ch'ango from my vision in the temple. The grisliest composite included my parents in their doomed autoboat, entangled with the treacherous toll unit that had led to Kurt's death.

I could see Nan, as vibrant and young as the Blood Dreamer, in the Stone Palace office that had been our schoolroom. She explained our family's influence with wry candor, "For ten generations, the Family has dominated the House of Doms, absorbing new Doms into the Family and creating token parliamentary seats out of the tiniest communities." A sense of crisp amusement masked the blatant disrespect of Nan's words. "The World Parliament has become a monster of over two thousand members, but the competition for power remains reasonably civilized. A new Affirmist seat can always be formed to accommodate the aspirations of a would-be Dom. Qualified Mastermages are sufficiently scarce to restrict the darker aspects of Mystic politics to a small group. Elections might be dishonest shams, but they generally remain free of outright violence."

Blood became Shadow. Nan became my father, complaining to my mother downstairs, as I eavesdropped from the shadows at the top of the stairway: "The factory failures of the last few years have undermined the traditional policies. Parliamentary seats have begun to disappear faster than they can be replaced. Where will an ambitious young family member like Toby find a suitable seat, unless an existing Dom retires prematurely?"

My mother answered with the steely voice that always seemed incongruous in a woman of such delicate beauty, "Toby covets Ben's position as your heir. You should send Toby back to Caiphas before serious trouble develops."

"I cannot offend Toby's father now, with the election pending and Ch'ango stirring trouble with her demands for a Mystic share of Tathagatan factory property."

"I do not want our children left alone with Toby."

I shivered in the darkness, as if I were still nine years old and resentful of my mother's dislike for my beloved cousin Toby. I had listened because of Toby's name and my childish attachment to him. I had paid so little attention to my parents' concerns, shunting them into the back of my mind along with all the other Affirmist intrigues that I despised. I had heard and remembered both the lessons and the warnings, but I had chosen not to understand them until tonight.

By the Mystic/Affirmist social contract, the Dom and Mastermage of each seat are charged with mutual protection against in-party treachery. The responsibility of defending my father from his own family had rested with Ch'ango, who had driven my grandfather out of office when *he* refused to cooperate with her. If my father had retired naturally, Benedict would have become his heir, because my father would never have admitted Benedict's unsuitability. Even if Benedict had denounced his intolerant Intercessor, Ch'ango would never have endured anyone as independent of thought as my brother.

Thus, Marita the woman thought, while Marita-the-child hid in the darkness. In vision, my mother cried and was gone. Shadow became Sable. My father became my brother. Benedict stood in a house of gargoyles, before an altar of nacre dragons, and Ch'ango shattered his bones with a spell that had toppled the Rit forum's standing stones. A gray cat raked her back and denied her spell its vicious finish. The Cat was made of Shadow, and I knew him as the man who slept beside me.

The ugly vision, strengthened by nightmares, would not leave me: Ch'ango, who valued nothing but her own power, enabling Toby, who was much more malleable than either my father or my brother, to claim one of the choicest parliamentary seats. Both seats of Rit had perpetual positions on the administrative committee, which dictated the items that reached Parliament's agenda, the speakers who were heard, and any legal changes that could be presented. With both Lar and Toby as her puppets, Ch'ango could retain extensive governmental control, even after retiring from public view in order to conceal her augmented Mage marks.

If my new theory came as a sending from Ch'ango, its motive was obscure. If it was a true extension of yesterday's vision, as I believed, it made my intention to award myself twelve lotus marks imperative. I wished I dared ask for Andrew's help. I did not like to contemplate his reaction to my decision, which directly defied his warnings about Ch'ango's methods.

While I debated what to say to my unpredictable lover, he propped himself on his elbow to look at me. The morning light made his skin shine like the bronze accents of the bedroom. He watched me with his Shadow Cat's eyes, neither speaking to me nor touching me. "Did you have a successful night?" I asked him.

"More or less."

"Do you intend to tell me anything about it?"

His guarded expression relaxed into a smile. "I have nothing very exciting to report. I devoted most of my time to that universal affliction: necessary, tedious chores. I verified the status of some of my local holdings, reestablished some useful contacts, and arranged a few sales of Prince Hiroshi's specialized products. Contrary to what you may think, Marita, my life is not a continuous adventure."

"Yesterday, you weren't sure you'd be able to return here. Were you testing my ability to worry?"

"Accidents can occur to anyone. They're a little more probable in my line of work."

"I'm pleased to see that you avoided them for another day."

"Thank you. I share the sentiment." He touched my hair, twisting the pallid curls around his finger. "What's wrong?"

"A vision," I answered.

He withdrew his hand abruptly. He hissed in frustration, "You might at least have waited for me to stand as guardian."

"I was not alone. I went to the Avalon temple."

The expression on his handsome face became derisive,

and his voice was scathing, "The relative insignificance of your particular Mage School does not reflect an inability to achieve rarified heights of corruption."

"*You* chose to take a house in the Avalon district."

"To give you access to the Mage supplies that you favor, not to encourage you to abandon all semblance of intelligence."

I matched his sarcasm, "Tathagata brings out the worst in you, doesn't it?"

"It has that effect on most people." He added pointedly, "Some submit more quickly than others." He left the bed and dressed with quick, angry movements. "I plan to pay my respects to your uncle today, whether or not you choose to accompany me."

"I'll come," I murmured, dreading the return of that terrible wall of suspicion between us. I was not sure that our fragile relationship could survive even a minor clash of wills.

"I am so glad that it is convenient for you," muttered Andrew, as he sat before the mirror, carefully equipping himself with a variety of Hiroshi's tiniest devices. The sheen of his golden vest concealed a multitude of irregularities. A breeze lifted the sheer curtains behind him.

I tried to pierce the antagonism that I had revived, "Did you know my father?"

Andrew continued to check the concealment of his Empire-inspired miracles, but he made an obvious effort to answer civilly, "Only from across the Parliament floor. Dom Hollis and I never moved in the same social circles."

"Do you know how he died?"

My question breached the wall of anger with unexpected ease. Andrew whistled quietly, and he turned to face me. "So that has finally occurred to you," he murmured, displaying more visible compassion than I had ever known from him. "Yes, I am reasonably sure that I know how Dom Hollis died."

"Ch'ango arranged the 'accident,' " I said calmly, though the tightness of my throat seemed near to strangling me.

Andrew nodded. "Ch'ango arranged it. With Toby's cooperation. Which placed him in her debt."

"Because my father refused to be her puppet."

"Ch'ango demanded that Dom Hollis disinherit his son, and Dom Hollis declined. Most of us believed that your father would eventually have recognized his outstandingly poor judgment about Benedict, but after Ch'ango's vociferous demand, your father could not rescind his decision without conceding political power to the House of Mastermages."

"Assassination . . ." I murmured, wishing I could bespell the word out of my memory.

"Or blood magic, considering Ch'ango's expertise in that area."

"Ch'ango would have killed Benedict, as well, but you stopped her."

"You did have a grimly thorough vision," murmured Andrew sympathetically. "Mages' Luck has allowed me to save Benedict from Ch'ango's blood spells more than once. As for your parents . . ." Andrew shrugged a mute apology. "Few of us expected Ch'ango to react so drastically to your father's refusal to cooperate with her, but she had gathered a sizable grudge against your particular line of the Family. Assassinations have become increasingly common in the last few years, largely because members of your family have begun to seek more Mystic help in furthering their own ambitions. Your father's removal was the most prominent instance of Mage against Dom—and one of the most thinly disguised incidents. Your parents never even boarded the autoboat that purportedly failed them."

I closed my eyes, remembering my father with his dreams of an orchard in Rit, my beautiful mother coaxing laughter even from her plain half sister, Nan. I presumed that my parents had been as flawed as other members of the Family, or they would not have held the seat of Rit, but I could only think of them as they had seemed to me as a child. I had continued to love them deeply, even when I rebelled against their Affirmist views of life.

Andrew came back to the bed and sat on the edge. I reached for him, and he held me. "Does Benedict suspect?" I asked him.

"I should think so," answered Andrew with a sigh against my skin. "He prophesied the event."

My muscles stiffened. "Benedict knows," I whispered.

"Your brother has remarkable Mystic gifts even without the aid of Mage marks. His healings and his prophecies have won many converts for his Intercessor, particularly among social paupers like privateers, fixers—and Prince Hiroshi's followers."

"Benedict did not tell me that he knew anything about our parents' deaths," I muttered, astonished and hurt almost as much by Benedict's omission as by Uncle Toby's treachery.

"I believe that you were attached to Lar at the time, and that relationship made Benedict feel very abandoned by you. He came to Tathagata to try to make your parents understand his prophecy and avoid its tragedy. When they would not listen, Benedict found solace in interpreting some archaic texts regarding an old religion—his Intercessor."

You should have told me, Ben. You should have forced me to listen. "Is this where you met Benedict?" I demanded, feeling paralyzed by an excess of lost possibilities and new suspicions.

"Yes. He was preaching on a street corner. His ideas intrigued me."

I could not restrain my cynical reaction, "He intrigued you, because you knew that he was the son of a prominent Dom."

"That added an extra dimension of interest," admitted Andrew. "He was obviously well educated. He could prattle for an hour about his Divine Intercessor and convey more data about pre-Empire cultures than most people learn in a lifetime."

"You wanted to know how he learned his 'Holy Word.' " I stared into Andrew's eyes, trying to read the thoughts that raced through his agile mind. "You used Benedict."

"Everyone uses everyone here. That is the nature of Tathagata. It's infecting you, right now." Andrew kissed me, but it was a gesture of irony and not affection. "You're using me, my dear. Do you realize how much you'd have to pay an information broker for what I've told you? The street rates for detailed, personal information about ongoing power struggles are extremely high."

"You're only telling me about my own family."

"My dear Marita, every Dom in Parliament is a member of your family, either by birth or by adoption."

"Isn't that why I'm here with you?"

"If I answer no, you won't believe me. If I answer yes, you won't forgive me."

The curtains billowed again, but the breeze had acquired a cold, sour taint. Andrew jerked his head toward the window, then he turned back to me, covering my face and his with his gold-banded arms. I had one painful glimpse of a white-hot flare smashing through the upper window pane. A concussion of force and sound accompanied a rancid smell of strong, russet Mage smoke. Fire oil seared the exposed skin of my arms, sending tremors through the nerves that fed my Mage marks.

Andrew pulled away from me, tore the covers from the end of the bed, and used the quilt to smother the fire that spurted in a dozen places from the carpet's maroon velvet pile. Fires were erupting from curtains, cushions, and the sheet that covered me. I shook free of the smoldering fabric before more of the fire oil could creep onto my skin.

I stretched across the bedside table to reach my philter purse. With a hurriedly concocted spell, I cast a storm of dry silver rain into the room. The beads of spell-borne philter powder hung near the ceiling, stealing moisture from the air, until each droplet shivered and plummeted. The droplets hissed as they met the fire oil, extinguishing the burning at the source.

A haze lingered in the damaged room, but fresh morning air gusted through the window. Andrew threw the quilt to the floor and growled in disgust, "Petty vandalism."

I wrapped myself in a blue silk robe that I found hanging in the nearest closet. I searched in vain for an unsinged chair and concluded that standing was safer. "Your friend Julia may not invite you to stay here again. You're a little hard on the neighborhood."

"I wouldn't be surprised if Julia arranged this as a welcome," grumbled Andrew, waving brusquely at the room. "In payment for damages, she'll have me renovate another house for her, a service that would otherwise cost her more than she could afford." He began to laugh. "She knows I have too many enemies to prove all of them innocent of any particular attack."

I shook my head. "Of all the men who have aspired to attach themselves to me and my family, you are undoubtedly the most troublesome." Cautiously, I tiptoed to his side. He had more enemies than I would ever know to name, and I was discovering too many enemies of my own. Past and present burdened both of us. I entwined my arm with his, wanting to recover the closeness of Tiare House, knowing

that our personal histories made the survival of such closeness nearly impossible.

"I don't need your family, Marita. I have power enough in
my own right."

With that indirect assertion of my personal worth to him,
we went downstairs, almost reconciled. I tried not to wonder
if he had created the morning's havoc to resecure my sym-
pathies. For all I knew, he suspected the same of me.

Talitha

10 Tiurai, 510

Scribe Purissima:

Your news of Scribe Gavilan's disappearance is most distressing to me. I am sorry that I cannot help you. Indeed, I did not receive the letter that you say he wrote to me on the 23rd of Tiunu. Do you know which courier he hired to carry the letter across town that night? I have no idea why Gavilan would have left Tathagata without telling you.

If I do receive his letter, I shall notify you at once. At this late date, however, I fear that the letter is lost.

Scribe Talitha

Marita

Uncle Toby lived in a dignified brownstone not far from the Site of Parliament. In Tathagata, an Affirmist dwelling as ostentatious as the Stone Palace could be viewed as hollow conceit, and important Affirmists spent large fortunes to acquire the simplest, most conservatively designed houses in the government district. There were no more than three houses as unadorned as Toby's on Parliament Street.

Individual dwellings might be simple, but the neighborhood was overwhelming. The diverse structures of the governmental cluster ranged from elongated white pyramids and mirrored obelisks to colorful Mystic temples festooned with gargoyles and plastone dragons. Official buildings did not follow the policy of austerity, and most Mastermages cultivated an image of extravagance as a statement of personal power.

I climbed the stoop to Toby's house alone. I had left Andrew, boldly cloaked in Mastermage violet, just down the street. In Tathagata's government district, the garment of the elite was common enough to constitute a effective disguise.

A white-haired doorman met me with a supercilious inspection of my Avalon attire. He took my name without comment and disappeared beyond an ornate bronze door on my left. He reappeared just long enough to close the main door in my face, but Uncle Toby himself reopened it almost immediately. Uncle Toby must have broken a personal record to reach the entry hall, unless he had been hiding directly behind the bronze door. I pushed my emerald cloak away from my arms and extended them for his official inspection. I was glad that I had not yet augmented my Mage marks beyond what Toby expected.

He did not even look at my arms. The perpetual geniality still glowed from his face, but he snapped at me, "Why are you here, Marita?"

"You always told me I would be welcome, Uncle Toby," I replied ironically. This selfish, conniving man, whom I had once adored, was my parents' murderer. Fury gave me the courage to persist in Andrew's plan, little as I understood its reasoning.

"Since you discarded your rights as family, you will refer to me by my proper title. By the law, you earned your brother's sentence when you arranged his escape. As your Dom, I could enforce that sentence."

I stared at the white marble floor, loathing my uncle's hypocrisy. He threatened as a matter of form, while his opportunistic mind seethed with the possibilities of using me. His selfish glee at seeing me here was palpable. When I met Toby's eyes again, I had completed my resolve. "Dom Toby, your only interest in my brother is the man who calls himself Andrew. If you still want Andrew, I can give him to you."

Toby sneered, "Will you serve your family as loyally in Tathagata as you did in Rit?"

"Must we hold this discussion in the doorway, where all of Tathagata can hear us?" Pretending a grudging hesitation, Toby moved aside to let me enter. He gestured brusquely toward an alcove equipped with two high-backed plastiwood chairs, more decorative than practical. I seated myself gingerly, spreading my cloak around me. "I will not lie and pretend that I'm sorry for having saved my brother's life. We both know that Benedict's irrationality would have precluded a sentence of execution, if you had not hoped to capture *Andrew* by holding Benedict as hostage."

The chair was so narrow that Toby had to straddle it to sit comfortably. He did not argue against my premise. "Nothing can excuse your methods for achieving Benedict's freedom. You have bargained with Aroha, the most treacherous man ever to disgrace the World Parliament with his presence. Do you deny it?"

"I do not deny bargaining with Andrew. I sold certain of my services to buy Benedict's life. That does not mean that I support Andrew in all things."

Toby offered a pinched smile. "Forgive my bluntness, Marita, but Aroha has never needed to pay to acquire a woman's services."

"Forgive *my* bluntness, Dom Toby, but I am not a brothel maid to sell my own flesh. I am the daughter of a Dom, and

I am a senior Mage of the Avalon School. You may dismiss my value, but I assure you that Andrew does not make that mistake." My haughty tone seemed to impress Uncle Toby, which pleased me. However, the most delicate part of my deception was yet to come. "Andrew values knowledge, wherever he finds it, and I have so far been able to appease him without conceding any information that he could use against us. That situation cannot last indefinitely, which is why I have risked his anger to visit you today."

"You have developed rare courage, niece."

Inwardly, I smiled at his acknowledgment of kinship. Outwardly, I wore a grim expression. "Every attempt to capture Andrew has failed because every attempt has been orchestrated according to Affirmist laws. Uncle Toby, there is not an Affirmist in this world who can begin to understand a Mage like Andrew. If you want to thwart him, you must proceed by his rules—Mystic rules."

"What are you proposing, Marita?"

"I can give you Andrew. I shall give him to you, but there are a few trades that I would ask in exchange."

"Give me Andrew," said Toby with a greedy, glittering stare, "and you shall have a seat in Parliament, if you wish it."

"A seat in Parliament would be acceptable, as a start," I answered coolly, though the prospect horrified me. "I would also demand a full pardon for Benedict, as well as for myself."

"You shall have it," agreed Toby. A door at the end of the hall opened, allowing me to hear the murmur of conversation and to glimpse a vaguely familiar face, before the door was hurriedly reclosed. Toby jumped nervously, although he immediately covered his reaction. "Where is Andrew?" he asked smoothly.

I realized that the face reminded me of my brother—which meant that Toby kept me in the hall because members of the Family were conferring elsewhere. He had met me quickly at the door because he had just admitted other visitors. I sensed no Mystic presence, but I feared to probe too closely. "Andrew is here, in Tathagata," I replied, trying to decide whether I should make a quick escape or force myself to complete the story that Andrew had bidden me to tell. If the Protectorate were meeting in that little room, Ch'ango herself might be present. That thought made my nerves tremble like water in a winter breeze. I concluded, however, that it was too late to retreat now. "I cannot give you a specific location, because Andrew does not inform me of his comings and goings, but I can tell you where he will be when the Parliament meets for its final vote regarding Prince Hiroshi. Andrew will be inside the Parliament building. Prepare a proper Mystic defense of the building, and you will have him." I handed Toby a smooth golden bracelet, set with agate, which Andrew had provided for me. "I stole this from Andrew, and stolen magic has power beyond its original. Use it. Mastermage Ch'ango can arrange the spell. She knows how to take advantage of stolen magic."

"You surprise me, Marita," said Toby slowly. At the mention of Ch'ango, he had wiped all signs of emotion from his plump face, and he did not otherwise acknowledge my use of her name. "You never showed any ambition until now."

"You weren't looking," I replied. "I have long held ambitions as a Mage, if not as an Affirmist. The two paths have simply merged recently."

Toby reassembled his artificial smile. He hefted the solid bracelet in his hands, testing its worth. He fixed his attention on the gold lizard bracelet that encircled my upper arm, though I believed that it was the door at the end of the hall that inspired him to say, "These chairs are dreadfully uncomfortable. Let's continue this discussion in my office."

"I need to be going, thank you." Andrew had instructed me to remain as near as possible to the main entry, and the possibility of Ch'ango secretly observing me made me all the more anxious to leave. "If you need to reach me, place a message among the prayer scrolls at the Avalon temple. Seal your scroll with brown wax, and mark it with your signet. I shall find it."

Turning my back on Toby and the unseen conferees required all the nerve I could muster, despite Andrew's assurances that he was observing and protecting me. I opened the front door, waiting for the sound of a stunner or the debilitating blow of one of Ch'ango's spells. I walked evenly down the stoop, turned right, and continued down the street. Only when I had passed the corner did I pause, lean against a lamp post, and exhale an overdue sigh of relief.

A woman in an Affirmist brown suit stared at me suspiciously as she strode past. She muttered several derogatory words regarding me, my Mage School, and Mysticism in general, totally disregarding the laws of universal tolerance. The open use of the colors of affiliation seemed to encourage antagonism as readily in Tathagata as in its less sophisticated, more circumspect cousins. Tathagatans did not obey laws; they made them.

I continued down the street, watching for Andrew. He had told me to walk directly toward the Site of Parliament after leaving Uncle Toby's house. Andrew could not have missed seeing me. Pedestrians were plentiful, but Avalon green was not that common. I saw half a dozen figures draped in Mastermage violet, but none of the robes around me covered Andrew's muscular figure. Andrew's absence worried me enough that I forgot to be annoyed with him for abandoning me.

I was within two blocks of the Parliament building, and I could hear the official criers shouting the public agenda and the day's progress. Their words were garbled by the intervening noise of people and traffic. Brass dragons, enhanced by Mage illusions, snarled from the minarets of the Lung-Wang temple beside me. I crossed to the opposite side of the street to avoid the clouds of musky incense that swirled out of the temple doors, and I gained an unobstructed, angled view of the Site of Parliament.

The actual Site of Parliament occupied the center of the government district. It was an enormous, rectangular building constructed of polished white marble. Along the right side, large squares of plain brown canvas were hung at regular intervals to honor the Affirmists. The left side of the building was covered by copper friezes representing great Mystic legends.

The usual crowds had gathered around the criers, jostling each other to hear the most timely and accurate Tathagatan news at its source. I saw no one entering or leaving the Parliament building. Uniformed guards, bright with their patchworks of official colors, flanked each door, and they were not dozing at their posts.

I decided to move closer in order to hear the criers' words. Because the criers' voices were not completely synchronized, I could not decipher their common message until I joined the crowd directly across the street from the Parliament building. I tried to remain inconspicuous in the shadow of the shops behind me, although I did not expect anyone here to recognize me.

"Special session continues all day," shouted the crier whose deep voice I had singled out from the rest. "Evidence of Mage Aroha's treason against society has been confirmed. A sentence of death has been recommended. Names continue to be solicited for the execution committee. Judgment of the crimes of Aroha's conspirators continues."

The members of the World Parliament excelled at making declarations. Action was not their forte, even for trivial causes. They had condemned Andrew, insulted Hiroshi by refusing to name him, and presented their pious stance in support of society's welfare. They had accomplished nothing, because they had decided against Andrew and Hiroshi years earlier. They were floundering in their own cowardice, greed, and ineptitude, as Andrew had predicted. The execution committee might never be filled, if it had to rely on volunteers. Other than Ch'ango, who would risk fighting Andrew on an individual basis?

The crier began to repeat his message, which would not change until the members of Parliament decided to release another fragment of information. The brevity of the information that I had heard only confirmed that Parliament was protecting itself from ridicule by keeping its discussions secret. I squeezed past the thickest part of the crowd, listening to the cynical speculations about the actual business being conducted inside the guarded Parliament building. The hypotheses ranged from a theory that Aroha did not exist (and the members of Parliament were currently enjoying the mindless pleasures of E-units) to a flat statement that Aroha had rebuilt the Empire arsenals and was currently on his way to bombard Tathagata into oblivion.

Unable to press farther through the crowd on the sidewalk, I ventured into the street, warily avoiding the numerous autobuses. As soon as possible, I returned to the safer walkway. I heard a low chuckle from a balcony overhead, and I glanced up. Andrew was seated comfortably on a cushioned ecru lounge, his braceleted arms crossed over the embroidered violet silk of his cloak.

Andrew grinned at me and glided to his feet. Apparently unhampered by his long cloak, he hopped over the balcony's rail and used the plastone ornaments of the adjacent building to climb to the ground. No one but me gave him more than passing notice. He took my arm and joined my interrupted journey down Parliament Street.

"You can always rely on Tathagatans," he murmured, "to concoct every outrageous explanation for any given subject. Every citizen in the government district has a solution for every problem, but not a single soul would ever deign to observe his neighbor closely. Looking at the surroundings might suggest a lack of self-assurance—or an affiliation with the information brokers of the less elite districts. Hence, no one notices when their much-bandied problem is sitting virtually on top of them."

"If one person happened to break your rule," I whispered, "you could find yourself in more trouble than even you could handle.'

"How is Uncle Toby?" asked Andrew so cheerfully he was almost fey.

"In the worst temper I've ever seen. He kept forgetting to be genial."

"Good. A bad mood will make him careless."

"He could have become 'careless' enough to use a stunner on me. I thought you promised to stay close in case I needed you."

"I was close." He touched my earring, the spiral shell that was his gift to me from Rit. "You must learn to trust in Prince Hiroshi's talents and in my ability to apply his products. I wish we'd had time to teach you more about his methods before we came here."

We had walked nearly half a block beyond the Site of Parliament, when Andrew said, "Let's cross here."

"Where are we headed?" I demanded, suddenly fearful, as my crescents began to tingle.

"To the Site of Parliament."

We were already halfway across the street. Terrified of being overheard, I whispered, "Andrew, they're planning your death in that building. Every door is guarded. What do you hope to achieve? You told me yourself that nothing happens mid-session."

"I still have a Member's key that will let us bypass the guards. The key codes are changed regularly, but they are fairly easy to decode. Mine is now current. I recorded it last night."

We were approaching the Mystics' side of the building. "You came here?"

"It's perfectly safe after the members go home. A few token guards and warding spells are easy to avoid. I wanted to check the landscape and make a few adjustments to my advantage."

"You planted some of Hiroshi's mechanisms?" I asked. The copper friezes glared down at me, the faces of ancient Mystic gods enormous and intimidating.

"I didn't like to think of all those bored parliamentarians suffering another day without diversion." Andrew shrugged. "There are several small observation rooms behind the main chamber of Parliament. That's where the most informed people spend their time." He pressed a philter vial into my hand. Its contents vibrated. "You know how to use this. Walk up to that door and ask the guard how to deliver a message to Scribe Talitha in the main chamber of Parliament. Apply the philter while he answers you."

"You just said that you could bypass the guards."

"As a precaution, I prefer to ensure that we reach the private door without being remembered. The philter produces a colorless smoke that will reduce the guards' attention span for a few hours."

"Why don't you administer it yourself?" I grumbled.

"You provide excellent distraction, and I'm too well known. You won't have any trouble. When you're done, walk toward the rear of the building. I'll meet you at the door."

I complied, hating every moment of false innocence. I performed Andrew's little task so easily that I felt tainted and corrupt. I left two smiling guards behind me. I knew that I had injured them with illegal magic, even if they were happily oblivious. When I rejoined Andrew, I muttered, "Why do I feel that every crime I commit on your behalf will rebound on us eventually?"

Instead of retorting lightly, Andrew answered with a sad, ironic grimace, "Every sin has a cost, my dear." He inserted a white keycard between two panels of a frieze depicting the world egg. A door swung inward onto a dim, paneled hallway striped with walnut-stained wood and silver runes.

He led me through empty halls that echoed disquietly with the voices of the members of Parliament. I heard the name "Aroha" shouted repeatedly, as if it were a curse. The name "Hiroshi" was spoken with resentment, envy, and awe.

We passed many doors, all indistinguishable to my eyes, before Andrew applied his keycard to admit us to a room that was hardly bigger than a closet. Three plastiwood chairs and a small matching table comprised the furnishings. The only light came from a row of tiny holes along the far wall.

Andrew touched the wall, and the lighted holes clicked into darkness. I heard another soft click. Instead of a dark wall, I faced the bright main chamber of the World Parliament. Every gilded column and carved ivory panel seemed to leap at me in unnatural detail.

We were positioned just beneath the crystal dome, slightly above the tiered rows of the Mastermages. I looked across the chamber at the Affirmists, recognizing many of my cousins, uncles, and aunts. Almost half of the brown velvet seats were empty. I could not see the whole expanse of Mastermages.

The current speaker, standing behind the podium on the mosaic floor far beneath me, was a cousin named Martin, Dom of Haumi. He was recounting the evils of Hiroshi and Aroha, making much noise but very little sense. At an ivory desk behind him sat Talitha and three other Scribes, all of them armed with notebooks and pens. I was mildly surprised to see Talitha in the position of recordkeeper, but I assumed that she was serving as a substitute, working with my uncle's approval. The official Scribes recorded such data as they considered appropriate to the permanent files of the Scribes' Guild. Talitha made few notes about Dom Martin's speech.

Andrew murmured, "Watch the sunburst pattern at the center of the floor."

As soon as he finished speaking, pillars of light erupted from the golden tiles of the floor mosaic and stretched in rainbow brilliance to the top of the crystal dome. Dom Martin stumbled away from the podium. Talitha whispered to her neighboring Scribe, a middle-aged man who jumped to his feet and raced to the exit. The door did not open for him. He rattled its handle furiously, then turned and leaned against it, his pinched face ruddy with anger.

The sunburst's halo dimmed to a faintly glowing curtain. In its center stood Andrew, tall and defiant in violet and gold. I looked twice at the man beside me to convince myself that the image in the parliamentary chamber was illusory. When the image began to speak, I laid my hand on Andrew's shoulder to assure myself that he, rather than the man in the chamber, was real.

"Greetings, my fellow parliamentarians," announced Andrew's image with an impudent smile. His audience, initially

stunned into silence, loudly began to demand action from
guards who did not materialize. The chamber seethed with
motion, but no one seemed willing to venture onto the chamber floor. Dom Martin had crept back into the tiers. Talitha
and the two Scribes beside her, a balding man and a silver-
haired woman, watched Andrew suspiciously.

Andrew's image raised his hands and commanded silence.
"Please, friends," he said, "restrain your panic. I have not
come to destroy you, though that is your ungracious intention toward me. I bring you opportunity."

The sunburst curtain brightened. When next it dimmed,
the man in its center was Hiroshi. Attired in the blue and
golden ceremonial robes of Empire royalty, he looked quite
as impressive as Andrew.

"I have spoken to you before," declared Hiroshi grimly,
"and you did not listen. This is your final chance to recon-
sider the narrowness of your perspective. We can afford to
waste no more time on your foolish delays."

I analyzed as I watched. The image projected the same
man I had met, but there *were* subtle differences, amplifica-
tions of the traits that had impressed me most. Hiroshi's
voice seemed a little stronger. His posture was straighter,
taller, and more sure. The sense of dominance was magnified. This was not a simple man with extraordinary talents.
This was an Empire Prince.

"I shall give you back your world," decreed Hiroshi with
regal confidence, "if you are willing to care for it properly.
Otherwise, you will forfeit everything you now possess.
Your Protectorate is a facade, the tool of an avaricious Mage
named Ch'ango, who will surely destroy you if you decline
my help. I offer knowledge, not threats. Heed my warnings."

The simple speech sent shivers through my Mage marks.
I felt that I was watching and listening to a ghost of the Empires, legendary scourge and near-divine creative genius
united in the shape of a man. The members of Parliament
seemed to share some of my sentiment, for they had grown
completely still.

The sunburst repeated its magic once more, creating the
image of Andrew at Hiroshi's side. "Thank you for your
keen attention, Mastermages and Doms," declared Andrew
wryly. "If any of you wishes to be saved from the coming
calamity, mark your door with this sign, and we shall allow
you to be part of *our* future." He raised his hand and drew

the letter "A" in fierce script upon the air. The letter expanded and multiplied spontaneously, until its duplicates covered the surface of the curtain of light.

A shattering sound from the crystal dome drew all eyes upward. A chorus of voices screamed, as a web of cracks in the crystal imitated the sunburst pattern of the floor. The light curtain flared blindingly.

I averted my face from the display. Andrew watched it impassively. "An adequate finale," he murmured critically, "but a trifle too abrupt."

Hesitantly, I returned my attention to the location of Andrew's spectacular presentation. The blaze of light had faded, and the images of Andrew and Hiroshi were gone. The sunburst was only an elaborate mosaic design. Light flowed only from the ceiling panels. The crystal dome was intact.

"I think we made a suitable impression," remarked Andrew quietly. He smiled at me. "Hiroshi and I spent several months developing that little episode. We had some trouble projecting images that looked realistic from all sides. Aside from a trifling persuasion spell, it was entirely a product of Empire science. Elaborate Mage techniques would be discredited too easily in this crowd."

I let my hand slide off his shoulder. "You've just added fuel to their accusations against you. If anyone still questioned whether you presented a danger to society, you've eliminated those doubts now."

"How often can they sentence me to death? As long as they're suitably intimidated, the condemnation remains meaningless. They may not mark their doors, but no one will volunteer for the execution committee." Andrew touched the view of the main chamber, restoring it to a gray wall. "There is also an element of fair play in Prince Hiroshi that insists on giving a legitimate last chance to his opponents. It is conceivable that someone, even in the World Parliament, has a hidden modicum of common sense buried beneath the usual blather."

"*You* were a member of Parliament."

"And I was every bit as arrogant as the rest of the lot," he finished for me. "But I've already told you what changed my perspective."

"Your arrogance has not evaporated. This exercise frightened people whom you already terrify. *Ch'ango* is not afraid of you." I glanced at the Parliament floor, where Talitha was walking the perimeter of the sunburst mosaic. "Neither is Talitha," I added.

"They both imagine that they know me 'too well' to be defeated by me. They are wrong."

Am I wrong about you as well? I wanted to ask, but I remained silent. While the parliamentary guards struggled to reopen the main chamber's door and free the members, Andrew and I left as we had come. The two guards whom I had bespelled continued to smile.

Den

Dear Brother Benedict,

We have arranged the retreat, as you requested. It will be ready when you require it. It is the only dwelling on an island that is not on any autoboat's route. There are edible fish in the local waters, and some tubers and herbs grow near the wetlands. The island will accommodate two in reasonable comfort, and no one will question you or your charge. You could live there indefinitely.

Would it be wrong of me to pray that you never need this retreat? We do not want to lose your wisdom, and I do not want to see my prophecy about you and your sister fulfilled. I am an old man, who has seen too much tragedy and despair.

May the Intercessor have mercy on us all,
Den

Marita

Leaving the Site of Parliament, Andrew ushered me away from the main streets of Tathagata, prowling through narrow alleyways that I would never have entered alone. The best of them resembled Janine's precarious domain, being equally dirty, decayed, and lifeless. The most disturbing routes included silent, loitering clusters of cold-eyed men, who acknowledged Andrew with restrained nods and watched me with dour suspicion.

"Do you know them?" I asked softly, after we had passed a particularly malicious looking crew. The filthy backsides of prosperous Tathagatan businesses loomed over us, blocking the sun.

"I know most of them," replied Andrew equably. "They all know me. Several of them work for me intermittently."

"In what capacity?"

"Smuggling, information gathering, observing select individuals, making my presence felt when I am absent from Tathagata, ensuring that my movements are not *too* well advertised when I *am* here." He kicked aside a pile of trash from a plasteel grate, reached through the grate, and removed a silver-gray box that barely fit between the mold-encrusted bars. He pried a thin wedge of silver from the box and replaced it with a similar object, taken from inside his vest. Restoring the box to its original position, he also arranged the trash with artistic care to cover the grate again. "We'll see if your uncle appreciated your gift to him," said Andrew, waving the silver triangle that he had retrieved.

"What is that?"

In answer, he handed me the triangle and tugged on my right earring, activating another of the shell's multifaceted gifts. I jumped in alarm, hearing Uncle Toby speak my name. Andrew smiled knowingly, and I calmed myself enough to listen as we walked.

"'If the villain does not control her, why did he bring her to Tathagata?" snapped a man whose voice I did not recognize.

Lar answered, as clearly as if he were beside me, "He flaunts her as a prize of conquest, Sev. His control of her gives him nothing but a captured pennant. Dismiss her visit. It is insignificant to us."

"I must inform Talitha," muttered Toby. "If there is any chance that Marita was sincere, we should prepare."

"Ch'ango already knows," countered Lar, "and Ch'ango is handling the situation. Aroha will be dead long before Parliament finalizes the vote against his wretched Prince, and all of us will sleep more soundly."

We had reached the end of this particular web of alleys. Before returning to a proper street, Andrew took the triangle from me, and the words of the stolen conversation ceased abruptly. "Anything of interest?" he asked me.

"Couldn't you hear?"

"Not while you held the data slip. I'll listen and transcribe the session later."

"It was my uncle and Lar and a voice I didn't recognize. I think Lar called him 'Sev.' "

"Dom Sevrin," replied Andrew, "another of your inescapable relatives. He is a major member of the Protectorate."

"I saw a man at Toby's house: He looked much like Benedict."

"That description fits Sevrin well enough."

"They hate you, Andrew. They want Ch'ango to kill you."

"Is that all you heard? Pity." We were back on Danu Street, not far from the temple yard. "I have one more stop to make. You might check the prayer scrolls at your Avalon temple, though I doubt that you'll find anything with your uncle's signature. I'll meet you back at Julia's." He brushed my cheek with a formal kiss. "Don't try any more seeking spells, and don't trust Avalon Mages above the rest. They are all Tathagatan here." He plunged into a crowd debarking from an autobus. Though I tried to watch his progress, he and his violet cloak disappeared without ever seeming to emerge from the knot of temple visitors.

I visited the bank of prayer scrolls, each tied by emerald ribbon to a section of the temple's eastern wall. Most were unsealed; a few dangled open, displaying Mystic symbols or the random dots of dactyliomancy. Of those that were guarded by imprinted wax, none wore any shade of brown.

I lit another candle at Merlin's shrine, but I did not stay. It was a busy hour of the day at the temple, and Mages all around me seemed to be jabbering excitedly of Mastermage Ch'ango and the Mystic revival that she would lead. The smoking incense of many offerings stung my eyes.

Julia's house seemed a refuge of quiet and peace when I reached it. Andrew had not returned, but Iron preened atop the desk that Andrew had used. Iron observed me with interest, as I opened one drawer and stared pensively at the bulging envelope Andrew had placed there. I allowed my mind to float into that tranquil state that precedes a planned seeking.

I heard the front door open. I snatched my mind back to my surroundings, rushing the process and giving myself a headache. Iron raised her head and angled her ears toward the quiet sounds from the entry hall. She settled atop her feet and wrapped her tail around her, evidently contented to tolerate the visitor.

I made sure that my philter purse was accessible, but I let Iron's reaction guide me. I seated myself on the brocade lounge, and I watched the door. A woman, attired in an ivory silk pantsuit, entered and raised her heavy eyebrows at me. She had bleached, tightly curled hair and coffee-colored skin with a white snake painted on one cheek. Her chin was too narrow, and her nose was too sharp, but her eyes were large, dark, and beautiful. She had an ample figure, but the plumpness was well placed. "Didn't you hear my knock?" she asked in a rich contralto voice.

"No," I replied. "Are you Julia?"

She smiled, an unexpectedly wide and generous expression for her thin face. "I am glad that you recognize your hostess," she answered with a slight sway. "Not all of Aroha's women are so courteous. What is your name?"

"Marita," I answered, trying to match her air of cordial candor.

"Can you tell me where to find Aroha, Mage Marita?"

"No. I'm sorry."

"Do you expect him to return soon?"

"No. I don't really know when he'll return."

"Aroha does not tell us much, does he?"

That brought an honest smile from me, though I did not

particularly like being ranked with Julia in Andrew's life. "No," I answered. "He keeps his secrets well."

"Very well," agreed Julia. "Will you be staying here long?"

"I'm not sure yet." I summoned Andrew's Mystic name with difficulty, hoping that I triggered no adverse luck spells thereby: "That depends on Aroha."

Julia nodded. "I always wonder if he's worth the trouble he brings. Tell him that I have some jobs for him in exchange for the damage upstairs."

"He expected that you'd want him to pay in service."

"Aroha knows my tastes," replied Julia. She glanced at the desk. I refused to do likewise, considering its uncertain contents. Julia said amiably, "Thank you for the information, Mage Marita."

"You're quite welcome."

Our very civilized conversation ended with Julia nodding toward Iron and remarking, "I never worry about Aroha's affairs, as long as Iron is happy." She did not define the type of affairs that might concern her if Iron were not happy. She turned to leave, just as Andrew materialized in the doorway behind her.

His golden vest glittered, unshielded by the cloak that he removed and draped across a chair. His arms were bare of their usual weight of wealth. Mage silver nearly encircled each strong wrist and patterned the skin all the way to the elbow. "Good journey, Julia. Your neighborhood has deteriorated. The vandals were busy this morning." He settled beside me on the lounge.

Julia returned his smile tolerantly. "No neighborhood is safe when you visit it." She leaned gracefully against the wall. "You attract trouble, Aroha."

"I pay well to keep it at bay."

"You are not the only rich man in Tathagata." She shrugged.

"Did you have someone in mind?"

"Mastermage Lar is generous."

"You've lowered your standards, Julia," said Andrew dryly. He glanced at me, but I maintained my stoic silence. Lar's selective generosity was certainly not a subject that I intended to discuss.

Julia traced the line of her white snake absently. "I am an Affirmist, Aroha. I do not judge people. I simply serve them and try to earn a few comforts for myself and my employ-ees. Lar is not without influence in Tathagata, and you have chosen unfortunate companions in recent years."

"You have prospered from my choices."

"I do not deny it. We would not be having this discussion otherwise." Julia spread her hands. "I like you, Aroha. I like what you pay me, and I like how you pay it. You know that I affirm everyone equally, even those who are encumbered by accusations of serious crimes against society. But your presence in Tathagata worries many of my best customers. When they worry, they lose interest in simple pleasures, and my income drops."

"They seek escape from their worries, and your income rises."

"They do not escape the Mastermage of Tathagata."

"Tathagata has no Mastermage."

Julia sighed, "I do not meddle in politics, Aroha. I repeat only what the criers announce to all the city, and I remind myself that even Aroha has overestimated himself occasion-ally. You once assured me that Tua'ana would bear a healthy child, and my poor girl died with a mixie suckling her breast. I would not like to be disappointed by you again."

Andrew did not answer her. He turned his head away from me and stared fixedly at Iron. He had withdrawn himself from all human company without moving from the brocade lounge.

"Don't stay long in Tathagata," suggested Julia with plasteel in her voice, "or you may have more than a little vandalism to concern you." She swayed into the hall, and I heard the front door close moments later. Andrew uncoiled himself from the lounge, stormed from the room, and thun-dered up the stairs.

When I tried to stroke Iron's soft fur, the cat hissed at me.

Talitha

10 Tiurai, 510

Mastermage Lar, via Scribe Meara,

I have conferred with Dom Toby and several other Protectors. We concur that Aroha's insolent message to the Parliament this morning requires discussion by all major members, as soon as possible. I have seen more than one marked door this evening, though I have found no one who admits to the placement of Aroha's infernal symbol of concession. We have scheduled a meeting of the Protectorate for tomorrow, during the second break.

If Ch'ango again declines to meet with us, I hope that you will still attend. You are a gifted, intelligent man in your own right, and the Protectorate needs you. Do not abet your detractors. You diminish your status by hiding behind Ch'ango, giving credence to Aroha's derogatory remarks about your capabilities as a Mage. You and I have often disagreed, but we cannot afford to indulge in petty differences. We both felt the sting of Aroha's attack in Rit. We cannot let him win simply to guard ourselves from the prospect of personal shame. Remember where Aroha learned his manipulative skills. When he insults you for serving Ch'ango, he mocks only himself.

Scribe Talitha

Marita

My second morning in Tathagata began more peacefully than the first. Andrew clung to me as if I were the ephemeral product of a Mage vision, hungrily sought and unrepeatable. There was an edge of desperation to his passion. He had scarcely spoken since Julia's visit the previous day. For once, I felt more needed than in need.

When he did speak, his question was quiet, calm, and deeply troubling. "Do you feel like visiting a monastery today?" he asked.

His left arm's scarab felt cold where it touched my side. His shells and lotus marks felt hot. "I'd like to see Shamba and Pachacamac," I replied, holding my deeper worries to myself, "but you've made that a dangerous destination, haven't you? After your deliberate inquiries, you'll be expected."

"Ch'ango has been observing me by Mystic means since we left the Site of Parliament yesterday. I'd feel safer meeting her on neutral ground, and that is the purpose of the monastery. It's a refuge from Mage feuds."

"Will Ch'ango respect a truce of tradition?"

"No. But the monastery enforces respect of its rules. Transmissive magic does not function predictably there, and that is more than a legend. Even receptive spells are difficult to control within the monastery's confines.'

My crescents shivered at his touch, betraying the turmoil in him. In such a rare, unsettled mood, he did not need arguments from me to compound his problems. "I shall go where you wish," I answered meekly.

"Forgive me, Marita," he whispered and said no more in words. Every Mage sense in me sang that he gave me love that morning, instead of passion alone, but it was a song of bittersweet joy. I did not understand why love brought him pain. I did not want to know.

We ate sweet chocolate and a fruit that tasted synthetic after the luxury of Ha'aparari. We walked together beneath an early morning sky that was soft with shades of mauve and buttery clouds. Andrew said little. When he did speak, it was of inconsequential things, like the first night we met and walked together in Rit. Beneath his violet cloak, his arms wore only two of his customary bracelets, positioned above the elbows to leave his Mage marks clearly visible.

As morning began to brighten, we reached Xilonen Plaza, the Tathagatan approximation of a park. The grass was pale and sparse, but Tathagatans were careful not to crush the sickly blades. Few of them even trod on the plastone cross between the grassy patches, though pedestrians frequently filled the walkways in the surrounding office district. A blank white column in the center of the plaza was revered as a memorial of the Great War's ending. According to my father, the column was all that survived of a Hangseng Prince's Tathagata residence.

Andrew did not circle around the plaza. He led me to the center column and stopped in front of it. He ran one hand across the column's stark, weathered surface. "We shall enscribe our names here, Marita," he murmured, "all of us who fight for restoration. The past should not be barren."

I heard Ch'ango's voice distinctly say, "You have become an arrogant fool, Aroha. By all the power in me, you will regret your very life before I am done with you."

Andrew did not react to the voice. My Mage marks provided no indication of Mystic spell. I did not wear the uncanny shell earrings this morning; I had bought my cascading bells for myself. As far as I knew, I wore none of Andrew's devices, except for the two gold bracelets, which had different gifts than sound transmittal. I searched around the plaza in alarm, but I did not see Ch'ango or anyone who showed the slightest interest in us.

Andrew struck the column lightly with his banded wrist. Nothing more than a wisp of gray smoke betrayed his action. Where he had touched the column, his cryptic, flowing signature, "A. of Purotu," was etched deeply into the marble. "Would you like to add your name to the list?" he asked me.

I shook my head, afraid to speak. I did not know if Andrew had heard Ch'ango's curse. The sky was so clear. The streets were so filled with ordinary people and their ordinary concerns. Andrew looked so strong, powerful, and confident.

The World Parliament might sentence him to death, but he had no fear of laws that bound the rest of us. He walked openly through the city of his enemies.

Andrew smiled crookedly. "You know the rules of Mystic challenge, don't you?" he asked, filling me with a horrible suspicion that Ch'ango's voice had prophesied truly. "If a Mage ignores three challenges from a rival, according to Mystic tradition, that rival gains Mage force from the recipient of the challenges."

I could not fathom his devious reasoning; however, by his words' effect on my Mystic senses, I understood too well what he was doing. Andrew was daring Ch'ango to take him. He had issued three challenges to Ch'ango and her Protectorate: the first, through me, to Uncle Toby; the second to Talitha and the Parliament; the third to Ch'ango directly by his present careless defiance. I assumed that Andrew had suggested visiting the neutral monastery as an added taunt, designed to pressure Ch'ango into a hasty attack.

"I'm not ready to lose you," I whispered to him as a plea.

"Make sure that Dom Toby provides you with that seat in Parliament, if I don't return," answered Andrew. He pressed his Parliament Member's key and a flat philter purse of aqua silk into my hands. He must have worn the purse beneath his embroidered violet sash because I had not seen the aqua silk previously.

"I do trust you, Andrew."

His dark eyebrows rose in surprise. "You jump to the most astonishing conclusions, dear Marita," he said wryly, but his kiss lingered, as if to press itself indelibly on his memory and mine.

He pushed me from him, when shrill chimes pierced the empty air. I tried to cling to him, but he pried my fingers from the silken fabric of his violet Mage cloak. The chimes battered my ears. Andrew raised one hand, tensed to hurl a warding spell. When he retreated from me, I could not follow.

The ice wind swept between us and spiraled in front of me, a hypnotic swirl of frozen water and dust. Andrew hurled one of his bracelets into the growing vortex. His action seemed to feed the spell, for the wind blew more strongly, pressing me backward against the white column. I could not move even to touch my philter purse. Andrew stood firm against the wind's icy pressure, though the wind tugged at his cloak and hair.

I squinted to protect my eyes from the stinging cold. I could see nothing beyond the plaza except a gray fog, and the sounds of traffic had likewise disappeared. I could hear the ice wind howling and the unnatural chimes deepening to a funereal bass. The tiny bells of my earrings trilled a high, frantic melody.

Andrew struggled forward into the wind, each step a minor triumph of determination. He forced his left hand deep into the vortex, until only a small portion of his arm remained visible. The muscles of his shoulder protruded in powerful relief, and the single gold bracelet cut into his skin. The wind emerging from the vortex became thick with crimson beads, and the ominous color splattered Andrew.

He snatched his hand out of the spell center. His fist was a mass of shredded skin, blood and scraped bone, but it gripped the bracelet that he had cast. The swirling wind diminished in force.

With a rumble and a flash, the plastone walkway beneath Andrew's feet shattered like brittle glass. The wind, which had thrust the folds of Andrew's cloak taut behind him, reversed. The vortex gulped the violet silk. Andrew stumbled forward. The ice, the dust, the blood, and the fog devoured him, then stretched thinly upon the spiral of wind and faded from my sight.

The sky was very blue. The autobuses growled, and the people of Tathagata shouted and schemed. One of the crossed walkways of Xilonen Plaza remained intact. The other was broken into uneven gravel.

I knelt to touch a small, dark pool amid the fractured plastone, and the liquid felt cold and thick. Its color was red. I rubbed Andrew's blood between my fingers, feeling that my own life had been drained from me.

I turned away from the sight of that bleak pool, but the view did not improve. The white column was equally stained. Blood dripped from the inscription of Andrew's name.

Several morning commuters were beginning to point at the broken walkway. A pair of frowning women in aqua Tangaroa robes crossed the street and headed toward me. I scattered a concealment philter and ran from the Tangaroans, the plaza, and the destruction.

My philter dissipated before I had traveled a block, but I found a shadowy corner in which to reappear without attracting attention. An autobus had just opened its doors, and I hurried to catch a ride to any destination that was distant. I squeezed into a seat between a slouching Affirmist boy and a fat, elderly woman in a neutral beige dress. I tried smiling cordially at both of them, but neither seemed pleased to share their bench with me.

At each stop, the pair of them looked at me resentfully. I kept expecting one of them to demand that I explain my presence or leave the bus. They may have been the two most harmless people in Tathagata, but I could not bear to stay next to them. At the fourth stop, I left the bus. After losing Andrew to an illusion-made-real, I felt that my paranoia was justified.

I refused to believe that Andrew could be dead, although I would have drawn that conclusion regarding anyone else in the same situation. He could be Ch'ango's captive. He could be entirely in control of his situation. I did not know if I should grieve, scheme for his rescue, or rejoice at his achievement. I looked at the dried blood on my fingers. Even if he had gone willingly to his attacker, he had paid a painful price.

Andrew insisted on guarding his secrets. If I had imagined that I had breached his independence, or that he had ever granted me his full confidence, I had been brutally disabused of my misconception. Andrew might, as Benedict had told me, force change upon those around him, but Andrew held stubbornly to his own defiant code. Confirmed in my doubts about Andrew, I discovered agreement with my brother's claim and Andrew's own injunction to me. Andrew *had* changed me—not necessarily for the better—but it was time that I accepted the result.

I selected another autobus with reason instead of panic. I would return to the house on Danu Street, where Andrew had left me a list. I would read the list and decide where to go next. I would not remain at Julia's house without Andrew. The house had already been attacked once to discourage its tenants from a lengthy stay.

Seated alone in the back of the autobus to the Avalon district, I remembered the aqua philter purse that I had tucked under my belt. When none of my fellow passengers were looking toward the rear of the bus, I lifted the edge of the aqua silk enough to see the gleam of silver nerve film inside the purse. I closed the purse quickly.

The purse that Andrew had thrust into my hands contained a fortune in Mage terms. It held enough nerve film to fashion a hundred sets of Mage marks. It must have held Andrew's entire supply. I could only imagine how much effort he had exerted to obtain so much of a scarce commodity, generally rationed even to Mastermages.

If he survived to see Ch'ango's marks, he would be unable to duplicate them without finding me. I hoped that he would be in a condition to locate me with his customary skill, but I needed a plan of my own. I needed to augment my Mage marks.

I smiled wanly through my misery. I still wanted to believe that Andrew was battling by his rules. I wished that I knew what cost he considered appropriate for his "sins." I doubted that he judged himself with the mercy of Benedict's Intercessor.

I debated changing my destination again and avoiding Danu Street altogether. I had the nerve film. If Andrew had valued his list of names equally, he would have included it in the aqua philter purse—unless he wanted me to return to Danu Street. Perhaps he had spoken of the monastery as a recommendation that I seek it as a refuge.

Keeping pace with Andrew's schemes made my head feel battered under the best of circumstances, so I forced myself to stop analyzing his possible intentions. I would go to Danu Street. Considering the breadth of Ch'ango's powers, I did not think Danu Street would be any more dangerous than my other options.

I had resolved not to yield to panic and the external forces that my crescents, shrunken tight against my skin, amplified. I practiced the breathing patterns and controlled sequence of mental images that Andrew had taught me, and the tingling of my crescents eased a little. In the Avalon temple, I had made my own judgments of what I needed to do in Tathagata. Andrew's disappearance, though it might devastate me personally, did not contradict my vision.

The autobus stopped in front of the Avalon temple. I decided to debark and walk the remaining few blocks. I entered the temple, bypassing the prayer scrolls. I wanted nothing from Uncle Toby, even if he should deign to make an offering.

Someone else knelt at the Merlin shrine and seemed disinclined to move. The other exposed shrines, scattered throughout the nave, did not appeal to me, and most of the altars along the walls were occupied. Byelobog, the White God, had only a rustic pillar, carved from old, fibrous plastiwood, to honor him, but he occupied a shadowy corner beneath a broken lamp. Though I did not know the Slavic mythology well, I equated Byelobog with benevolence. I knelt on the frayed rug in front of his neglected image.

I laid my cloak and veil on the floor beside me. With trembling fingers, I opened the aqua philter purse and removed the sheaf of nerve film. A pair of lotus marks had already been etched onto the top sheet of film. I tapped the outlines gently, and the silver lotus blossoms fell into my hand.

They had no perceptible weight, but they felt cold. I held them, steeling myself for their insertion. If I used a numbing philter to make the process painless, I would be unable to guide the attachment accurately. Incorrectly applied, nerve film could cause paralysis or permanent agony.

I knew the techniques and had practiced them on several occasions. Less than a year ago, I had given Kurt his final lotus marks. The twelfth lotus position was easier to locate than the lower ranks, because the twelfth lotus formed the tip of the pyramid. It was, however, a particularly delicate attachment, because the twelfth lotus rested directly upon the underside of the wrist.

I laid the aqua purse and one lotus atop my folded veil. I removed a vial of penetrating fire oil from my own philter purse. Deciding that the right-hand mark would be most difficult to apply, I positioned the first lotus on my right wrist. I inhaled deeply and squeezed three drops of oil onto the lotus.

The silver film sizzled into my skin, and I gasped at the burning and reshaping of nerves, as the fire spread through me from my fingertips to my brain. Tears overflowed from my eyes, and I sniffled helplessly. My left hand still held the unstoppered vial of fire oil. I did not dare to move my right hand until the lotus had attached completely.

The level of pain, compounded by the reconfiguration of my nervous system, made conscious thought impossible. I was a helpless, injured animal. I snarled at a temple visitor who approached me too closely. The girl retreated with a stark, sick look of horror on her pale face, as if she had witnessed one of the more dreadful rituals of blood magic.

The imbalance of an unpaired lotus kept me dizzy even when the waves of pain began to slow. I endured it for long minutes, hoping that my senses would settle back into order, but Byelobog's shrine continued to reel. I stretched my right hand tentatively, and the lotus moved with the same suppleness as the skin. The first attachment was clean.

I had difficulty picking up the second lotus, and placing it seemed impossible. Yet I had no choice but to finish what I had begun. Several times, I traced each of the eleven existing lotus marks, losing count and wandering from my thumb to my elbow. When I finally thought I had established the pattern of eleven, I positioned the twelfth lotus. I was not sure that it was anywhere near my wrist, but I could make no better guess through the distortion of imbalance.

The first drop of fire oil landed on bare skin, and the odor of singed flesh compounded my distress with nausea. Gagging, I threw drops of fire oil wildly. Puffs of acrid smoke erupted from Byelobog's shrine, but some of the oil did reach the lotus, and the anguished process of attachment began once more.

The pain could not exceed the terrible level of the first attachment, but the second ordeal acquired a sense of nerves writhing against nature. I had positioned the lotus imperfectly. Whatever the outcome, I could not correct my error. My entire body began to shake.

A man's voice penetrated slowly. "Who is your Mastermage?" it demanded with what seemed like interminable persistence.

I muttered, "Andrew," without knowing what I was saying. I must have garbled the name, because the man insisted that I repeat my answer.

"She's incoherent," said a woman.

"A bad attachment. The lotus is crooked," replied the man.

"It's amazing that she placed it as well as she did. She must be mad to have tried applying her own Mage marks."

"Mad with ambition," grunted the man. "I've seen her kind before in Tathagata. Not many of them last beyond the first attachment. Most of them swallow their fire oil, killing themselves to end the pain."

Byelobog's shrine stabilized. I could see my final lotus. It was skewed slightly, but it had merged adequately with my skin and nerves. My mind cleared, except for the minor disorientation of adjusting to a new pair of Mage marks. "I am not mad," I informed my listeners irritably. "I succeeded, didn't I?"

The man and woman stared at me with unflattering disdain. They were both twelve-lotus Mages robed in emerald with the silver and black sashes of temple overseers. He was tall and bony with a jutting chin, protruding gray eyes, shoulder-length brown hair, and a severe burn scar along one side of his neck. She was a small, blonde woman with a red face and high forehead. In addition to his lotus blossoms, the man's arms wore a star, an unusual specialty mark of authority to interpret Mystic law.

"Who is your Mastermage?" demanded the man again.

"Lar of Rit," I answered, because that half-truth seemed less harmful than any attempt to explain my connection to Andrew.

"We must report this violation to him," declared the woman, pointing at my inflamed wrists as if they defiled the temple. "He should fine her a year's servitude, at least."

When I named Lar, the man's expression lost its angry furrows. "I can take care of this matter, Hanna," countered the man. "You may return to the office. Reassure Vesta that the situation is under control, and send someone to cleanse this shrine."

"As you wish, Mage Connell," answered Mage Hanna stiffly. She bobbed away from Byelobog's shrine at a brisk, determined pace. She seemed like a structured woman, upset by my interruption of her routine but too disciplined to react with more than a stern remark.

As Mage Hanna disappeared beyond the great doors, I realized that the temple nave had emptied except for myself and Mage Connell. Observing the direction of my gaze, Connell said, "The morning ceremony is taking place in the courtyard. If Mage Vesta had not returned inside for her wand, you might have started a serious fire. I must fine you for the damages."

I offered two gold coins from my pocket, moving my stiff hand with care. "Is this adequate?"

Connell widened his bulging eyes. "Quite adequate." He took the coins from my hand with a cautious delicacy. "These are Tangaroa designs," he remarked, observing the crashing wave pattern. "Mastermage Lar is Lung-Wang, is he not?"

"Yes," I replied, "but I work with many Mages." I did not understand the purpose of Mage Connell's question, and uncertainty made me wary. Gold had equal value in any currency, and the coins were used interchangeably. I had not even made conscious note of the nature of Andrew's coins.

Connell nodded. "I have some healing salve. If you will accompany me, I shall treat those wrists of yours."

"Thank you, but I have my own salve." As my head continued to clear, I became increasingly aware of the aqua silk purse resting on my emerald veil. Was that splotch of color the only reason for Connell's questions about the Tangaroa coins? Trying to move naturally, I gathered my cloak and veil, and I clutched them over the aqua purse against my breast. I rose to my feet, surprisingly steady. "I am sorry about the damage. Good journey, Mage Connell."

"Please, Mage Marita, don't leave so hurriedly."

Had I told him my name in my confusion? No, but I had admitted being an Avalon Mage of Rit. By now, the entire Protectorate knew that I was in Tathagata, and I had suggested the Avalon temple as a place for Uncle Toby to find me. Alerting the officials of the Avalon temple to watch for me would be a reasonable action for Uncle Toby to take. I cursed myself for my lack of foresight.

"I have already inconvenienced you too much," I said.

"Mage Marita," whispered Connell, glancing guiltily around the temple, "I want to help you. Aroha is my friend."

I wished that I had looked at Andrew's list. Connell seemed like an earnest man, but I remembered Andrew's warning: Trusting a Tathagatan was generally unwise. "I appreciate your kindness," I responded, smiling weakly, "but I'm really not feeling very well. Perhaps we shall meet later."

I expected an argument, but my reluctance seemed to have struck Connell like a blow. He shuffled nervously, and mumbled the rote offer of his official position, "I keep the vespers vigil alone each Jovesday, if you ever want to talk to me. Grow in wisdom, Mage Marita."

"Good journey," I murmured. Clutching my cloak with its precious contents, I left the temple. The public ceremony had just ended, and I was able to skirt the fringes of the dispersing crowd without attracting questions.

Silently, I reiterated to myself, half disbelieving: *I have made myself a full twelve-lotus Mage.* I would need to work with my new skills to become adept with them, but I could already feel the depth of change within me. If Andrew was right about Ch'ango's methods, she could now reach me with greater power and menace. I had good reason to believe, however, that Andrew preoccupied her for the moment. My opportunity must arise before she could look past him.

I would allot myself a few hours to practice the skills of twelve lotus blossoms, and I would then claim one more set of Mage marks. I would wear scarabs, and I would use them. If Ch'ango could make a Mastermage of Lar, I could make the same of myself. After all, power was my family's specialty.

I encouraged myself bravely, but my crescents knew the lie. They stung like nettles.

Talitha

11 Tiurai, 510

Mastermage Ch'ango, via Scribe Tsao-wang:
  I am unable to accommodate your request for postponement. The Protectorate's next meeting will occur as previously scheduled. We have much to discuss, involving the insolent demands that Aroha and Prince Hiroshi presented to the Parliament yesterday morning. I shall be pleased to provide you with a copy of the detailed minutes of the meeting. I am sorry that you will be unable to attend.

Scribe Talitha

Marita

Julia's house seemed desolate without the hope of meeting Andrew there. I was not sure what implicit arrangements he had made with Karam regarding the duration of our tenancy. He had demanded an indefinite term from the property broker, but Julia had clearly indicated the conflict of her own ideas.

Iron was curled on the desk, asleep on top of a folder that had not been present when I visited the room earlier in the morning. If I accepted Julia's correlation between Iron's moods and Andrew's welfare, I could interpret the cat's contentment as a favorable omen. I tried to encourage myself accordingly, but I could not make myself feel greatly cheered.

Before disturbing Iron, I opened the desk drawer to retrieve the envelope that Andrew had placed there. The bulky envelope was unsealed, and I shook the contents onto the desk's polished surface. The sketches of Julia's furniture, extremely well drawn for quick camouflage, looked harmless. I hated to damage the drawings—valuing their broad strokes for the sake of the artist as well as for the artistry—but a temporary existence had been Andrew's intention in creating them.

Iron had opened her eyes to watch me with lazy curiosity. I reached toward her and scratched her chin gently, intending to nudge her away from the folder. She purred, until I nudged, at which point she hissed and struck at my fingers, drawing blood. My hands were too swollen and sore to endure much more abuse. I decided to let Iron keep the folder a little longer. Considering Andrew's rapport with her, Iron might well have been enacting his wishes.

I spread the contents of the envelope on the desk beside Iron. She began to groom her paws and face, apparently satisfied that she had disciplined me. I sprinkled binding powder on a corner of one sketch, then added a drop of vision oil, trying to implement Andrew's vague instructions with a whispered spell to aid me. I produced nothing but a dampening of the paper and a Mystic abrasion of sore nerves.

I applied several grains of various philters to the clear stain, testing common and uncommon blends. Most of them had no effect at all, confirming that Andrew had treated the paper with a sophisticated mixture. Trying to recall early Mage lessons, I continued my delicate experiments, until I achieved a combination that transformed the paper into pearly translucence. With care, I applied the philter to a larger area. The sketch of a chair became a dim outline, overlaid by Andrew's list.

The list contained more than names and addresses. It included political affiliations, romantic attachments, personal strengths and weaknesses, and Andrew's terse assessments of motives, current schemes, and goals. As I treated the remaining twenty pages of Andrew's "brief" list, I became increasingly nervous about having such information in my possession.

Most of the names meant nothing to me, although I recognized a few relatives whom I had met as a child. The part of the list that interested me most concerned the Protectorate, its statement of purpose ("to eradicate all venal knowledge, synonymous with the science of the Empires, and all who cultivate and spread such knowledge"), and the frighteningly short roster of parliamentary members who had *not* signed the official statement of support. Most of the abstainers were described as indifferent Doms or Mastermages who had not visited Tathagata since their installation ceremonies.

Seven names were listed as the dominant forces in the official Protectorate: Ch'ango, Talitha, Toby, Lar; Dom Elayne of Uthlanga, Dom Sevrin of Nara, and Mastermage Cuycha of the Kinebahan School in Colom. I had met Cuycha once in my parents' company; he was a formidable Mage. Elayne was a cousin of my mother. Of Sevrin, I had already heard enough to make me dislike him.

The document was a terrifyingly effective blend of dry data, unsavory speculations, and a few heart-wrenching transcriptions of old letters. The letters, reflecting Andrew's private concerns, insights, and discoveries, made my crescents ache for the breadth of burdens he had carried for so long. In a letter dated Titema, 496, Hiroshi provided instructions for a factory repair that "should prevent the recurrence of your son's tragic condition." A note from Benedict described his foreknowledge of our parents' death and their unwillingness to accept his advice to distrust Toby. Benedict's note, dated Tiunu of the year 494, was addressed to me; in the margin, Andrew had scribbled, "found in Ch'ango's house among Dom Hollis' personal effects." I nearly stopped reading, blinded by my own tears, but I persisted.

The name of Mage Connell of the Avalon temple in Tathagata, who had claimed to be Andrew's friend, was notably missing from Andrew's list of allies, tolerant neutrals, and "aid for a price." The property broker, Karam, was included in the mercenary category. Julia was listed as a tolerant neutral; Andrew's notes included the addresses (and names of regular patrons) of five brothels that Julia owned and operated. Among the allies, most were privateers, fixers, scroungers, or shopkeepers, whose names I did not recognize. None of the allies or neutrals were Doms. Only one ally was a Mage: Shamba of the Inianga School, formerly of Rit, formerly a major supporter of the Protectorate. Mage Pachacamac of the Kinebahan was listed as "neutral, possibly sympathetic but too defeated by Ch'ango to be of use." The other neutral Mage was Gaia, the abbess of the Tathagata monastery.

I felt queasy considering Julia's earlier visit. This house did belong to her. As she had pointedly mentioned, Andrew's gold was not the only coin to buy information in Tathagata. She had named Lar, and I did not doubt that he paid well—on Ch'ango's behalf or for his own schemes. Julia could have returned when Andrew's folder had rested openly on the desk. She could not have read its contents, but she could easily have deduced that he had left it for someone who would see more than furniture sketches. Andrew listed Julia as a tolerant neutral, not an ally. The quiet, elegant room lost any remaining appeal for me.

As I finished reading Andrew's list, Iron leaped off the desk and wandered across the room to the window ledge. I had never believed legends of animal familiars who shared the soul of a Mage, but Iron's behavior unnerved me. I opened the folder that she had guarded.

More furniture sketches greeted my eyes. I applied my philter blend. As the paper acquired its translucent sheen, Andrew's letter to me emerged boldly.

"Dearest Marita," his letter began, "I am in Ch'ango's

custody by now. You may hear much about me from those whom I have fought and those whom I have served: mostly bad and mostly true. You will judge me for yourself. Let these documents, my gift to you, mitigate your condemnation."

The introduction stirred so much confused emotion in me that I delayed a full minute before continuing. With blurred eyes, I resumed reading, "If you feel you must wear scarabs, do not attempt to apply them yourself. Go to Mage Gaia at the monastery, and tell her that I authorized the procedure. I have enclosed instructions for a memorization procedure that I would encourage you to use before destroying these papers.

"If I succeed against Ch'ango, I intend to remake our world's government with Prince Hiroshi as its leader. To you, my dear, I would gladly give whatever position you might wish. If I fail, claim your place in Parliament as Mastermage or Dom with the aid of anyone who can assist you. If I am lost, so is Prince Hiroshi, and our sorry Parliament will be the last obstacle against Ch'ango's doomed, destructive autocracy. Try to educate all of those who will listen. Talitha may become reasonable, once I am gone.

"Do not try to take Iron with you. She can survive on her own in Tathagata, where actual vermin are as plentiful as their human counterparts. Iron will wait for me as long as I live. If I die, so will she.

"I never lied about my love for you, Marita of Avalon, with or without your spells of binding. I am sorry that our time together was so brief." He had signed the letter with the initial "A" in the same script that had filled the Site of Parliament. The signature was written in gold.

The rest of the folder's contents consisted of complex philter formulas, twelve-lotus and scarab spells such as only a truly exceptional Mastermage could impart, and instructions regarding the usage and locations of various "common" Empire devices. Andrew's folder and envelope provided enough power to create a dozen Mastermages or Doms. I employed his memorization process, a combination of philters, spells, and association techniques, to engrave his gift of knowledge in my mind. I burned the documents, including the envelope and folder, with fire oil in a blue porcelain bowl. When the last paper had curled into smoke, I dusted the ashes into the fireplace. A trace of gold clung to my finger.

Watching Iron with her enigmatic stare, I remembered one of my mother's comments about Tathagata. She had said that it was possible to be more alone in crowded Tathagata than anywhere else on Earth. My mother never liked Tathagata, which was why Benedict and I were raised almost exclusively in Rit.

I was less alone than Andrew. Perhaps a twelve-lotus Mage could detect him, where a ten-lotus Mage had invariably failed. I turned my sights inward to explore the potential of my new lotus marks, but the connections were still too tender to sustain concentration. I achieved only a smearing of my physical perceptions. The Mystic seeking would have to wait. I withdrew cautiously from my tentative vision.

I went upstairs to collect my few belongings into the canvas bag that I had brought to Tathagata. The bedroom had been straightened slightly, but the carpet and furnishings were still singed. The curtains still billowed over the smashed window. Everything belonging to Andrew, including the gold and philters that he had hidden behind a loose wall panel in the closet, was gone. Perhaps Andrew had left his treasures as deliberate, surreptitious payment to one of his mercenary allies, but my concern about Julia revived and sped my departure.

I took my bag and left the house to Iron. The throbbing of my arms had diminished. The new lotus marks, the left mark slightly askew, seemed to belong to a stranger. Every Mage mark altered its wearer in subtle ways, beyond increasing the number of spells that could be wielded. I had never heard anyone try to define the internal differences except as an awareness of a change of self. In that respect, I had not yet accustomed myself even to my eleventh set of lotus blossoms.

As I walked through the quiet neighborhood of the Avalon temple, I constantly expected someone to stop me, accuse me of conspiracy or illegal magic, and march me into a court such as Benedict had faced. I kept one hand on my philter purse, and I made sure that the gold lizard bracelet was oriented correctly in case I needed quick use of Prince Hiroshi's brand of magic. In my mind, I reviewed the processes and spells that Andrew's letter to me had described.

I readied myself for conflict, certain that I must eventually confront Andrew's enemies. I was less sure that they would approach me. As Julia and other evidence had indicated, Andrew attracted many women and did not hesitate to enjoy the results. My best protection rested in the perception, which Julia had apparently shared, that I was only one of the many women who allowed Andrew to use them. My ego cringed from the idea of being seen as so weak because I had *been* that weak for too long. However, I could not afford to pamper my self-esteem in the midst of a war.

I transferred autobuses twice en route to Tathagata's Mystic monastery, which occupied several acres of desolate land northeast of the city. I was the only passenger on the bus that traveled inland along the walled road. The high, plastone walls guarded supply factories from visitors and view. It was a claustrophobic journey. Emerging from the prison of the walled road, even the monastery's brown, barren fields looked inviting.

I pressed the signal button, and the autobus stopped in front of the monastery gate, where I debarked. The monastery building was a low, pale ocher structure in the center of the fields. The ubiquitous factory walls surrounded the monastery land on three sides, the road side being fenced with long strands of twisted wire. As I struggled to reach the plasteel gate's broken latch, the autobus abandoned me to the dry fields and the hot, empty wind that stank of burned plastic.

As I crossed the hard ground toward the building, a grayrobed figure emerged from an arched door. The sense of recognition, strong and unsettling, jarred me. I stopped walking in order to examine my reaction to the greeter, but closer examination did not change what I knew. The man approaching me from the Mystic monastery was my brother.

"Gaia has been expecting you," announced Benedict in calm greeting. His yellow hair shone brightly in the sun. His thin, folded hand rested lightly on the white cord that bound his robe. "Andrew sent a courier yesterday, warning her that you would come."

Mystic prophecy or informed speculation? With Andrew, who could distinguish the difference? "How long have you been here, Ben?"

"We arrived in Tathagata this morning."

"We?"

Cheryl J. Franklin

"Hiroshi, Anavai, and I."

"Prince Hiroshi has come here?" I demanded, honestly appalled. "The World Parliament is ready to execute him on sight. Andrew has insulted the members into a frenzy of personal anger against himself and Hiroshi, both."

Benedict nodded. "It is for the purpose of stopping Andrew that Hiroshi has risked his own life to come here. Andrew has never listened to advice from anyone else. No one but Hiroshi has a chance to influence Andrew now." Benedict's thin hands began to twist the belt cord, worrying its fibers. "The prophecy came to me just after you and Andrew left the island, and a disciple of mine confirmed it."

"What prophecy?" I asked, uneasily hesitating to share my own scant knowledge of Andrew's schemes. The wind moaned accusingly.

"You should speak to Gaia first," said my brother, after an indecisive pause.

He turned and strode away from me rapidly. I ran to catch up with him, before he could pass beyond the thickly plastered monastery walls. He stopped at the plasteel door from which he had emerged. He unlocked the door with an iron key and gestured for me to enter.

Ivory tiles lined the arched entry and the twisting hallway that we followed. I glanced into rooms that we did not enter, and I received incurious glances from many pairs of despondent eyes. The monastery cells were cool and dim, small and sparsely furnished, and nearly all were occupied. The supply units were simple plasteel models, lined neatly against the whitewashed walls. Gray-robed men and women sat in desultory clusters on the plastiwood floor of the discussion hall, through which Benedict led me. The building and the quiet, weary figures within it had a uniformly tired look, as of long waiting for a grim event. Only my brother seemed alert and alive. Despite the nervousness of his constantly mobile hands, his blue eyes shone almost radiantly.

"We house the refugees," declared a woman who awaited us past a turn of the narrow hallway. She was slightly built, as gray as her robe, and so frail that she seemed barely capable of standing unsupported. Her eyes were dark, bright beads in a wide, shriveled face. Her bony arms wore nine sets of lotus marks and crescents. The crescent placement was of an old style—the horns of her crescents were directed toward her body instead of away from it—a style not used by any official Mage school since the final days of the Empires. "Do you seek sanctuary with us, Mage Marita?"

I shook my head. "I seek information, Mage Gaia."

She did not dispute my use of her name, nor did she seem surprised by my answer. She said calmly, "You understand the dangers of such seeking, so I shall not try to deter you."

Aware of my brother beside me, I continued defiantly, "I was also told by Andrew of Purotu that you could assist me in applying Mage marks." Looking at her, I was not sure that her hands could hold any steadier than my own, but I would not dismiss Andrew's recommendation lightly.

Gaia's wrinkled lips curved into a gracious smile, but it was not a happy expression. "Have you the silver for the scarabs?" she asked.

I withdrew a sheet of Andrew's nerve film from my philter purse and offered it to her. She accepted it and nodded at my brother. "It will be well," she said to him.

"The test of wisdom has not yet come," he answered.

Benedict's reply seemed to compound the distress of the aged abbess. She clucked softly to herself as she disappeared through a narrow doorway into another hallway, muttering, "Prepare. Prepare."

I gulped back my own nervousness, which the eerily ancient abbess had not improved. "Will you tell me your prophecy now?" I asked my brother.

Benedict sighed. "You do not need to hear it." His hand sought my shoulder timidly. "I prayed that the Intercessor would ease my path, and He responded by providing you to share my burden. You carry the vision within you, Marita. It has reunited us for the fulfillment."

The certainty ran throughout me, confirmed by the new silver lotus marks on my arms. "I'm not sure what my vision means," I responded slowly, but I did not doubt that Benedict was correct about the sharing of it—for whatever cause.

"We will understand, when understanding becomes necessary. Until then, we need only obey the Intercessor's guiding Word." Benedict's hand fell back to his side, but the contact between us remained in our intangible *sharing*. We viewed the phenomenon differently, but it flowed, true and vital, between us. "I shall take you to Shamba now. He can tell you about Ch'ango—and Andrew."

Benedict's quiet insights into my private questions could not amaze me. Our perspectives diverged fundamentally, but

I knew that we had regained our lost twinship. All of my
Mage marks tingled with the confidence that Benedict and I
belonged together in this time and place, just as a mutual
need of companionship had long ago sealed us in childhood.
The feeling warmed me, but it was perilous, drawing me
near to my brother's form of obsession, isolated from all reality but our own.

Benedict took me to one of the monastery's cramped con-
templation rooms, a cell poorly lit by a high, narrow window
in the thick plaster wall. Incense, sweet and thick, smoked
from a brazier of bronze. Two dark old men, enveloped in
the uniform gray robes of the monastery, sat in the manner
of solitary meditation, though they faced each other across a
braided rope rug. I had seen both men often across a sapphire pentacle in Rit, surrounded by the blazing orange and
crimson of their respective Mage schools. They had
dimmed, either by their own choice or by Ch'ango's design.

Shamba and Pachacamac whispered together, too intent to
acknowledge interruptions, until Benedict said, "Shamba, I
have brought my sister to see you, as we discussed."

Despite Benedict's words, Mage Shamba did not expect
me. His head snapped upward, throwing his cowl from his
thick, black crown of hair. His amber eyes widened. The
force of my vision made me wonder at his surprise, but
enough of me still reacted like the Marita of a year ago: I
felt relieved to be greeted by astonishment, instead of by
prophetic assurance or a privateer's devilish deductions.

The monastery's gray robe did not suit Shamba's ebony
skin. It dulled the vividness that Inianga orange had always
enhanced. The greatest change, however, had transpired inwardly. In less than two years, all the vitality had ebbed
from Shamba. The man I remembered from Rit had seemed
younger by decades.

The Avalon cards associated Inianga with the suit of
Blood, meaning life, empathy, and spirituality. The symbolic
associations of his Mage School belonged equally to
Shamba, the individual. I could not look at Shamba's lean,
bearded face without feeling that this man possessed much
more depth than Mystic lore and Mage marks could convey.
In Rit, he had always intimidated me, for he presented an
imposing figure, both physically and as a true leader of a
significant Mage School. Now, I regretted that I had not
tried to know him better. Mage Shamba had retained his un-

assailable dignity. He still conveyed the impression of incorruptibility, which seemed all the more rare and precious in Tathagata.

Benedict explained me in his own fashion, informing Shamba mildly, "The Intercessor has called Marita to lead His plan to fulfillment. To accept this difficult blessing, she needs to know more about the Protectorate. Please, Shamba, accept your own call from Him and help her."

An expression of terrible pain contorted Shamba's weathered face. He whispered, "How can I comply? Benedict, you *know* what you ask!"

Mage Pachacamac, who had not heretofore acknowledged our interruption, suddenly raised his hooded head and scowled at my brother and me. Mage Pachacamac, the Kinebahan leader whom Ch'ango and Lar had brazenly cheated, did not appreciate my brother's request.

Pachacamac had aged more conventionally than Shamba, for the Amerind's braided black hair contained liberal streaks of white. Pachacamac was a tall, broadly built man, but he had lost considerable weight since I had seen him last. His obsidian eyes had retreated deep beneath his sculpted brow, where they seemed to look on uncomfortable vistas a lesser Mage could never have endured.

"Do not torment Mage Shamba," growled Pachacamac.

"He inflicts his torment upon himself," replied my brother.

Shamba raised his powerful hands quellingly, silencing both men. Having completed his stern gesture, Shamba composed his creased features with undisguised effort. "Why did you never come to me in Rit, Mage Marita, when time might have allowed us to devise an honorable outcome?" Grief overflowed his words and made them forcibly tragic.

Guilt assaulted me, though Shamba's suggestion would have struck me as ludicrous at the time he referenced. "You were, by far, my senior."

"You are of the Family. You could have made yourself heard."

"The truth had not yet visited me," I answered, though my voice faded as Mage vision prodded my attention. As Shamba spoke, my image of Talitha as Blood Mage revived spontaneously in my head, and the sense of *rightness* about her had strengthened. Our vision—Benedict's, Shamba's, and mine—had begun to coalesce. The prospect frightened me. I took an unconscious step backward, and my spine met the cold plaster wall. "I knew little about true prophecy, and 'destruction from Rit' held no meaning for me. Why did *you* never come to *me,* Mage Shamba?"

"Sable and Shadow blinded me to the role of the Ice Prince," sighed Shamba, generously employing Avalon references that few Inianga knew or cared to acknowledge. The Inianga had no formal counterpart for the symbolisms of Avalon's Mage cards. Pachacamac glowered at my impassive brother. Shamba tugged at his coarse beard. "I surmised only that *Ch'ango* was the name of the destruction."

"Not *Aroha?*" I murmured, aching for denial and dreading it.

"The Shadow Mage misleads, diverting attention from the truth," answered Shamba, dismissing Andrew's significance with an impatient confidence that impaled my heart. "By stealing Mystic energy from the Kinebahan, Ch'ango began her spell to claim the earth power that your Avalon Sable symbolizes. I did not predict that Benedict would be the condemned who would walk free." Shamba ended softly, "Or that Talitha would represent the lawful, enslaved by a false ideal and a treacherous Mage."

Mage instincts cried: *Do not envision Andrew, broken by Ch'ango and used by her! Do not let that imagining become possibility!* I knelt humbly before the two senior Mages, and I forced my mind to a quieter path. "Why did you dismantle your Mage Schools in Rit?" I asked, directing the question at Shamba and Pachacamac both. "What did you achieve by scattering your Mages?"

"We weakened Lar," answered Pachacamac, more gently now that I had given proper homage by lowering my position, "which is comparable to weakening Ch'ango."

If Shamba could minimize Andrew's role, I could allow myself to disregard Lar equally. "You could have fought Ch'ango," I argued, though I kept my voice deferential, as was befitting before these two honored elders. "You led many strong Mages."

"We could not fight her successfully," countered Shamba, "not then, not from within the city that gave birth to her. She controls too many Mystics—and Affirmists—either by deception or intimidation, and they serve to spread her villainy. If we had tried to fight her, she would have corrupted more Mages. I know the strength of her methods. She dominates the Lung-Wang and Tangaroa Schools even beyond Rit because she rules the Tathagatan temples." Shamba waved his limber hands at the braided rug, and I seated myself cross-legged between him and Pachacamac. Benedict remained standing, a still and silent sentinel. Surrounded by these three men, I felt secure until Shamba continued bitterly, "Believing in Ch'ango, I helped build her 'Protectorate.' I did her bidding when I no longer believed, because I feared her. I deluded myself that I served from honorable loyalty to my Mastermage, until she proved her depth of treachery by stealing the Kinebahan spirit jar."

"I had always refused to share with her the spells of our ancestors,'" growled Pachacamac, "because I feared that she would desecrate the spirits. So she took them, and she broke them, and I have failed my people and my Mystic vows. If I had not challenged her about Lar, many Kinebahan spirits, now lost, would have remained intact. My proud Mage challenge achieved nothing but the breaking of two great Mage Schools."

"It is her cruel influence that speaks through you, Pachacamac," murmured my brother, "and blinds you to hope."

Pachacamac merely shook his head. Shamba hunched his shoulders from doubt or from despair. My crescents hurt for them both—and for all that Ch'ango had cost me.

She had taken Andrew—possibly. She had murdered Kurt. She had corrupted Lilith. She had stolen from me all that Lar had left me of my innocence.

A wisp of harder sympathy ran through me. If Mages like Shamba and Pachacamac could fall to Ch'ango's schemes, how could I condemn Lilith for her weakness? Lilith had sinned less than I, who had yielded to Ch'ango by way of the same crippling despair that I witnessed now in Shamba. Under such a spell, I nearly sent my own brother to his death. "You were very close to Scribe Talitha at one time, weren't you?" I asked Shamba, hoping to remind us all of a happier time.

Shamba did smile, a warm, genuine expression that smoothed the lines of sorrow from between his curling brows. "Talitha and I shall always be close in spirit." His pride was obvious. "She is my daughter."

"I did not know," I said, truly astonished.

"You are not alone," admitted the Inianga Mage with wry regret. "Talitha's mother was a Scribe, which entitled Talitha to receive that privileged training and rank. The Scribes' Guild, however did not want a Mage to live with a Scribe, and they placed a condition on Talitha's education: After Talitha's birth, I was forbidden to see either mother or child. It was a cruel restriction, but I complied for Talitha's sake, until Talitha's training ended in her twentieth year."

"Talitha is a major influence in the Protectorate," I observed quietly. I awaited Shamba's response with raptness close to desperation.

His answer was frustratingly brief. "For this injury to my daughter, I will not forgive Ch'ango."

"Ch'ango's crimes are too many and too great," interjected Pachacamac, "to earn mercy from any of us. But she craves our fear, not our forgiveness, and she achieves what she desires."

My brother murmured, "Mercy is given, not earned."

I begged Shamba, "Do you know where to find Ch'ango?"

"No. As far as I know, Ch'ango sees no one but a few Scribes like my daughter, and Scribes keep their secrets well."

"Would she confide in you?"

"Not willingly."

I could not make demands of this self-punished patriarch, but I could continue to beseech him. "Where does the Protectorate meet?"

Pachacamac shook his head at me, disapproving my intentions without attempting to influence his Mage brother aloud. Shamba answered with a sigh, "Usually in a room behind the main chamber of Parliament. There are several such rooms, used by various factions and individuals. It is a measure of power and influence in Tathagata to be able to appropriate a room within the Site of Parliament."

"Andrew took me to one of those rooms," I admitted.

"Ch'ango taught Aroha how to interpret and overcome every runic barrier in the Site of Parliament before he left her faction. Such knowledge is difficult to retract."

"I did not know that he worked with Ch'ango," I replied hollowly. Considering Andrew's faculty for subterfuge, I should not have felt such dismay.

Shamba's gaze tightened on me in sorrow for my ignorance. "To understand the prophecy, Marita, you must recognize the nature of Mastermage Aroha and realize how he acquired so much power at such a young age. His methods were as ruthless as any in Tathagata. He made many enemies."

"I *did* gather that he had enemies." I glanced at my placid brother, who clearly did not share my surprised reaction at Shamba's claim about Andrew and Ch'ango. Benedict knew all that Shamba would tell me. Benedict had brought me to Shamba simply to let me hear the truth from a fellow Mage, whose Mystic perspective would be more likely to convince me.

As Shamba smiled wanly at me, he reminded me of Andrew, decrying my naïveté. Shamba tented his long fingers and explained with patient care, "Three major enemies have persisted beyond the rest. They actively hate Aroha because of his behavior in his term as a Mastermage. Ch'ango is the first. She *fights* Aroha because he works with Prince Hiroshi against her. She *hates* Aroha because he betrayed her personally. This, in part, is why Aroha has managed to combat Ch'ango more effectively than the rest of us. He learned many of her secrets while working for her faction. He also was her favorite, which is why she hates him yet spares his life."

"He has changed his ideals," I murmured, "but he has not lost his charisma."

"I do not know if he has ideals," responded Shamba with a frown, "or simply too much intelligence to let himself become deeply indebted to someone as destructive as Ch'ango. She chose Aroha as her official successor to the choice seat of Rit, a much more significant post than Purotu, a year after he came to Tathagata. Undoubtedly to her surprise and fury, he abandoned her when she decided to 'retire' from public view, shortly after Prince Hiroshi first approached the Parliament. She substituted another candidate quickly. Ch'ango selected Mage Lar, though she still wanted Aroha, and envy transformed Lar into Aroha's second bitter enemy. Out of hatred for Aroha, Mage Lar made himself virtually Ch'ango's slave. Whatever individual capability Lar once possessed, he has emptied himself in order to let Ch'ango work through him to destroy Aroha."

Shamba became silent, and his expression twisted into pain. Pachacamac reached past me to lay his hand on his friend's shoulder. "Shall I tell her of the third enemy?"

asked Pachacamac kindly, and Shamba nodded without
speaking.

No kindliness entered the look that Pachacamac gave to
me. He informed me sharply, "Aroha never met a woman he
would not seduce, if he thought she could aid his ambitions.
Such calculated affairs are common in Tathagata, but Aroha
succeeded better than most at achieving what he wanted.
Few women or men in Tathagata expect sincerity in their relationships. Hence, few were disillusioned by Aroha.
Scribes, however, are not usually targets of such manipulative dalliance. Talitha trusted Aroha, and he wounded her
cruelly."

Shamba murmured, "He did not gain what he wanted
from her. She was wise enough not to share her Scribe skills
with him."

"She was wise enough," added Pachacamac, "to learn
from Aroha and make herself a major force in Tathagata.
She hates him, nonetheless."

"Thus, Ch'ango is able to use her," muttered Shamba feebly, "because my wise, just daughter is blinded by her hatred
of Aroha."

"She trusted him," I whispered, trying not to picture myself in Talitha's beguiled, betrayed position. I knew I had
shared such a role at least once, in my adolescent relation
with the ambitious Lar.

The incense hissed in its brazier, releasing a spiral of umber smoke. "The Protectorate works to eradicate Hiroshi and
his Empire-inspired ideas," said Benedict from behind me,
"and all of the Protectors view Andrew as the major obstacle
to their cause. Most members of the Protectorate would relish Andrew's death. Lar seeks Andrew's humiliation. Neither Ch'ango nor Talitha will be satisfied with any penalty
but torture for Andrew, even if they destroy themselves,
their Protectorate, and the rest of the world in the process."

My vision swirled in my head like the ice wind. "Ch'ango
has entrapped Andrew," I cried, "just as Hiroshi feared." My
head began to pound, the vision forcing itself upon me.

I could see them both: Mage of tainted Sable and Mage of
purest Shadow, Ch'ango and Andrew. A plastiglass wall, re-
inforced with plasteel bars, separated them. She wore the
citron jacket and silver bracelets that I had seen before. She
relaxed in a high-backed judge's chair. He sat on the concrete floor of a filthy, stifling cell. Andrew's violet cloak had

been stripped from him, along with his gold. Oozing scabs covered his hands and arms. Ch'ango's hollow cheeks had swollen with burns.

They exchanged no words. Each stared unblinkingly at the other. A welt appeared spontaneously on Andrew's chest, and a bleeding gash snaked across Ch'ango's hairline. In their battle of Mage spells, Andrew was the prisoner, but he was torturer as well as tortured.

"Their battle will escalate beyond them," grieved Benedict, equally caught by the vision of horror. "Ch'ango sacrificed all that she once possessed to create her own Mage marks, but she cannot truly master them without a teacher. She has wielded their unique, distorted power for only a single spell, a remote projection that threatens the targeted Mage into a needless, self-destructive retaliation. Ch'ango did not learn enough from Hiroshi to interpret the full manuscript."

"She sacrificed the Brass magic that was hers, and she is left with only stolen magic, venal and corrupt," I wept. "She craves completion, and she knows that Andrew can master the skills that defeated her."

"She baited him with the hope of *her* knowledge, but she will learn from *him* and feed on him. He will devise new weapons, and she will master what he creates, and they will both become blind to any possibility but destruction. Such a war cannot remain private. It will shake the world, as surely as the final rivalry of the Empires did."

I looked at my brother. Andrew and Ch'ango became transparent images like reflections in a dark glass, and Benedict frowned through them. "We must find them," I pleaded, "before Andrew sees her Mage marks. I do not know how he plans to manage it, but he expects to duplicate her marks without leaving that cell."

Shamba's concession trembled with remorse, "We must persuade my Talitha to lead you to them."

"You do not have the strength to intervene between Ch'ango and Aroha," argued Pachacamac against us.

We three, who shared a vision, did not heed Pachacamac's despair. "We shall find the strength," I answered firmly. "Ben, please take me to Gaia." Benedict nodded sagely.

Marita

The silver scarabs looked fragile in Gaia's withered hands. Across the worn, wooden table, her face seemed dim and distant. The flame of the single white candle licked at a stubborn spike of wax, and shadows danced throughout the room.

Gaia poured three vials of fire oil into a celadon porcelain bowl. "Both scarabs must be applied simultaneously," she told me. "The mind cannot tolerate the imbalance of a single scarab."

"I understand."

"It will not be pleasant," said Gaia, "even with the numbing philter. Scarabs never attach easily. Unhealed lotus marks will compound the usual problems. The scarabs may negate your crescents, since the powers are antithetical."

"Apply the scarabs," I answered.

"Drink the wine."

I tried to stop my trembling as I raised the drugged wine to my lips, but the rim of the glass rattled against my teeth. A few drops of the rosy liquid trickled down my chin. The philter made the wine taste sour.

My nerves quieted, and warm rivers of peace flowed through me. When Gaia asked me to extend both arms, I flung them toward her with exuberance. I yelped when her fingers clamped the unattached scarabs tightly against my wrists, tacking the nerve film to my skin with hot wax.

"Hold still," ordered Gaia sternly. She plunged two glass droppers into the bowl of fire oil, and she squeezed the contents onto the two scarabs.

I screamed. The haze of false peace abandoned me. The fire oil burned only my skin. The scarabs bit into every nerve of my body, infecting and inflaming. They were merciless.

The shadows of the room closed upon me, suffocating me

in blindness, while foul beetles crawled inside of me, devouring me. A pendulum's rhythm pounded in my head, crashing, crashing, tearing the bone from my skull. My feet trod fire. I drowned in a sea of bitter salt.

I choked and thrashed. The beetles would not leave me. Their spindly legs skittered through my veins and sinews, stabbing a path into the chambers of my heart. They plucked the tissue from the arteries, and blood erupted into my brain.

The room turned crimson, dripping with the blood that filled my eyes. I tried to claw the scarabs from my skin, but they had embedded themselves too deeply now. They had become part of me.

The pendulum pounded. Thunder reverberated between my ears, crashing and ringing like deadly chimes. I counted the pulses: one, a hundred, a thousand. Stones split, and mountains thrust fierce crowns from the ocean. Creation and destruction merged into a single process.

Gaia's voice whispered across a lightning-streaked sky. "Count with me," she demanded. "One, two . . ."

"One," I echoed but could not continue.

"One, two," she repeated slowly.

"Three," I answered.

"Marita, can you see me?"

"No."

"Try." She fluttered her hands in front of my eyes. "Can you see me?"

"I don't know." The room smelled like cinders. The gray robe that Gaia had given me clung to my skin. I tried to see more than the blur of Gaia's fingers. I grabbed her hand to immobilize it, so that I could focus. Her skin felt smooth, like paper.

"Marita, can you see me?"

"Yes," I answered. The candle had burned to a stump. Gaia's face was pale and drooping with fatigue. My arms wore scarabs, embraced within my crescents' horns, atop each reddened wrist. "Are these mine?" I asked foolishly.

"What do you feel inside of you?"

"A resonance. I am part of all things."

"The scarabs are yours. Use them wisely. Use them rarely."

"Do I belong here?" I asked, frowning at the windowless room.

"No, Mage Marita. This is a place of peace." Gaia sighed. She rose to leave the room. She moved with difficulty.

The scarab-marked Mage did not belong in the Tathagata monastery. Equating myself with that dangerous Mage required effort. The mental struggle cleared my head. I said thickly, "Mage Gaia, I am grateful for your help."

"To repay an old debt, I helped Aroha," she answered, "not you." She left me. My Mage marks assured me that I would not see her again of her volition. I sensed her quiet spirit retreating.

I stared at the scarabs until the candle guttered and died. This powerful Mage was not Marita. This power was nothing that I had ever wanted for myself. I had become an instrument of prophecy—my brother's prophecy, which now was mine.

In the darkness, I began my seeking, certain of my goal and my defenses. Andrew had included several watching spells among his letters to me. The most powerful of the spells was uniquely his creation, exploiting Mage and Empire arts conjointly. It seemed appropriate to apply such a spell first to him.

The monastery tolerated receptive magic but did not facilitate it. I felt the monastery resist my active spell, but I delved through that stalwart barrier easily by leaping through an Empire network that only my Mystic senses understood. Andrew seemed so bright and vivid to me now, as clear a presence as if he lay beside me in Tiare House. The shield around him was hard and strong, but it resembled clear Avalon Ice instead of Lung-Wang Brass. I touched his recent Mystic memories lightly—recent enough to remain accessible on the surface of his mind, but not so current that his physical reactions would cloud the sense of them. Even if I had worn the shells of greatest Mystic dexterity, I would not yet have trusted myself to study Andrew in the present, where he would be most likely to detect me.

I heard Andrew taunt, "If your skills have grown so great, Ch'ango, why do you show me nothing but the least of tricks, such as you would have scorned to use in our more intimate days? Lar the Less could do as well as *this*." Andrew displayed his bleeding arms, as if the wounds were insignificant. I felt the sharp, cutting pain that his insolent gesture cost him.

"Where is your genius at discovering secrets?" mocked

Ch'ango in return, her cruel eyes glittering. "You have lost your edge, my pet." I felt her bitterness and her cunning.

"Why don't you kill him now?" growled Lar, a bleak vessel of envy, vanity, and soured pride. "You do not need him." I felt Lar's desperation, and I felt his honest fear of what Ch'ango and Andrew wrought between them.

Ch'ango dismissed Lar irritably, "You will be late for your meeting."

"Give my love to your fellow Protectors, Larless," gibed Andrew. "Tell them to expect to see me soon."

"You are going nowhere," snapped Ch'ango.

Andrew answered with an arrogance that belied his initial words, "I am a servant. I go where my master goes. When I have conquered, it is to Prince Hiroshi that I will give the victory."

"You serve *me*, Aroha, as will your idealistic Prince Hiroshi. You belong to *me*."

Andrew's laughter fueled Ch'ango's anger and her hatred, but it also fed her fear. Andrew knew her well; I felt his confidence. It was Hiroshi whom Ch'ango dreaded because she could comprehend nothing about the Empire's heir. She did not fear Andrew as a Mage, for she had decades of experience to countermand his force of relative youth and quickness of mind. She feared Andrew because he understood Hiroshi, and she equated Andrew's rebellion against her with his attachment to Hiroshi's mysterious Empire ideas. She equated her conquest of Andrew with the eradication of all the difficult questions that Hiroshi represented to her.

Ch'ango, the embittered old woman who had made my grandfather quake, strengthened her spells with her virulent hatred. What Mystic could not be awed by her? What sane person could not be repelled? Ch'ango's mottled hand threw a Lung-Wang dagger spell at Andrew, and it sliced through his shield and drew blood from his shoulder. Andrew's laughter deepened, and the intensity of *his* hatred made me recoil.

I withdrew from the ugly, violent emotions that filled all three Mages in that dismal prison. Benedict sat across the plank table from me, waiting quietly for me to complete my journey. The plasteel door was open, and the hallway's sconce spread yellow light upon us.

"All of it is wrong," sighed Benedict. "There is no justice

in what Ch'ango wants, nor in what Andrew does to thwart her."

"Why didn't you try to dissuade me from wearing scarabs?" I asked him, wishing that *someone* had prevented my irrevocable step. I had employed Andrew's watching spell with a clarity and ease that terrified me; I did not want the responsibility of such abilities. I did not share Andrew's obsessive craving for knowledge in all its forms. "You warned me against their power."

"I obey the Intercessor's will," replied Benedict with sympathy furrowing his brow, "and I observe the truths that He sends me. If you ask why He has chosen you as His instrument, I would say that it was your innocence and reluctance to take the power available to you. That may not be prophecy, but it is my discernment."

"I understand the force of a clear vision, Ben."

"Your understanding is not the same as wisdom," murmured my brother, smiling to soften his criticism, "but it may suffice to achieve the Intercessor's will."

"It must suffice for us," I answered, mustering a trace of asperity. "It is all that we have to unite us."

Benedict touched my new scarabs. The raw skin did not feel tender to me, thanks to Gaia's philter. "I refused to wear them, Marita, when the Intercessor asked it of me," he whispered, smiling at me sadly. "Andrew tried to give me Mage marks years ago. I feared that I would lose myself in striving for Mystic power, just as I once dreaded the thought of becoming Dom of Rit. Father never did understand *why* I feared the responsibility of such power: I wanted worldly power too much to trust myself to use it fairly."

"Toby had no such fear," I said with bitterness.

"I have hated Toby for his part in our parents' deaths, but I have never envied him the status that Ch'ango arranged for him. Even as Mastermage Aroha, Andrew understood that I did not seek Affirmist rank. He saved me from Ch'ango, when she would have slain me after killing our parents, though he had not yet become wise enough to leave her faction."

"I know. That truth visited my dreams."

My brother nodded. "Even in the Rit prison, the Intercessor offered me authority. I felt the truth—and fought it. If my faith had been stronger, I could have walked free of the

Rit prison and carried Ch'ango's enmity away from Andrew and from you."

"You have tremendous Mystic strength, Ben, but you are not a Mage."

"This battle should have been mine. I never meant to cause you to bear my burden. I am truly sorry, Marita. The Intercessor answers our prayers in unexpected ways."

My own self-pity abated, made to seem ridiculous by my brother's odd, altruistic fanaticism. I hurt for him because he believed in his guilt. "You may have the physical potential to become the greatest Mage of our history, but you haven't the temperament for that role. It would destroy you."

My brother offered me his hand. I accepted his support as he accepted mine. "Since the day we arrived on Ha'aparari, I knew that the authority had been given to you, Marita. I shall be obedient to it."

"Guard me, please, Ben, as you guarded me in Rit before I understood. I must perform one more seeking. This spell will be more difficult because I seek to watch events that are occurring now."

"I am always beside you, my sister."

Marita

Even when Talitha pretended a maternal care for me, I had recognized her as a strong, intelligent, and beautiful woman not so many years older than myself. Aunt Nan had perceived her as a rival from their first meeting, and Nan had accepted defeat. Knowing that Talitha had once loved Andrew, I found myself conceding likewise in my heart. Andrew had used Talitha, but I could not say that he had used me less or cared for me more.

If any of us survived beyond this day, I would expect nothing from Andrew. The sharing of passion between us could not have held much significance for him, who had charmed so many. I no longer imagined that I knew what Andrew valued or loved, except knowledge. I thought I understood his letter to me, his gift and his farewell. And I concluded that I did love him, would always love him, but could not allow that love to dominate me.

Seeing Talitha by Mage sight, I yielded Andrew. My vision was clear now. The members of the Protectorate, too, must be made to turn their eyes from Andrew, the Shadow Prince, and see the truth.

Prince Hiroshi's work and ideas must survive and spread. To save Hiroshi and his cause, we must defeat Ch'ango, and we must awaken all who serve her to the folly of what they do. These essentials gave life to the joint prophecy, and disobedience to this wisdom would doom us all.

Secure that Benedict stood with me, by whatever strange gifts he possessed that needed no Mage marks, I reached into the Protectorate. I touched its core, the conflicting ideals and aims of its creator and diverse members. When I had defined the form and content of its brittle shell, I began the process of dismantling it.

They met, as Shamba had led me to expect, in one of the private rooms at the Site of Parliament, a larger and better furnished room than that to which Andrew had taken me. Except for Ch'ango, all of those identified on Andrew's list were present: Talitha, Lar, Toby, Dom Elayne, Dom Sevrin, and Mastermage Cuycha. I recognized eight of the nine attending Doms as relatives, though I could not match names to all the faces. Of the seven Mages, I could identify only one in addition to Lar and Cuycha. Mage Connell from the Avalon temple sat between a hound-faced Dom and a stout Tangaroa Mage.

Uncle Toby was speaking with such agitation that his face was flushed and damp. His public Everyman mask had succumbed to the dynamic, ruthless, driven man who had taken Rit and held it at the expense of my parents' lives. "The original Protectorate did not rely on themselves to execute their enemies," he argued fiercely. "They plied the anger of the populace, and that is how we must proceed. While Aroha has distracted us with showmanship, such as that buffoonery in the Parliament yesterday, Prince Hiroshi's trinkets and ideas have managed to spread to every island. The scope of contamination has become a plague, less direct in its attack against us but just as dangerous as Aroha at his worst. We can't even count how many E-units have been abandoned in favor of the privateers' 'curiosities and wonders.' If the people begin to look beyond themselves, they must be made to support us and not our opponents. If we cannot keep the people faithful to the social contract, we may as well concede now and let Prince Hiroshi have his factories and schools."

"You make our victory feel like defeat," complained Lar with a stern frown, but his sidelong look toward Talitha held a wistful quality.

Talitha nodded, as if deeply grateful to Lar for interrupting Toby and sparing her the effort. An unusual weariness hung about her today. "Prince Hiroshi cannot deal with the privateers himself," she sighed heavily. "Without Aroha, Prince Hiroshi is an isolated, unrealistic man who threatens no one, including us."

"We have no victory to celebrate," snapped Cuycha, a stocky, twelve-lotus Mage whose appearance was dominated by bushy black hair and a mustache, "because Aroha is not yet dead. When will Ch'ango finish with him?"

"I have spoken to her," muttered Lar. The Mastermage of Rit might have achieved a supercilious tone, indicating that the privilege of addressing Ch'ango belonged to him alone, but this was only an unhappy man. I pitied him, amazing myself that I could view him without stronger emotion. "Ch'ango still hopes to extract some useful information before disposing of Aroha."

"Aroha will tell her nothing," countered Elayne scornfully, "just as Ch'ango admits nothing to us." Dom Elayne was a plain woman of middle years who resembled Nan before age and Toby took their toll. She turned her keen gaze on Talitha, clearly expecting leadership and wondering why it hesitated to manifest itself.

"We must rouse the people," announced Toby, clinging to his pompous theme, but he looked as miserable as Lar. "We have confiscated a large number of Prince Hiroshi's devices. Lar knows how to make them deadly. If we can deploy a few more of the sabotaged versions, Prince Hiroshi's popularity will decay quickly and he will be loathed, as he deserves."

"You would use these mechanisms?" asked Talitha without expression in face or tone. "Then the tools and techniques of the Empires are not evil when they become valuable to us? Prince Hiroshi's point is won, and we only battle him as the nominal employer of Aroha, an ambitious man who threatens our collective power." If she had shouted, she could not have made her ironic observation more clear. The room became quiet, although Toby and several others shook their heads helplessly. Dom Elayne seemed thoughtful.

The dislikable Dom Sevrin interpreted Talitha's remarks as an uncomplicated condemnation, and he tried to placate her, "We must match our enemy's weaponry. How else are we to eradicate the poison that Hiroshi spreads? Would you rather return to Empire tyranny and let someone like Aroha use and abuse the world and its people?"

Tailtha only looked at Sevrin with a disdainful tilt of her proud head. Elayne examined her agate ring and murmured, "Dom Sevrin, I do not think that you have completely understood Scribe Talitha." Sevrin stared at Talitha, as if he had just considered the possibility that her comments could bear a literal interpretation.

I barely nudged the group with a spell of dissension. Cuycha, the most sensitive member, lost his reticence and spoke his undiplomatic inner thoughts: "Talitha defends the false prince. She speaks heresy."

One of the older Doms responded for Talitha, though Talitha seemed indifferent to the man's support, "None of us can doubt Talitha's loyalty to our cause, Cuycha."

"I cast no aspersions on my fellow Protectors," countered Mage Cuycha in a tone of unlawful contempt, "even when they assure me that they will capture Aroha without my help, and they repeatedly let him slip from their grasp."

"I might wonder if *those* Protectors had adequate skills to lead us," muttered a bald Lung-Wang Mage. He stared with particular intensity at Lar. "We may debate Mastermage Ch'ango's faults of character, but she would have handled matters capably."

"Capably?" mocked Talitha. "Ch'ango would willingly destroy the world to achieve her own desires, as you well know, Mastermage Tsi. We should thank Mastermage Lar for applying some restraint to her bloodthirsty methods. Aroha learned from *her*."

A ruddy-skinned Dom with a paunch snapped, "We have too many Mystics trying to dominate the Protectorate. Where is our balance? Let us hear more of Dom Toby's suggestions."

"Dom Toby's methods have failed us repeatedly," growled Mastermage Tsi. "He prattles eloquently about rousing 'the people,' but we cannot regain the confidence of 'the people' now, when we have ignored and abused them for decades. We might stir a few gullible patriots, but they would need sophisticated arms to police for us against Prince Hiroshi's followers. We have already proven that we cannot use Empire weapons effectively, because we do not understand them—and that is Prince Hiroshi's point. The Affirmists have nothing to offer to 'the people' or to us."

"Why are we bickering over the past?" demanded Elayne, making an obvious effort to staunch the rampant flow of unlawful accusations. I tried to discourage her peacemaking, but she lacked any clear Mystic senses and remained impervious. "Aroha has been a difficult foe, but Ch'ango has imprisoned him. Lar is right. Instead of moping over how to proceed next, we should rejoice. We have achieved a great victory."

"When I am sure that Aroha is no longer a threat, I shall rejoice in our triumph," declared Talitha grimly, stiffening her back and regaining the focus of the Protectors. "Until that time—and it is not yet here—the war is far from complete." She glared at Toby, whose geniality seemed to have frayed into morosity. "We win nothing if we create and use the very weapons that we denounce. We must decide what we Protectors truly represent: Are we defenders against the Empire sciences, or have we become merely foes of Aroha? If it is the latter—and after all the evil that we have condoned in the past year, I am no longer sure myself—then Prince Hiroshi has won his case, and this Protectorate persists only to finalize Aroha's defeat. We must decide now and commit ourselves accordingly, because if Aroha is dead, we must deal with Ch'ango."

I would have expected arguments against Talitha's words, but even Cuycha seemed willing to accept her "heresies" now, since no one else had joined him in denouncing them. Like any true Tathagatan, he adapted easily to majority opinions. "What do you propose, Talitha?" asked Toby, leaning back in a brown velvet chair, as if retreating from responsibility for a situation that had grown beyond him. I shared his anxious curiosity and let my meddling spells abate.

"I propose to talk to Prince Hiroshi," answered Talitha slowly. "Ch'ango says that he is here in Tathagata. Once the information brokers know that Aroha is our prisoner, I think that Prince Hiroshi will come to us. We shall see how threatening he appears without Aroha beside him." She added dryly, "Prince Hiroshi has always been eager to explain his creations to the honorable members of Parliament. If we intend to exploit his contrivances, we may as well ask him how to use them intelligently and constructively, instead of deliberately converting them into tools of violence. That does not imply a sanction of Empire techniques, Cuycha. It is no more than our customary, lawful application of the Empires' legacies. We have tolerated as much from fixers since the Great War."

Several of the Protectors nodded and looked wise, as if each one of them claimed secret credit for Talitha's suggestion without fully understanding the profound rationalization that it signified. Toby distanced himself by studying the ceiling, and Cuycha assumed a dangerous glower. The reaction of Dom Elayne and two of the silent Mages seemed to be relief. I realized that Talitha had made verbal what these three had been thinking: Toby's proposal was too blatantly destructive to settle well, but Hiroshi's knowledge of Empire techniques offered power that no Tathagatan could easily reject.

The turn of the conversation had stunned me. Time, as Hiroshi had predicted, had worked in his favor. Over the years since first he approached the Parliament, his ideas had begun to lose their radical flavor, even to the Protectors. Regrettably, all of the Protectors seemed to perceive Hiroshi as defenseless without Andrew, and that attitude would prevent any real acceptance of Hiroshi's teachings in Tathagata. However, tolerance was all that Hiroshi had demanded of the World Parliament; he would be content to achieve that much

The Avalon Mage, Connell, raised his hand. When Talitha acknowledged him, he cooed with an unctuous humility, "Honored leaders, if your servant may repeat himself without offense, let me say again, Mage Marita still serves Aroha. She has not been defeated, so he is not defeated."

"Perhaps you have not understood," explained Lar impatiently, rubbing his head with his amethyst-adorned hand, "that Aroha is our prisoner."

"And Marita," added Toby gruffly, "is weak and easily manipulated. She will soon forget Aroha and return to her family."

Connell tried to support his floundering argument, "Honored leaders, some strength is required to apply one's own Mage marks." Most of Connell's superiors in the Protectorate talked among themselves about Talitha's suggestion, and they did not listen to him. Lar seemed on the verge of speaking, but he glanced instead at Talitha.

Talitha, at least, had heard Connell. She replied to him with a trace of bitterness, "Even if Marita is so besotted that she continues to try to help Aroha, she will fail. Lotus marks count as nothing against Ch'ango, and Ch'ango tolerates no one who works against her." Talitha ended softly, "We all know of people who have vanished after antagonizing Ch'ango, and we all know why those people never reappear."

"Ch'ango is unfailingly capable and efficient, especially in her use of blood magic," muttered Mastermage Tsi, reiterating his sardonic support of the absent Protector.

Lar aired his fragile pride, "If we did decide that Mage Marita endangered us, we would not need Ch'ango's assistance to conquer her." The faintest flush of embarrassment colored him. "I have possibly underestimated her in the past, but she is still a lesser Mage. I could eliminate Marita without a moment's effort."

"Yes, Lar," sneered Toby, "we all know how much you deserve to be a Mastermage."

An outburst of dickering ensued, but I did not follow it. Benedict touched me, just as a sense of something cold and dangerous stirred on the horizon of my consciousness. I returned to the monastery's safety without delay.

My brother said, "I believe that Mastermage Cuycha detected you."

"He did not identify me," I answered confidently. "The monastery does provide a significant measure of defense, and Cuycha does not have Ch'ango's aptitude for long-range spells."

"Nor do you, Marita. You have worn scarabs for less than an hour."

"I have the advantage of Andrew's expertise."

"Do not depend too much on Andrew or his Mystic teachings. By his own admission, he developed many of his most potent spells while he abstained from active magic, and he has tested them only in a theoretical sense. Ch'ango has her own great store of knowledge, and she will defeat him. She has deceived him already."

"They deceive each other," I replied, but I understood my brother's point. Ch'ango probably knew Andrew's *verified* Mystic spells and techniques better than I, and she had far more experience as a Mage. I must rely on the methods and knowledge that Ch'ango did not share. "Where is Prince Hiroshi?" I asked.

"I do not know. I have not seen him since we arrived in Tathagata," answered Benedict. "I believe that he is searching for Andrew."

"He must not go to Ch'ango!" I responded in alarm. "That is what the Protectorate wants." Even as I protested, however, I saw clearly the image of Hiroshi with one of his infernally clever devices, tracking Andrew. Seated beside him on an autobus bench, Anavai leaned over her husband's shoulder, watching with him as a green circle of light traveled across a fist-sized screen. The circle's diameter shrank. "Ch'ango will kill them both," I whispered, as my vision turned and showed me its bleak alternative: destruction, desolation, a lifeless world with only the wind to stir the dust of ruined cities. Hiroshi's Suit was not Sable but the Ice of mental discipline, crystallized by his passionate ideals. In my sad alternative vision, his Face was not the Empire Prince but the Dreamer that meant folly and sacrifice. Without Hiroshi and Anavai as leaders, the revival of Empire science would wither like my father's failed orchard.

"With the Intercessor's help," said my brother, "we shall not fail. We shall reach Ch'ango before Hiroshi finds her."

"I cannot sense Ch'ango's location—or Hiroshi's," I said, frustrated and frightened. The effects of Gaia's philter had dissipated. I became aware of the raw, tender state of my nerves and mind. My confidence in my vision wavered.

"We can find Talitha," replied Benedict.

"Yes. Of course." What was I trying to achieve? Who was I to fight a Mage like Ch'ango or to think that I could offer help to a Mage like Andrew? I must go to Talitha, yes. She was wise enough to know what should be done.

Benedict jumped to his feet and raised his arms toward the stained ceiling. "Leave her, Ch'ango!" demanded Benedict sternly. "By the Intercessor, be gone from here!"

I shuddered, and the wave of self-doubt fled from me. "She is gaining strength," I whispered fearfully, meeting my brother's steel-blue eyes, "or she would not have been able to defile this sacred place with her attack. She is learning from Andrew, and she knows what he has given me." I stared at my own new scarabs, bleakly silver against my inflamed skin. "We must return to Tathagata."

"I shall ask Gaia to summon an autobus."

III.

MAGE CARDS:

Ice Prince

Shadow Mage

Blood Everyman

Brass Dreamer

Sable Mixie

Marita

The autobus seemed to creep like the tide of Rit's bay. Benedict and I faced each other across the narrow aisle. Mage Shamba sat in stiff dignity beside me. Grimly, Shamba had promised to plead with Talitha on our behalf. All of us hoped he could convince her to give us Ch'ango's location willingly. None of us wanted to injure Talitha. Her survival was critical to our fragile vision of hope.

The high-walled street conveyed no sense of our progress. When the barricades ended and the view opened onto the dry, moonlit valley that edged Tathagata, all three of us sighed aloud in relief. Soon, we could see the towers of the city.

Shamba declared, "My daughter will listen to me." He was trying to reassure himself, as both Benedict and I knew. "I should never have left her. She needed my guidance, not my anger."

"She is not without wisdom," offered Benedict kindly, "though she is misguided."

"Yes," replied Mage Shamba eagerly, "Talitha cannot be blamed. She is a daughter to make a man very proud." Then he twisted his lean, bearded face in disgust. "Ch'ango lied to her. Ch'ango lied to all of us."

Benedict murmured more sounds of vague comfort. I exerted no similar effort to console Mage Shamba. I needed to prepare myself inwardly. To realize the potential of my augmented Mage marks, I should have studied and exercised new skills at length. I had worn the new marks for only a few hours. The watching spell had come easily, aided by infernal Empire gadgetry, but other spells might prove more difficult. I could already feel the clash of my crescents, rebelling against the scarabs that had superseded them as my arms' foremost marks.

By the time the autobus rumbled onto the streets of Tathagata proper, I had worn a hole in a bench of the autobus, where I had practiced a directed energy spell. The bus glistened with the light nacre that I had painted—with the aid of a few philter grains—over dull plastic and plasteel surfaces. I had practiced old spells and new, and I was as prepared as time would allow. I wished that I had learned more from Prince Hiroshi's people when I had the opportunity.

We three seemed such a humble army, debarking and racing to catch a transfer bus to the Site of Parliament. Shamba had replaced the gray robe of the monastery with his proud Inianga orange, but his robe was a frayed Rit garment. Benedict's yellow hair stood on end, and he was as pale and emaciated as ever, battered by past contests with Ch'ango. I still wore the Avalon finery that I had purchased with Andrew's gold, but my arms were streaked with burns and inflammation from the recent, unorthodox application of Mage marks. All of us looked harried.

Every city noise seemed magnified a thousandfold. The Tathagatan crowds seemed oppressive, angry, and rude, jostling us and impeding our progress. The streets smelled sour and dirty. Every star in the sky beat its mote of light upon us, nagging us with reminders of the passage of precious minutes.

The moon rose high above Tathagata's skyline before we stood beside the Site of Parliament. The criers had gone, and the crowds had thinned to a few stragglers. I looked at the balcony where Andrew had sat, mocking the World Parliament, the Protectorate, Ch'ango, and himself. The temptation was strong to summon him in my imagination, to allow myself to recall the feel of him against me, but I shunned all such memories quickly. They were a trap, as sure and addictive as any E-unit's powerful illusion. Benedict glanced at me with a frown of concern, but I nodded and smiled to reassure him. Ch'ango could not reach me so easily now.

"There is a private entrance on this side," I told my companions, leading them past the great Mystic friezes. The guards of the day were gone, because the public doors had been locked for the evening. "Andrew left me his key." When we reached the depiction of the world egg, I inserted the key as Andrew had done, and the door opened for me. I entered the Site of Parliament with Mage Shamba beside me. I turned to look for Benedict. He had remained outside.

"I shall wait for you," announced my brother mildly, "and I shall continue to pray a defense around you."

I did not argue. I did ask, "Why must you wait?"

"Years ago, I made a vow to the Intercessor that I would never enter the Parliament." He grinned with a touch of embarrassment. With his flaxen hair standing on end, he looked very young. "I should have worded my vow more carefully, but I shall fulfill it in all respects. The Intercessor will understand and defend me in obedience."

I hated to leave him, but I nodded as if I agreed with his reasoning. "Don't loiter too close to the building. The night guards may tour the perimeter."

Since I lacked my brother's faith in divine protection, Benedict's safety concerned me. For Mage Shamba and myself, I had little fear of discovery by any mere guard or parliamentary official. I had the advantages of scarab marks, Andrew's spells, and Andrew's descriptions of Empire monitors, secret locks, alarms, and weapons embedded in the Site of Parliament.

According to Andrew's notes, most of the devices had existed before Andrew's enhancements. I wondered how many members of Parliament would have felt secure in their chambers if they had realized the lethal potential of their surroundings. I also wondered how much that knowledge would have increased the use of assassination as a substitute for parliamentary debate. Andrew's tools could make the Dons, as well as the Mastermages, more efficient in their rivalries. The cruelty of our world's leaders would remain untouched.

I grimaced, realizing how deeply the past few months and Andrew's cynical views had corrupted me. The Mystic/Affirmist social contract now seemed fatally flawed. Lawful tolerance had become hypocrisy to me. My vision demanded as radical a revolution as Prince Hiroshi had ever proposed, and I had become as critical and openly opinioned as my brother.

The Protectorate had ended its meeting, but the members had not yet disbanded. I could sense the squabbling, ruthless crew not far from us, but Shamba and I did not take that route. We wanted only Talitha, and she led a very orderly life. She would not leave the Site of Parliament without visiting her office to store her Scribe's notes of the meeting. Shamba guided me through empty hallways to his daugh-

ter's office. The door was locked, but Andrew's notes had
described the means of deactivating such simple, interior
barriers. I squeezed an acidic paste into a slot a few meters
away from the office door. A harsh odor trickled into the
hallway, but the door of Talitha's office opened to us.

Her office was quite large, but plasteel files and bookcases consumed virtually all of the floor space. A
plastiwood table, which served as a desk, and four beige
chairs were the only other furniture. The quantity of stored
material surprised me, although I knew Talitha's thorough,
meticulous habits. The official parliamentary records had
their own library, maintained under close scrutiny by the
Scribes' Guild. All of Talitha's files were locked, and I did
not feel justified in breaching them for the sake of nosiness.
The bookcases were likewise secured with plastiglass
doors, and the spines were identified, according to the custom of the Scribes' Guild, only by varied placement and
repetitions of the Guild's quill emblem.

"She keeps inventories, census data, and records that the
Guild would otherwise discard," said Shamba, assuaging my
curiosity a little.

I seated myself at Talitha's desk. Shamba tried to pace,
but the room was too cluttered. "She will come soon," I assured him, moving a brass lamp from the table to the floor.
"We shall summon her."

Shamba scowled, unhappy with the prospect of bespelling
his daughter even so mildly, but he took the chair across the
table from me. "She is my daughter. I shall direct the spell,"
he told me firmly. "Guard me, please."

He untied the bindings of his philter purse and spread a
square of linen, striped in shades of orange and russet, upon
the table. He positioned brass disks at each corner of the
scarf. In the scarf's center, he placed a polished black stone.
He held his left hand, palm down, above the stone, and he
began to chant the summons of the Inianga spirit guides.

I scattered pearlized motes of protection powder over
Shamba's head, and I built my sentinels to accord with his
Inianga magic. I had not performed guardian magic since my
novice days, when detecting any form of magic had required
effort. Sensitizing myself now, the entire universe seemed
thick with stray spells and strong emotions. I could even
identify Mages and Schools of origin.

I recognized the remnants of an old spell, wrought over

five years ago by my little Avalon group. I remembered the exercise, a cleansing of a set of crystals that Dory had discovered beneath a vestment chest in the Avalon vault. Kurt had dropped a cold spike of quartz down the front of my robe, and I had yelped and broken the concentration of the entire group. Dory had chastised Kurt, who had continued to grin impudently, and she had restarted the cleansing from the beginning. The fragment of spell, never properly completed, still rattled through the atmosphere.

The vicious, amused inspection of Ch'ango filtered nostalgia and random spell noise from my attention. "You are childish," she informed me condescendingly, "imagining that you could ever vie with me as an equal. Aroha is mine, as he was meant to be. Go back to concocting love philters for bored Affirmists."

My nerves shivered, but I did not let my fear drive me. "Sorry," I retorted with crisp disdain, "but it is time for the Prince of *Stolen* Sable to yield to the Prince of Ice." Ch'ango's maddening chimes rang deafeningly in my head. I raised my own version of one of Andrew's Tangaroa spells, a writhing eel of Tangaroa Shadow and Avalon Ice, and I opened its jaws to consume Ch'ango's scarlet tide of hatred. Our spells hurtled toward each other, mental illusions that constituted reality to us. Before our spells could meet, a dagger of gold split the air between them.

"Don't let her provoke you into rashness," hissed Andrew. I could not be sure if he addressed me or Ch'ango. Each of us reacted to his warning. The crimson fury of a distorted Kinebahan spell, strong with the power of its stolen origin, dripped into bloody runnels and flowed back to its source. I let the eel become a mist and memory.

I ached to touch Andrew, but he needed his focus elsewhere, and I had an obligation to Shamba. The Inianga Mage had nearly completed the summoning. The spirit guide had made its gentle suggestion to Talitha. Conscious or unconscious of her father's work, she was headed for her office.

Shamba lowered his hand until it touched the black stone. I cast a philter powder for shadows throughout the room, so that Talitha entered her office and closed the door before she saw us. She wore a flowing skirt and blouse of amber silk, threaded with gold, and the gold turban that I had once envisioned covered her hair. She looked first at me, crossed the distance between us with three long strides, and slapped my face stingingly. "Liar and traitor," she snarled, "I do not want your presence defiling my office."

"Talitha," snapped Shamba, "your condemnation offends the law and my ears."

Talitha inhaled deeply, but her dark eyes continued to glare at me. "Father, why are you here with this betrayer of all decency?"

The father stood and intercepted his daughter's bitter gaze at a comparable height. "I am here because I failed to discipline you, Tali, when you lost sight of reason and honor. I accept the blame for letting you stray so far from what is right and good, and I am here to correct my error."

Talitha shrugged past her father, and she pointed accusingly at my arms and Mage marks. "What have you done, Father?" she demanded furiously.

I answered her, "Mage Shamba did not apply my marks, but he shares my vision."

For an instant, Talitha seemed startled into belief, but old hatred resurged. "Your vision?" mocked Talitha. "Is it not Aroha's vision that rules you?"

Both Shamba and I replied, "No."

Mage Shamba continued, "It is you who are deluded by another's vision, Tali. Ch'ango has done this to you."

"Ch'ango did not write the laws of our world," retorted Talitha proudly, though she studied her father with care. "She did not cause the Great War."

"Nor did Prince Hiroshi," I countered, "even if Ch'ango presents him as the enemy of society simply because he is more educated than the rest of us."

"I thought that preaching was your brother's prerogative," muttered Talitha with contempt, as if she had never spoken the brave words that I had heard in my earlier seeking. She flung her sheaf of notes upon her father's orange spell cloth, causing the black stone to rattle.

"Prince Hiroshi has a vision that we must all embrace or perish," I replied, "and you know it as well as I. As a Scribe you have read the histories." I inhaled deeply, before plunging into confession, "You need not deny them. As a child of the Family, I read the same histories." I could feel Talitha's shock, though she showed her reaction with only a blink. Shamba's shock ran more deeply, for it countered his faith, but he did not speak against my claim. "You know the cruelties that the original Protectorate inflicted, as bad as anything that the Empires ever caused. The Protectorate, like its present incarnation, was nothing but a political tool of a few ambitious people, taking advantage of the postwar chaos."

Talitha crossed her silk-clad arms sternly, and she faced her father. "I do not want to arrest her while you are with her, Father, but my tolerance has limits. Mage Marita is a criminal, the willing inheritor of her brother's sentence of execution, since she conspired to free him."

Mage Shamba placed his strong hands on his daughter's stiff shoulders. "Daughter, you have acknowledged the falseness of your Protectorate's stated premise. Your own purpose is complete: Aroha is Ch'ango's captive. Do not cling from obstinacy to something that you no longer believe."

Father and daughter stared at each other, while I forced myself to remain silent. Talitha would be far more likely to express herself honestly to him than to me. I did not expect Talitha to become my eager ally, but I hoped that Shamba could coax her into admitting her own fear and loathing of Ch'ango. My alternative was to enslave Talitha's proud will via one of Andrew's most diabolical spells. I abhorred the idea, but I would implement it, though Shamba would detest me, and I would despise myself.

"What do you want from me, Father?" asked Talitha at last, and she sounded even wearier than in my watching spell.

"Tell us where to find Ch'ango," responded Shamba.

"That will serve her, not you," grunted Talitha. Her emotional reaction, almost horrified, told more than her words about her opinions regarding Ch'ango. "She has killed for lesser offenses than your disloyalty, Father."

"If I might choose, I would accept such death rather than see you do her bidding. If I might free you by the sacrifice of my own life's blood, I would die gladly."

She berated him, "Do not speak so wildly, Father," but my crescents felt the inward shiver of her guilty reaction. She loathed Ch'ango only a trifle less than she hated Aroha.

"I will not die at Ch'ango's hands, unless it be from grief that she has won. I do not plan to confront Ch'ango, unless those who *must* face her have failed," replied Shamba. "That task is not given to me. I have served the vision only until the true Blood Mage could accept that burden." He smiled wanly at Talitha, but his Mystic explanation had meaning only for me. By lotus and crescent, I felt his private Mystic rite take shape.

I wished that I could spare him such sacrifice, for it would leave him emptied forever of his Mystic self. I wished that I could dispute his wisdom. I could do neither; I respected him too well. He made his grand offering from trust of me, as well as Talitha, and I could only repay such faith by returning it.

Inwardly dismembering his Mage essence, Shamba offered his spirit guides his own Inianga power to strengthen the daughter who meant everything to him. With his offering of all that made him a Mage of Inianga, the vision's Mage of Blood would be freed to assume its deeper, necessary character as prophecy's living fulfillment. If Shamba's hope succeeded—which required my success, as well—Blood, which is life, would evolve from Mage to Everyman. Talitha would become what the vision required her to be.

Talitha glanced at me, wonderment contending with the distaste she felt for the decisions I had made. I felt her confusion: Her undeveloped Mystic senses reacted to her father's silent spell, though she could not identify the cause of her unsettled emotions. "You are not Ch'ango's equal in any respect," she informed me acridly.

"I know." By all the Mystic gods that ever existed, I *knew*. "But I am not alone."

With thick scorn, she told me, "You are still a spoiled, naive child, Marita." Her words did not cut me; I hurt for her father and for her. Though she could not know what her father had already commenced, she regarded him with the grief of loss and the turmoil that had shaken her confidence. Her words were bitter: "If you wish to pass sentence upon yourselves, I shall not keep you from your executions. You facilitate the Protectorate's goals." She hefted her father's black stone, as if she might throw it in frustration. "I shall direct you to Ch'ango. She has been expecting you."

Marita

This is the house of Ch'ango, who would make herself Earth Empress, a Sable Prince in truth: It is a domed structure, white with age, though its chipped mosaic tiles hint at a colorful past. The wind blows through it constantly, whispering through vast rooms and pillared hallways that are at least half ruined. The Great War, or the riots and catastrophes that ensued, left the building vandalized and hollow. It is a house without comfort, but it is large and stalwart, and it squats possessively atop many even rows of prison cells, for it was once a house of pre-Empire justice.

The house lies hidden by the massive walls that engulf a supply factory a few kilometers outside of Tathagata. The transport system from the factory no longer functions properly, and the factory itself produces a tiny fraction of its former output of synthetic comestibles. Except for the little that Ch'ango consumes, these products fall into an excess vat, are reprocessed and are reissued in an unending cycle of futility.

This is Ch'ango's house, hermitage, and throne: pre-Empire wreckage that fuels her dreams of domination. Long ago, Ch'ango became drunk on the power games of Tathagata, and she is drugged by the desperation of an aging woman who dreads the approach of her own ending. Her personal power writhes between a corruption of classic Mystic extremism and a villainy of her own perverse invention, a twisted justification of her Hangseng pride. Benedict has said that a demon possesses her soul.

I perceive her as an unusually adept Mage who partook too deeply of the same amoral ambition that my family considers lawful and respectable. Uncle Toby is as vile as Ch'ango, but she is more intelligent, more talented, and more dangerous. Their crimes differ in degree. He is contemptible, but she is unendurable. Our society's laws decline to denigrate anyone's personal philosophy, but I join my brother in condemning Ch'ango. Even tolerance must have boundaries.

My brother and I crossed the bleached sand that surrounded her house, and sharp salt crystals sliced the soles of our shoes. Our eyes burned from acidic fumes out of the faulty supply factory, the air's taint harsh enough to foretell the birth of more mixies. Foul smoke clouded the night sky, and few stars were visible. The setting moon glowed just short of fullness, but its face was murky

Ben and I had debarked alone from the autobus. We might never know another night, nor ever again share this precious certainty of mutual understanding. For this one night, Mystic vision united us in mind and spirit, urgent in a need to exorcise Ch'ango. Together, tonight, we were more than a pair of battered, idealistic siblings. In the cause of Hiroshi, we were the Prince of Ice.

Talitha would follow us soon, though Shamba delayed her forcibly on the autobus to let us have at least a few minutes' lead. We felt Hiroshi, already within the gates before our arrival, though he took a more circumspect path than ours; he approached Ch'ango's house with caution, while we walked boldly to the door. The vision, that Mystic force which bound us by whatever diverse names we each gave it, would draw all those whom it required.

We could not have prevented Ch'ango from summoning Lar or other Mystics who might serve her, but Benedict and I knew that she had *not* called them. She would rely on her own prowess for direct personal combat, because she was a jealous woman. She had Aroha, and she would not share even his destruction.

I could feel Lar dimly, for his Mystic senses focused on this place and fragile time. Ch'ango denied Lar; she had Aroha. Stripped of her guardianship, Lar could not use his scarabs, nor the full power of his lotus marks. He could only hate, envy, and regret. I could pity him; I could not imagine how I had ever thought him worthy of devotion. He had dwindled to Brass Dreamer, as lost to himself as Ch'ango's inner fire was lost to the honorable Lung-Wang. As once he had represented a small part of the Ch'ango-dominated Sable Prince, so now, abandoned, he contributed merely an element of the Brass Dreamer that was the lingering energy of Ch'ango's many sacrifices.

Ch'ango's war had become a solitary undertaking. Like two champions of old, each dueling for the victory of an entire culture and its country, Ch'ango and Andrew had positioned themselves as lonely rivals. Each would risk the world to win, and each had forgotten any cause but deluded self-importance.

"Sable and Shadow rarely meet peaceably," I murmured.

"The Intercessor knows what may come of such a conflict," replied my brother, understanding me, if not my words.

As our feet touched the cracked marble terrace that surrounded Ch'ango's house, the spell barriers flew against us. The Dragon Kings rode against us, bright, dark, leather-winged, and saber-taloned, citron and Brass, sulfur and smoke. Their numbers were uncountable, blocking sight of all but their furious legions. Their bellows shattered the sky. Their great scaled tails lashed against us, and we ducked and dodged them. Their passage stirred the sand into whirlwinds.

With fingers that trembled, I cast a cloud of emerald philter dust. I whispered a spell, as Benedict shouted a prayer. Emerald touched the Dragon Kings, and the sky became flame. The flame became ice, and the ice turned clear. Old and hollow, the flaming dragons faded into glassy etchings. My scarabs tingled, and I whispered, "I am no longer so weak, Ch'ango, that you can conquer me with fear alone."

Illusions, undying, altered and assumed a new form of anger. The Ice wind howled against us, but it had lost its power to terrify me. I recognized its Mystic signature now, though Ch'ango had corrupted the spell to her own vile usage. It was Dory's spell, stolen like the Kinebahan spirit jar. I raised my hands and absorbed the wind's harsh energy. Stronger than Dory, I reclaimed the Ice that belonged to Avalon, accepting its cold pain, though it racked my body. Benedict steadied me.

This is the house of Ch'ango: Its whispering hallways are dark. The stairway to the prison level is wide. Many steps are broken, and they crumble beneath incautious weight. There is no railing.

I carried a Mage light in the bowl of my hand, but I had dampened only a few grains of rosy philter powder and did not let the glow extend far. Benedict moved by feel. His pace was more assured than mine. He had divined our destination.

We heard Ch'ango's laughter before we saw her. It was a guttural sound without beauty, and it echoed from the hard planes of concrete walls. Confident from my success against her guardians, I refashioned my own Ice wind and threw it against Ch'ango's cold heart. The blow of her counterspell knocked us from our feet. Already at the base of the stairs, I did not fall far. Benedict, who had walked behind me, fared less well.

My brother fell headlong to the floor with a crack that broke my frail confidence. Frantically, I arose and cast my Mage light toward him, seeking him also with hand and urgent plea of Mystic healing. The Mage light found him first. His head was bruised and bleeding, but he was conscious and struggled to stand.

Ch'ango's pitiless mirth mocked us, and I saw her, as the scattered powder of my Mage light floated across the room. Topaz and ruby pins held her silver hair tight, baring every crease and sag of her skin defiantly. She wore a Mastermage's violet robe, embroidered with citron and crimson dragons. She sat erect on her carved wooden chair. Her smile was thin and cruel. Her arrogant eyes declared her victory.

Seeing her, I knew her symbols fully: Her Suit resembled Sable, but it was corrupted Brass. It was both dark and bright with the energy and Lung-Wang power that were her gifts, before she warped them. Her Brass Face was the Dreamer of folly. Her Sable Face was the Mixie of misfortune, waste, and loss.

My Mage light drifted farther and touched Andrew, seated cross-legged on the floor of his bare cell. He wore a wrinkled linen vest and trousers of white, the color of neutrality that some Mages say is void of power. His jewelry-bare arms shone with Mage-mark silver. His Shadow Cat eyes were narrowed, and his expression was unreadable. He did not speak.

These were the visual images: an aging woman, an imprisoned man, a dim and ugly room divided by metal bars. The two warriors did not bleed visibly, just as the color of their magic did not match the colors that I saw them wear. Their wounds were made of Mage spells, terribly real but internal.

My crescents felt the power of Ch'ango and cringed. Ch'ango did not doubt that she could defeat me. She had shackled Andrew in body and in mind. She had dismissed Benedict as an easy casualty. Indeed, his fall had injured him badly, though not irreparably. I tried to build a spell against Ch'ango, but all of my thoughts and words became garbled and ineffective.

Two stubborn forces coexisted inside of me, tearing apart my mind. They were both dark, both determined, both wrought of scarab-marked women. By her domineering spells, Ch'ango drew me to her, and her crabbed fingers tore my gold earrings from me, splitting the flesh of my ears. My blood dripped down my neck, and I cried, but the physical pain afflicted me remotely, unable to compete with the torment of Ch'ango's methodical dismemberment of my Mystic self. Before Ch'ango, I felt as helpless as the Stone Palace's statues of the vandalized past, and I was equally besieged.

The lesser force inside of me struggled to usurp command, but it/I failed pitiably. As a Mage, Ch'ango exceeded me by greater measure than I had ever imagined Mystic skills could reach. My proud new scarabs mocked me. I had claimed them rightly; I *could* use them; but they counted as nothing before Ch'ango. She smiled thinly, because she knew my defeat, and it pleased her. It confirmed her power over the Family—and over Andrew.

I sagged in front of Ch'ango's throne, groveling to her by her will. Her cold, twisted fingers marauded across my deadened flesh. She tried to strip both bracelets from my upper arms, and she hurled the floral bracelet to the floor. The metal rang against the concrete, then dwindled to silence. The clasp of the lizard bracelet stymied her. She tugged in anger, tearing my skin as she spell-shattered the lizard's mechanism. "Whore," she cursed me, "Aroha has belonged to *me* since before you earned a lotus."

A blaze of white illuminated the bars of Andrew's cell, and the bars were gone. My body reawakened to ordinary pain, freed from the two, equally startled, contending forces that were Ch'ango and my own resistance. Andrew still did not speak or move except for the enigmatic shifting of his eyes toward the stairs. I followed the direction of his emotionless gaze.

"Marita, move away from Ch'ango, please," ordered Prince Hiroshi, waving a black cylinder. I could not obey Prince Hiroshi, for Ch'ango clutched me anew, and she had hoarded years of her ambitious life-force for the fulfillment of this cruel magic. Hiroshi hesitated, and I felt his revulsion for the weapon he had created in the image of the most violent, denigrated aspect of Empire science. He stood uncertainly on the bottom step, for he was teacher and not warrior, but he was also Andrew's staunchest friend. With cruel relish, Ch'ango twisted a spell of deceit around Hiroshi's reluctance, immobilizing him.

Anavai, her delicate face knotted with determination, knelt beside my brother, helping him to rise. In Anavai, I sensed none of her husband's doubts. In Anavai burned a frantic anger against Ch'ango and all who had worked against Hiroshi's vision. Anavai had not come to save a friend but to fight for Prince Hiroshi's cause, which would give their son his future. Her emotions matched Benedict's for single-minded purity.

"The great Empire Prince recognizes his conqueror," mocked Ch'ango. "Inform your less perceptive servants, Great Prince, that the war is ended, and our world is well Protected once more." She began to laugh her throaty triumph. "Your cause dies here with you, Prince Hiroshi, and my Protectorate will eradicate the evidence of your existence more absolutely than the Great War erased the Empires."

Anavai shouted fiercely, "Do not heed her lies, my husband." Benedict gripped her arm, restraining her.

A deeper voice overlaid both Anavai's defiance and Ch'ango's vicious laughter. "You boast prematurely, Ch'ango," declared Andrew with sudden strength. He rose to his feet, abandoning his pretense as a beaten prisoner. My scarabs responded with a flare of eagerness, but my crescents trembled from the angry strangeness in him. He hurled himself bodily at the aged Ch'ango, but she did not bend. Andrew did not free me from her spell, which left me huddled at her feet. Hiroshi muttered his frustration.

Ch'ango looked frail beside Andrew's strength and height, but she did not cower. She remained erect, proud, and imperturbable, even as his powerful hands ripped the sleeves from her robe. Ruthlessly, he bared the panoply of Mage marks that made her arms silver from wrist to elbow: twelve lotus blossoms, ten shells, scarabs, and a complex series of irregular polygons that I did not recognize. Linked with the scarabs, the geometrical shapes completely encircled her forearms and drew twin arrows through the lotus triangle.

Prince Hiroshi commanded, "Andrew, cease this madness!" Hiroshi's voice was stern, but I felt his pain. He had already realized what my crescents sought to tell me, and now I saw it also.

Andrew did not heed his Prince, for Andrew was not present. Ch'ango *had* won that long Mystic battle. She had recovered what she wanted: not Andrew but Aroha. The man in Ch'ango's cell had shifted altogether to a remorselessly ambitious Mastermage, who was a stranger to me. He was not, however, unknown to me.

He was the archetype of the Shadow Mage, magic upon magic, tainted by Ch'ango's blood spells—not living Blood but Sable, which signified dust and death as well as earth. I tasted every bitter sacrifice that Ch'ango had made to bind Aroha to her: from Lar's independence to her own twisted pride, from a gray cat named Ava'e to a Dom named Hollis of Rit, from the sundering of Benedict's bones to Kurt's wasted death.

"You pressed me to learn blood magic, Ch'ango," whispered Aroha, his rich voice a caress. His fingers traced her strange Mage marks with a cunning seductiveness that I knew well. His vicious, aged enemy enjoyed him like an infatuated girl. "Savor the results!" he cajoled, drawing her against him by enticing Mystic spell.

As she embraced him, his hand swept upward in one swift blow. Wielding his lean fingers like Mystic talons, Aroha clawed blood from Ch'ango's face. He turned her own blood's dark magic against her, deepening the initial scratches into ragged gorges of pustulent flesh. She slapped her hands against her jet-black eyes, which streamed with tears of pain from Aroha's vicious spell. She wailed, releasing me from Mystic shackles.

Before I could struggle to my feet, Aroha cast Ch'ango back into her chair and snatched me from the floor with his remorseless strength. "Andrew," I pleaded, but Andrew did not exist to hear me. Incoherent sounds from other voices—Hiroshi, Anavai, Benedict—failed equally to deter Aroha. Hard, cruelly familiar muscles imprisoned me inarguably. Aroha ripped both emerald and aqua philter purses from the cord at my waist.

With fluid agility, he confiscated his own nerve film and my vial of fire oil, and he discarded both purses without any token of proper Mage respect for them. He discarded me likewise, and my shoulder struck the floor painfully. With the adroitness of a rehearsed action, Aroha wrapped his wrists in silver nerve film. Crying her fury, Ch'ango shook free of his blood-wrought spell, and she blasted the room with the Ice wind.

"A hi'o na!" laughed Aroha in a Tangaroa spell that deflected her Ice wind and left him untouched. Where their spells crossed and clashed, the tempest roared with thunder. I *felt* my brother's prayer, and I met it with my own spell of protection, but neither of us could temper the furies of Aroha and Ch'ango. Benedict, touching Anavai, extended our defense to her, but we could not reach Hiroshi.

Assaulted by that terrible storm of will, Prince Hiroshi dropped his black cylinder and fell to his knees. Anavai, stumbling away from Benedict, now snatched the weapon and raised it coldly in defense of her Prince and husband. Slight, pretty Anavai aimed at Ch'ango the force that our world had dreaded since the Empires failed, and she fired without regret.

Ch'ango raised one gnarled hand peremptorily. Her Mage spell deflected the spray of Empire energy, and the concrete ceiling absorbed the blow. Thrown backward, Anavai landed hard against Benedict, who braced her, though he struggled to retain his own balance. My brother's strength left me, and my protection spell shimmered into a void.

I could not reach or help anyone. I wept, but my crescents could not respond, for scarabs blocked them, and I could not think clearly enough to use the scarabs. Ch'ango had paralyzed me anew. With hardly an effort, she controlled all of us, except Aroha, whom she watched with unfathomable calm.

He had drenched his wrists and two entire sheets of nerve film with my fire oil. I smelled his skin burning, but he did not even hesitate from the agony that he must have felt. Aroha grasped Ch'ango from her throne, and she yielded like a doll of limp rags. He pressed his wrapped, burning wrists against Ch'ango's geometrical marks.

She tore free of him within seconds, but the likeness of her Mage marks had been etched onto him. His silver glowed, for the polygons had already embedded themselves in his nervous system. He crouched, cradling his arms, and he exercised his rare skills to accelerate the process of absorption.

I felt the transformation taking place in Aroha, building in him a Mystic power that no human host should ever have attempted to contain. Ch'ango stood over him, watching as well, greedily drinking his skill and insights, as her wounded face seeped crimson. By her rapt expression, she seemed as amazed as any of us by his cold, horrifying self-discipline, but she did not hesitate to seek her own advantage. "You will not master *my* marks, fixer boy," she hissed, goading him with her scornful words. I felt his Mystic power surge with anger, and his silver glowed ever more brightly.

Between Ch'ango's waving hands, a curved silver knife took shape from black fire and crimson air. Her spell-knife poised above him, readied to steal blood from him and share his burgeoning Mystic force. The hem of her robe slapped my arm, but I could not touch her Mystic essence. Aroha, racked by his own extraordinary undertaking, seemed unaware of her.

Ch'ango's knife wavered and fell, but it did not find its target. I felt her awe of Aroha in that brief instant. My crescents trembled, sensing Ch'ango's anxious passion for Aroha and the gifts that he alone could provide for her. My scarabs recognized her ironic secret. Ch'ango could barely begin to use the marks that she had created for herself. Though she retained greater Mystic skills than any other Mage of my knowledge, save possibly Aroha, her powerful spells were few. Even the abilities of her early training had begun to fail her, and urgency augmented her hunger for power. She could not master her unique Mage marks alone. She had failed to confiscate Aroha's power by stealing his blood, but she learned from Aroha, as he taught himself.

Raw Mystic power, not Hiroshi's esoteric teachings, was what she had always craved from Mastermage Aroha. It was Aroha's exceptional ability to learn and understand that would restore her, augment her, and make her Empress. It was Aroha's vast knowledge that would enable her to subjugate the knowledge of others. I could not let him finish his work, for it was hers. It had always been hers.

Benedict watched me; Hiroshi and Anavai watched only Aroha and Ch'ango. I stopped fighting against Ch'ango, sure that she was too consumed by Aroha's internal discoveries to make use of my surrender. In a burst that channeled all my new scarabs' Mystic force, I regained some mobility, enough to let me retrieve my philter purse from the floor. I did not threaten Ch'ango. She ignored me. Since her spell-knife had failed to take Aroha's blood, she had chosen a more dangerous course. By Mystic bonds, she had locked herself to Aroha, risking his pain in order to reap the gifts of his tremendous knowledge and cunning.

I knew the vulnerability imposed by self-inflicted Mage marks, and I knew the desperation for relief from pain. Aroha might quicken the process, but he could not escape the suffering. I reached toward Aroha, offering ease. I had served him as he wished and expected, coming to him with the nerve film when he wanted it, and he trusted me.

I cast the delusion oil before he could stop me. He screamed my name in rage, recognizing my betrayal. Ch'ango, too, regained awareness of me. Her compact body stiffened beneath violet silk, as she realized her own unexpected danger. She had linked herself to Aroha, and his defeat would be hers. She reacted instinctively and decisively in her panic. Her threatened Mystic senses overwhelmed her hope of learning more from him, and she aimed her spells for his quick death. I recognized their battle for an instant; then I recognized only my own desperate position.

To survive, Aroha needed to focus his greatest powers against Ch'ango, but that mortal combat did not spare me his anger. If Ch'ango had not confiscated his bracelets with their burdens of Empire ingenuity, I would not have lived beyond that moment. Despite his anguish and divided attention, Aroha struck at me with the overwhelming force of an Empire-educated Mystic genius, whose marks exceeded scarabs.

The barriers that I built were shaky, for Ch'ango had battered my inexperienced powers. Aroha's Tangaroa serpent coiled and struck, sinking poisoned fangs into my flesh. I felt the blood seeping from the scars around my new Mage marks, as Aroha pounded his will against me. He inflicted Mystic wounds that were deep enough to manifest themselves in physical reality. The blood that poured from my arms was more than Mage perception, and he used it to enhance his magic against me and Ch'ango both. My blood pooled on the floor of the ancient prison, and it stained my emerald robe, weakening me dangerously by spell and bodily loss. My senses blurred, and I believed that I was dying.

Aroha's deadly Mage serpent slowed in its strikes, as the delusion oil began to take effect. Not even Aroha could counter delusion oil, Ch'ango, and my imperfect defense while his own body protested the awful contortions of the self-inflicted polygons. He lashed out at an illusory foe, and one wall of his former cell exploded loudly, shooting fragments across the room. A concrete chip drove through the calf of my leg, but I hardly felt its effect, for I was reeling jointly from Aroha's spell and his personal pain.

Shrapnel had pierced his strong, exquisite body in a hundred locations, but his blood gushed only from his Mage marks. Both new and old patches of silver nerve film had begun to curl and darken, ripped unnaturally from their bonds by a rebellion of his own mind and nervous system, besieged by philter-borne delusions. The mental tortures would soon drive him mad, if he did not first die from loss of blood.

Not even Ch'ango could have destroyed Aroha by solitary, direct attack, but Aroha could not withstand his own skills. All of that tremendous power of his mind and body was devouring itself. When Aroha completed his self-destruction, I knew I might go mad with my grief at losing Andrew, but I could not reach to him again.

We pay a high price for our sins, dearest Andrew. You knew, for you warned me when I bought your help in Rit, that you and I could only bring each other suffering. Benedict and Hiroshi—and even Anavai—knew, as well. Only I was slow to understand.

Aroha was fading, weakening, and rending my heart from my soul. He struggled so close to the end, but he continued to fight. Unable to stand, he sank to his knees, his bleeding arms pressed against his head, but his head remained unbowed. I was glad when he closed his clouded green eyes, for the anger in them was too bitter.

"No!" shrieked Ch'ango, realizing what she was about to lose by her own twisted designs. "You will never leave *me*, Aroha!" She knelt beside him, attacking him now only with her helpless, angry, flailing fists. She, too, was riddled with shrapnel and weakened physically and mentally. She could not own him; she could not destroy him; she could not commit to either choice. She tried once more to reach him, to salvage him and his accursed abilities. Her effort sufficed to drag her into Aroha's maelstrom of agony.

Aroha's hatred of her survived amid his delusions. He immobilized her with a spell of bondage, and his bleeding arms dragged her to the floor. Ch'ango's arrogant eyes bulged in terror, as he choked her, and she renewed her battle against him with a new desperation. Their Mage spells clashed, shaking the building and the earth beneath it.

Benedict shouted over the roar of breaking concrete, earth, and air, "In the name of the Intercessor, cease this demonic work!" I did not know if he addressed Ch'ango, Aroha, both, or neither. Their spells cracked the stairway, and the wall separated into blocks that shifted, threatening to collapse.

"This is an abomination of power," growled Hiroshi, his voice quivering with emotion. Anavai wept openly, for pity had stolen her anger. An equal depth of sorrow was in Hiroshi's eyes, for they had both loved Andrew.

Prince Hiroshi raised his hands. Between trembling fingers, he held his black cylinder. Ch'ango could not immobilize him again with her deceit. The weapon sprayed a haze of gold upon the two combatants, locked in their deadly, private war. Ch'ango and Andrew slumped together, his torn fingers still fastened around her neck.

The room became silent except for the creak of rubble settling in the rooms above us. Someone stumbled hurriedly down the broken stairways. It was Talitha, and she measured Prince Hiroshi, the reluctant conqueror, with her stern, keen gaze.

She did not hesitate long. She chose to come to me. She wrapped an Inianga scarf around the bleeding scarabs of my right arm. She gripped my other arm, applying pressure to stop the flow of blood.

Benedict rose stiffly to his feet. He limped to the entwined, brutalized bodies of Andrew and Ch'ango. He began to chant a prayer of mourning.

Hiroshi took Anavai in his arms. I did not know which of them most needed comfort. Hiroshi grieved for a friend, and Anavai grieved for her husband's loss. They had impaled the Protectorate's corrupt heart, but they would never rejoice over the price of conquest. Hiroshi, his clever black eyes desolate, apologized to me, "I am sorry, but it was necessary."

Talitha murmured, "They were both destroyers. The rest of us could not fight against either of them. Marita, child, how can you grieve?"

I did not try to answer. I was empty. I pulled free of

Talitha and pressed my wounded arm for myself. I shuffled haltingly toward the stairway.

Benedict's voice paused in its droning prayer and told me, "Marita, he does not need to die."

Prince Hiroshi, Anavai, and Talitha turned equally solemn faces toward my brother. I sympathized with their ignorance, for I knew what it was like to move blindly through someone else's vision. They still did not understand what they had witnessed. They had neither Mage skills to enable them to see, nor the peculiar prophetic blessing of Benedict's Intercessor to guide them.

I answered Benedict, "Ch'ango is gone, and she was Aroha's life, as he was hers. Try to heal him, if you deem that course wise, but he will neither help nor thank you. Look at his arms. Every Mage mark has been burned from him, and those marks were linked to every fiber of his body and spirit. Do you truly believe that Aroha will endure a cripple's life?"

My brother replied simply, "It is Andrew whom I wish to see endure, not Aroha."

One tear rolled down my cheek. I tried to sense Andrew, but I perceived only Aroha, the Mage who nearly mastered the greatest Mystic power of all time. "I would pray to your Intercessor myself, if I thought that anyone could restore Andrew, after what I have caused him to suffer. I do not have that hope, Ben. My vision goes no further than this, the end of the war between Aroha and Ch'ango." I added, glimpsing a final prophetic fragment, "The Blood Everyman signifies life, contentment, and plenty. The Blood Everyman is Talitha and Prince Hiroshi. They will unite to resolve the peace, as they begin to learn respect for each other," as if those of whom I spoke were not present. I did not disregard them intentionally. The vision had passed to them, and all of us knew it. It was I who was absent, as absent as Andrew.

I left them there in the final scene of my vision. I had no more schemes or goals or hopes within me. I had no vision left. Within the hour, I was on an autoboat bound for Rit.

Marita

Two years have passed since Andrew and Ch'ango fought their final battle. Toby is still the Dom of Rit, and Lar remains the Mastermage. The World Parliament continues to govern much as before, but Talitha's meticulous files contain an amendment to the laws of our society. Empire techniques may now be used for all purposes of repair, restoration, and non-injurious developments; fixers are even allowed to own tools and property. Prince Hiroshi has received the government's legal blessing to form his own Guild of workers, researchers, and educators. The amendment passed with relative ease, once Talitha and a few of her supporters convinced crucial Doms and Mastermages that Prince Hiroshi was a worthy ally, whose devices could profit them. Many who had feared and envied Aroha became eager to take his place.

Prince Hiroshi's achievement constitutes a revolutionary change in our social law, but most of our society has accepted it without the faintest tremor of self-doubt. I would like to imagine that our world's people are wise, but I fear that they are simply too ignorant to understand the past, the present or the possibilities of the future. The Empires mean little to them. Those who learn henceforth will be taught from Prince Hiroshi's perspective. Like Talitha, I may always distrust some part of Hiroshi's work, but I know that our world needs him, his science, his curiosity, and his creativity. We have slept too long.

I do not go to the Mage Center. I sell a few philters to old, loyal customers, but I have conveyed the remainder of my office lease to Janine. She was eager to augment her image and clientele. Rodolfo often works with her. A year ago, Lilith moved away from Rit, from Lar, and from me.

I live with Nan, the birds, and the orchids. We are two Ghosts, Shadow and Ice, insubstantial remnants of the past.

Toby does not leave Tathagata to disturb us, and we have dismissed the staff. Most of the Stone Palace is closed and empty. Nan and I seldom speak.

Sometimes in the greenhouse, I remember Ha'aparari, Tiare House, and the man I loved there. Those memories are precious to me, but they always lead to pain. I am convinced that he must hate me, for I hate myself.

Benedict wrote to me a month after I returned to Rit. The letter appeared in my pocket, having reaching me, I think, via a scruffy young boy who passed me in the street. Benedict informed me that Andrew would live. He said that he had found Ch'ango's book and stored it safely, where no unwise Mages will be tempted by it. I have not heard from my brother again.

Talitha writes occasionally, as does Anavai. It was Anavai who told me that Benedict and Andrew had disappeared from Tathagata, and not even Hiroshi admitted to knowledge of their whereabouts. I tried only once to locate Andrew and Benedict by Mage spell. I failed to discover any sign of them. For several months, I felt guilty for my Mystic approach, and I was glad that I had not succeeded.

No one has ever described to me the extent of Andrew's permanent injuries, but both Talitha and Anavai have indicated that Andrew lived under Benedict's constant care in Tathagata. I am not sure that I want to know more. Whatever my brother salvaged, I doubt that it resembles the Andrew whom I loved, or Talitha would not be so forgiving toward Prince Hiroshi. If anything of that Andrew remains, I am certain that it includes bitterness against me.

I often wish that I had stayed with him or returned to him while I had the chance. I remind myself that I was his destroyer and that remaining with him in his weakness would have been an added cruelty. I would not want him to think that I would take pleasure from my bitter victory.

I cannot think of him without wanting him. A strange, acute emotion takes root in me. I ache to hear, see, meet, and touch him. I also long to be free of this urgent need to sense him near me again. Every word he ever spoke to me resounds inside of me as if it were some priceless gem of praise, sustaining my life. I do not want to hope for anything from him now, but he is part of every thought and dream inside me.

I cannot justify this feeling as love. It is nothing selfless, fine, or pure. I do not even know if I do love him. The memory of him excites a hunger in me that only he can satisfy, but I know that I must fast, perhaps forever. Whatever I admired and desired in Andrew may be altogether vanquished. It is certainly unattainable for me. I cannot believe that he would want my love now, if he ever did.

I am foolish to debate my feelings for a man who is lost to me, but this is the cycle of my days. I rise, I walk, I think of Andrew, I cry, and I sleep. I am almost as oblivious to the present world as an E-unit addict.

I try to focus on now. Nan is in the greenhouse, dividing orchids. It is a clear, cool morning. I shall walk on the beach and think of nothing but the waves.

As I descend the iron stairs to the courtyard, I dislodge a pebble from the ridged surface of the lowest step. The pebble flies, and a cat emerges from beneath the stairs and pounces on it. The cat is gray.

I see the man kneeling in the empty, broken fountain. His head is bowed, so I cannot see the face beneath that thick, black hair. The color of his long-sleeved shirt is a neutral cream, and it hangs loosely across his back. He is thinner, but his muscles still look strong.

I almost turn and flee upstairs. He raises his head. The dark eyebrows tilt quizzically above the gray-green eyes. His smile is wry. "The fountain can be repaired," he says.

I force myself to approach him. "What about you?" I ask, every nerve in me shaking. My crescents are numb.

Andrew shrugs and rolls up his sleeves. His arms are twisted with scars where once there were Mage marks. His laugh is abrupt. "Benedict never did approve of my Mage skills. He maintains that I am less subject to temptation now, which he calls a blessing of the Divine Intercessor. Benedict assures me that suffering has moved me closer to the Intercessor's wisdom."

"Is he right?"

"Perhaps I have learned something about forgiveness."

"I'm sorry, Andrew," I whisper.

He meets my gaze and holds it, as surely as if he could still bespell me by Mage's art. "You're not sorry that Ch'ango failed," he responds briskly, "and neither am I. You both learned more from me and about me than I expected. I tried to use you in my battle against her, and I paid for my own manipulative methods. If I had maintained my vow to abstain from magic, Ch'ango would not have reached me, and you would not have needed to intervene." He gestures with his damaged arms. "This only impairs my vanity."

"When you left Tathagata, you didn't even tell Prince Hiroshi where you were going." I need to let him know that I wanted to find him.

His expression becomes sober, but he is not embarrassed to admit a weakness. "Benedict's disciples had arranged a place of retreat. I was not ready to see anyone."

"Except Benedict?"

"Your brother is not quite like other people, is he?"

"I suppose not." I sigh, "Neither are you."

Andrew grins, and I realize that shrapnel scars make his grin permanently crooked. "Benedict is preaching in the forum again. He had acquired an attentive audience of seven persons when I left him."

I cannot smile. I am too close to tears. "Nan would like to see the fountain working again."

"Would you?" asks Andrew softly. We both know that he speaks of more than a broken fountain.

My heart is pounding. I try to calm its pace, but my Mage marks are playing tricks on my sense of time. My love for Andrew is new and eager, instead of impossible. I answer him earnestly, "Andrew, I would like it very much."

Andrew bends to turn the dolphin wheel, which squeaks and barely moves. "It will take some time. Two of the dolphins require extensive work. I'll need to replace the pivot and readjust the balance. I may have to spend a month here—or more." He looks at me with his old, impudent gleam.

"There is no shortage of rooms."

"Do we need more than one?"

"I don't know," I answer.

The pretense of confidence disappears, and he meets my eyes probingly. "No," he murmurs after a moment. "We don't really know each other all that well, do we, Marita?"

"I don't know," I answer again, and now I cannot keep the tears from falling.

He climbs out of the broken fountain. "We're both quick learners," he says, his crooked smile returning cautiously. He touches my hair.

I fling my arms around him and bury my face in the soft

fibers of his shirt. "No love philters this time," I promise him.

"No binding spells either," he murmurs in my ear.

A door creaks above us. I hear Nan emerge onto the balcony. "Is it true," she calls, "that your friend Hiroshi has grown flowers in the open air?"

Andrew and I look at each other, and we both begin to laugh for little reason. "Quite true," he replies across my head. "Would you like me to restore this courtyard as a garden, Nan?"

"That would be quite suitable," she answers. She whistles a tune, which sounds like birdsong, and returns to her greenhouse.

Appendix 1:
The Cards of the Avalon Mages

Suits: Blood, Brass, Ice, Sable, Shadow
Faces: Prince, Mage, Dom, Cat, Everyman, Hound, Ghost, Mixie, Dreamer

SYMBOLIC ASSOCIATIONS

Suit	Intrinsic	Extrinsic
Blood	life, spirituality, empathy	a person of ruddy coloring, a child
Brass	fire, energy, will	a person of light coloring, a youth
Ice	water, discipline, mental agility	a person of very pale coloring, an elderly person
Sable	earth, wisdom, artistry	a person of very dark coloring, a middle-aged adult
Shadow	air, magic, changeability	a person of medium coloring, a person who has died

(especially the card of the Shadow Ghost)

Face	Meaning
Prince:	Hangseng or Nikkei ruler, Empire science, powerful force
Mage:	Mystic power, prophecy, luck
Dom:	Affirmist power, law, wealth
Cat:	mystery, uncertainty, beauty
Everyman:	equality, contentment, plenty
Hound:	certainty, prosaic events, continuity, neutrality
Ghost:	the past and its products, material things
Mixie:	misfortune, loss, ugliness
Dreamer:	folly, sacrifice

Mage Schools	Mythos	Suit (Intrinsic)	Mage Color
Avalon	European	Ice	Emerald
Inianga	African	Blood	Orange
Kinebahan	American	Sable	Crimson
Lung-Wang (aka "Dragon Kings")	Asian	Brass	Citron
Tangaroa	Pacific	Shadow	Aqua

Derived symbolisms (from social customs)	Card	Color
Mastermage	Mage	Violet
Affirmists	Everyman	Brown
Neutrality	Hound	Cream or white
Factories, things of the past	Ghost	Cream or white
Empire	Prince	Blue
Security, safety	Dom	Black

The Avalon deck consists of 45 cards in five suits. The suits are indicated on both the front and the back of the cards, either by color or symbolism according to the individual Mage's preference. (The decks may be highly individualized.) The faces are shown only on the front. The basic method of Avalon reading uses the following cards:

1) **Significator** — If a significator (i.e., a card representing the person for whom the reading is made) is used, it is withdrawn from the deck before shuffling and placed at the top of the reading layout.
2) **First primary** — The deck is shuffled, and the top card is placed face-upward on the table, beneath and slightly to the left of the significator (if present). This is the first primary card.
3) **First primary's support cards** (optional) — If the next card belongs to the same suit as the first primary, it may be set aside or stacked face-downward underneath the first primary. This step is repeated until a card of a different suit is encountered.
4) **Second primary** — The card of the second suit is placed

face-upward beneath and slightly to the right of the significator (if present). This is the second primary card.

5) **Support cards** (optional) — Cards are repeatedly drawn form the top of the deck. If such cards match one of the suits that is already represented in the layout (excluding the significator), they may be set aside or placed face-downward underneath the representative card.

6) **Secondary cards** (three) — As one of the remaining three suits is encountered for the first time, its representative is placed in the second row of the layout. Steps (5) and (6) are repeated until all five suits are represented. If desired, the remaining cards may be sorted as supports, thus using the entire deck. (In general, support cards are either omitted or used only for the primaries. When present, the order of the support cards is used to clarify a reading.)

The resulting layout may look something like the following:

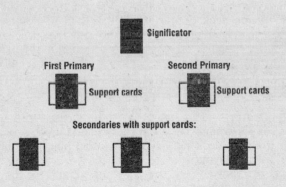

Significator

First Primary   Second Primary
Support cards   Support cards

Secondaries with support cards:

Appendix 2:
Glossary

Several of the names, as well as the dates, are taken from the Tahitian language. Accents, which effectively double the vowels, are omitted (for convenience of typing). The apostrophe is used to represent a glottal stop. A few definitions are provided below:

'A hi'o na!	Behold!
anavai	river
aroha	good feeling from the heart
feti'a	star
ha'aparari	to break
iti	little
nui	large
purotu	beautiful
roa	long
tiare	flower

Months of the year:

Tenuara	January
Fepuara	February
Mati	March
Eperera	April
Me	May
Tiunu	June
Tiurai	July
Atete	August
Tetepa	September
Atopa	October
Novema	November
Titema	December

Several other names are taken from a variety of mythologies and cultural histories, e.g.:

Ch'ango	goddess of the Moon; Chinese
Chaac	rain god; Mayas

Cuycha	rainbow deity; Incas
Iniangas	magicians with the power to make rain, discover thieves and spell-binders, etc.; Bantu tribes of southern Africa
Kinebahan	mouth and eyes of the sun; Mayas
Lung-Wang	"Dragon-Kings," rulers of waterways and rain; Chinese
Pachacamac	god who animates the earth; Incas
Shamba	a king famed for wisdom (King Shamba Bolongongo of the Bushongo people of the Congo)

Cheryl J. Franklin

☐ **SABLE, SHADOW, AND ICE**   UE2609—$4.99
The Mage's cards had been cast—but could a destiny once
foretold ever be overturned?

The Tales of the Taormin:

☐ **FIRE GET: Book 1**   UE2231—$3.50
 Only the mighty sorcerer Lord Venkarel could save Serii from
the Evil that threatened it—unless it became his master. . . .

☐ **FIRE LORD: Book 2**   UE2354—$3.95
Could even the wizard son of Lord Venkarel destroy the
Rendies—creatures of soul-fire that preyed upon the living?

☐ **FIRE CROSSING: Book 3**   UE2468—$4.99
Can a young wizard from Serii evade the traps of the comput-
er-controlled society of Network—or would his entire world fall
prey to forces which magic could not defeat?

The Network/Consortium Novels:

☐ **THE LIGHT IN EXILE**   UE2417—$3.95
Siatha—a non-tech world and a people in harmony—until it
became a pawn of the human-run Network and a deadly alien
force. . . .

☐ **THE INQUISITOR**   UE2512—$5.99
Would an entire race be destroyed by one man's ambitions—
and one woman's thirst for vengeance?

Mickey Zucker Reichert

☐ **THE LEGEND OF NIGHTFALL**   UE2587—$5.99

THE RENSHAI TRILOGY

☐ **THE LAST OF THE RENSHAI: Book 1**   UE2503—$5.99

☐ **THE WESTERN WIZARD: Book 2**   UE2520—$5.99

☐ **CHILD OF THUNDER: Book 3**   UE2549—$5.99

THE BIFROST GUARDIANS

☐ **GODSLAYER: Book 1**   UE2372—$4.99

☐ **SHADOW CLIMBER: Book 2**   UE2284—$3.99

☐ **DRAGONRANK MASTER: Book 3**   UE2366—$4.50

☐ **SHADOW'S REALM: Book 4**   UE2419—$4.50

☐ **BY CHAOS CURSED: Book 5**   UE2474—$4.50